HOTMAN'S INNOCENCE
(Subtitle)
LOAFER'S GLORY

First Edition of author Peter S. Hotman's first book.

Saul and Jane Hotman in 1959.
At ages four and three-years-old
their stormy saga of childhood
survival began.

HOTMAN'S INNOCENCE
a family saga/memoir

HOTMAN'S INNOCENCE, a family saga spanning three generations, one hundred years, from homesteading in the early nineteen hundreds to Rock 'n' Roll and the twenty-first century. Based on true stories told to the author Peter S. Hotman by his aunt Delena and other relatives. The last half of the narrative continues as a memoir of his turbulent early childhood in the 1950's, and 60's. Appearance and names of the characters have been changed to protect the innocent. The author clearly demonstrates how iniquity of the forefathers, family blessings, and curses are generational. The cycles of abuse can be broken. This book is based on truth.

The Hotman and Bip Families' Legacy Predisposes Saul's and Jane's, Survivors' Story.

by
Peter S. Hotman

Copyright 2002 by Peter S. Hotman

All rights reserved, including the right of reproduction. No part of this book shall be duplicated in whole or segments, or transmitted in any form or by any means, electronic, mechanical, recording, video or audio, photocopies, photographs, or by any information storage and retrieval system. No reproductions at all are allowed under this copyright without permission in writing from the author and publisher. Although every precaution has been taken in the preparation of this book, the publisher and author assume no responsibility for errors, omissions, or discrepancies in statistics, historical events, facts about places, individuals and incidents in the lives of the characters described herein, as the book is a collection of memories and maybe out of time sequence. All names and appearance of characters have been changed for privacy and to protect the innocent. The character, Bill Hotman represents many Klansmen of the time. This book is based on truth. The author has taken a few artistic liberties for the flow and development of the stories. Neither is any liability assumed for damages resulting from the use of information contained herein.

First Pet Me Goose Press edition 2002

Designed by Peter S. Hotman

Manufactured in the USA

The Library of Congress has cataloged the Pet Me Goose edition as follows:
Hotman, Peter
LOAFER'S GLORY/HOTMAN'S INNOCENCE/ a family saga/memoir

Scriptures from the Holy Bible King James Version. Permissions obtained to base the book on family stories. Statics from public domain.

ISBN 0-9721614-0-6

DEDICATION

This book is dedicated to my sister Jane, her son Damian, and the loving memories of Delena, Enoch, and Jake, as well as every victim of childhood abuse, domestic violence, mental illness, religious persecution, and racism.

Acknowledgments

THANK YOU:

Susan, for edits and development help.
Steven, for the hundreds of hours of reading.
Kayte, for writing the Preface.
Merrilee, for the positive professional feedback about the writing.
Jane, for allowing me to use her story.
W.M.M., for firing up my determination to NEVER BE SILENT.
Diana, for the Afterward.
Elisabeth, my wife, for input and patience during the three years it took me to finish the book.
Leve, for being a guiding light most of my days.
Kathy, for the encouragement and many email.
Nancy, my second sister, always positive.
Gary, for the words of strength and encouragement.
Momma, for forcing me to learn how to love the unlovable. I forgave all.
God, for helping me to glean wisdom and knowledge from the tragedies that Merl Judas' evil brought into many lives.

"The sound of distant African drums, and chains of slavery, an Indian war cry, and bagpipes. The feel of wooden Dutch shoes when walking. The taste of English tea and a Pilgrim feast. Spanish horses, Allah, Jehovah, the Holy Ghost an unknown tongue, oppressed and persecuted peoples, the gift of Lady Liberty, and Freedom, all were the legacies of my forefathers. Their blood flowed in my veins. Momma said I was a thoroughbred–All American! Proud of my heritage. God Bless Us All In The USA!"

PREFACE
by Kayte Vincent

To reclaim life requires acceptance of past experiences rather than denial of painful memories. Also, it demands the Hope of Faith in a future that is and should be guided by a Power far greater than mankind. This book is exhilarating and provides a creative prose in subject matter that portrays love and respect for others in a rural family characterized through poverty, hard work, and severe physical and mental illnesses. The blessings revealed as one absorbs this reading shows these family members though poor, possessed something that the world's fortune cannot purchase: A FAMILY OF LOVE AND SUPPORT FOR THEIR CHILDREN.

The beauty of this novel is manifested in the author and main character coming to terms with his victimized past of physical, emotional, and sexual abuse. He energizes his life by circumventing the failure of society to protect him and those innocent of potential and on going maltreatment. SILENCE, MOTIVATED BY FEAR AND SHAME IN THE VICTIMS AND THEIR LOVED ONES ONLY EMPOWERS THE ABUSER/PEDOPHILE, AND HE/SHE WILL VIOLATE AGAIN IF NOT CONSTRAINED. A VICTIM SHOULD NEVER BE SILENT OF THE TRUTH.

This nonfiction novel--family saga/memoir has candidly and honestly confronted communities who have been guilty or unfortunately unknowledgeable of bigotry. Social prejudices and injustice are noteworthy throughout this reading, citing hardships for the mentally challenged, those in slavery, those crucified with labels. There are various chapters which present those perpetrating and discriminating within social stratus as well as bearing sarcastic and carnal attitudes, forcing no choices for those limited in resources and political power, and seeking to teach generations in a familial undertone which undoubtedly projects anger and abuse to other.

Society has tonal qualities displaying guilt from past generation failures, but the nature of this novel is to confront and apprise the present that these prejudices must not be repeated in families who are responsible as protectors and supporters of children and youth. After reading this novel, my heart rendered a recommitment to protect those who cannot protect themselves, young, old, able or disabled.

May you as a reader become convicted to teach and become responsible for humanity....there are no shortcuts in giving your best to others.

PREFACE BY KAYTE VINCENT (pseudonym) PROFESSIONAL AND EDUCATIONAL BACKGROUND: Kayte Vincent graduated from the University of Central Arkansas with a Bachelor of Science in Education. She has a Master's of Science in Home Economics/Child and Family from Southern Illinois University, Carbondale, Illinois.. Her thirty years of career have been in related fields of family preservation, child maltreatment assessment, safety/health protection of children, and permanency plans for children's stability and human welfare. She also has a Master's Degree in Special Education and has worked intensively with the developmentally disabled.

INTRODUCTION

Little Saul Hotman's Closure

My family came from a land of extremes. Isolated, the Ozarks' hills attracted many criminal factions in the 1800's. Part of Jesse James Gang settled near Loafer's Glory, changed their names, and raised families after James was killed. Gangs of horse thieves also ran from the law in Alabama and homesteaded near Loafer's Glory throughout the same time period. Many of their descendants inherited the criminal attributes and personalities from the gene pool.

The Ozarks lured puritan-ethic religious Christians into the area as well. Cherokee Indians came to the hills in an effort to escape persecutions and the Cherokee Trail of Tears. They called themselves Black Dutch, implying they were dark-skinned Europeans. They were the Lost Cherokee Tribe. Some settlers brought Negro slaves. Farmers, immigrants, and their slaves homesteaded alongside roughneck law breakers, Native Americans, and mountain men. Together, all of these peoples, good and evil, pioneered a new life and created a civilization out of the wilderness. They mixed and mingled and local gene pools became a combination of morality and corruption as mixed raced dark and light complexioned offspring proliferated. Half-breeds, quadroons, octoroons, blacks passing for white, and whites with a speck of darkness inherited the ebony color and are ostracized. In coming generations the lines of right and wrong were as blurred as the races.

The colorful tapestry of mixed nationalities and cultures woven together created the Ozarks' society by 1900. It was a sacred place because of the love found in the good populace, one neighbor for the other, though tainted by scoundrels, domestic violence, child abuse, and moonshine addictions.

In the early 1900's, citizens reported Bonnie and Clyde hiding out in the hills during their campaign of crime. Ma Barker (Bloody Momma) and her boys also had a cabin near Yellville, Arkansas, their hideout nestled in the hills about thirty miles from my family's old homestead in Loafer's Glory.

The beautiful, scenic hardwood and pine forests held a natural splendor and the rich serenity near multiple, deep blue freshwater springs, streams, creeks, and the Buffalo river in the Ozark mountains were in great contrast to the standards of living for most residents.

The wicked were very wicked and many of the religious were radical in their beliefs and zeal. The human spirit struggled against the carnal. Cover the sin and put on the face of a saint or be rejected and ostracized. Rules of endearment and backwoods social etiquettes bled the truth and joy out of the spirit. One had to live a lie for survival, for that was what it took to be affirmed as one of the good ol' boys.

To belong was the desire, to be respected preferred. But that meant losing one's own identity, which was replaced with a duel character. Thus a guilty Christian complex took hold in the heart. Two choices: conform, or reject the harsh culture and move on to other places. Any man considered kindhearted, gentle, and soft-spoken the community appraised as having a weakness in his nature. The type did not stay around long, a contradiction of terms for existence.

The Ku Klux Klan persecuted anyone with a dark complexion, including Native Americans after the Civil War. The ebony Negroes were forced to leave the district by 1920. But the Black Dutch-Cherokee were allowed to remain. A sign posted on the outskirts of Racoon Springs read: "No Niggers Allowed Beyond This Point!" Some African American folks traveling through the area years later were lynched. Their bodies left hanging for days, dangling from bridges and trees along the main thoroughfares--murdered in cold blood the "killers," never found or prosecuted. Negroes stayed out of the region for decades.

Cohabitation by unmarried couples was not tolerated. The fornicating pairs were left a calling card in the night as a warning--get hitched or get out of the county! Small burning crosses made of two cat-of-nine-tails was placed on their porches. If the warnings were ignored, the couples were publically humiliated and escorted to the county line. Shackin' up was strictly forbidden. Vigilante justice ruled!

Illegal moonshine stills proliferated during prohibition, and bootleg whiskey sold to out-of-state gangster organizations became the financial stay for many families. Tempers flared easily, as drunken brawls in the settlements were common. Unsolved murders accumulated over the years, several bootleggers involved in the moonshine wars having a hand in them.

Shackin' up may not have been stomached but lots of women were rough as cobs with loose morals. Prostitution and houses of ill-repute were well known, just not publicized. These institutions--deemed a necessary evil.

A majority had religion, including the bad guys. Squabbles in the churches over doctrine were common. Verbal confrontations, between preachers and congregation members, happened on occasion. Some tussles began when the sermons got a little to hot and conviction of sin crept into to the wayward souls. A few pastors were caught in backsliding scandals. The feuds in churches over doctrine sometimes escalated into fistfights and split congregations. Self-righteous religious folks shunned the wayward souls in the community while slander ruled and ruined many good men's names.

The Ozark people's resistance to change and tolerance remained. Stern religious beliefs, social customs, racism, and superstitions were passed from one generation to the next. Community gossip and slander nipped at individual self-esteem. Strength in body, mind, and pocketbook commanded respect. Noble in character or loathsome, the majority of the people had one thing in common--the extreme poverty.

Natural splendor and prosperity mingled with poverty and degradation. Good and evil, carnality and sanctity of spirit clashed in the hearts of men. Descendants of these strong harsh peoples my parents grew up in this civilization.

This old breeding ground where I was conceived and born was no place for the faint of heart. Lack of educational opportunities and no work skills other than manual labor contributed to the harshness. Contrasting extreme shades of gray were the standards for good and evil. Depending on the last name every family had a label. To be deemed a saint was seldom. The labels remained for generations whether correct or not. A serendipitous wash of righteousness and wickedness became the sign post of behavior for this people who lost and found truth and the law on a whim.

Plagued by extreme poverty and lack of educational and economic opportunities, Loafer's Glory community lagged behind the times by more than twenty years in the 1950's when I was born. Only the strong survived.

With snuffed dreams and abandoned lands for the promise of a future in another state, her young spilled out from the hills to make their abodes in more prosperous towns with hope of a gentler face for survival. Loafer's Glory was my home. My parents would meet here at the breeding grounds and they too would journey afar in hope of the promise of an easier life before my fifth birthday.

My mother and father should never have married.

Nevertheless, they did when Ora Bip turned thirteen, one year after Enoch Hotman's head was split open with an axe during a logging accident. The ill fortune leaving him progressively disabled with brain damage, and then succumbing to schizophrenia. These beginnings provided the witch's brew for my impoverished, turbulent, miserable, and sometimes phenomenal childhood.

The forefathers were as closely connected to their splendid rocky land as they were to each other. My family's influence was both a blessing and a curse. From their legacy I found strength, courage, and wisdom. I gleaned knowledge from their mistakes so as not to succumb to the generational banes. Their distinctions are part of the weave in my tapestry of life. Their very existence caused me to understand the meaning of compassion and forgiveness. I could not hate them for their weakness but I learned to love them even more.

Colors of their tumultuous culture and the lustrous callous lands helped to make them who they were. The hardships and joys they experienced prejudiced how their lives touched mine. For better or worse, they influenced my development and character. They were a flawed, impoverished and illiterate, harsh but good people, hardworking, god-fearing, backsliding Hard Shell Baptist, Pentecostal Hillbillies.

Then, there was Merl Judas, our king of terror. Through fear and ignorance we kept our mouths shut and endured a private hell. My younger sister Jane, and I had no teacher or protector in such matters. We were at Merl Judas' mercy. Our aunts Delena and Leve would eventually give us what our teenage mother Ora was incapable of sharing, a mother's love and a home. We were strong children, or perhaps our struggles made us tough. Old beyond our years, we were survivors, but it would take a miracle to liberate us from the destruction, and heal our broken spirits. The blasphemes began long before Jane and I were born.

My childhood was a complicated struggle filled with insecurity, abuse, and lack of trust for many adults around me. God became a help in times of trouble after I lost my parents to the tragedies that were their lives. He was my comforter when Merl Judas robbed Jane and me of our innocence. We weren't alone in our suffering.

I am convinced that God truly is a father to the fatherless. At age nine, the greatest of all miracles changed my destiny forever when I had an encounter with the Prince of Peace.

My childhood was never boring.

Today, as a grandfather, I share my long-silenced report. The lives of the first and second generations were entwined with mine, but separate, different, and disconnected. For decades many had anguished in silence. Every child and adult victim of abuse should be heard. Often those in control had the loudest say, and the victims were silenced. Many times the cycles of abuse were generational, hidden crimes. Where does justice make her abode? There was my case.

In 1995, anger shattered my chains of secrecy. The old humiliation and memories turned to outrage when I discovered Merl had allegedly molested, and attempted to rape yet another child, a seven-year-old girl. I would never be silent again! With God's help, I found courage, determined I'd no longer be muzzled about the truth, and I began to write this book. I broke the hush by presenting the ancestors' stories for them, just as they were told to me. As Aunt Delena had asked before her death, my quill became their voices. The impact of incidents in their lives would invade mine, decades later. Nothing in my childhood had fit the standard mold. My inner child, Saul Hotman would speak as well. His voice was muted early on, here, an important articulation in the family's saga. This epic wouldn't be complete without all accounts.

As my pen whispered across the pages I decided to break the literary rules--flawed the manuscript on purpose. This giving symbolism, disruption of order, and disconnection. Just as it had been for my immediate family. The ancestors' tales in "Section One," told in third person would bring congruity to "Saul's Memoir," told in first person.

Scribbling of the pen, and the annals glided into "Section Two." The subject matter was socially taboo for decades. This broken rule literally screamed, "You can't do this!" Exactly my message to society about pedophiles, rapist, and abusers. I was a survivor.

A perpetual outsider among my kinsmen. Never able to bridge the gaps that were my differences, or remove the labels. The acting out that followed Jane's and my childhood terrors left us ostracized auslanders into adulthood.

I was unwanted? Perhaps it was the responsibility of taking in an abandoned child that was undesirable. Their litters were huge and the culture was poor. I was an extra financial burden, more than they could afford. Connected to my biological people, though only on the fringes of their fond emotional attachments. In that, my heart was broken. I was the son of troubled souls. My parents and their offspring were considered to have no value. They received little respect.

The rejections and slanders were ultimate. My immediate family was at the bottom of the pecking order with the kinsmen. I wasn't the only one on the fringes. I hold no grudges or bitterness toward them today. Truth is harsh some times.

Saul Hotman had endured, and now he found the courage to rise above the emotions, labeling, and social handicaps connected to an impoverished, disadvantaged, and miserable childhood. No self-pity, here. He'd speak as I wrote down the words coming from a child's heart. It was okay now for him to break the silence--no more monsters. He didn't have to be afraid, or ashamed any longer. He'd reveal the taboo.

Countless childhood horrors that paralyze are generational, in every hometown. The subject matter was universal. Maybe this would help others–imparting hope through a survivor's account. Love as you would want to be loved was the message.

Some believed that men don't tell. Bad things happen to everyone in this lifetime, and some shouldn't be revealed, or discussed--just buried. That was the rule for the forebears. The guidelines needed to be broken.

Not wanting to knock off the emotional scabs. Not only my silence but tens of other victims were guilty of keeping our mouths shut about the abuse. I had to repent for my silence. Many young lives were ruined during Merl Judas' life span. The tragedies didn't have to happen. They did though. In part, because of this author's muted years. Merl's many other adult victims of childhood abuse maintained the code of silence. His intimidation tactics worked. The fear and shame kept our lips sealed. We wouldn't tell. Not until it was too late.

There is no known cure for a pedophile. Symbolically I would speak now, through HOTMAN'S INNOCENCE, for the silent victims who never found justice. Sadly, Saul Hotman's narrative should have been told forty years ago! But who would have listened then? Who would have believed him/me?

Public awareness and education about the overwhelming frequency of this crime could help bring changes. The social stigma for a victim must be removed in a caring society. One should never remain silent about the crimes. I'm not a psychologist, but personal experience tells me our children must be taught at a very early age what is inappropriate touching and sexual behavior out of adults toward juveniles. Parents and children's care-givers should research and educate themselves to be familiar with the silent language of children acting out. There are many non-verbal signs displayed by those who have been violated. This book wasn't an information manual about the signs. Though parents should educate themselves about acting out. An informed mind and keen eye can understand this language. Acting out speaks loudly, and can tell the story of a crime without spoken words. It is a silent cry for help in many cases.

Justice is instrumental for the healing process of any victim, even a child! Ignorance, secrecy, and silence of victims, their loved ones, and care-givers only empowers abusers. Habitual pedophiles know this! Immediately, authorities should be contacted when abuse is suspected, evidence gathered and saved, or more times than not the pedophile gets away with his crimes and he will violate again. This evil is not selective as it has no specific race, religion, gender, or economic boundaries. A pedophile could be anyone. A crime of secrecy.

If Jane's and my care-givers would have known the signs, and encouraged us to talk. Perhaps they would have reported the crimes. That might have prevented Merl Judas from violating many more children during his life-span. Perchance he would have gotten help, or been incarcerated. Maybe not. Merl was not unlike other pedophiles as many are skilled manipulators. He fooled the majority.

HOTMAN'S INNOCENCE would remain for decades after I was gone. Maybe a beneficial impact would come of the effort. Today, I am a trouble maker for any abuser!

World wide, one in three girls, and one in seven boys are raped and molested before adulthood, an epidemic. One pedophile violates an average of one hundred children during his lifetime. Ninety-six percent of all pedophiles find new victims. This is a cancer on modern society. It was time for HOTMAN'S INNOCENCE, an act of my social responsibility. I would tell the story through the voice of a child, and adult victims of abuse.

I'd also address universal social issues of addiction, domestic violence, persecution of the handicapped, extremes of religion, and racism. These are many times generational. Abuse of any form is a crime. It is an act of stripping individual power and control from the victims' lives. Most times it is a struggle to take back one's own life after being victimized.

HOTMAN'S INNOCENCE, my victorious battle cry against every child's King of Terror--pedophiles and domestic violence. This book was not written with malice, or as a form of revenge--a declaration of HOPE. Bitter victims suffer. Truly, forgiveness and kindness are greater than vengeance. That doesn't mean one should not have to take responsibility for the crimes he commits against the innocence. NEVER BE SILENT! Those who protect a pedophile at the expense of a child had might as well be accomplices to the crimes.

Merl Judas stole little Saul Hotman's dignity. As an adult, I fought back! I took back what was rightfully mine. In helping others to do the same–I'm only getting started. The truth sets men free. Perhaps this is where Justice lives.

This book was final liberation, and closure for a traumatized childhood.

HOTMAN'S INNOCENCE
SECTION ONE
THE ANCESTORS' LEGACY

(In Third Person)

1997: A Letter From Delena To Saul

Dear nephew, Saul:

I hope my many letters have given you enough information to write the stories about our forefathers. My short term memory seems to be slipping a bit these days. The past is more appealing now, that I am old and homebound. Concentrating isn't as difficult when remembering long ago. Maybe you will be able to write that book now. I'd hate for the family legacy to be lost.

Had to get help writing this letter, and took three stabs at finishing it. My brain isn't working right. Can't seem to focus on a task for long periods.

I love you like a son. You and Jane brought a lot of happiness into my troubled life. Ricky and I should have adopted you. Though Leve did right by you for a time. She and Jake should have adopted you. It just didn't happen that way. You survived though. Despite the rough start, you did good, Saul. You and Jane, both are strong.

Guess we're a family of survivors. Don't ever forget the family stories. Yours will be added to the legacy by the next generation. Competent with words, just know you can organize and put this together appropriately. I'll be waiting to see you make good on your promise. Exposing evil is a moral, and social responsibility. Hope I'm able to read a copy before I die.

Hey, be sure you describe my character as colorful as I really am. I've always said what I think. I gave everyone hell at least once.

Maybe you could start by telling about Pa, your grandfather Isaiah. He was my dearest friend. I miss him still, some sixty-five years after his death.

Your momma Ora, what a stupid and silly, rebellious girl. She didn't deserve you kids. I could have strangled her and Merl. Maybe you can devote half the manuscript to that story. God only knows people need to wake up. Expose the evil.

I had some horror stories too. Oh, that wicked man, Newton! I finally got past it. Even found solace in something that feels like forgiveness. Heard he really did repent. Too bad his son's turned out to be town drunks. Better to be a drunk than a rapist, though both are loathsome.

The family legacy, maybe its a curse. Too much pain. Gotta find some good in the tragedies. I just know you can discover a way to do that. Be brave!

None of us Hotman kids were saints. Ma, your grandmother Anne came the closest to that title. She prayed herself to death, ya know. Put that in the book. Ma was a saint.

Bitterness is a conniving bitch. She's a thief, robbing precious moments, with help from her wicked sister Hatred. I've known them in my time. Stay clear of those old whores! Shake the dust off when the jerks do you wrong and go on to happier times when your heart is broken. They'll get their comeuppance. Don't ever let them get your anger out of you. I failed there a time or two.

Wisdom is quenched when two devilish sisters named Insanity and Tyranny rule a man's soul. Take it from one who knows. Don't fall under their spell. The human spirit is resilient when we allow ourselves to learn from bad experiences, and not go insane with rage and anger. The pain can make us strong, better people, if we don't get bitter. Instead choose to learn. Don't get mad, get smart is what I always said after I found out anger only hurt me.

I'm losing my mind. I may not be able to write another letter. But before that happens I wanted to encourage you to tell it all. Our story will be a blessing to others. I just know it will!

Now I forgot what else I was going to say. That has happened after every other line. Thanks to my aide I was able to organize my thoughts enough to send this to you.

Bye for now. Love you!

Your old cantankerous aunt, Delena.

While clutching the paper and walking away from his home-office window Saul adjusted his glasses and smiled. Placing the letter in a drawer he sat down. Reaching for a note book next to his computer, he sighed. "I love you too Delena. I'll write your story, and mine. The family legacy won't be lost," he whispered.

Sturdy middle-aged fingers ran through his short dark-hair flecked with tiny strands of gray. Switching on the computer and glancing over his notes he began to type, writing "Section One" of HOTMAN'S INNOCENCE.

Part One
The Hotmans
1910 to 1933
Anne, Isaiah, Delena and Leve
The Early Years

Chapter One

As the strong men harvested timber for railroad cross ties, Isaiah, twenty-six, a tall handsome bulky lumberjack, paused, wiped the sweat from his brow and ran his stout fingers through his black hair. Muscles bulging, the air entering his lungs broadened his chest. His torso extending even more when he forcefully drew the heavy axe handle high over his head and powerfully swung downward. With a crashing blow crackling sounds echoed across the hollows as steel-embedded green hard oak and the log split full length.

His older brothers, mean-spirted, burley, hairy Bill who was as ornery as a wild Arkansas razorback and smaller whiney Jimmy skidded logs with the mules. With a crack of the whip and a holler, "Gee! Haw! Woe! Get up there, you ol' bawd!" they commanded the beast. But their voices were muffled by the clamor and whistle of distant steam donkeys. Wood-fired steam engines used to hoist and saw. The primitive mechanical power-horses roared at the mill over the hill. In the nearby forest were other lumberjacks. The booming slams of falling trees vibrated the earth beneath the soles of their heavy work boots.

Using a crosscut saw, the brothers pulled and pushed, and the colossus trees fell. They wielded heavy metal wedges and a broadaxe while chiseling ties out of fallen hardwood oak timbers. The rhythmic ring of steel against steel became the constant daylight song in the forest as lumberjacks worked. These were the sounds of money, food on the table, shoes on their feet, and clothes for their families. A dozen today? Ten tomorrow? Fifteen the day after? This was a good day's work, and the buying agent would be pleased. He'd short them some. But that was the way it was. He'd make the profit off their sweat when he sold the ties to different railroad lines and the Hotman families would survive another harsh coming winter with the supplies the meager money would buy.

When they broke for lunch and sat on a fallen log to eat their beans and cornbread, Bill and Jimmy told Isaiah that the time had come for him to take a wife. They told him smart Anne Hunter, Bill's young sister-in-law, had a shine for his company.

In a bass voice, big Bill slapped his knees and teased, "She's ripe for a man now!"

Isaiah blushed.

Jimmy chuckled and punched Isaiah in the side. "Darn good-lookin' too. Ya can't go wrong there!" He pulled a handkerchief from his overall pocket then loudly blew his nose and stuffed the hanky into his pocket again.

Bill whacked Isaiah on the back with his gigantic palm, smiling sincerely. "She's got religion too! Ain't no bloody Jezebel. A good girl! The marrying kind! Strong too. She'll give you sturdy sons to help ya in the fields. Don't need to wait too long or someone else will snatch her up."

Isaiah smiled still blushing and nodded.

"Fine then, I'll tell my wife May Bell and she'll tell her that you are coming to court Saturday at noon," Bill said, smirking.

Jimmy said, "It's about time, Boy! I was beginning to think you weren't natural! You should have married eight years ago. Hell your life's half over and you ain't got one young Hotman to your name."

"Oh, I'm natural all right, just shy around the girls," Isaiah said, head down.

"Then it's settled! You'll start courtin' on Saturday," Bill said as he scarfed down the last bite of his cornbread and followed it with half a quart canning jar of fresh cow's milk.

Isaiah wolfed down the last of his beans and placed the bowl back inside the one-gallon metal lard bucket used for a lunch pail. Smiling he rolled off the log onto the ground in front of his brothers, stretched out, and placed his hands under his head. "Ya know, I've had a crush on Anne since she was fourteen. I hope she likes me."

Bill and Jimmy chuckled.

As Isaiah gazed into the forest canopy of lush green red-oak and white-oak leaves he noticed a bald eagle take flight from one of the upper branches fifty paces away. The majestic bird soared high in the bright blue cloudless April sky. "I hear there are flying machines now that can take a man up there where that eagle soars," he said.

Bill and Jimmy laughed hysterically.

"Isaiah Hotman you've been into the niggers' white lightenin' again! Drunk you are!" Jimmy said.

"Next thing you know you'll be telling us that one day soon some maniac will fly one of those contraptions to the moon and back!" Bill joked.

"That's right brothers, and they'll power the contraption with Ozark Negroes' moonshine!" Isaiah said and laughed as Bill and Jimmy playfully rolled off the log on top of him and they began to wrestle. Isaiah chuckled again. Then he howled, "Well boy's, you've gotta admit the Kick-A-Poo-Joy-Juice is mighty powerful sauce."

They continued laughing hysterically while scuffling in the leaves.

Chapter Two

Dense splashes of colorful pink and white tree blossoms from Dogwoods and Redbuds surrounded the Hunter house in the near woods. The clear blue sky was tipped in silver as the warm midday sun reflected off the rushing pristine creek waters a hundred feet from their log cabin. Shy, pretty, sixteen-year-old Anne watched out her bedroom window and waited impatiently as Isaiah rode his mule the mile to their home at the edge of the oak forest. She was hoping for the beginnings of romance.

Isaiah came courting that Saturday with liquorice-flavored rock-candy. His large rough calloused hand clinched a bouquet of wild flowers as he dismounted Silk, his mule. Waving the flowers above his head, confidently smiling, he yelled from the front yard of the Hunter home, "Mr. Hunter! I come to court your daughter Anne."

Anne giggled. He was prompt as the clock over the fire place mantel.

The elderly, pale complexioned Mr. Hunter, limping from an old Civil War injury, hobbled out of the house supporting his right leg with a cane. His face wrinkled and stern from age, he smiled with no teeth and pointed his cane up while propping himself against the door facing. "Come on in, Boy. Anne's waiting. You're welcome here," he said with a slight quiver in his voice and faltered back to his rocking chair inside, lit his pipe, and resumed reading his worn Bible. Tobacco smoke swirled over his head.

Anne nervously admired herself in the looking glass before Isaiah walked inside. Never satisfied with her appearance she pinched her cheeks and fiddled with hair combs. Glancing downward at her feet to see her petticoat wasn't showing, she tugged at her ankle-length blue leaf-print skirt, handsewn from flour-sack material. She adjusted the lace around the neck of her white puffed-sleeves linen blouse.

Her lustrous light brown hair was braided, up off the shoulders, rolled in twirls around her head and secured with combs. Her Swedish bloodline came through with rosy cheeks, fair skin, and refined facial features. She was deeply religious, Baptist, a virgin. One look and she melted with desire when Isaiah spoke.

Restlessly squeezing his sweat-stained gray brim hat in his large hands, hesitating, stuttering shyly, he said, "Miss Anne, I think you're a fine strong pretty woman and I'd like to get to know you better. If that would be all right with you?" He dropped his gaze.

Anne secretly fantasized about him since she was thirteen, and finally they were courting. She felt faint with excitement, as she blushed with a girlish smile, and dimples pierced her cheeks. She held a lace handkerchief loosely in her hand while wiping the nervous perspiration off her brow, and then covered her mouth as she continued to giggle.

Her high cheek bones were inherited from her Black Dutch Cherokee grandmother, other than that she had the features of the Swed. "Isaiah Hotman, I think you are a right nice man, and I'd be proud to get to know ya better," she said while batting her eyelashes and blushing. Consciously she made the effort to stop uneasily biting her lower lip.

When he glanced up smiling and looked into her face, she reached for his hand. Grinning, he grasped her calloused field-worker hands in his brawny large fist, and they stepped onto the front porch.

She looked over her shoulder to see if Mr. Hunter and her ma were watching and then sat down on the porch swing. Ma and Pa Hunter quickly turned their heads back to what they were doing. But Anne didn't mind them watching. Their presence made her feel safe.

Anne stood, peeking through the open doorway again wanting her mother Zoe's approval while still holding Isaiah's sweaty palm. "Ma, do you need me to help?" she asked and winked.

Dark complexioned, Anne's mother was smaller framed with strong Cherokee features, though her father was a full-blood Swed. She wore her mostly black salt-and-pepper hair pinned up and a floor-length full flour-sack print green dress. Smiling, she nodded and winked and went back to preparing the meal.

Content, Anne sat back down beside Isaiah. He placed his arm around her shoulder. She was happy that Ma approved of her choice and with his arm draped over her as she snuggled closer and smiled.

They sat on the porch swing chatting, getting to know each other. As they continually held hands, her heart fluttered in her throat. He was her first beau.

He charmed her with his heavy jovial voice. His large, deep-blue eyes held her spellbound. His healthy olive complexion, shimmering soft black hair, tall strong physique with broad shoulders, powerful chest, and muscular arms complemented his warm sincere smile and full set of sturdy teeth. His handsome chiseled face, square jaw, chin with cleft, refined nose, and long lashes accented his eyes. In his faded bib overalls and red plaid shirt, his masculine stance resembled a Greek god she had seen etched in a book.

They married within a few short weeks. She loved him after their first courting, and would love him until she died.

Anne and Isaiah purchased 120 acres from his brother Jimmy near the settlement of Loafer's Glory, thirteen miles from Red Hill. Harsh spoken, smaller framed than Isaiah, light complexioned, ash brown hair with a slight red cast and freckles, Jimmy was not nearly as good looking as his younger brother.

He suffered from allergies, frequently clearing his throat, coughing, spitting, and blowing his large long nose on a soiled handkerchief. Some thought Jimmy had the consumption but he smoked, which made the condition worse. Jimmy and his fat middle-aged wife Hanna were Anne's and Isaiah's nearest neighbor.

Old-growth timber cloaked the grounds where their newly purchased property lay. They constructed a crude two-room wainscot shack. Later, as the family grew, they built a larger rough-plank cabin and cleared their ground. On the average, Anne had a child every two years for the next twenty.

Anne's first child Delena was born in 1912. Isaiah wanted a boy. Having to make do with a girl he nicknamed her, Son. She was Daddy's little girl with an attitude. Isaiah spoiled Delena. Twice more he was disappointed when Tina and then Leve were born in 1914 and 1917.

Anne was eight months pregnant in the spring of 1918 with their fourth child when Isaiah hitched a team of mules to the wagon as he did once a month to fetch supplies in Dinktown. Anne crouched at the kitchen table peeling potatoes, frowning, preoccupied and frustrated, she sighed, lay the knife on the table, and put forth her rough hands toward Delena, whom she watched rushing through the yard toward the back porch. She smiled. Delena was a beauty.

Anne's pampered first born, vivacious cotton-top Delena, almost seven, had a light complexion and steely blue eyes. Her long blond hair trailed past her shoulders, trimmed square at the ends.

Delena bounded into the house and crawled onto Anne's lap. Kissing Anne on the cheek, she threw her arms around her ma's neck. "I wish you could go with us Ma," she said.

Anne's rough hand stroking Delena's hair. "Child, you make your pa head home before he gets too liquored up. I want you back before dark. Ya hear!"

Giggling she said, "Yes Ma."

"Okay, now I won't worry. You're a good girl Delena," she said while playfully kissing Delena all over the face.

Isaiah stepped inside. Anxious to head out he was gruff. "Son, get in the wagon. It's time to go."

Laughing, Delena kissed her ma on the cheek again. Her long gray wool coattail flying high behind, she leaped toward the wagon outside.

"Anything special this trip, Honey?" Isaiah asked.

"Yes," Anne said, continuing to peel potatoes. She glancing up at him, smiling. "I need cloves to pickle, cocoa, sugar, and ginger. Tell Delena, she'll help you remember. Take your coat. There's a chill in the air." She leaned forward and turned to peek out the kitchen window. Dark angry clouds rolled in the distant sky. She sighed with a frown, "Looks like we're in for another cold snap. It may rain again."

"No, I mean something special." Grin lines surrounded his lush lips, and he ran his fingers through his hair then put on his hat.

Beaming, she said, "New needles, and one of those pretty blue sacks of flour. That material would make a lovely Sunday dress for Delena. Maybe you could get some blue buttons? Not too big now."

He folded his arms and leaned against the door facing and grinned. "Is there anything else?"

Leve, fifteen months, was crying in the next room. Anne dropped the potato and knife on the table, scooped her off the floor quilt, cradled her, sat in an oak rocker and rocked with great gusto to quiet the baby. She didn't want to awaken four-year-old cotton-top Tina asleep on another pallet.

Her composure changing to agitation, she whispered forcefully, "Yes, don't you come home drunk, and be here before dark! Dinktown is Sin City! I don't want Delena around roughness. You watch her!"

She sensed he was humiliated and angered by her prohibiting posture as guilt boiled up from his belly. Wrenched faced Isaiah squirmed, removed his hat and run his fist around the brim. He said nothing but glared back at her.

Her hostility over his craving of booze gave her gratification when she made him grope under conviction. Scowling, she thought he was resisting penitence. Obviously he hated her scathing tongue. A different approach might work better next time. Maybe?

She knew he adored her. Jovial most of the time, but head strong, she ruled the perch to his rancor. Exuberant in her religious zeal to change his ways made him revolt even more but backing down this time wasn't an option. He twisted his hat again, saying nothing in defiance to her commands. She saw that he abhorred her hammering him over his guzzling of the corn squeeze as his brow wrinkled and he hatefully leered back at her when she sternly said, "All drunkards are bound for hell!"

Maybe he'd come home sober this time. He had to watch out for Son. Maybe he would escape her tongue lashing this evening if he would just come home sober. She didn't like being crabby with him anymore than he liked getting chewed at.

Afraid the rough ride could bring the labor a month early, Anne reluctantly remained at home with the younger children. She continued to rock Leve, and hummed a lullaby while watching out the window as Delena and Isaiah rode the wagon out of sight.

Leve quieted and slept. Anne fretted that Isaiah would come home drunk until they returned.

Chapter Three

Delena stood up on the moving buckboard. Overwhelming joy and excitement surged through her young mind as the Galloping Goose's lonesome whistle screams echoed across the hollows. She was exhilarated and began to jump about as they approached Dinktown. Her arm extended, index finger pointing to the column of black smoke rising in the direction of the whistle beyond the next hill she shouted, "Look, Pa! It's the Goose!"

Firmly and gruff, Isaiah snapped, "Sit, Son, before you fall off the wagon."

Slowing into Dinktown, the steam locomotive chugged. The clatter of moving railcars and screech of heavy steel wheels against the tracks as she came to a stop brought the hustle and bustle of waiting merchants and customers around the depot. The locomotive delivered passengers at the terminals and took on new ones. The air was heavy with a hot slick haze. Steam blanketed the train. The odors of soured wood and crates of fresh garden produce waiting for a haul, mingled with the vapors of burning coal used to fuel her engine. Sooty, grey-black smoke came from the locomotive stacks, drifting downward onto the loading docks.

Isaiah parked the wagon then he and Delena went inside the depot to check for mail at the new post office.

Returning to the buckboard Delena coughed, and Isaiah cleared his throat, spitting on the street when they sat with the mail in hand and a new Sears and Roebuck catalogue.

Black and white workers on the docks stepped out of the intense toxic fumes for fresh air and then returned to work moving freight. Cargos were unloaded and replenished. Materials for sale by the local people fill her cars. Dock workers unloaded commodities and supplies to the Dinktown store shelves, while other workmen transferred communal inventory onto the train. Delena watched intently from the wagon seat as they labored.

In Dinktown the grand Galloping Goose locomotive met the runtier Dinky train. The Dinky's wood-fired steam engine was half the size of the bigger Galloping Goose's. Dinky lugged slower but her mighty three cylinders were enough to climb the craggy hills with weighty loads. Chunga, screech, and moans rang out as she labored down the tracks to and from the forest.

Dinky belonged to Broosters Mill the world's largest whiskey and wine barrel manufacturer. Hundreds of Negroes had moved to the area in the past few years. They worked at the mill, kept Dinktown alive, and had even laid the tracks Dinky ran on. She blustered along tens of winding and curving miles into the dense hardwood jungle, and along the Little Red river. The little iron horse always left a trail behind, hickory smoke bellowing out from her bantam locomotive exhaust stacks. She carried precious cargo, fresh-cut stave bolts, logs, and Negro workers.

Delena never rode the Galloping Goose but her husky uncle Bill had secretly stowed her away on the Dinky. He filled in for the sick engineer that day a year ago, on her sixth birthday. He could get fired if anyone found out. But they never did. Bill was her favorite uncle, except for when he and Isaiah got drunk together.

Bill resembled Isaiah in height and build but his hair was light brown and he sported a heavy black beard and mustache. He unconsciously and frequently scratched the thick chin hair and picked at his mustache with tough, large lumberjack fingers while gazing off into nowhere in deep thought. Hot tempered with the Negroes, he lost his patience easily, and was openly racist. But he was completely different with children, both blacks and whites.

Bill provoked Delena to laughter with his playful childlike personality. His fondness for spinning silly stories and jokes kept her and the other kids intrigued and giggling.

He spoiled her too. She liked that. Maybe she would get to see uncle Bill today.

Isaiah drove the team of mules and the wagon came closer to the whiskey barrel mill as Delena continued to happily take in the sights.

He groaned.

Leaning her head on his arm and looking into his face as he glanced down, she asked, "What's wrong Pa?"

Grimacing, he sighed. "I was thinking about my youngest brother Buster."

Delena sighed. "Pa he'll be all right. Don't worry your mind." She smiled.

Isaiah smiled and winked at her. She giggled.

Delena remembered Isaiah pleading with Buster not to join the army. She sensed the ache in her pa's heart. She had heard him mention many times he thought Buster would be killed.

Buster, twenty-one, was fighting on German battlefields. Tall, slim and redheaded with a black beard, he was different from Delena's older uncles. Not as harsh. A kind hearted spirit and generous to a fault, he hoped to be a doctor someday. Maybe the Army would help him with the training.

Delena thought about Buster's bothersome habit of clicking his little pinky and thumb and rolling his thin lips inward and pressing them together when in deep thought. This annoyed her. But another thought ticked her off more. She had heard Isaiah more than once say that he felt like a parent to Buster, not a brother. Buster was a grown man and didn't need a daddy, especially not hers!

In the distance several brawny black workers hoisted bundles of staves and she remembered the first time she saw black people two years earlier. They bewildered her. She flashed back to that moment.

"Pa! What's wrong with that man? He's all muddy!" she exclaimed, when one of the Negro dock workers walked out of the engine smoke that settled around the Galloping Goose.

"He ain't muddy, Son! He's a Negro. That's just his natural skin color. His ancestors come from Africa. A wild dangerous land, far, far away from here."

"Is everybody from Africa muddy color?" she asked.

"No, they some white, pink and tan and yellow folks there too. But most are black like that Negro."

She giggled at the memory as Isaiah jerked his hat back down to his brow when the wind picked up.

The early morning rain turned the streets into a gooey mess. Black mud was flung backwards from the wagon wheels as they slugged along. The acrid smells of burning coal from the Galloping Goose, soured bleeding trees' sap from cut logs, fermented white-oak staves, and railroad ties filled their nostrils. They coughed and her nose burned inside. Pungent wood smoke from stoves in the homes, sweet horse manure on the rugged streets, outhouse latrines, and moonshine stills perfumed Dinktown, populated by ten thousand residents.

Delena pulled a clean white handkerchief from her coat pocket, and covered her nose, hoping to lessen the offensive odors. Her stomach churned. Their eyes watered from the haze of smoke.

Loud noises of industry, mules braying, cattle mooing, lumberjacks cursing, singing laborers, saloon hall music, and the clanging trains roared inharmoniously. This was a loud, nasty, violent, and smelly place. Not peaceful and clean like home.

On a side street stood Doctor Ben, his goat cart stuck in the muck.

She watched him hesitate before jumping off the cart to help lessen the load for the pair of billy goats that drew his small wagon. She tugged at Isaiah's coat sleeve. "Pa, there's Doc Ben. I think he's stuck."

Isaiah snapped his head around and began to chuckle as Doc's stubborn goats refused to budge an inch. Doc, forcefully tugging on the harness to drag them ahead, slipped in the mud and went sprawling backward onto the street.

Delena giggled hysterically and Isaiah rolled with laughter as Doc crawled to his knees cursing, his new suit covered in mud. Isaiah said, "Is he ever gonna learn? When is that rich fool gonna get a mule or a horse? Even a donkey or oxen would be better than goats."

"Pa, I don't think he's rich. Folks mostly pay him in chickens and eggs and pelts and firewood. That's what uncle Bill told me," she said, laughing.

"Think folks need to take up a donation and buy him a mule. That would be better than goats in case of an emergency. Goats are too slow."

Wide eyed, smiling, Delena cupped her hand over her ear."Listen, Pa. Hear how pretty they sing?"

Isaiah nodded.

Muffled, holy singing of Negro spirituals reverberated to heaven above Dinktown as workers sweated on their jobs. She liked the soulful tunes that hummed under all the other clamor. Mill saws moaned, buzzed, and shrieked, barrel saw blades screamed grated on her nerves. But the singing was soothing.

The warning-cry sounded: "Timber!" Then old-growth hardwood rumbled like thunder crashing to the earth on the surrounding hillsides. The trees surrendered to men's sweat, saws, mules brute physical strength, and the Brooster company's determination. Mill saws, and blades turned by clanging steam donkeys ripped through giant white oak logs ten hours a day. The trees had no voice to moan. The blades did their jobs and cried for the forest with loud mechanical sounds. Implications of prosperity and economic good times for the people faltered as the rich got more wealthy. The poor had jobs to provide regular income, which was security and prosperity enough. Just to survive was good.

Most of the blacks were religious. Delena saw one of those holiness black ladies washing clothes in Willey's Cove creek near where the Galloping Goose refilled her boilers. The towering wooden water tank was five hundred feet from the depot and stood six feet above the Goose's stacks. Delena and Ma had overheard some ebony church women talking during earlier visits while they shopped in the mercantile. She remembered the women huddled around the bolts of dress-making material, and conversing about a Negro prophet named William J. Seymour as they checked out the pretty prints. She heard them enthusiastically say Seymour started a new work of God in California.

They were dressed like pictures of penguins she had seen, basic black dresses with white aprons and tied bandanna caps covering their kinky hair. The sight of the wash lady reminded her of that day in the mercantile.

The women had talked about a ghost. He was a good ghost. They called him Holy. She shivered, the memory evoked the same response of fear as the first time. The ghost sounded scary and weird.

Lifting her gaze toward the distant highest hill to take her mind off the ghost, she observed Backbone Mountain, now crowned by a rainbow after the morning's shower. The hills were alive with color. "Look, Pa! It's a rainbow!" she yelled.

Isaiah glanced up to see. "Ah, the wee people are moving their pot of gold," he teased.

"Oh, Pa, don't be silly! There aren't any wee people. Ms. James at school told me that last week."

Isaiah chuckled and popped the mules back. "Get on up there!" The mules trotted a little faster.

Delena loved springtime. The leaves had returned after the harsh Ozark's winter. The hills sang with new life, baby birds and critters, new beginnings and young growth. Colors of hot pink, tones of blue, shades of yellow, purple, and white splashed a tapestry of happy hues, mingled with new leaves. The bright glory of flowering foliage painted the promise of a good growing season. She would pick a bouquet of tree blossoms for Ma before returning home.

Drunken brawls and fights inside taverns and on saloon streets caused commotions. Drawing closer to the barrel mill she heard cursing as they rode past a tavern. Delena didn't understand those words. Ma didn't allow that talk in their home, but Delena knew they were ugly words filled with hate.

Innocently she tugged at Isaiah's coat sleeve. "Pa, what's a bastard?"

Snapping his head around, glaring angrily, he snarled, "Girl, I ottar wash your mouth out with lye soap! Don't you ever use that word!"

He was mad and she knew better than to ask again. Trembling fearfully she said. "I'm sorry, Pa." Dirty word! I don't need to know the meaning, and that is that, she thought, while counting her blessing for not being paddled. Good decent folks weren't suppose to say them, ma said.

Lots of things were fascinating and fearful in Dinktown and she had many questions for Isaiah that afternoon. But she never asked the meaning of another curse word.

Musicians, and pretty, easy women entertained. Honky-tonk pianos, fiddlers, and banjo pickers played lively tunes in the taverns. Dinktown pubs, jute joints, and the big white brothel houses in Rumley a few miles down the road were wicked places of wine and song. Spirits flowed freely until the wee hours of morning. No wonder Ma wanted them home before dark.

Sometimes the place frightened her, the people looked mean with scowled sad faces, fear and hate radiated from their eyes. Many of the scruffy men were sick, coughing and puffing on rolled tobacco anyway. When the wind was right, she could smell them before they came up the street.

Ma never let their family go without bathing. She insisted on tub baths every Saturday afternoon whether they needed one or not. Sponge, spot baths every evening before bedtime, Ma insisted.

She was glad Pa was big and strong. He would protect her if anyone tried to mess with her. She snuggled closer to him on the wagon seat when they passed another saloon and two brawling drunks making fools of themselves in the mud.

On many occasions she waited outside the tavern for her pa. This trip without Anne was no different. He parked the wagon on a side street off the town square. "I'm going in the pub to have a visit with the rail agent. You stay put. I'll be back in about twenty minutes."

She smiled. "Okay, Pa! Bring me a sweet drink, will ya?"

"Sure, Honey," he said while securing the brake on the wagon. He tied the reins down then jumped to the street and strolled half a block to the nearest pub.

Delena crawled to the back and moved a folded tarp. She thought to hide under it if he stayed too long. Happily, standing at the end of the wagon, she listened to the lively music drifting out of the saloon. She ran her fingers through her long hair, pulling it behind her ears. She tapped her toes and her worn black slippers made clunking sounds against the wagon-bed to the beat of a honky-tonk piano playing "Buffalo Gal." Hesitantly, she began to jig dance.

She drew a crowd as passers by smiled and clapped while throwing pennies into the wagon. She liked the attention and the smiling faces. She cut loose with full confidence moving her feet quickly. Her dress tail flying high showed her long bloomers when she spun around. After twenty minutes of jigging, exhaustion set in and she collapsed onto the tarp.

Just as she fell, her intrigued audience of six gaily dressed pretty saloon gals, three black church ladies, and a couple of old wrinkled men scattered when a husky bartender pitched a burley cursing drunk onto the muddy street, face first. Pedestrians laughed loudly when he pulled himself from the black ooze.

Struggling to stand he cursed thunderously, wiping the mud and horse and ox manure off his face. Raging, he pulled a large knife from his boot, threatening everyone who continued to laugh.

Shaking in terror, crawled under the tarp. He couldn't see her and she couldn't see him.

Delena hated waiting. Her heart was sad as his twenty minutes ticked away to pass an hour and fell asleep. She awakened with Isaiah tickling her in the rib. "Wake-up, Sweety. I have your lemonade," he said.

They climbed onto the seat. Frowning, she could smell the whiskey every time he exhaled. "Now Pa, don't you get drunk! We gotta be home before dark!"

He didn't answer.

She sipped on her sweet cold lemonade and shivered in the cool abrasive spring air while trying to disregard the fact that her pa was a little tipsy.

Out of the corner of her eye she watched him repositing his hat further down on his brow. He popped the mules back with the reins. "Get up there," he said. The mules and wagon sloshed through the muck toward the mercantile.

Pa was going to get drunk and Ma was going to be angry with her. She snapped her head around to focus on the people and trains, hoping to get the sad thought out of her mind.

The trains and the black people fascinated her. She thought, while counting the pennies collected for dancing, I'll purchase peppermint candy sticks and share with Tina and Leve. Ma will kill me if she finds out I was dancing. Baptist don't dance is what Ma says. I won't tell her! She doesn't have to know. I just won't tell her.

The mules pounded through the mud down the street past the mill toward the new mercantile. Isaiah parked the wagon. They jumped off and strolled into the store.

Her pockets filled with peppermint sticks and the wagon loaded with fresh supplies, Delena was glad to leave town, away from the foul smells of commerce, and before alcohol got the best of Pa.

Ma would be proud of her! They'd be home before dark. She and Isaiah sang old folk ballads as they rode to the outskirts of Dinktown.

A shot rang out! Bewildered, she jerked, startled, clutching her chest. Pa trembling, as though a cold chill had traveled down his spine. He was scared!

"No! Buster! No!" he shouted.

Frightened and frowning she shrieked, "Pa, are you all right? Are you shot!" She fearfully held tight to his coat sleeve.

For a few seconds he was out of touch, gazing off into nowhere.

"Pa! Pa!" she cried, tugging at his coat and tapping his face with her small hand as the mules slugged along.

People were running toward the mill. In the excitement she heard a bearded elderly man shout from the street, "Get the sheriff!"

Isaiah snapped out of the trance and frantically parked the team near the blacksmith shop. "I'm okay, just a weird feeling, I think I had a vision of Buster being shot," he said when he pulled the wagon over and stopped.

Delena watched him shake his head again and place his face in the palms of his hands. Pa had too much to drink. She fearfully held tight to his arm as he shook his head as though tossing the thought of Buster out of his mind, like she tossed the Ghost out of her thoughts earlier. He nodded, pulled loose from her grasp, adjusted his hat, anxiously jumped off the wagon, and ran toward the Mill.

"Pa?" she cried, "Pa don't leave me here alone! I want to go home!"

He raced for the mill as she watched him looking back at her alone on the wagon. She heard him yell, "Stay put!" Then he hurried up the street to blend into the large crowd.

Saddened, sniffling, angrily, she squirmed to the back of the wagon and crawled under the tarp that covered the supplies. Her hands trembling for fear of being alone on the outskirts of town. Be brave. She reclined on a fifty-pound sack of flour. Pulling a peppermint stick from her coat pocket and swirling it around inside her mouth, she sucked out the fresh sweet taste while trying to hold back her tears of fright. They'd never get home before dark! Just like Ma, she was gonna give Pa a piece of mind when he came back. Then she softly cried.

Chapter Four

Bill was a Klan member and some of the Negroes knew. Fearful that Bill was the one shot, Isaiah ran wildly to find his brother.

When he arrived, the lifeless body of a dead Negro lay in the muck. Sickened and weakened by the scene, nausea churned in Isaiah's bowels.

Sadly he regarded other solemn grieving Negroes gathering around the body. Some were crying. Hate glared out of their eyes but they could do nothing to retaliate for their dead coworker. They restrained their rage as three husky grimacing white foremen standing off in the distance pointed shotguns in their direction. There wouldn't be trouble out of the black workers today!

Listening to the growing mixed-race crowd's comments, Isaiah learned another white worker had shot the Negro during an argument. The shooter had run off.

The crowd continued to grow around the gruesome sight as Isaiah worked his way through the sea of people, getting closer. Buster popped into his mind again as Isaiah stared at the dead man fifty feet away, lying center the mill yard. He shook his head to bounce out the thought, turned in the opposite direction facing the large assembly, nervously nodded, and adjusted his hat to one side as his hands trembled. He craved a shot of whiskey.

Relieved that the body wasn't Bill and realizing he could do nothing, Isaiah tried to leave the scene, struggling upstream through the river of people pressing forward. The mournful image of the Negro's bloody body fresh in his mind grieved him. He was eased when he saw the stocky sheriff deputy running down the street.

Panting to catch his breath, the deputy ordered the curious swarm to move back so he could access the crime scene, and the crowd cleared a path for him. "Well I'll be darn! Dumb nigger, shot dead in the head," he said while gazing with out compassion at the pool of bloody mud around the victim's lifeless form.

Isaiah could tell the deputy was thinking as deeply as possible for such a shallow mind as the officer removed his hat, exposing his bald head and scratching behind his ear with his stubby fingers.

The middle-aged pudgy and short officer slapped his new tan hat against his leg. Glaring hate with wrinkled-brow, he squinted. Lips taught in anger covered his clinched teeth as he never once took his hand off the gun and holster strapped to his leg. Frequently his cautious fearful eyes flicked toward the group of black workers who moaned and glared back at him.

Isaiah pressed his way back through the crowd, waited an at a distance watched.

The officer sighed, nodded, and took a deep breath. Addressing the black men around the body he said harshly, "Don't you boys think you need to get back to work? You aren't being paid to stand around and gawk!"

Without speaking, eyes downcast, obediently the blacks returned to their labors.

The deputy swerved toward the crowd and chuckled. "Its all right folks. Everything is under control here. You can go on back to you business. Go on! Break up this crowd, now. I do not see any shot dead man! Why am I called out here? There is just one of those lazy niggers. Don't call me again unless a real man is shot!" He stormed away cursing under his breath.

The mumbling onlookers moseyed back down the streets.

Saddened for the blacks, and relieved it wasn't Bill, Isaiah ambled down the muddy street toward Delena. Wanting to protect her young mind, he wouldn't tell her what he had seen.

Back at the wagon he didn't see Delena at first. His hands were shaking as he grabbed the tarp. His voice quivered, "Dear God, where are you Delena?" But then she moved slightly under the canvas. Seeing her lumpy little wiggling form under the tarp he sighed. "It's nothing, Honey. Just an argument at the mill. Bill is okay." He jumped back in the wagon and released the brake.

Delena crawled out from under the canvas and sat down beside him, pouting. He decided not to play her game so he ignored her.

He didn't like the idea of Bill being in the Klan. One day the blacks wouldn't submit and they would kill him. He couldn't do anything to change Bill. Troubled about how the blacks were treated and wanting to change things for the better, Isaiah felt his hands were tied. They were tied if he wanted to live. No one crossed the Klan!

He sensed big trouble on the horizon as tensions between the blacks and whites intensified. He was worried more that chaos and rampant lawlessness would ensue if prohibition laws were passed in January. More killings would come. He shook his head to toss the vision of the dead Negro out of his mind while grasping a small whiskey flask in his coat pocket.

Delena demanded his attention, and he had to chuckle as he gulped a shot and felt instant relief from the trembles.

Frowning, pulling her hair in frustration, she said, "You don't need that, Pa!"

He put the flask back in his pocket after downing another sip. He knew Delena was curious about what happened at the mill from the scowl on her face. But he also knew she was upset over him drinking and leaving her alone. He shouldn't have left her alone. Now he sighed feeling guilty and gently pinched Delena on the chin. "I love you, Sweetheart."

Forcing giggles she said, "Lets sing, Pa. That will take your mind off it."

Smiling, he wrapped her in a strong embrace. Holding her close with one arm, and the reins in the other hand, he popped the mules back.

"Get up there," he said. The wagon jerked, and away they went.

He felt powerful and important when Delena innocently lay her head against his sturdy arm. Powerful, because he knew her life and future were in his hands.

He hated himself for liking the booze so much. I'll quit drinking soon, he thought, as he popped the mules back again and they trotted homeward.

Wailing off key, he tried to teach Delena an old Irish folk ballad. They sang most of the ten-mile ride to Loafer's Glory.

Stopping a mile from home he let Delena snap floral branches off the Redbuds and Dogwoods alongside the trail. He helped her. Finally, after her constant questioning got the best of him, he told Delena a Negro man was shot.

Her brow wrinkled. "I remember great-grandmother Liz's death last year. Pa, death is final, sad and lonesome. I miss her. I don't understand."

He patted her on the head and looked into her face. Smiling, tenderly he said, "I know, Son, but you will understand someday."

She nodded and squinted as the first hues of purple evening light began to embrace the scene as the sun slipped behind the mountains. Curiously she asked, "Pa, did that Negro have any children and a wife?"

"I don't know, Honey. I'm sure he had somebody to love him." He handed her a short limb of dogwood blossom he had snapped from a high branch.

Grin lines appeared around her lip corners and dimples pierced her cheeks. "I'll bet he went to heaven. God loves Negroes, children, and even those KKK men. Ma told me so. I believe her," she said and broke off another branch two feet long covered with a cluster of redbud blossoms.

Isaiah smiled. "Your ma is right, sweety."

"Pa, why was Granny so cold when I touched her at the funeral?"

"Well, Sweety, you know when we gather mussels along the Buffalo, and sometimes when we open one there is a freshwater pearl inside?"

Smiling she said, "Yea, such pretty things to be in those ugly shells."

"That's what death is like. Some folks, like your granny, are pearls inside. God harvests the pearls and leaves the empty cold shell behind."

Skipping around a small Redbud and smiling, she sniffed the large bouquet in her arms. "Ma tells me good folks go to be stars that light the night, and some go to be angels when they die," she said. "So death isn't a bad thing if you are a pearl inside?"

"I think that is right."

"I wonder if Negroes can be pearls? Pa how can a human be a pearl?"

He chuckled. "I really don't know how pearls get inside the shells. But I think being a good-hearted, honest, hard working person makes us pearls."

"Ma says ya gotta have Jesus in your heart when you die or you go to hell."

"Your ma says so then it's so! I reckon!" He plucked a dogwood blossom from a limb and squatted down in front of her. "Come here," he said.

She nodded. Then in confusion as she stomped the ground and tossed an armload of tree blossoms into the back of the wagon. "Why do blacks and whites hate each other, Pa? What's a KKK? Ma says they were mean to great-grandma Liz because of her dark skin."

How could she understand racism? Even he, the adult, couldn't comprehend how racist hate overwhelmed people's lives.

Isaiah knew better than to express his feelings about the KKK openly in Dinktown or Loafer's Glory. He had to be careful how he answered her question in the likelihood she would repeat his statements. He wanted to protect her, and himself. Motioning for her to come closer while he held the flower in the palm of his large unfurled hand. "See this?"

She nodded.

"See those spots on the corners of each petal that look like dried blood?"

She nodded.

Pointing to the Dogwood tree he said, "See how twisted and small the trunk is?"

She glanced over at the tree and nodded.

"Look here." He lifted the blossom and pointed. "See how the four petals make a perfect cross. See the stains? They look like blood. The story is that God cursed the Dogwood because it used to grow as big as the oaks and man used it to make the cross Jesus was crucified on. The blossom represents the cross and Christ's blood that spilled from his head, hands and feet. Now that the tree is cursed, small and twisted, it can never be used to make another crucifixion cross."

"Pa now it's better than an oak. The blossoms compel people to happiness. I just know Ma will love her bouquet," she said and snapped more redbud branches.

While humming another folk song, he hoped she would loose interest about her racism question and he wouldn't have to reply. Bill was getting hard. He didn't like what the monster hate, and what the KKK was turning him into. "Honey, let me think about your questions a while before I give you an answer. You do want the right answers don't you?"

"That's okay, Pa. I think they are all just dumb for hating each other. Hate makes everybody sad," she said, as they climbed onto the wagon and headed home.

There, hoisting a fifty-pound sack of flour thrown over his shoulder and a package bound in brown paper and twine, Isaiah marched inside. Anne's smiling, dimpled face shined with delight when Delena came skipping through the doorway behind him and handed her the huge bouquet.

Anne smiling, pecked Delena on the cheek, hummed and lit the kerosene lamp, while he watched her place blossom branches in a gallon fruit jar filled with water. Delena ran for the wagon again. She centered the arrangement on the kitchen table and stepped to the door. "Come here, child! These are lovely!"

Delena rushed to Anne standing on the front porch. While holding tight to the sack of spices she carried in one hand and more blossoms in the other she threw her arms around Anne's waist.

Anne hugged and kissed Delena again, then went inside and unwrapped the package Isaiah laid on the table.

He felt proud of himself at her sparkle, and knowing he didn't forget the special supplies she requested. Maybe she wouldn't be cold toward him, knowing he had done as she requested. He even brought lace and extra material for additional dress making. Surely she would be pleased.

Delena ran her small fingers over the flour sack on the floor near the cookstove. He could tell she liked the blue print as he smiled and placed the tail of the faded dress she wore on the sack to compare the two materials.

"Ma, you gotta hurry up and get my new dress made! This is so pretty!" she said as she ran her hands over the blue sack again.

He imagined the finished dress on Delena. Anne would do it up right.

Anne's cheery face made clear her happiness to have them home and for the dress-making material. But when she kissed him and smelled his breath, she glared at him in silence. The stiff greeting, with a dead-fish kiss of appreciation, let him know her disapproval. But at least she wasn't nagging him about the booze.

She shook her head. Lines of frustration streaked across her brow but they smiled at each other and kissed again. Isaiah placed his hand on her swollen belly. Grinning, he said, "Maybe this one will be a boy?"

She nodded, smiled again, and placed her hand on his as their attentions turned to the next room where Delena was pulling Peppermint sticks from her pocket and placing them in three stacks in front of happy-eyed giggling Tina and Leve.

Anne scowled and turned to Isaiah. "You shouldn't waste the money on candy."

He grinned. "I didn't, Delena said the religious Negro ladies gave her pennies."

She scowled again. "Why on earth would they do that?"

"Just look at her! And you have to ask that question?"

"You're right. She is a friendly sweety. But who could resist!"

Chapter Five

A month had passed since Isaiah and Delena made the trip to Dinktown. Late in the afternoon a knock came at the door, and the sound of soft deep howling outside reminded Anne of old tomcats growling. She struggled to raise herself from the rocker. Her labor pains were light. She'd send Isaiah to fetch Hanna in a couple of hours. Ready to give birth any time, she waddled across the floor to open the door. Jimmy stood there. His face grief contorted, he cried bitterly.

She yelled for Isaiah. Jimmy came inside the house.

Isaiah stepped into the livingroom with Delena at his side. Anne had never before seen waspish Jimmy weep. Compassionately, she with drew a clean handkerchief from her apron pocket and gently placed it in his hand. "What has happened?" she asked.

He nodded, unable to speak, choking back his tears.

Isaiah placed his strong, large hand on Jimmy's shoulder as he sat at the kitchen table.

Calming some, he grimaced. "Buster is dead!"

Anne poured the men hot coffee. Jimmy blew his nose and stuffed the handkerchief into the pocket of his overalls as he went on fighting to restrain his sobs, and told them he had received word from the Army. Buster was shot in the head and killed the month before, the very day Isaiah and Delena had gone to Dinktown for supplies.

Astonished, Anne's and Isaiah's gazes locked together.

"Now I understand," Isaiah said, "I had a vision of Buster dying when the Negro was murdered. Now, I know why I missed him so much that day," then dropped his grief-stricken face, a tear silently working its way out of his eye. "My heart has been ripped out by the roots," Isaiah moaned.

Placing her free hand on his shoulder while pouring coffee, then she lifted her half-skirt apron and wiped her tear-filled eyes. "Sweetheart, your vision was a gift from God. It was the power of your love for Buster that allowed you to be with him in his last moments. This is a gift from God."

Isaiah wrapped his arms around her waist as she stood beside him.

Instantly her water broke, and her labor intensified as she doubled over in pain, dropping the blue-speckled enameled coffee pot. Scalding coffee mingled with the birthing-puddle on the floor. She screamed. This birth would be different. Her water had never broken this soon into the labor.

Isaiah and Jimmy scrambled to get her to the bed. "Go for Hanna!" she yelled.

Jimmy ran out of the house so fast Delena's dress tail move slightly in the breeze he stirred when he shot past her, and leapt out the front door. They could hear him coughing as he trotted on foot a quarter a mile down the road.

Anne waited impatiently as Hanna, Jimmy's tall, fat, middle-aged, bubbly wife, came riding bareback.

Delena shouted from the front door. "Hanna is here!"

Anne sighed as Hanna stormed into the house.

Hanna twisted and rolled her salt-and-pepper hair tight into a bun then secured it high on her head with hair combs she pulled from the pocket sewn on the front of her long gray plaid skirt. "Well it's about time, gal! I thought you were going to bust before this baby came. It's gonna be a big one!" she said.

Anne squeezed Isaiah's hand, and panted as another intense pain hit. Grunting painfully she whimpered, "I hope not too big." She relaxed as the labor subsided until the next came a few seconds later.

Hanna shook her head while tapping Isaiah on the shoulder as he sat next to Anne on the edge of the bed. She scowled. "Isaiah get!" she growled and glared at him. He promptly left the room.

Anne heard Delena giggling in the next room and chuckled as Isaiah cowed at Hanna's forceful presence.

"Child, let's see where we are," she said as she helped Anne remover her clothing and laid a clean white sheet over her naked body. When Anne was eased a bit Hanna fluffed the pillow. Smiling, she said while patting Anne's hand, "Honey, this looks like it's gonna be a quick delivery."

Anne cried, "Oh I hope so!"

Hanna glanced around the room. "I need an apron. The baby has already crowned."

Anne grimaced as another sharp pain hit and she grunted while squeezing Hanna's hands. The pain passed and she pointed toward the kitchen. Panting, she said, "On the wall by the cookstove is a clean one."

Hanna patted Anne's arm and smiled. "I'll be right back!" She waddled into the kitchen.

Hanna returned a few minutes later carrying a large butcher knife, cup of moonshine, and clean white rags. She placed the knife under the bed. "There, that'll cut the pain in half!" She gulped a swig of moonshine and ran her forearm over her face to wipe away the perspiration.

Anne grimaced, grunted, and nodded.

Hanna folded a rag, dipped it in a pan of cool water, wrung out the excess, and patted Anne's forehead.

Anne groaned again as she began to push.

"You're doing great, Honey!" Hanna said.

Anne grimaced, then tried to smile and screamed again.

Isaiah soon returned and handed Hanna another cup filled with moonshine. He winked. Turning his attentions toward Anne he trembled.

She struggling and crying, "You ol' drunkard! If you ever do this to me again I'll divorce you!" Anne snorted.

Hanna scowled and took a sip from the fresh cup. "Now get! This is a woman's time. You men cause us nothing but great travail!" He darted out of the room. "Put on a pot of creek willo tea to kill the pain!" she yelled.

The baby arrived with no complications two hours later.

Hanna cleaned the screaming child, and placed the newborn in Anne's arms. Smiling, she towered over them beside the bed as Anne examined the healthy, strong infant.

His powerful set of lungs wailed. Red faced expression of anger announced the beginning of a new life.

Isaiah, Delena, and Tina waited anxiously to see the new arrival in the next room. The suckling continued to cry loudly, and Hanna heard Leve began to cry. "Isaiah, quiet that child!" she yelled.

Isaiah scooped Leve off the floor, and rocked vigorously to quiet her, the oak rocker creaking on the plank floor. Anne let the baby nurse and they slept.

She awakened after thirty minutes and motioned to Hanna. Sweat beaded on Hanna's fat face as she dragged her forearm across her brow again to wipe away the perspiration from running into her large brown eyes. Exhausted, and panting, she smiled and said, "You can go in now.

Anne had an easy delivery. She should be fine, but I'll stay the night just incase there is a problem."

They all trailed into the bedroom. Anne was cradling the sleeping newborn on her chest above the sheet. Hanna took her seat again by the window as Anne motioned for Isaiah to sit down on the edge of the bed.

Delena, Tina, and Leve sat in the floor bunched together near the head of the bed. They impatiently picked at their clothes and ran their fingers through each other's hair. Tina pulled Delena's locks, and she squealed. "Ma, make her stop," she said.

"Quit, Tina! Quit!" Anne snapped, and Tina stopped. Anne gestured, and Hanna gently placed the baby in Isaiah's arms.

The girls fidgeted again. Hanna snapped her fingers, scowling. "Now girls, calm down or I'll switch ya good!"

Tenderly, Isaiah peeled down the diaper. Beaming, joyfully he whispered, "It's a boy!"

Anne smiled as Hanna handed her a cup of hot creek willo tea. Swaying as she stood over the bedside, Hanna said, "Drink this, it will ease the pain!"

Thanking her for the tea, Anne sipped and frowned. Hanna was drunk.

Smiling Hanna lifted the thin cup to her puffy lips and downed the last drop of moonshine and staggered back to her seat.

Anne grimaced and turned. "Go on," Anne said to the girls who timidly approached the baby.

Wide-eyed and pointing, Delena asked, "Pa, what is *that*?"

Hanna chuckled with Anne and Isaiah as he responded, "Oh that! Honey, that's his wingy." The adults tried not to laugh too loudly and Hanna belched. "Excuse me!" she said leaned back, relaxed and rocked.

"Wingy? It looks like a grubb worm," Delena said.

Tina took a closer look at the baby, kissed him on the forehead, and sat down beside Leve fast asleep on a hook rug in the floor. Delena leaned over a little closer to get a better look. The newborn sprayed her and she jumped back, crying. She pulled up her dress tail and wiped off her face. "I don't like him! Take him back!"

Hanna, Anne, and Isaiah could not contain their laughter.

Anne motioned for them to hush as she reached out to comfort Delena. The other adults forcefully held back their chuckles. "Come here, Child," Anne said, as she caressed Delena's small tender fingers. "It will be okay, Baby. He has no control over that. He didn't mean to spray you. It just happened. You peed on me and Pa lots when you were little like him. So don't you hate your baby brother. Okay?"

Delena nodded and rubbed her eyes. The baby awakened and opened his eyes for a moment.

"Look, Delena! Just like you!" Isaiah said.

Reluctantly Delena came closer and gazed into the baby's dark steely blue eyes. Timid to get too close, she smiled and laughed.

Hanna staggered into the kitchen and brought back a clean wet washrag. She wiped off Delena's face, hands, and ran the rag over her pee-soaked hair.

"Finally, Isaiah has his male child." Anne said.

Isaiah kissed Delena on the forehead.

"Now isn't that sweet," Hanna said as they tried to ignore her.

"Pa, I think Hanna is drunk!" Delena whispered and rolled her eyes.

Trying to act sober, Hanna said, "I'm just tired, need a nap. What will you call your son?" Hanna asked.

"My name is Delena!"

Hanna and Anne smiled as Isaiah reached out and waved his rough hand over Delena's head, fuzzing the top of her hair. "Now, Son, no reason for you to be jealous. You will always be Daddy's little girl."

Delena smiled and sat on the edge of the bed beside Isaiah. She leaned against his strong arm.

"What should we call him, Delena?" Anne asked.

Delena placed her index finger against her cheek and rolled her eyes, intense concentration on her face. "How does Chad sound?"

Anne and Isaiah nodded. He smiled, and asked, "And Buster?"

The others solemnly gestured their approval.

"Then Chad Buster Hotman he is from this day forward," Isaiah said as he pulled the cigar from his pocket and fumbled for a match in the other shirt pocket. He struck the match on the bed rail and lit the cigar. Smoke writhed around the room over their heads.

Anne sipped the tea, and set the cup back in a saucer. "Your ma loves you, Chad," Anne said while blowing him a kiss.

Hanna passed out and snored. The family roared with laughter.

Chapter Six

World War I and prohibition brought the beginning of an era of sorrows and hardship for most families. Heartache and deprivation only escalated after the war. A serious paucity in spirit and pocketbook remained for decades. Belief in God, religion, and the churches became an even more powerful stabilizing and sometimes destructive force as racism and the production of moonshine proliferated.

Prohibition became law in Arkansas, January 14, 1919. Delena said as direct result the barrel mill shut down. The booming tree harvest came to an abrupt close. When barrel contracts were lost nationwide and overseas, turbulent economic times turned to fear, hate, and violence. The Ku Klux Klan decided all Negroes must leave now.

Tensions ran high between blacks and whites. A white girl accused an unemployed black man of raping her on the outskirts of Dinktown. Later she recanted, but too late. During the night the Ku Klux Klan hunted him down and hanged him in a tree near the Galloping Goose depot on Wiley's Cove Creek.

Terror, fear, and hate gripped the peoples' hearts, both blacks and whites. The Ku Klux Klan members decided to clean up the county, intimidating blacks to move on. The KKK set fire to shanty town. The blazes roared out of control and the barrel mill burned to the ground. Within a few days no blacks remained. Both peoples had two things in common--the loss of income due to prohibition and the evils of racism.

After the Negro laborers fled, left behind was only a handful of hardy local Caucasian residents who had money and those poorer whites whose ancestors had lived in the hills since before the Civil War.

Many white families left in search of jobs. The impact of black society remained but they would never again return. The barrel mill was never rebuilt, months later a pallet mill was constructed. But not before the Dinky railroad ceased to run. The Brooster family sold her within two years passage of the prohibition laws . The subsequent lack of paying jobs forced many families to secretly cook-off moonshine for income. Homebrew became a widespread multiple-family business.

Some Klansmen turned to moonshine production. Bill built a still. Rival bootleggers' moonshine wars escalated around Loafer's Glory.

Oftentimes Bill and other bootleggers deflated the tires on their jalopies, centering the wheels on the abandoned Dinky rails, and transported hundreds of quart fruit jars of the contraband whiskey through the forest by way of the deserted rail system. They used secluded drop-off points on rough logging trails in an attempt to escape local "reveneuers" (A.T.F. agents).

Since the track widths were no further apart than the wheels on Model A pickups, moonshine runners centered their truck wheels on the Galloping Goose tracks to transport the illegal cargo. This worked perfectly for distant deliveries, usually made in the middle of the night.

On occasion when the Galloping Goose arrived earlier than

scheduled, Bill narrowly missed head-on-crashes between the train and contraband transport vehicles. He soon learned to wait until the train passed and then traveled in the opposite direction of the Galloping Goose on the tracks.

Bill's criminal involvement with the Ku Klux Klan and moonshine running labeled him a backsliding Baptist drunkard. Definitely a racist and probably a murderer! Nevertheless, he was just one backsliding drunk among many. With alcoholism as a generational curse on the Hotman bloodline, religion became the family hope.

The family's Baptist roots ran deep but that all changed in 1921. William J. Seymour's revivals years earlier in California ushered in a new work of God. The Pentecostal experience spread like fresh torrential rains among minorities and poor working-class folks across America.

As one result of Seymour's revivals, in 1914 the Assemblies of God founded their Arkansas headquarters in the town of Hot Springs. By 1921, the tongue talkers from several newly formed Pentecostal organizations came to the old breeding grounds. Arriving by way of the Galloping Goose they held open-air brush arbor meetings in the surrounding communities, some of which the Hotmans frequented.

Anne insisted Isaiah take the family to these Holy Roller gatherings. She listened intently to their sermons. She tugged at Isaiah's shirt sleeve as they sat on a rough bench under the brush-covered arbor. "Isaiah they are talking about the experience of William J. Seymour, the same black holiness preacher Delena and I overheard the Negro women talking about."

"I'm not impressed!" he said as he watched Anne taking in the sermon. Beholding the operations of the gifts of the Spirit in these meetings his disgust grew, but he could tell Anne longed to know such things herself as she held on to every word the charismatic preacher yelled, and nodding she shouting back at him, "Amen! Praise the Lord!"

The Pentecostal way of worship was not for him. He thought they were all nuts as he observed newly converted Pentecostal folks enthusiastically praising God.

Happily, believers clapped and sang to lively soulful music while hillbilly musicians played on this sultry August night in 1921. He was determined Anne would not drag him to another one of these dog and pony shows.

Isaiah beheld, reserved dignified folks cutting loose, wailing uncontrollably then sometimes falling, rolling, shaking, and lying on the ground in a trance-like state. Others under the power moved their feet quickly while doing something like a jig before succumbing to unconsciousness, and flopping limp to the sawdust beneath their feet.

Total pandemonium set in as the people's cries became louder. The bewildered, frightened Hotman children huddled close to their parents. Delena tugged at Isaiah's other sleeve. Trembling, she whined, "Pa can we go home now!"

"You take the children and make a pallet in the back of the wagon. We'll leave in a minute," he said and gently patted her on the back.

Happily Delena grabbed crying Leve and Tina, and they ran hand in hand for the wagon fifty feet from the arbor as Isaiah sadly watched the preacher and abhorrently shook his head.

Smiling, Anne continued to hold baby Chad, bouncing him on her knees while he slept through all the goings on.

"Amen! Praise the Lord!" she yelled again along with other congregation members.

Snarling, cursing under his breath, Isaiah's agitation and disdain grew as he watched the runners and screamers.

Worshipers shouted, "Praise God! Glory!" then frowning disbelieving others got up and left. A few began speaking in unknown tongues, and others laughed uncontrollably when the emotional hell-fire and brimstone preacher got more excited. Waving wildly to make a point, pounding on the Bible, and flapping his large thick lips as tiny sprinkles of spit spued while he shouted, he reminded Isaiah of a braying mule.

Isaiah surveyed, the rows of people on the other side of the arbor. His husky dark-haired friend Tom squirmed as his wife, handsome tall April, shot to her feet and gave out a message in the unknown tongue. At that, silence and reverence washed through the arbor as quickly as the mighty clamber of discordant noises began. When she finished speaking, a long reverent silence.

Humbly, the visiting bald fat missionary gave an interpretation. Weeping prevailed in their midst at the kind words of Scripture he spoke, ending his speech with, "Thus says the Lord!"

Isaiah coughed in disbelief.

The preacher under the anointing couldn't contain himself, stepping from behind the pulpit with his eyes closed, babbling in an unknown tongue he took off running toward the congregation seated in the pews. But instead of detouring down an isle he leapt to the back edges of the first rough bench and ran to the back of the arbor by taking this short cut through the seated parishioners on the backs of the church pews. Isaiah gasped. Someone could get hurt!

Powerfully towering over them, the big rawboned German preacher skillfully walked and ran the backs of the church pews with each large step, eyes closed. Isaiah had seen enough.

Of the many antics he observed, the pew walkers made his stomach churn. This was no way to act in the house of God! He craved a shot of moonshine. Forcefully, hatefully, he shook Anne's shoulder. Scowling, he motioned for her to get to the wagon as he stood.

Frowning, she nodded.

He left, kicking sawdust above his work boots while exiting the arbor and strolling rapidly for the wagon.

Reluctantly, Anne followed.

Delena smiled and crawled into Isaiah's lap as they headed home while Leve and Tina slept on a pallet in back.

Leaving the arbor behind he heard some testifying of being physically healed. He chuckled.

Anne frowned, and poked him in the side. "Be careful! Don't mock the Lord! His recompense can be severe!"

He nodded and adjusted his hat. "Ah! They're all fools to believe in that funny shit!"

Anne said nothing.

He could tell she knew he wanted a drink when he patted his coat pocket where he usually kept the flask but he had taken it out before leaving home.

She pouted and cradled Chad close to her bosom, refusing to speak again.

Isaiah concluded they had all lost their minds, or demons had hold on them. He chuckled again.

Anne scowled.

He didn't think women should be falling at all in church. He loathed watching women's skirt-tails fling over their heads showing "Possible." God was not in that! He remembered how embarrassed Anne was at the sight two weeks earlier. Then there was the meeting three weeks before when another group of religious maniacs pulled rattlesnakes and copperheads out of a black box, handling them as they supposedly danced in the Spirit. He didn't have to pressure Anne to take their leave from that scene. Even she said those folks were tempting the Lord as the family ran for the wagon that night.

Isaiah scowled and nodded. Definitely not the presence of the Holy Spirit. The Pentecostals were too confusing and frightening for the children; too radical. To be a Baptist was safe, familiar, comfortable, and a family tradition. He determined the Hotman clan would not turn away from their religious roots. He would not take them to any more Holy Roller meetings. "Anne, surely you don't believe this horse crap?"

Ignoring him, she glanced at the girls sleeping on a quilt pallet.

Chapter Seven

Anne gave birth to Grant, then she rebelled in 1921, believing the Holy Rollers did have something genuine and she would have it, whatever it was. To Isaiah's embarrassment, his protective efforts were useless.

Anne received the baptism of the Holy Ghost with the evidence of speaking in tongues during a service in their Baptist church around Thanksgiving. She was then promptly escorted out of the building by two brawny deacons, and Isaiah was told not to bring her back. He had wanted to crawl under a church pew.

Anne's conversion, coupled with Isaiah's alcoholism, made for some rocky years in their marriage. Isaiah fell prey to the ethers, and became a mean-spirited drunk when provoked, beating Anne in front of the children and mocking her new-found religion. On one occasion he dragged her around the yard by her hair. She was his property. Beating wives and children was tolerated, common place. He wanted to beat that Holy Ghost stuff out of her! He damn sure tried on numerous occasions.

However, when Isaiah wasn't drunk Anne ruled the roost with her stern-tones and religious fervor. In-between their squabbles more babies were born and the older children received the Baptism. Delena was thirteen when she had the experience and a few years later, Leve. Isaiah eventually repented, accepted the Pentecostal beliefs in 1929, and he quit drinking.

Pentecostalism became a way of life for the family by 1929. The Hotmans attended a small Pentecostal church regularly that October.

On a warm night, by the light of a bright autumn harvest moon, Anne and Isaiah who were standing on the church steps. Delena and Newton the pastor's handsome son, holding hands came out of the church.

"Mr. And Mrs. Hotman, if it's okay with you I'd like to walk Delena home tonight?" Newton asked then smiled at giggling Delena.

Isaiah winked at Delena, turned to Newton and frowned.

"Stop it, Pa!" Delena said and turned back to Newton. "Pa's a cut up, I think that was a yes," she said and squeezed his large hand. "Well, can we?"

Anne smiled, cleared her throat and looped her arm through Isaiah's, she said, "You be home within an hour."

Isaiah nodded and smiled at Delena then squinted at Newton. Anne pulled Isaiah down the steps.

"Thanks, Ma, Pa! I'll be home in an hour." She grabbed Newton's hand and they ran out of the church parking lot.

The younger children filed crawled into the back of the wagon. As the mules pulled the wagon onto the gravel road dark haired Leve asked, "Where's Delena, Pa?"

He chuckled. "She's a courtin'!"

The children began to giggle. "Delena's gotta beau beau! Delena's got a...." They all sang in unison but Leve scowled, saying nothing and sulked the entire trip. The family sang "I'll Fly Away" while the mules trotted homeward.

Anne patted Isaiah's leg as the children continued singing. She pulled her shawl tight around her shoulders. Placing her hand on the back of her head to make certain her bun was still in place, she said, "Honey, our little girl is all grown up."

They had known Newton since he was born twenty years ago. Anne lay her head against his shoulder. Isaiah sighed, pulled his gray brim hat up and back off his brow. He placed his arm around Anne. "I think that Newton is a fine young man, just like his pa. He'll be good to Son. She deserves the best!"

"Delena is such a headstrong tomboy, any husband she gets will make her a good wife," she said, "Isaiah, we should never have started calling her Son. She looks like a beautiful woman but she is strong willed like a man. We raised her to be too independent! She'll always have a problem submitting to a husband's discretion."

Patting her on the hand he said, "Ha! Son will be fine. She's daddy's little girl! She'll be fine."

Chapter Eight

Trekking the long way home, the giggling, boy-shy Delena and her suitor Newton held hands and swung their arms together as they walked and talked. Out for a courting stroll with her Honey, Delena thought.

Newton was tall with broad shoulders. Tonight he had dressed to look notably dignified, perhaps just for her? He had on his best Sunday attire. His curly short blond hair glistened as it caught rays of moonlight. He wore navy-blue trousers with a white shirt, red and black checked bow tie, high polished black dress slippers with white socks to match his shirt, and one of his father's black suit jackets.

Strolling down the rugged logging road they ducked as a screech owl flew overhead. Crickets chattered, bull frogs croaked and splatted into the creek running alongside the primitive road.

When they were alone, she let him gently pull her close and he tenderly kissed her. Delena had never let a boy do that before. But she liked

Newton. She had a crush on him for the past year. Finally, they were courting and the kiss was good. But she had nothing to compare it to.

Seventeen-year-old Delena was considered an old maid by some in the community. She curled her glistening dishwater-blonde shoulder-length hair every day. Her tall thin but curved body made her the object of many a young man's fancy.

She wanted no part of them. Her steely blue eyes were hard and cut to the bone with rejection toward most of the young men showing interest. She felt they were beneath her and cruelly rebuffed their efforts of courtship.

As they sauntered down the trail, she thought that Newton was a true believer. Self-consciously, she tugged at her ankle-length green print dress to cover her bloomers that were slightly showing below the dress line. She watched every step so not to scuff her new black slippers on the rocks. She didn't want a man that wasn't a believer, or a believer who couldn't live by the godly rules. He had to walk the talk. Her parents accepted him. They had the highest of respect for his family. She was happy to be with him. He made her feel good inside, and she trusted him.

They walked a while and kissed again. But when he shoved his tongue inside her mouth during a surge of passion, she nearly gagged and pushed him away.

"Why did you do that?" she asked. Repulsed at the thought of his tongue being inside her mouth, she spat.

Chuckling, he said, "Come on girl, you aren't that ignorant." She let him gently take her hand again, resisting a bit, "I'm sorry. I just thought with you being older than some girls who are already married, you knew about French kissing."

Delena felt stupid, because she didn't know for certain what he was doing. She was ignorant about those things. Ma never talked about that with her, she had no romantic experience at all.

As he pulled her close again, she remembered when she became a woman at age fourteen. No one had ever told her about the blood. She sat by the pond washing herself all day and crying. Because she thought she had become a bloody whore, like the drunks in Dinktown talked about on the streets. She remembered how ignorant she was back then, thinking that the blood made the Jezebel. Not until Anne came searching and found her weeping did she learn blood was normal for all women. She was glad to know she hadn't turned into a Jezebel.

Now, she felt ignorant again but didn't want him to think she was so dumb. She said nothing as he pulled her close, her mind spinning, she wanted to push him away but she also wanted him to kiss her again, without the tongue.

Smiling, he said, "I'll teach you how to French kiss."

She nodded. He proceeded to show and tell all about kissing as she listened intently and cooperated, but she was still embarrassed. He kissed her again with the tongue. She didn't push him away this time. Instead, she wrapped her arms around his stout neck and ran her fingers through his soft curly hair, imitating the way she caught Isaiah and Anne kissing when they thought no one watched.

They walked a little further down the road visiting and getting to know each other. Newton's sense of humor made her laugh continually as he told silly jokes and flirtatiously tickled her from time to time. He seemed patient with her insecurity around boys and her ignorance of the courtship game. And the kissing she was really beginning to like.

When he won her confidence, he lured her into the woods near a spring to get a drink. There he threw her on the ground.

Horrified, she jolted upright. Why he was doing this? Why had he suddenly changed? Did she do something to cause this?

She screamed, clawed, and fought for her life. But he was too strong for her. She struggled to get up, yelling for help. He beat her head against a rock while forcefully holding his rough hand over her mouth to muffle her cries. She bit his hand. "I'll kill you! Pa will kill you!" she shouted. He hit her in the face with his fist.

When she realized there was no escape she pretended to be unconscious. In sheer terror she struggled no more when he tore off her underclothes and ripped her flesh in penetration.

The preacher's boy, Newton, was suppose to have the Holy Ghost but he brutally stole Delena's innocence. In silent rage she endured the fear and pain. When finished with his nasty job the preacher's son washed himself in the spring water.

She lay motionless, terrified. How much she loathed herself for ever trusting a man. She vowed to never see the world through eyes of innocence again. She would never believe anyone was a Christian until he proved to her it was so for many years by walking the talk. If she survived, she promised herself not to ever let her guard down again. She wanted to open her eyes. But she dared not for fear he'd see the terror now surging through her soul and have the mastery over her body again.

"You hard-to-get high-and-mighty gip!" he said, slapping her face to make her open her eyes. "If you can hear me, your darn well best keep your mouth shut. Tell no one! This is your fault, bitch! You shouldn't have been such a tease! I won't have my parents' reputations ruined. Pickled pig feet! I bet ya enjoyed every minute," he said, laughing while crouched over her motionless body. "Next time I'll get some of that Leve stuff if you tell! Guess, I need to go repent now." He sighed. "But what for? You enticed me!" He stood and kicked her paralyzed form, stepping over her. He whistled while leaving, singing:

"Well, I love the Kitty Chuchu.

Doodle diddle dee doo doo.

Fiddle my wingy wang.

Does Kitty me too?

My heart pines away.

Yonder's another young filly to tease.

Citta Marie Citta Marie.

I'll play again.

Maybe I'll win.

Well, I love the Kitty Chuchu.

Doodle diddle dee doo doo."

Delena lay motionless until she could no longer hear his singing. In sheer panic she opened her eyes, bounding to her feet. Crying, she ran home, her bloody, soiled, and tattered dress barely hanging onto her body.

Thirty minutes later she crept into the house where the others were sleeping, forcefully holding back her sobs. She had run through the forest and avoided the road thinking the preacher's boy would be waiting to have his way with her again.

Her hands and hair were sticky with drying blood that had oozed from the wounds on her head and body. Scratches zig zagged her legs and arms from the blackberry briars she had run through in her panic to find the safety of home. Her new slippers ruined. Ma would be mad. She grabbed her night-gown from under her pillow on the bed where twelve-year-old Leve was sleeping, a bar of her mother's homemade lye soap from the kitchen cupboard, and a wash rag.

She quietly tiptoed out and ran a hundred yards into the hollow toward the spring-fed pond where her mother often prayed during warm weather under the shade of the oaks and willows. This was Anne's holy ground.

On the edge of the pond bank, she washed herself over and over and cried and prayed for a couple of hours before returning to the house and crawling into bed next to Leve. Had she done something to bring this upon herself? Was Newton crazy? How could she have misjudged him so completely?

Leve, twelve, rolled over and mumbled, "Delena, Ma has been worried sick about you. You had best have a good explanation for coming in this time of morning, or you'll get it good!"

Delena tried to hold back her tears. "Preacher's boy raped me tonight!"

Leve pushed back her long shimmering black hair, draped her arm over sobbing Delena's waist and held her hand tight. "I figured as much! He's been touching the young girls at church. He won't get away with this!"

"Don't tell!" Delena murmured in desperate fear and shame. "He said if I tell he will come after you."

Leve snuggled closer and batted her long dark lashes against Delena's arm. "That sorry polecat! I'll give him some of my stuff! Folks around here will call him Squeaky when I get through with him!" Leve held Delena to comfort her until they fell asleep talking in whispers with silent tears streaming down both their faces.

When morning light came into the bedroom, Delena arose to began her chores. Isaiah had already left to work the fields. When Delena walked into the kitchen, Anne was washing dishes in an enamel pan on the table.

Running her long fingers through her mussed hair, dreading to face her mother, she choked out a whisper, "Ma."

Anne turned, glared at Delena, and dropped the cup she was washing. It crashed to the floor and broke into several tiny pieces. Anne caught her breath while throwing her hand over her mouth. Tears weld up in her eyes. "What have you done?"

Delena knew she was a frightful sight for her ma with bruising on her face in the shape of a hand, busted lip, and lacerations visible on her body.

Delena, felt the anguish in her mother's heart when Anne began to nervously tremble, and could not hold on to the wet dishes.

Leve strode into the room. "Tell her Delena!"

Delena hesitated. She could not keep this from her mother any longer.

As the story unfolded, the color faded out of Anne's face. Delena watched as the reality of betrayal settled into Anne's mind, her eyes squinting in rage Anne scowled and the wrinkles on her brow told the war of conflicting emotions eating at her soul. Anne clutched her chest. Tears streamed down their faces. Anne pulled a chair from the table and sat down.

Leve finished washing the dishes, then dried and put them in the cupboard as Delena sat down at the table beside Anne to finished the story, tearfully waiting for her mother to respond.

"Don't tell your father, if you tell this, he will kill the boy!" Anne said.

Delena screamed with angry hot tears streaming down her face, "Good! I want him dead!" She pounded her fist against the table.

Shaking her head and then hiding her face in her hands as she leaned over her knees and folded her arms under her head, she then snapped upright again and said, glaring, "Delena, I can't believe this, you should not have enticed him. He is the preacher's son!" She sobbed again. "How could he do this to my baby?" She wailed loudly.

A great wave of bitter emptiness swept through Delena. When she needed her mother's comfort, it was not there.

Anne stood and pulled Delena to her feet, placing her arms around her eldest daughter in a strong embrace and sniffling. "Son, God knows the truth, vengeance belongs to the Lord," she said.

Delena pushed Anne away and ran toward the front door. She heard Leve come to her defense as she ran out of the house toward the barn. "I believe Delena, Ma. He is a polecat! He put his hands on me two years ago, and tried to play with my thigh while you were leading song services one night. I whispered to him to pull his filthy hand away or he'd draw back a nub! I said I'd tell. He never bothered me again after that. But he did others. That's probably why so many quit the church this past two years."

Anne tearfully screamed in agony and embraced Leve, "You should have told me!" she said and cried, as Delena looked back and saw them through the open door.

As she had on other occasions, Delena crawled into the loft and cried bitter tears. When Delena returned to the house to do her chores, she rejected Anne's efforts to comfort her. "Honey, a lot of bad things happen to people in this world and some things should never be talked about," Anne said. But these words did not quench the flames of hatred welling up inside Delena's soul. Several in the preacher's extended family were members in good standing with the KKK and Delena hoped they would kill him. She would tell uncle Bill! He would kill the skunk!

By evening Anne and Delena had dealt with their grief and were speaking again.

When Isaiah returned home and saw Delena's bruises. The family was glad, he no longer got drunk. He controlled his temper better when sober. Delena was afraid he'd go back to drinking if she told him about the rape. The family couldn't endure his drunken belligerence and abuse again. Raising an eyebrow he trembled and took deep breath to hold back his emotion of rage as he asked in suspicious tones, "Who did you get into a cat fight with?"

"I fell out of the barn loft while collecting eggs."

Isaiah gazed into her darkly bruised face with embittered, steely blue eyes, waiting for her to tell him the truth.

She said nothing.

"Did Preacher Boy do this to you?" he asked.

Anne and the rest of the children were so quiet that a leaf falling on the tin roof, tic, sounded throughout the house.

"Pa! He's a good boy, I fell," she answered, head down in shame.

His piercing blue eyes mirrored the rage in his soul, as though he knew her lies. Then he smiled, wrapped his arms around her and held her tight. "Son, you better watch your step next time."

Delena began to cry hysterically while he held her. He showered a father's love into her heart without speaking as he held her tight and gently patted her on the back.

A few weeks later Isaiah insisted Delena and the family return to that same Pentecostal church one last time. Naturally Delena resisted but her father firmly insisted. He knew the truth! How he could be so cruel-- making her face the rapist? Reluctantly, Delena forced herself onto the wagon with Isaiah, Anne, and Leve while the rest of the family walked to another church up the road. She rode in the back, sulking all the way.

To the *Hell Church* and the *devil* Newton? There is no God there, she thought. They arrived. Dread and loathing engulfed her soul. Hesitating, she stepped through the chapel doors and ran her long fingers through her well-groomed hair, pulling it forward to cover a small scar on her cheek.

She saw the preacher's boy. First fear surged through her and her stomach quivered with nausea. Trembling, she took a deep breath. She turned to walk out of the chapel, afraid of her own hate and the ability to kill at that moment.

Isaiah gently took her arm, smirking as he winked at her and the family strolled arm and arm toward Newton at the front.

Both his eyes were blackened, he had a busted lip, spots of fresh blood on the crotch of his pants, and a few teeth were missing. Isaiah's hands also appeared to be swollen, cut, and bruised.

Someone stepped up behind her. She turned. Uncle Bill. He was a Baptist! They had worked Newton over for her! The crazy bastard didn't get away with rape!

Although no one ever said, she knew her father and Bill had fought to defend her honor. A guilty Christian complex taunted in the back of her mind as she basked in the fruits of revenge. She knew she should forgive. But she wasn't ready to forgive; finding satisfaction in revenge felt good.

The tall thin pastor had bruises and cuts on his hands also. Newton's dad? He fought for me? Or did he try to protect Newton?

Newton would not now follow through on his threats to rape Leve. If you try, Pa will castrate you if he hasn't already, then kill you, you pig, she thought. Fire and sparks of resentment kindled violent emotions in her belly that seemed to leap out of her dagger eyes. This was no place for her to feel this way! This was God's house. But Newton was the pastor's son! He didn't honor his parents. He shamed them all and the entire congregation. This was the devil's house!

Standing against a wall in back with two other girls her age, Leve smirked at Newton. Delena saw her staring as they stood beside preacher's boy in front of the first pew. The growing congregation of about thirty began to gather behind them.

The preacher's boy raised his bowed head. Terror shone from his large blue eyes, fear and intimidation on his solemn bruised, skinned face. His distended busted lips trembled when he tried to speak. No words came out, only nervous gurgled whispers. Newton's skinned hand quivered as Isaiah forcefully reached forward, grasping his arm and hand while appearing to share a friendly handshake.

The boy cringed but made no sounds. He trembled and swallowed, unable to reply when Isaiah sarcastically asked, "What happened to you, Boy?"

His pa slapped him on the back of the head with such force he stumbled forward a step to catch his balance. "Answer Mr. Hotman, Boy!"

Head down, he softly stuttered, "I fell out of the barn loft when collecting Ma's chicken eggs."

"You had best really watch your step, Boy!" Isaiah yelled. "Next time you might not be so lucky! If you had fallen on a pitchfork, ya could have been dead!"

The pastor fought for her honor! His pain and shame must have been as great as hers.

She and Isaiah leered at Newton, hard. When he glanced up at her to speak, she spat in his face. The family turned and left the church as the congregation behind them began to sing. Delena was not in the mood for "Amazing Grace," but was rather happily intoxicated by sweet revenge.

Chapter Nine

After the rape Delena suffered emotionally, at first refusing to date or get involved with any man. She became increasingly dependent upon Isaiah. In his presence she felt safe.

Though Delena wasn't a lesbian, she no longer trusted her own instincts when it came to men. As a result she cocooned herself within the family until 1932. Refusing to date or be alone without a family member present when away from home.

Delena's suspicious bitter attitude, and deep dependancy on the immediate family concerned Anne. She didn't know how to break the oppression. The fear that possessed Delena after the rape.

Anne hoped that perhaps *her* good news would be the turning point for Delena to get on with her own life–overcoming the trepidation.

One beautiful August day in 1931 when the peaches were ripe and the family gathered the fruit off the small orchard trees near the barn, Anne announced she was pregnant again. This was their ninth child. Hoping to see smiling faces to share her joy, Anne was quite disappointed. No one spoke. The gay voices of happy children giggling, jabbering, and playing as they worked ceased. Not even the birds chattered, the instant silence startling and abrupt. Everyone frowned and turned leering at her. Delena was less than pleased above all the rest and mumbled, "This we don't need." She pouted and whined, "Not again Ma!"

Anne glared at Delena and threatened to paddle them all. Woe filled the air and silence roared with reservations about Anne's joyous news. None of the siblings really wanted another baby in the house. But one by one they began to ask questions.

Timidly, voice quivering, Leve asked, "When is it due?"

Smiling, Anne said, "In the early spring, next year."

Eight months along by springtime 1932, Anne swung the milking pail half full of clean warm water, and a rag as she strode to the barn. Bonnie, their pet jersey was in the stall waiting impatiently. Her udder filled with milk and nearly dragging the ground, she mooed while shaking her head when Anne walked inside the barn and patted her on the hips. "That's my sweet faithful Bonnie. You are always on time," she said, as she filled the feeding bin from burlap bags of dried corn and oats.

Sitting on a handmade stool Anne pulled a clean wet rag from the pail and wiped off Bonnie's bursting to be relieved bag, dumped the fresh water out of the pail, and placed the bucket under the cow's teats. She twisted the soiled dampness out of the rag and shoved it into an apron pocket. When she finished maneuvering her long ankle-length skirt and heavy-petticoat up in her lap to keep them off the filthy barn floor, she grasped Bonnie's teats with both her large rough hands, squeezed, and pulled firmly. The milk came down, squish squash, pings, pangs. The warm white liquid splashed continually into the enamel pail with every rhythmic pull on the four teats. To the musical beat of the squirting milk Anne hummed a lively gospel song.

The weather was unusually warm. Flies swarmed. As Bonnie slung and shook her head around to protest the hoard of biting pest, one of her sharp long horns tore through Anne's blouse, pierced the skin, ripping deep into the muscle inside Anne's abdomen.

Anne held her composure. Stay calm. Bonnie could rend her apart if either of them panicked. She stopped the milking. Agonizing, through clinched teeth she groaned, "Oh Bonnie, what have we done!"

Bonnie was a gentle cow. The children even rode on her back sometimes. Bonnie didn't flinch. Her horn lodged inside Anne's belly. She froze with her head twisted in an awkward position. Anne sensed that Bonnie seemed to know something was wrong. The cow never resisted but allowed Anne to lightly maneuver her head and horn. Painfully, fearfully, gently, silent hot tears streaming down her face, she said, "Easy girl, don't move Bonnie, don't move." She took both hands and pushed Bonnie's head back to remove the four inches of horn that rested inside her midriff below the belly button. Blood ran from the wound and seeped between her fingers as she made her way back to the house hunched over and holding her lower gut.

Anne called to Delena working in the garden a hundred yards from the home, "Delena! Come quick! I need help!"

Delena came running. "Bonnie gored me," Anne cried as Delena frantically removed her apron, folded it several times into a tight square, and pressed it against the wound.

"Oh, Ma, we gotta get you to Doc Arnold."

"No doctors," she said as Delena helped her up the three steps onto the back porch and inside the house.

"Holler at Leve and tell her to fetch the pal of milk."

Delena yelled from the porch to Leve working in the garden "Leve, Ma says for you to go finish milking."

Leve nodded and dropped her hoe.

Delena cleaned the wound with vinegar and then homebrew while Anne squirmed on her bed, forcefully holding back her screams as the disinfectant burned like hot coals inside the open wound. Easing some she allowed Delena to apply a fresh bandage while she quoted *Ezekiel 16:6*, over and over: "A*nd when I passed by thee, and saw thee polluted in thine own blood, I said unto thee when thou wast in thy blood, Live; yea, I said unto thee when thou wast in thy blood, Live."* Delena continued to fuss over her to see the doctor. Anne believed the scripture would arrest the bleeding.

She stopped quoting the verse, agitated by Delena's carping. "Stop it! Now! Where is your faith, Delena?"

Delena slung the bloody apron into a dishpan on the floor beside the bed. "Ma, you got to stop believing every word that these out-of-state evangelist say. They're not all right. Some of them are dangerous," Delena warned. "It's not sin to get medical help from the doctor!" She slapped another clean white rag over the bleeding wound.

"I have to submit myself to my pastor and he says medicine is of the devil, witchcraft! I won't go to the doctor, they are evil. So just hush. Pray for me. I'll trust the Lord," she said, through the clinched teeth of her pain.

"Please, Ma!" Delena pleaded.

Glaring, she said, "I am not going to the doctor! I choose to trust the Lord. You and Isaiah can harp all you want but I am not going." She went back to quoting *Ezekiel 16:6*.

Isaiah returned from the logging woods, and they did harp and protest most of the evening. Anne was resolute, she would not see a doctor. She was as stubborn as Delena and Isaiah both. She commanded them to just get out and let her rest. Anne remained in bed the balance of the afternoon and night. She could hear Delena angrily banging pots on the stove, and mumbling in the kitchen as the girls prepared the evening meal.

Anne was grateful Delena kept the stabbed sight cleaned and dressed for her until it knitted back together. The wound healed without the aid of a medical doctor. Anne believed God had answered her prayer and helped her to recover so quickly before the baby was born. Though she was still in pain from the goring when the birthing labor began a month later.

Could her unborn child be marked by the cow horn? Could he be deformed or mentally ill? But she had no complications with the pregnancy. No spotting. No out of the normal sickness she hadn't experienced eight times before. Trust the Lord, and after his birth she was relieved to see he had no physical deformities. Time would tell whether the horn had marked his mind. Nursing the infant for the first time, she mumbled, "No, I must not be double minded. God will keep him whole. Devil, you get out of my mind! My son will be fine," she said while lovingly gazing into the baby's eyes. "Won't you Enoch!"

Chapter Ten

Superstitious and having heard many old wives' tales, Enoch's older siblings surmised the cow horn mark had to be in his mind. They anticipated mental problems to manifest as he grew.

Their cousin Witty was said to be marked by a stud horse when his ma was nearly trampled while she carried him in the sixth month. Though declared to be well endowed in certain areas, Witty never was right, a halfwit. He looked normal at birth, but he lacked a portion of brains when grown. The children figured this might be the case for Enoch as well.

Older siblings resented Enoch's presence. They reasoned another child placed more demands on what few resources they had. A baby meant more chores and harder work. At twenty Delena, quietly seethed contempt for the new baby.

When Enoch was a month old, one Saturday afternoon Delena's silence erupted. "Momma is too old to be having another kid! We all have to work hard enough and never have anything to show for it. The rest of the young ones are as poor as rails. I'm tired of being as wretched as an outhouse mouse and working like a slave! Now we got another mouth to feed! Hammered hog slop! Give it away!"

Anne had hoped the baby would motivate Delena to find someone, and start a family of her own. To her surprise Delena's response was negative. Sadly, tempestuously rocking while cradling Enoch and holding back her rage and tears, Anne shouted, "Girl, you shut your mouth! You won't disrespect your pa or me that way! Now shut it up."

Delena rolled her eyes in disgust. Ignoring Anne's wishes, she continued her ravings.

"Isaiah!" Anne whispered across the room.

Frowning, without a word Isaiah bounded to his feet, forcefully grabbing Delena by the arm and dragging her screaming out of the house. Anne watched from a window with the others as he busted her posterior with his rough hand.

Eighteen-year-old Tina brushed back her curled blond hair and scowling she said, "Ma, you needed another baby like we need frost on the crops in summer."

Anne glared.

Chad asked, "Why did you and Pa do this to us?"

Anne snapped, "Boy!"

Rebelliously Chad said, "Delena doesn't deserve the whipping!"

Tina seethed, "Chad's right!"

Anne frowned and they hushed their whining. Anne made it clear with her staring, that they would be next if they didn't silence their tongues.

Delena's screams echoed across the hollow as she begged Isaiah to stop the whipping, apologized and promised to take it all back. The family heard Isaiah yelling angrily, "Girl, you won't ever get too big or too old for me to bust you butt. Don't you ever say anyone in my family is not wanted! You will apologize to Ma and tell the other children you are wrong. Don't you ever be so cruel to baby Enoch! Do I make myself clear?"

"Yes Pa," Delena answered through her tears. Anne smiled, satisfied.

Delena immediately returned to the house and apologized to the family.

Anne hated that Isaiah had spoiled Delena. It was about time he gave her a thrashing. He hadn't paddled her since she was ten years old.

Being flogged by her father was uncommon. Spoiled, Delena became hot-tempered if she didn't have her say over the littlest of things. More times than not, Isaiah let her get away with her antics and ravings. Anne didn't like the rebellion she saw growing in Tina and Chad. She'd have to take care of that at another time. For now, correcting irreverent Delena was most important.

After Delena's attitude adjustment, Anne made her hold little Enoch while she and the other girls prepared dinner. She watched as Delena tearfully apologized to him. Compassionately, Anne embraced sobbing Delena and kissed her on the cheek. Anne was contented Delena would never be as disrespectful again with her over the birth of Enoch or any other child she might have in the future.

Remarkably, to Anne's surprise, and the entire family, Delena began dating occasionally after Isaiah whipped her that day. Though only those men she could have the mastery over. She had to be in control.

Chapter Eleven

Mother Nature's indecision to let go of autumn's warmth held throughout an Indian summer two weeks before Christmas. The bare trees began to bud. Then the jet stream came down, bringing killing cold as the north winds blew fine crystals of freezing rain and snow. The land would need the deep freeze for weeks to exterminate the vermin ticks and fleas.

The day after the first wintry storm Delena and Isaiah pulled their shotguns off the wall near the fireplace mantel, bundled up, poked gun shells inside their coat pockets, and headed out the door. They walked uneasily over the three inches of snow that covered patches of ice as the warm midday sun was melting away the frozen precipitation. The ice laden tree tops sparkled as diamonds against a royal-blue sky. Dripping frozen foliage on white rolling hillsides would no longer hesitate hibernation, but it would die, remaining dormant until springtime.

Enoch was nine months old when winter winds howled and Delena and Isaiah tromped through the snow to the edge of the fallow field near the woods. They were out to snare a turkey for Christmas dinner.

The Workers Progress Administration under the New Deal of the Great Depression era planned to build roads, federal buildings, and courthouses in the Ozarks. But that was months away. Isaiah need work now.

Isaiah crawled over the rail-fence near the woods while Delena held his gun. He said, "Son, I gotta find work somewhere or we'll have some bad times. Come spring I'm gonna try and get a job on the WPA. Surely they could use my lumberjack skills."

Delena handed him both their firearms, pulled up her long skirt and held it tight. Her bloomers showing as she climbed over the fence. She said, "Pa, maybe I can get a job too on the WPA."

He chuckled, "Don't know about that, Son. I think WPA work is for men only."

She sighed as he handed her the gun and they marched into the woods searching for game markings. The holidays were upon them. They had no money. Sales of railroad ties were down. Isaiah hadn't sold one in months. Christmas would be slim. To make times more solemn, a widespread flu epidemic hit, and some of the Hotman's neighbors died the weeks before Christmas, but no one in the family had contracted the illness. Delena said, "I guess all families are suffering right now. The Great Depression they call it. It is depressing. To bad you lost all the money in the bank."

Sighing Isaiah said, "We didn't have that much to loose. We're luckier than rich folks. Our confidence isn't in our money, but in each other and our faith. We'll make it through."

She said, "I heard Mr. Dayton hanged himself when he lost his life savings. Though his children said he fell off a horse and broke his neck. I didn't believe it. He hanged himself. Now those high fluting Dayton kids are poor just like us. They're havin' a hard time adjusting to simpler ways. Can't look down on us poorer folks anymore. We're all in the same boat now. We'll survive because we know how. They might not."

Isaiah whispered, "Yep! Count our blessings everyday!"

Delena whispered, "Our neighbor, poor Mr. Yuman." She sighed "He is sure taking hard the death of his wife Lisa. Yep, Pa we're blessed. Don't know what I'd do if you died with that flu like Lisa. Ma might go nuts."

He said, "Hush up girl. God knows I got eleven mouths to feed. I ain't gonin' anywhere for a long time. Now be quiet. I thought I heard a turkey." They stopped dead in their tracks.

Before returning home they shot a monstrous wild tom turkey and over a dozen fat rabbits, which happened to be covered in fleas. They carried the wild game through the woods and across the barren corn field back to the house.

Standing near the cistern in the back yard cleaning the day's kill, Delena clawed herself. Scowling Isaiah said, "These darn fleas!" He cursed while running his bloody fingers inside his coat to scratch. "I don't know which is worse, the cold or the fleas!"

Laughing, agitated, clawing, and scratching from countless bites they skinned and gutted a dozen cottontailes.

"Pa, we can't take these vermin inside. They'll get in the beds and on all of us." Delena said, running her bloody hands up her dress tail to scratch her posterior. "Oh! Poo! Got them in my hair and drawers!"

Isaiah said, "We needed this cold snap. Hope it stays a while. If not, by summer the pest will eat us alive."

Anne walked out carrying two enameled blue-speckled water buckets and drew water from the cistern. "My, you did your selves proud this hunt," she said, gazing at the half-dozen skinned rabbits already in a dishpan setting on the ground next to Isaiah. Then she slapped her arm. "A flea! I was wondering why you two were cutting such squirming shines. Now I know. Take those pelts off down in the hollow. And burry them when you're through." She turned and carried the heavy buckets of water to the kitchen. "You both will have to strip and bathe! I don't want fleas in my house!" she yelled out the door.

Grimacing as she scratched, Delena said, "Okay Ma." She yanking the guts out of another rabbit, tossing them into a bucket beside Isaiah. The splash of raw fresh meat into salt water and internals being pitched created blood trails that stained the snow red to and around the containers.

After a bit Anne returned with another bucket filled with boiling hot water. She set it at the edge of the porch. "Here, for to loosen fat gobbler's feathers," she said, while walking cautiously across the snow to the dead bird lying on the ground next to Isaiah's feet. Delena watched her hoist up the turkey.

"Do you want me to help pluck?" Anne asked. Smiling, she grunted and laid the gobbler back on the ground. "Fat indeed! Bet he'll weigh a good twenty-five pounds dressed out!"

Isaiah scowled and nodded. "Nope, you'll be covered in fleas too," he said.

Anne went inside and stood in the doorway. "Guess I do need to stay away." She chuckled and slapped her arm.

Delena smiled. "Were gonna have a great Christmas dinner. Turkey is the biggest I've ever seen, Pa!"

Isaiah nodded while backing away from the rabbit pelts, he pulled up his pants leg and rubbed vigorously. "Anne!" he shouted, frustration ringing in his tone.

Anne stuck her head out the door, giggling. "What you want?"

"Boil lots of water for to bathe. I'll washup on the porch. Can't wait for Delena to finish first in the house. I gotta get these fleas off me." he said, scratching his rump.

Isaiah and Anne chuckled while Delena laughed hysterically.

Anne raised an eyebrow and said, "Isaiah you'll catch a chill bathing in the cold on the porch."

He said, "Fill the tub. I gotta have relief! Cold or not."

Anne nodded.

When the rabbits were skinned Delena placed the last of the killed fresh meat in the dish pan and carried the game inside for Anne to prepare for cooking. "Here Ma, we'll all eat our fill tonight." She set the pan on the table.

Anne's gaze traveled up and down Delena's bloody long skirt. "You and Isaiah get those flea-infested pelts out of the yard and then your baths will be ready," she said.

While they dressed out and hung the turkey in the smoke house, Anne began filling the bathing tubs and boiling rabbit dumplings. By the time they had buried the remains and returned, the tubs were filled with steaming hot bath water and lye soap.

Shivering on the back porch, Isaiah stripped down and jumped in. Anne hung one of her crazy quilts over the passageway between the living room and kitchen to give Delena privacy. Delena heard the other children marching into the house as they finished daily farm chores.

Behind the quilt, in the living room Chad grumbled, "Delena always gets to hunt with Pa. I don't know why he calls her, Son. I'm the oldest son. Not her! I get stuck tending to hogs!"

Leve said, "She's a better shot, and we need the meat. Pa

is fair. He'll take you next time just for fun. I promise! Now stop being jealous before Ma hears and smacks you good."

Delena shouted, "Chad wish you were covered in these fleas and not me. Consider yourself lucky this time."

Chad didn't answer but jealously mumbled, "Lucky my rear! Pa's not fair."

Scowling Anne folded back the quilt and stuck her head through the opening and snapped, "Chad! What were you saying?"

Chad didn't respond. He sighed, eyes downcast. Anne nodded and returned to her cooking.

After tossing her flea-infested clothing out the back door, Delena splashed in a wash tub.

Isaiah yelled, "Anne get Delena's clothes off the porch!"

Delena laughed while leaning back to relax in the warm water. She heard them fussing on the back porch. Anne chuckled as Isaiah continued to bellyache while scrubbing and clawing himself. She watched through the glass door panes as Anne picked up her clothes and tossed them into the iron wash kettle out back. Returning to the kitchen Anne opened a bottle of pungent horse liniment.

Ointment vapors filled the house and mingled with the scrumptious odors of hot rabbit dumplings and cherry pie baking as Anne applied the liniment to Delena's many bites. Delena dressed and Anne checked the cooking food while they continued to giggle at buck-naked, shivering, grumbling Isaiah. They couldn't see him from the kitchen but they all could hear him.

Anne grabbed the bottle of ointment off the table and stepped onto the back porch. She growled, "Get out now if you want this ointment. I haven't got all day to baby you, Isaiah."

Delena heard him squeal as he shivered dancing out of the tub. When cold air rushed against his wet naked flesh he cursed, "Hammered hog crap woman! Hurry up I'm about to freeze to death," he said.

Anne continued to fuss on him while she applied the burning ointment to his bites. She snorted, "Hush! Your worse than a child!"

Scowling Isaiah shouted, "Let me see your wet naked behind standing out here in thirty degrees." He chuckled.

Anne said, "Next time you can wait til Delena finishes and bathe inside. I hope you don't catch your death."

Chad continued to mumble in the next room while building the night's fire as Delena finished combing and rolling her long blond hair. Anne took down the quilt and carried clean clothes to Isaiah. Leve and Tina were tending to the youngsters and then they helped Anne set the dinner table.

Smiling Delena said, "Chad you really are lucky. By the next hunt most of the fleas will be dead," as she scratched her arm pit.

Chad puckered his lower lip and dropped his gaze. He said nothing and tossed another log onto the fire.

Clean, relieved from the infernal itching, and dressed, dinner was served. The family of eleven gathered and took their individual places at the table. Anne held baby Enoch on her lap. She chewed a chunk of rabbit, withdrew the pulverized meat from her mouth and placed it to Enoch's lips. He swallowed the food and giggled.

Delena said, "I think Enoch likes the rabbit."

Isaiah then placed a pulverized morsel into Enoch's mouth. Enoch swallowed as Isaiah laughed and said, "This boy of mine is going to grow up to be a cottontail."

Enoch giggled and made a buzzing sound.

Nodding, smiling Isaiah said, "Nope, maybe I'm wrong. Sounds like a June Bug. Buzzzz."

Giggling Enoch said, "Buzzzz!"

They all roared with laughter then filled their plates with double portions.

Isaiah stopped eating and said, "Boys I'm taking you all deer hunting after the first of the year. Son and I spied a twelve-point buck up on the ridge this afternoon."

Anne cleared her throat and said, "Isaiah Hotman, little Lanny is too young. He can't go. He could get hurt."

Four year old Lanny's face wadded up like a dried fruit as he was on the verge of tears. Isaiah said, "Lanny, I need you to stay home and be man of the house. These women just can't survive without a man to protect them. Can you do that for me?"

Lanny dropped his gaze.

Isaiah said, "Being man of the house is the hardest job of all. I'll expect you to take good care of the place while we are gone."

Lanny smiled and nodded.

Thirteen-year-old Chad and eleven year old Grant began to play shoot at each other using their fingers as pistols.

Anne growled, "Calm down boys! Finish your supper!"

They went back to eating.

When dinner was finished Delena helped Anne sort through the box of old handmade Christmas ornaments. Delena and Isaiah would find the perfect holiday tree and cut it down tomorrow.

Christmas morning when the children awakened they were pleased to find gifts under the crudely decorated cedar tree. Delena was happy for the younger ones that Anne had managed to scrape up enough money to buy every sibling an orange. She had also knitted them each a scarf and mittens, wrapped in old newspapers. Joyously, the younger ones tore into the packages and pealed their oranges.

Anne baked cornbread dressing and warmed the smoked turkey while Delena and the girls helped prepare the meal. They loaded the Christmas dinner table with a roaster of dressing, bowls of canned garden vegetables, and blackberry cobbler for desert encircling the wild smoked turkey.

Both Delena and Isaiah thought they might be coming down with the flu and took to their beds after dinner with fever and chills. Two days passed and the glands swelled all over their bodies. By the new year worst hit on Delena was under her arms. Falling in and out of consciousness she heard Anne kneel by her bed and weep bitterly, petitioning the Lord to let her daughter and husband live.

Delena repented of her rebellions and bitterness while in this semi-conscience state and rededicated her life to the Lord. Totally out of control and helpless, she had felt these same emotions once before. Her mind began to wander to events three years earlier. She had to get past the rape, forgive Newton, and get on with her life. Determined, she would put it behind her when she recovered—if she recovered.

She remembered the many good times shared with Pa. They would never again go to church, hunting, work in the woods, or take monthly trips to Dinktown together. He would not be there to protect her, the family, or her honor if he died. Silent tears drenched her pillow.

The next day Delena heard Pa struggling for every breath. His glands swelled in his neck and cut off his breathing as he gasped one last time. Momentarily, silence filled the house then she heard Ma, overcome with grief, screaming and weeping.

Her beloved pa gone. She thought of his last words two days before. He had spoken again of getting work on the WPA in spring. But now those dreams would never see the light of day. Delena silently wept.

She heard Bill cursing in the next room. "Little brother, I sure am gonna miss you. Those darn rabbits! Those damn fleas!"

Now Delena knew why Isaiah had died and the reason she was sick. Rabbit fever. Motivated by fear and rage she vowed to never hunt or eat rabbit again. The rabbits and their fleas had taken her pa from her.

She heard Anne preparing his body for burial through her tears in the next room. Bill and Jimmy built a pine coffin and the families came to pay their respects. Still unable to move or speak, Delena heard them talking as four strong men carried Isaiah inside the pine box out of the house and loaded him on Jimmy's flatbed truck. She could hear her ma's and siblings' agonizing travails as they left the home and shut the front door behind them. She was alone in her silent grief. On this windy, bitter cold day in January 1933, her pa, her best friend, was gone forever.

Chapter Twelve

Anne's family crouched, encircling the coffin on the back of the truck. She sat in the cab with whiskered, burley weeping Bill and skinny howling Jimmy. Her grief was silent, but tears drenched her lace handkerchief as she wiped her eyes one more time. The snow and ice had melted, but the windy ride to Red Hill Cemetery was bone chilling for the kids in the back. She held Enoch close and sighed, "I will miss him always. I will love him always. I will never marry again," she said.

They buried Isaiah next to Buster. No other shouting Baptist was there to show respects, and no Holy Rollers wept at his internment. Only Anne, his children, and brothers cried for Isaiah.

Sixteen-year-old, Leve held baby Enoch close to her chest. She pulled the blanket over his face to protect his tender skin from the stinging cold as the strong north winds howled and whipped her waist-length raven black hair. All the family snuggled close together on the north side of the grave with their backs turned against the piercing wind. Rubbing hands, flipping heavy coat collars up, and pulling knitted sock caps over their ears, they shivered in the biting cold. And wept.

Pulling her linen head scarf tight against her ears and tying a knot under her chin, Anne adjusted her green wool neck scarf to seal out the cold. She took off her matching mittens, shoved them into a pocket on her ankle-length black wool coat, and pulled a small worn Bible out of the same pocket. She flipped through the pages to find a passage.

Anne silently read and then dog-eared the section so not to loose the place. Her marriage to Isaiah had been harsh she thought as she stepped away and herded the younger children a distance from the grave. They watched Jimmy and Bill lower the pine box into the hole.

Compared to many wives in the settlements her beatings were seldom. Life was rigorous for everyone at the old breeding grounds. His problems with the moonshine made for rough days. She believed he truly loved her and the children despite the drunken temper tantrums and occasional fisting. She hoped he made it to heaven. She thought he did. She was glad he had quit the booze in 1929. Maybe just maybe he did make it to heaven.

She considered her freezing, teary-eyed children, gave a brief eulogy, and read the Scriptures from Psalm 23:1-6. She flipped the pages to the next fold. Choking back her sadness, smiling she said, "Be of good cheer my children!" Glancing down she read aloud: *"For God hath not given us the spirit of fear; but of power, and of love, and of a sound mind. 2 Timothy 1:7."* When finished she closed the book and held out her arms toward the brood. Smiling she said, "Isaiah loved you all and he would want you to be strong. Make him proud! After all Hotman blood flows in your veins. We will not be afraid or grieve for long. Isaiah has gone to be a star and he will watch over us always!"

She and the younger juveniles stepped away from the grave. They huddled close together while Bill, Jimmy, and the older boys began to shovel the dirt. Chad wept bitterly as he helped to fill in the pit where his father's body rested. She would need a miracle to keep this family together. She would not let the children see the depth her grief. She had to be strong for their sake.

Widowed at age thirty-eight in the middle of the Great Depression with nine children, she knew survival for the family wasn't going to be easy. And Delena who was so devoted to her Pa. Would she die too? "Give me strength Lord. Be brave. Give me wisdom to provide for my young ones. Sustain me, shield and comfort them to cope with this great loss. God you have to help us," she whispered.

Part Two
1933 to 1943
Keeping the Family Together

1998: A Letter To Saul From Leve

Dear Saul:

Hope my thoughts and memories helped answer your questions. Just wanted to add a few lines here. After Pa passed away we hit some real hard times--as if they weren't bad enough before his death. Survival was tough in the hills for most every family during the Great Depression. We scratched with the chickens to survive. Didn't throw away anything.

Ma saved every scrap of cloth to tailor clothes, and make quilts. I recall she was up until the late night hours sewing by oil lamplight, that after putting in a long day's field work. Then there was her preaching and praying. Where did she find the time and stamina?

Ma was stern after Pa died. Guess she had to be. We kids were no angels. Our rebellion drove her insane with worry at times. She was harsh but she sure loved us. Worked laboriously, scrimped, and saved to keep us together. We all had to do our parts, and sometimes that still wasn't enough. Ma's prayers sustained us through those rough years.

When we killed a hog nothing was wasted! Ma even had us to clean the internals. She'd boil them afterward and then stuff the guts with sausage. Rusted nails, old planks, scraps of tin, bits of paper and wire had a use. Nothing was thrown away. Ma was frugal and ingenious, or we we'd never have survived.

Many today talk about the good old days when we had no running water, jobs, or easy access to automobiles. Forget it! They can have them!

Your uncle Jake and I are failing in health. Seems we may have to ask for your help in our old days, if it wouldn't be to much bother.

You'll always be my little boy. Wish I could roll back the years and do a few things differently, but can't. Got to get some things right the first time cause ya don't get a second chance. Like raising a child. They grow up and those moments are gone forever. Only memories are left. I hope we gave you a few good ones.

Well, I know you love me and Jake despite our flaws. Somebody did right by you along the way. I don't think it was us, maybe the Lord. I just know you forgave us for letting you down.

I love you like a son, always.
Your aunt, Leve.

Saul smiled as he held the letter against his chest, and thought, Leve's and Jake's personalities swung as pendulums but he loved them. Yes, the stories helped, though everyone in the family tells the same account from a different perspective. The truth was in them somewhere. I trust yours Leve, and Delena's most. He returned to writing. I won't forsake you and Jake. You gave me the happiest, most secure years of my childhood. Except for your addictions. Loved me like a real mom and dad. I will gladly return the devotion. You saved my life!

Chapter One

The family survived on the farm the next two years. Delena slowly regained her strength. Feeling the Lord had called her to preach, Anne evangelized in local Pentecostal churches. She and the children raised huge gardens to feed the clan. With money very short and Isaiah gone, life nevertheless went on. They were still together.

Chad and Leve began to sneak around and sip the hooch. They too called it "Kick-A-Poo-Joy-Juice" after an Ozark's Indian tribe, just like Pa had. Use of homebrew became a worsening community problem for young and old alike. Chad and Leve warred in their spirits continually to serve God or the demons of booze. Anne preached hard against the use of liquor.

Delena slurped moonshine a time or two but never acquired a liking for the ethers. She was more interested in attempting to walk in Pentecostal holiness to please her mother, and the Lord. The strict clothsline doctrines she found oppressive. Though she publically adhered to the teachings, secretly she and Leve thought the rules were ridiculous.

Awakening concepts that true holiness was a condition of the heart and not the rags on her back danced in Delena's head. Fear of being labeled a Jezebel, ostracized, or hammered by congregation members, she chose not to breath her true feelings and submitted outwardly to the holiness doctrine. Other young women in the community made fun of her and her sisters because of their prudish, restrictive religious beliefs.

Delena hadn't completely recovered from the debilitating effects of the rabbit fever a year after Isaiah's death. Four years had passed since Newton raped her. She hadn't seen him since 1929 as he left the area after the beating. She heard through the grapevine he had returned. It was only a matter of time before their paths would cross again. While shopping on the Racoon Springs town square with Leve, Delena saw Newton and his new girlfriend Sally Beaton necking as they rounded the corner at the newspaper office. Delena trembled with rage and fear when Newton glanced up and winked. Sally scowled and gave them the BIRD. Pa was dead. Had Newton come back to torment her?

Delena and Leve returned their leering, then walked away. Delena mumbled, "Figures Newton would get tied up with that white trash Sally. No woman with any self-respect would have the bastard!" Unknown to Delena, Sally overheard. Delena glanced around and smiled.

Sally yelled, "Bitch! I'll kick your sorry butt!"

Delena laughed as Newton held tight to raging Sally who struggled to get free. Revengefully Sally frowned and yelled, "You just wait!"

Leve whispered, "Delena, I think she heard your nasty comment. You always seem to open your big mouth and say the wrong thing at the wrong time. Bridle your tongue girl!"

Delena rolled her eyes and bristled, "Right is right and wrong is wrong! And Sally Beaton is white trash!" She sighed, seething she said, "They won't bother us. If he tries I'll have Uncle Bill take care of him once and for all!"

Leve said, "I thought you had forgiven him."

Delena grimaced. "I thought so too. But when I saw him, the rage and memories flooded my mind and heart again," she said.

Two weeks later, Sally made good on her threat. While the Hotman girls walking home from church Sally and two of her drunk companions ambushed them.

Tall with dark-blond unkempt hair to her shoulders, Sally's common plain pale blue flour-sack dress with no lace was dingy and tattered. Anger burned in her drunken gray eyes. Her rage-contorted face, with thick makeup and red lipstick, reflected orange rays of the setting summer sun that late afternoon in August of 1934. Sally and her comrades, one red headed and the other with ash-brown stringy hair, jumped out of the bushes, screaming, and wielding knives. The three women knocked unsuspecting Leve and Delena to the ground.

Hotmans' tempers awakened with a vengeance. The cat fight was on! Hair flew, fists swung, and blood flowed. The felines clawed and scratched. Screams and cursing echoed across the hollows as Leve and Delena fought for their lives.

"Delena, I've been stabbed!" Leve raged as she grabbed a mop of red hair and began to spin round and round to gain momentum before releasing the girl into a patch of poison oak on the side of the road. Blood spued from the gash on her arm as she fought the other drunk stabbing her in the thigh.

Adrenaline surged through Delena's weak body. Strength to defend herself came from rage and fear as she realized the drunken wildcats were intent on homicide. After she was stabbed in the shoulder, Delena screamed, "These bloody whores! They're trying to kill us. Fight dirty, Leve! Get a limb! Pick up a rock! Take their knives!" She snatched up a palm size stone, smashing Sally's face. She then knocked the knife out of her hand.

Leve doubled up her fist and busted the brunet in the face with a right hook. Down they both went and Leve grabbed the knife, holding it to the woman's chin. "You ol' drunken hag, I ottar slit your throat here and now!"

Delena let Sally up and kicked her rump. "Newton must have beat your brains out, girl! You should know better than to mess with us Hotman girls! Git! Before I kill ya!" Delena yelled and Sally staggered over to the redhead crying in the poison oak. She helped her up.

Delena picked up another rock and threw it at them.

Red leaped angrily on Delena's wounded shoulder when the rock missed. Delena flipped her to the ground and grabbed her hair as the girl screamed in agony, struggled free, and bounced to her feet crying hysterically.

Leve was on the verge of slicing the brunet's throat.

"Stop Leve! Don't do it!" Delena shouted.

Coming to her senses Leve tossed the knife toward Delena and grabbed the brunet's hair and yanked out a wad. Then she let the crying girl up.

Finally their defeated bushwhackers ran off into the woods. Both Leve and Delena had fists full of hair that didn't match their own when the rumble was over.

Leve proudly pulled her tangled black hair back, and ran fingers over her scalp. She searched for bald spots, then checked on Delena who was panting with exhaustion. They examined each other from head to toe. No wounds were mortal but they needed medical attention. Realizing most of their locks were intact, they laughed victoriously.

Hobbling homeward, bloody, bruised with handkerchiefs placed around bleeding arms and leg lacerations, Leve said, "Guess we showed those ol' harlots!"

Delena pressed charges the next day after the local Doctor stitched their wounds. Sally and her accomplice received probation. Though Delena could never prove their motivations for the attack, she believed the assault was Newton's instigated revenge. The thought never crossed her mind that her acid tongue might have caused the incident until Leve told the judge, "Delena's big mouth gets her into trouble. She's just to darn independent!"

Everything in Loafer's Glory, reminded Delena of Pa or the rape. She wished to leave the old breeding grounds forever. Bridling her loose tongue was not an option. She'd say what she thought when she wanted to say it, no matter what the consequences, as long as Ma didn't find out. She was quite ticked off at Leve for telling the judge she had a big mouth. She'd get her back.

Chapter Two

Anne accepted an invitation in 1935 to pastor a Pentecostal church, and relocated the family fifty miles from Loafer's Glory. They moved to Rae Valley, along the White River. She pastored and the family sharecropped cotton.

Neighbors helped move household belongings to the sharecropper shack. Anne and Delena herded on foot the milk cow, her calf, and three hogs the fifty miles to Rae Valley. Staying nights with Christian friends, the trip took them three days.

Anne proclaimed often that the Holy Ghost revealed secrets she needed to know. She believed in the gifts of discernment and word of knowledge. The kids said she had eyes in the back of her head. While Anne and Delena were gone, Chad and Leve nipped a little Kick-A-Poo-Joy-Juice with other sharecropper teens whose parents also worked on the plantation. They'd try to conceal their misbehavior, promising the younger siblings candy for not telling Ma. But Anne already knew.

The second day of the trip Anne sensed something was wrong. She stopped, scowling. She sighed. "Delena, Chad and Leve are up to their tomfooleries again. We've gotta get home. I'm worried about the little ones," she said.

Smiling Delena said, "Ma they'll be okay. Tina will see to them."

Anne pulled a lace handkerchief from her apron pocket and wiped the sweat from her brow, "I know, but I suspect Chad and Leve are into the spirits again. I thought drunkenness in my home was over when Isaiah quit the moonshine. I guess iniquity of the father has visited my children."

Delena switched Bonnie the cow on the rump. She said, "Get up there," while turning toward Ma who was poking the sow with a stick. "Now Ma, maybe your just fretting for nothing."

Frowning, Anne tickled the slow friendly sow behind the ear. She said, "You stubborn beast, just as contrary as my children. Go on now." The hog squealed and charged forward when she twisted it's ear. Anne chuckled. Glancing up her expression changed to seriousness and her brow wrinkled. "Nope! I know the voice of the Holy Ghost. He said they are into the moonshine," she barked.

Concerned, frowning Delena sighed. She growled, "I hope it makes them sick!" Their strides lengthened as the livestock moved along at a faster gait.

On the last leg of the tiresome journey, Anne and Delena waded the animals across a shallow creek, a stone's throw from the sharecropper shack. Smiling, they waved at Chad, who was tossing hay from the loft. They watched him rise from his work to wipe the sweat from his brow with a dirty blue bandana. He ran strong fists through his ash brown hair and waved back. "Ma!" he shouted and the other children came speeding out of the house.

Looking onward, they watched excited faces charging delightfully down the hillside to greet them. The Hotman brood raced as hard as they could to embrace and kiss their long-missed mother and sister Delena.

Anne shook her head as Delena, such a touch-me-not, while trying to escape their affections fell into the stream and drenched herself. "Look what ya'll roughens have done to me!" she screamed, struggling to get on her feet again. The clutch of youngsters laughed and started a splash fight.

"I'm gonna whip your behinds with a hickory switch," Delena ranted as they doused her again in the cold water.

Seventeen-year-old Leve, now a vivacious elegant young woman, was built like a stone outhouse. Her beauty was unique, long black hair, large breasts and a slim curved body that accented her innocence angel face, which hinted of Native American roots. She gracefully strolled out of the house and met them on the shoal with three-year-old cotton-top Enoch bouncing on her hip. She stood him on the bank. Her long, delicate, refined but calloused fingers twirled back her waist-length hair out of her face. She watched after him intently and squatted by the water's edge to splash her cheeks. Leve had a drunken hangover.

Anne sensed Leve's head hurt when she softly moaned, sat down and placed her brow in one hand. Letting go of Enoch's palm as she looked up, then shamefully dropped her gaze as Anne glared back.

Enoch began to flip his small fingers in water, laughing hysterically with his older siblings when eleven-year-old Lou and eight-year-old, Sonny pushed Delena. She lost her balance and fell into the creek again.

"Momma!" Delena cried.

Anne joined in the fun and excitement with as much joy as the children. "Stop being such a poot, Delena. The babies are just happy to see us," she said, as she splattered Delena with a hand's scoop of water in the face and giggled.

Soaking wet in a mad rage Delena pulled herself out of the brook grumbling, "Stop! You just wait. I'll get you all good!" She flouted off to the house to change her wet clothes.

Lou and Sonny mimicked Anne through their child's play and giggles. "Don't be such poot, Delena!" they shouted as she angrily stomped up the hill toward the shack.

Fifteen-year-old Chad, who was looking more like Isaiah every day, and thirteen-year-old Grant, with dark hair, eyes, and complexion like Leve came running from the barn. They too joined in the fun.

Anne sniffed and caught the slightest scent of soured moonshine sweat as Chad hugged her. But she said nothing. He was sober. She would deal with him and Leve another time.

Blond, large boned, and heavier set than all the other girls, Tina bounded out of the house with a bulky basket of dirty laundry to wash in the branch and took part in the gaiety.

Enoch began to cry when Anne picked him up on the shoal. He held tight with arms around her neck. She kissed him all over his face many times and began to laugh. Soaking wet Chad and Grant herded the livestock to the barn while the others went into the house.

Leve had prepared a huge pot of pinto beans and corn cracklin' bread for supper. When they finished eating, the family dressed for church.

Sunday nights, they walked four miles to services where Anne preached. Hard field-labor, chopping, picking cotton, and gardening kept food on the table.

The local sawmill hired Chad a month after they arrived in Rae Valley. Money was short but the family was all together and Anne was doing what she loved best--preaching. Like a freed lioness and aggressive in her religious zeal, she knew if Isaiah were alive, she couldn't preach or move in the spirit as she did these days.

Though he had converted to Pentecostalism, he believed like most Baptist that it was ashamed for a woman to preach. She missed him but loved her religious freedom more.

They ran short of supplies before cotton harvest. Deluged with rain for a week, roads were muddy. Without work at the mill for Chad because of the bad weather, Anne ran out of money.

Desperate for basic supplies she and Chad walked the mucky country road toward Elbo Town five miles away, hoping to secure credit at the mercantile. They waded across three shallow creeks and several dry washes along the way.

Evidence of how high the brooks had swollen. Leaves, sticks, and trash were strewn several feet onto the road and along the stream banks where the waters had receded. As Chad approached the edge of one of the rivulets, he spotted green paper sticking out of a pile of drifted leaves and bent down to get a better look. Hardly visible in the rubble, was a sopping wet five-dollar bill.

Jumping into the air, waving the money high over his head, he shouted, "Ma, look what I found! This is ten days wages at the mill!"

Anne's heart raced for joy when she saw elation on Chad's face. She prayed silently every step of the journey, and having the money appear on the way to the mercantile at a time when the family needed it most did not happen by chance alone. "The Lord who has answered my prayers! Praise God!" she shouted. With her hands thrown heavenward she did the Pentecostal dance of rejoicing, and speaking in the unknown tongue. When she stopped, she saw Chad glaring hatefully.

Frowning, he shook his head as he shoved the five bucks inside his overall pocket. Adjusting Isaiah's old gray brim hat on his head and then angrily ramming his fist into his pockets, Chad said, "Ma, I wish you wouldn't do that in public! What if someone happens by!"

Several of the children had mixed feelings about her Pentecostal experience. They think I make such a fool of myself, she thought. "Boy, don't you back talk me or make light of my Lord. The curse of God will come upon you. God is not mocked! And neither is your ma! Ya here me!"

"I'm not mocking. I'm embarrassed," he said. Trying to get in her good graces again he pulled the five dollars from his pocket, and placed the bill in her hand.

Smiling gratefully she slid the money into her apron pocket. "Thank you, Son," she said. So many souls came to Christ in the little church she pastored. It was God's will for them to be in Rae Valley. "The Lord shall provide!" she shouted and squeezed the five dollar bill.

Chad finding the money was another Rae Valley miracle. She hoped God would mellow his harsh spirit. She didn't want him to grow up to be an abusive drunk like Isaiah.

She sighed, patted his hand and smiled, raised her chin and with a lilt in her voice said, "Well, Son! Your going to see many Rae Valley miracles before we leave this place. You might even get the Holy Ghost and then you will certainly understand."

He dropped his gaze.

She thought about when Bonnie and her calf were stolen the month before and how the Holy Spirit gave her the names of the thieves some forty miles away. She recalled how the older children had thought she belonged in the lunatic asylum when she began asking around the community about the names of the cattle thieves the Holy Ghost had spoken to her during prayer. No one had heard of these people, knew them, or where they might live. Chad was dumbfounded when it was true, and the Holy Spirit led her to find the thieves and the missing cattle. She chuckled at the memory and realized at that moment how much like Isaiah he really was becoming.

"Son, remember Bonnie?"

Chad nodded.

She said, "I haven't said anything to you and Leve, but I know you were into the moonshine. The Holy Spirit told me. I couldn't prove it. The younger ones said they didn't know. But they lied to me. I should switch you all!"

Chad squirmed as his eyes widened, surprise and guilt, head down, "I'm sorry Ma. It won't happen again," he mumbled.

Frowning, she barked, "It best not! Honor your mother! Your rebellion is worse than witchcraft."

He sighed. Under conviction, unable to deny Anne's spiritual gift he shrugged his shoulders and grimaced.

She scolded, "We may be poor but we aren't white trash. I expect better out of you children than this."

Smiling he said, "I know Ma." He couldn't abnegate the power of the Holy Ghost! Shaking his head, he frowned. "I'll resist the temptation a little harder. My friends are the only pleasure I have Ma. Maybe if we were rich I could make better friends. Just wish God could give us a *big* break. A million bucks right now!"

Anne scowled while quoting Scripture. *"It is easier for a camel to go through the eye of a needle, than for a rich man to enter into the kingdom of God. Mark 10:25.* I'll whelp you good if this happens again! There are young people who find happiness in each other's company without having to take the low road! Rich and poor! You can do the same. Now stop trying to change the subject."

Chad nodded. They sat down on the edge of the creek bank and removed their worn work boots before crossing.

He sighed and rolled his eyes. "I don't know about that Ghost. I won't be walking the backs of church pews! I won't be shouting and running in circles! He's always telling you my secrets! I don't think I like him," he said and chuckled.

Placing her hands on his shoulder she drew him near. "If the Holy Ghost gets a hold of you, you won't have any pride left. You'll worship God with all your heart, mind, and body. I hope one day you will grow to love his presence."

He pushed away her hands while bounding to his feet and stepped back. "I won't be making a public spectacle of myself!"

She needed to pray a little harder for Chad. "You need the Holy Ghost," she said as she motioned for him to come close. "He'll give you power to resist the devil booze!" He reached out and she took his hand. "Help your ma up, Son." She grunted and he tugged as she stood.

She checked her bun to make sure it was still in place and handed him his boots. "God blesses our labors with bountiful crops. The fieldwork is never ending but, Chad, we're still together and healthy. Look at the five bucks he just placed in your hand. That ottar make a believer out of you. God said he would supply our needs." She sighed, "I should have named you Thomas. Doubting Thomas." She chuckled.

He grinned, "Guess I have no faith unless I see the signs. I'm not a genuine Pentecostal. Maybe I'm a Baptist. A poor wretched sinner Baptist like Pa and you were in the beginning," he said.

Anne placed her arm around his waist, and they waded the creek, continuing on to Elbo Town.

"Me and the other's have nicknamed Rae Valley, Bug-Tuffy because the bugs are tough and so are the times here, Ma."

The shallow but swift stream splashed over their bare feet as they crossed to the other side. Anne giggled and kissed him on the cheek. She said, "Your pa was a good man but demon liquor had him bound. You're a good son! But I worry about your liking the corn squeeze. It will bring you nothing but ruin and heartache, Son."

Watery-eyed Chad hugged her. "I love you Ma," he said.

Chapter Three

Chad's drinking problems continued. His secretive consumption of moonshine worsened when he went off to work in the CC camps while they lived in Rae Valley. Leve wrestled to resist the "Kick-A-Poo-Joy-Juice" after the homesick family returned to Loafer's Glory in 1938.

Strawberries and tomatoes became cash crops with farmers and The Strawberry Grower's Association was formed in 1938. The neighboring town of Racoon Springs was proclaimed the Strawberry Capital of the World. Chad had sent money back home. Anne saved part of the cash and bought hundreds of strawberry plants. They planted strawberry and tomato fields on the homestead acres.

Hundreds of Mexican and Caucasian migrant worker families swarmed to the area during strawberry harvest to earn the meager wages of one and a half cent per quart. Growers got the good price of one dollar and ninety cents per crate. Crops were sold and transported to distant canning factories on the Galloping Goose.

Enoch, six, now worked alongside his older siblings in the fields. Anne toiled the crops and preached at every opportunity. After returning to Loafer's Glory she started having prayer meetings three times a week in the home. She became increasingly stern in her holiness beliefs and clothesline religion.

When invited to minister in local churches, her preaching became heightened with heavy hellfire and brimstone messages, loaded with lots of "Thou Shalt Nots." Her zealous preaching frightened Enoch. But he wasn't the only one her harsh strict doctrines was making miserable.

In 1939, when Lou was fifteen Anne caught her wearing makeup. Returning home late after a date, Lou hadn't washed off all the face-paint and lipstick her friends secretly applied.

On the porch Lou trembled when she was met by scowling Anne at the front door.

"Go to bed! Now! I'll deal with you in the morning," Anne said while glaring at Lou.

When the sun peeped over the horizon Anne pecked on Lou's window. Harshly, "Lou! Out of that bed now! I promised you a whippin'. Come here! Now," Anne ordered.

Slim, blond, and pretty, Lou reluctantly crawled out of the bed. Anne waited impatiently while trimming a Hickory switch as Lou dressed. Most rebellious, Lou knew the drill better than the other girls. Though Anne never spared the rod, stubborn Lou remained headstrong.

Anne's religious wrath overpowering her reasoning. Breathing heavily, she firmly grabbing Lou's arm, held on tight-and whelped her legs and behind several times. They awakened the whole house. Anne cried with every stinging lick of the switch as Lou screamed and danced around.

"No child of mine will burn in Hell's fires for wearing makeup! Don't even think about wearing jewelry! I'm not raising a harlot. Your forbidden to see your moonshine sipping boyfriend Martin ever again. That family has corrupted you. This hurts me more than it does you!" Anne shouted

"Yes, Momma! I won't do it again! I promise, Momma! Ple, oh, no, stop! Pleeee-ase, Momma. Momma, stop!" Lou cried.

Shaking her finger in Lou's face. Anne said, "Lou, you will work twice as hard, and I will use the switch more often if you don't start minding me!"

Tearfully Lou nodded, and ran toward the barn-loft as hard as she could run.

Two months later Anne sat in the oak rocker where she had lullabied each of her babies to sleep when they were small. Fretting over Lou because she hadn't come home the night before. She leaned forward and glanced out the window while holding her place in the Bible.

Martin's large boned and fat mother came stomping through the front yard, bounding onto the porch she knocked. Anne stood and opened the door. Martin's mother, Bonnie had a scowl on her face like when the children bite into bitter green persimmon fruit.

She squinted and shouted, "Anne did you know that girl of your's has run off and married my Martin? They have eloped!"

Anne's heart sank as she fought to hold back her tears. Had she been too harsh with Lou?

Bonnie said, "To make matters worse that ol' girl of your's got herself knocked up! Well, if its Martin's baby–if. I guess this is for the best."

Anne regained her composure and swallowed the lump of grief lodged in her throat, she asked, "Are they going to stay with you?"

Bonnie said, "Nope! No way! They wanted to but I don't allow whores in my house. Martin left me a note and explained their plans. Nope I won't allow them under my roof if they come back."

Anne's anger was kindled, her face flushed red as she tried to bridle her tongue without insulting Bonnie. She said, "Well, this is a good thing if we are going to be grandparents. I certainly wouldn't want Lou to marry just *any* no-count. They are welcome in my home."

Bonnie rolled her eyes and said, "Martin could have done better than Lou."

Anne clutched her Bible and smiled, "Bonnie, God knows best."

Bonnie snorted, "God hasn't got a darn thing to do with this. Youthful lust has carried off our children. I needed Martin at home to help in the fields. Now he has gone off to help raise a little bastard child!"

Anne took a deep breath to subdue her anger, "Thanks for letting me know. I've been worried sick about sweet Lou. Would you like to come in for coffee and a little prayer?"

Bonnie said, "This isn't a social call. Besides your religion must not be any count or your daughter wouldn't have turned out the way she has!"

Anne sighed. "Bonnie this is my prayer time. I have to go now," she said.

Bonnie scowled and stomped off the porch mumbling to herself as Anne shut the door. Anne ran to the other room, fell upon her bed weeping for over an hour.

A month later Anne received a letter from Lou. They had moved to South Bend Indiana where Martin found a job and trained to finish drywall.

In 1940: Delena and Leve left the homestead and traveled to many states together, harvesting various kinds of fruits and vegetables. When not in the fields or orchards the two women waited tables. They moved to Amarillo, Texas to work at a military armaments plant during the war effort in 1942. Leve made her home in Amarillo throughout the war. Delena stayed with her for a time but eventually traveled to California then to Oregon and Washington state harvesting crops. Neither kept in touch very often with Anne and the others.

Chad, an authority figure for his siblings and a surrogate father, he had a hard time accepting and following orders when sober. Nevertheless, he could shout out the commands. No one back-talked Chad in Loafer's Glory. Woe unto those who tried. His words were law, second only to Anne's in the house. Chad had many fist fights with local boys over the years, and Anne warned him to lay off the booze and control his temper when he was drafted into the army. Anne told him that she feared he'd die drunk and go to hell before he, Grant and Tina's new husband Roscoe shipped out for Europe.

Tina had married good-looking Roscoe when they sharecropped in Rae Valley. She and her husband built a home across the road from the Loafer's Glory school house before the war started. By winter of 1943 only Sonny, Lanny, and Enoch were left at home.

Autumn brought the cotton harvest. For the next several reaping seasons, Anne and the younger children migrated to the bottoms around Jonesboro Arkansas. They picked cotton and returned to the old breeding grounds at Christmas. In the winter of 1943 Anne secured a job with Racoon Spring's garment factory, sewing military uniforms. Every winter morning during World War II she walked the six miles to town. The youngsters attended Loafer's Glory school from January til April.

Part Three
Enoch and Merl
1943 to 1953
Enoch's Troubled Youth

1999: A Note From Enoch To Saul

My dear son, Saul:

I'm having a good day. The voices have subsided--only an annoying roar inside my head but I'm able to think with out interruption for a while. The new medication seems to be working.

I am grieved that I was not there for you kids. Had problems for so long. Sickness in body and mind robbed the pleasure of my family, and a life. I am grateful for the love and care you have given, and shown to me over the years. Seems our roles have been reversed.

If only things could have been different. But life handed me a basket of rotten fruit from the start. Then there was Merl Judas. I wish I had never known him. None of us deserved the treachery. My friendship with Merl was my final undoing.

I did try but my life was doomed to failure from the beginning. Forgive me for not being there for you kids. Though I have always loved you. Always!

Your father, Enoch.

When Saul finished reading the note he hugged graying and frail Enoch. "I love you Daddy! Now don't worry your mind about what could have been. We have each other, now. Lets enjoy these days together. Your no burden on me. You are a blessing."

Enoch sat down in the chair next to Saul. He smiled and then removed his false teeth. He said, "Can't wear those darn things. They make me gag." He mumbled, "No! No! Howdy! Howdy! I love you too, Peter Saul." Sipped coffee from a mug and then asked, "How's the book?"

Saul patted him on the leg. "You know, Dad, I've come to the part about you, and I need you to fill in some blanks for me. Tell me about your youth and when you and Momma got together."

Toothless Enoch smiled. He said, "I was a wild one back then before the accident. Your Momma, she was a raving beauty, and a bitch on wheels!" He chuckled, and said, "God, I loved her!" He sighed.

Saul reached for a note pad on the computer desk. He asked, "Is this going to bother you to talk about it?"

Enoch nodded. "Nope! I'm past the pain now. I forgave her. Howdy, howdy!" he said, "I forgave them all."

Chapter One

Enoch's siblings said his mind wasn't right. After all he was marked by the cow horn. They told him the story many times. Especially when he became angry, they disparagingly brought up and teased about his cow-horn marking. This intensified his insecurities, and resentments. Prodding from those around him worsened his defiance. A rebellious sort all of his young life, his emotional problems escalated the older he got.

Anne's preaching he wished to avoid but he was trapped. The antics in the Pentecostal church and talk of the Ghost spooked him.

His bitterness and dread deepened after Anne turned over all disciplinary whipping to his older brothers when Enoch was eleven years old. She no longer had the stamina to run after him in the woods in order to correct his rude conduct. Though there were times when she would sneak into his room while he slept and belt him in the bed. When Anne promised the children a whipping, she was always as good as her word.

Enoch woke to the sound of Anne snapping in the doorway, "Get up! The days a wasting! I'm not gonna call you again!"

"Okay, Ma! I'm up already!" Enoch growled.

"It's past five. Get dressed and do your chores! Don't be skipping out of school again or I'll whelp you good!" she barked, stomping back into the kitchen.

Enoch slid out from under the covers. Shivering in the frigid March morning air, he sighed while clutching his clothes. His depressing exhale lingered as frosty mist.

Enoch dreaded facing his tormentors another day. Older children attending the one-room school house picked on him. He was painfully shy, insecure, and freckled. They laughed at his appearance, and his learning disabilities made his life miserable with teasing and bulling. But he was not to be out done when they got him angry, or when he decided he wasn't going to take their prodding. He threw rocks, kicked shins and groins, and pulled hair.

He was now two years behind the other students. They mocked him when the schoolmaster made him stand at the black board with his nose in a ring while wearing a dunce hat. The thirty-five year-old schoolmaster, tall, skinny, premature graying Mr. Obey, often whipped Enoch with his belt in front of the other children, pulled Enoch's hair, shook him violently, and yanked on his ears while making derogatory remarks. He called Enoch a moron, an idiot, and a dunce. Enoch hated school and he hated Mr. Obey even more.

"I'll play sick again this morning, and Ma will let me stay home," he mumbled as he slid into his worn flannel shirt and patched overalls. After tying the laces on his scuffed work boots and licking his palm to run spit over the cowlick standing straight up at the crown of his head, he put on his ragged work coat and reluctantly shuffled into the kitchen.

Anne was lighting the kerosene lantern. She smiled and ruffled his hair as he picked up the clean milking pail off the bread closet. "Good morning, sleep head," she said.

He grinned. "Morning, Ma."

Sixteen-year-old Sonny stepped away from the wood cook stove while preparing breakfast. "Milk Babe good!" she shouted as Enoch darted out the back door.

Enoch kept his pace never looking back. "They all try to boss me! Why did I have to be the youngest? Bullies! They're all bullies! And Mr. Obey is a chicken shit! They're all chicken dookie!" he mumbled.

Fourteen-year-old, lanky Lanny was chopping kindling by lantern light as Enoch trotted past him toward the barn. "Get with it, you lazy dunce! Ma doesn't want you late for classes again!" Lanny said, and then went back to splitting kindling.

Enoch pretended not to hear.

When he returned to the house Anne, Sonny, and Lanny were waiting at the breakfast table. Enoch set the pail of fresh warm milk on the bread closet counter and washed his hands.

"Did you give Babe extra grain?" Anne asked.

"Yes Ma!" Enoch snapped.

Lanny leaned back in his chair and glared at Enoch. "Boy! That's no way to talk to Ma! Apologize now!"

With downcast eyes Enoch took his place at the table. "I'm sorry Ma," he said.

Anne nodded, reached out, and the family held hands while bowing their heads and she said grace. Ending her prayer, "And Lord look after my boy's Chad and Grant. Keep your hand of protection on Leve and Delena. Save rebellious Lou's soul. Amen."

Sonny stood and strolled into the living room. She grabbed an envelope off the what-not shelf near the Coo Coo clock. She took her seat at the table and handed the letter to Anne. "Ma, this came in the post yesterday. I meant to give it to you last evening but forgot."

Anne smiled and looked at the letter post marked from a town in England. "A letter from Chad!" she said, smiling. Hurriedly she opened the envelope and began to read aloud:

"Dear Ma: Hope all is well with the family back home. Gosh I sure am

homesick! Want to see all of you so bad it hurts. Just a few words to give you my new address.

"You may reach me at this address for a few weeks. Seems you were right Ma. The booze got me into lots of hot water here in England. I'm sending this note to you from the NUT HOUSE."

Enoch's eyes widened. The children said in unison, "Nut House!"

"Did he get shot in the head?" Lanny asked.

Enoch grinned. "Well, now at least I'm not the only one that's crazy!"

Anne scowled.

"Hush up! Let Ma finish reading," Sonny snapped.

Enoch bowed his head in shame as Anne continued:

"I'm not really crazy. Booze just let my temper get the best of me. Back in February is when all my troubles began. I got drunk and refusing to follow officer's orders. The Sargent shouted commands in degrading tones while I was at an allied air field delivering fuel. He kept yelling at me to move my truck so other vehicles could pass. The thing wouldn't start. I had been nipping demon liquor, lost my temper and reasoning in the heat of inebriate anger.

"Rage instantly surged through my entire being. I wanted to kill the bastard. I glared back hatefully and shouted at the Sargent then grabbed my machine gun and jumped out of the truck. I fired off a round into the air. The officer fled for cover as I made chased while opening up the gun with a shower of bullets into the air again. I laughed hysterically as other service men dove for cover. You should have seen the fear on their faces. I knew what I was doing. Damn! You know me Ma. Never did take to being bossed around or talked down to. I just wanted to come home.

"I wasn't so drunk I didn't know what I was doing. Quite the contrary. I just didn't care. Got tired of being ordered around so I gave close pursuit on the heels of my superior who ran for his life off the tarmac. When the gun ran out of bullets, I was subdued, but not without a fist fight. Took four to wrestle me to the ground before I was arrested by military police. One hit me in the face with the butt of his machine gun and broke my jaw.

"The incident very nearly cost me many years in prison. Being labeled nuts has its benefits Ma."

Enoch raise his head and giggled.

Anne continued reading:

"A way of escaping a lengthy prison stay or Court Marshall. Guess I got Pa's and uncle Bill's temper when I'm drunk and their harsh personalities. My anger only intensified in drunkenness. Pray for me Ma. Demon liquor got me into lots of trouble. Hoping to get out of the hospital soon and will be home for a few days this spring.

"Our neighbor, cantankerous old Stetty Beaton sent me a letter. Her son's Buck and Dub are getting discharged on medical disability this week. They'll catch the next ship home. She sent me a recipe to make myself sick so I can get discharged too. She told me to eat bar soap and handfuls of aspirin. But she added at the end of her letter that the plan made her boys spend a lot of time in the latrine. She said this would last awhile after they get home. Just one of the bad side effects of the recipe. But hopefully their bowels will begin to heal when they get home.

"I threw her menu in the trash, deciding it is better to calm down and bide my time than to squat and puke the rest of my young life. Beside the girls would avoid me if I did that!"

The children laughed as Anne smirked, nodded. and rolled her eyes followed by a big sigh.

Enoch slapped the table and stomped his feet, laughing hysterically.

Anne went back to reading and Enoch quieted while listening intently:

"I'll learn to submit myself to commanding officers for the remainder of the war. I'll see you all in a couple of months. I love you Ma. Your son, Chad."

Anne chuckled and whispered a prayer while folding the letter and stuffing it back into the envelope. "Lord, help poor Chad get his temper under control. Deliver him from the booze," she said.

"Squat and puke!" Enoch giggled. "Pass the biscuits please," he said.

Lanny chuckled and passed the plate to Enoch.

Tossing her long dark hair over her slim shoulders Sonny giggled and said, "Dan has asked me to the rodeo Friday night."

Anne scowled.

Smiling Sonny asked, "Okay, Ma?"

Anne nodded.

Enoch scarfed down his chocolate gravy, buttered cat-head biscuits, and eggs. Elated Sonny then turned toward Enoch. "Slow down! You'll have a belly ache."

Anne sighed, "Those poor rodeo animals. Don't know how any one can find pleasure in the torture. But you enjoy your time with Dan just keep your legs crossed and be home by ten."

Enoch slowed a bit.

Sonny nodded. "Enoch! Slow down!" she shouted. He paused and glanced up. "Did you get all your homework?" Sonny asked.

"Nope! Didn't understand all those figures?" Enoch mumbled.

Lanny smirked. "Mr. Obey will thresh you good again!"

Anne finished eating, pushed back her plate and patted her lips with a cloth napkin. She sighed and frowned. "Son, education is so important these days. You gotta learn these skills to survive as a man. Your Ma won't always be here to take care of you. I want you to start trying a little harder. Maybe I should talk to Mr. Obey."

Enoch pushed back his plate. "I'm sick to my stomach, Ma. Do I have to go to school today? I promise to study if you let me stay home."

"I told you to slow down!" Sonny sneered.

Lanny chuckled.

"No Son, you go on to school." She gently placed her hand on his forehead. "You don't have any fever," Anne said.

The coo coo bird jumped out of the clock and sounded six a.m.

"All right, Ma. I'll try harder, but my stomach sure hurts." Enoch said.

"You'll feel better after your breakfast settles," she said. "Now you run along and put on your good clothes for school. I've got to head for work or I'll be late."

Enoch walked toward his room. Sonny cleared the breakfast dishes and Lanny changed his clothes. Anne slipped on her old black coat, kissed the children goodbye, and headed out the door. Enoch stood in the open doorway and watched as Anne put on her mittens, pulled her neck scarf half over her face to cut the cold bitter wind, and waved bye one last time. He continued gazing down the main road as she strolled out of sight around the near curve.

One of the few school friends Enoch made in 1943 was with a boy named Merl Judas whose family moved to the Ozarks from the Bijou's of Louisiana. Merl was forever shy of or stretching the truth. Stubborn and mischievous, he had a way of making anyone and everyone like him at first. With his large blue eyes, warm joyous smile, olive complexion, and black hair he was an exceptionally handsome eleven-year-old. His good looks accented his charm. He had manners when he chose to use them. They became fast friends when Enoch started school after returning from cotton harvest.

Anne ran short of money in autumn of 1942 and sold ten acres of her homestead to Merl's mother and father, Bertha and Luke. Bertha's, frightening demeanor was amplified by a swarthy complexion, her long face, sharp nose, and chin. She cackled when she laughed. Convinced that Bertha really was a witch, Enoch stayed his distance. She had the habit of running her long bony fingers through her salt-and-pepper stringy locks that fell to her hips. Nervously, she placed an end hair-tuft inside her mouth and wet it with spit, then rolled the strand around her index finger.

Luke, a quiet man, was polite with everyone. Husky with bit of a paunch, his premature white curly hair and short gray beard were the makings of a rejected dark-skinned Santa Clause. Especially when he hardily laughed while placing his hands on his jiggling fat belly.

The Judas family built a two-room shack on the property. Along with their seven children they lived only a quarter mile away from the Hotmans. Enoch was delighted to have a friend about his age living so close.

Merl and Enoch met on the road in front of Judas house before the school bell rang every morning. They had known one another for three months in March 1943.

Enoch and Lanny ambled down the road carrying their books and met up with Merl waiting for Enoch. Enoch stopped to greet Merl but Lanny kept walking. "You better go to school, Enoch. Ma will whip your tail if you and Merl skip out again."

The school-bell rang. Bertha stuck her head out the door and yelled, "Merl Judas, you and that Hotman boy get to class! You're going to be late!"

"Shut up, Moms! I heard you three times ago," Merl shouted back at Bertha and grinned at Enoch. "Nagging old bitch! Lets walk out of sight. Can't stand her bitchin'!"

"I'd never get away with talking to Ma that way," Enoch said.

"Ah, she likes it. Just gives Moms something else to whine about." Merl grinned proudly.

"Ma would beat me to death," Enoch said as he and Merl picked up their pace.

Merl said, "I'm part Negro!"

Enoch crinkled his nose at Merl's tan arms then nodded. "Ya are? You aren't black! I thought all Negros were black."

"Well, I am and that's the truth! Ma and Pa say, I am French, Cajun, Creole, and Cherokee. My great-grandmother was a freed Negro slave turned to prostitute in New Orleans after the Civil War."

Scowling in disbelief, Enoch said, "Best not tell any folks around here! Most hate niggers! But it's your hide if you tell! Not mine! Nigra my big toe!" He nodded. "Well, my daddy is the man on the moon! Merl Judas, you sure spin a yarn. I think you're a liar! Don't ya know you'll go to hell for that?" Enoch asked while laughing.

Wide-eyed Merl said, "Moms says she is a black witch, an Indian herbalist. She can cast spells on people she don't like. Don't get on her shit list!" He scowled and continued, "Her magic is powerful. I've seen folks get down and die from her spells when they tick her off!"

"Well, she looks like a witch!" Enoch said as he tapped Merl on the arm. "You're it!" he shouted and took off running from the main road down the hill to the Baptizing Hole at the bottom of the hollow with laughing Merl on his heels.

"I'm not going!" Enoch shouted.

Merl yelled, "That ol' bastard Obey can kiss my ass too."

"Race you to the Blow Hole!" Enoch said.

They ran past the Baptizing Hole and half way up the next hill to an obscure cave opening just large enough for the two of them to shimmy through on their bellies. This was Enoch's secret place. He named it Blow Hole because warm air whistled out of the entrance in winter and cold in summer. Once inside Merl pulled a tin of Prince Albert tobacco from his back pocket and handed Enoch a fold of Old Country Boy roll-your-own papers.

Enoch reached into a coat pocket and pulled out a match to light a lantern on the small cave floor, shielding the lamp with his back from the breeze behind him. Another small opening spread ten feet from the mouth at the back of the cave where they heard the sound of running water and felt the rush of wind gushing through.

Enoch sat on a folded burlap feed sack and tossed one over to Merl who sat with the lamp between them. "Merl Judas, you stole tobacco from your older brother Ely again!"

"Yep! Sure did. That fool is a halfwit. He'll think he lost it at the sawmill. He'll never know!" Merl laughed.

Enoch said, "I haven't ever took up the smoke."

Merl yanked the papers from Enoch's hand. "I'll teach you!" Merl rolled a cigarette, struck a match on the hot lamp globe, lit the smoke, and puffed. "Here this is good stuff!" Merl said as he coughed, exhaled, and handed the cigarette to Enoch.

Enoch puffed and coughed. They sat inside the warmth of the cave near the opening in the dim light and puffed away until they both were green with tobacco overdose, at which point they whirled their breakfasts. The sick boys managed to crawl out of the cave and staggered down the hill to the Baptizing Hole where they washed their faces in the frigid running waters.

"I'm going home and back to bed," Enoch said.

Merl placed his hand on his growling stomach. "Me too," he said as they stumbled up the hill toward the main road.

Enoch heard Merl curse his parents if he didn't get his way. Bertha always cursed back but Luke kept his mouth shut. Bertha was the disciplinarian. His own would kill him if he were so disrespectful.

When they got to the road, pale faced and dizzy, Enoch turned to Merl. "Ma will beat me if she finds out. I can't lie to her. She sees through my lies. Wish I were more like you, Merl. Just can't cuss her. Love her too much for that. I can't do this anymore. I don't like the tobacco."

"It takes a while to acquire the habit, Ely says," Merl said and wobbled into his yard.

Enoch said, "If Ma finds out I might run into the woods if she tries to spank me. Just like you."

"Boy, you gotta learn how to charm them," Merl said as he stepped into the house.

Bertha yelled, "What the hell are you doing back home!"

Merl whined, "I'm sick Moms."

"Poor baby! Come sit in Moms' lap."

Enoch stood at the edge of the road frowning, guilty for his rebellion. Merl could charm his enemies and elders but Enoch didn't have those skills. He dreaded facing Ma that evening. She was always tired and grouchy when she got home.

Too sick to run Enoch reeled home and crawled back into bed with his clothes on.

Sonny graduated eighth grade the year before and was now in charge of the house when Anne was at work. She stopped her cleaning and check his forehead.

"Well, sure enough you are sick." She sniffed. "I smell tobacco smoke! You been smoking!" she said and then smiled. "I won't tell. Cause you didn't tell Ma about my smoking. Ma won't be angry. I promise. I'll tell her you're coming down with the flu. You just sleep now."

He rolled over and groaned when Sonny sprinkled him with a splash of lilac water.

"There, now Ma won't smell the tobacco," she said and left as Enoch drifted off to sleep.

Merl continued stealing tobacco from his older siblings as he and Enoch became the best of pals. They took up the chaw, smoking, and eventually demon liquor. Enoch did run from Anne every time when she tried to paddle him after that day. Within a few weeks Lanny was Enoch's disciplinarian because Anne couldn't catch him.

Chapter Two

The end of World War II brought the beginning of a new way of life. A veil of short-lived prosperity invaded the area after the soldiers returned home and went to work building homes, planting crops, and harvesting in the timber. The poverty remained, only less so.

Leve met and married tall, husky Jake, in 1946. Delena met sophisticated, of Hawaiian-French decent Shawn, fifteen years her senior, and married after the war. Still neither of the girls kept in touch very often. Lou now wrote occasionally to Anne as their relationship was mending.

Grant returned home after the war and married a local girl. He and his new bride moved to Hamilton, Illinois where he secured a job with a whiskey-barrel manufacturer. Grant and his family lived the remainder of their lives in Hamilton.

On September 1, 1946, the Galloping Goose came to the end of the line. Having served the people in the Ozarks for almost forty-five years, now she was obsolete. She could no longer make a profit on her runs through Racoon Springs, Dinktown, Rumley, and other destinations south because of competing new trucking lines, easy access to automobiles, and improved highways. The lonesome whistle scream of the Galloping Goose would no more echo across the hollows. The old coal-fired steam locomotive was retired to a museum in a northwestern state and replaced with the Blue Goose diesel-powered engine. The Galloping Goose was gone forever. The Blue Goose ran the northern tracks from Harrison, Arkansas to Joplin, Missouri for an additional fifteen years.

The same year the Galloping Goose's southern tracks were shutdown, Anne developed a heart condition. Her long hours of field labor were cut in half due to her health. She refused to see a doctor or take medication.

Pretty, sneaky, shy Sonny married Dan, a handsome ladies man and gambler who was raised two miles from the homestead. Soon all the Hotman children would be on their own. Only teenaged Lanny and Enoch were left at home by the end of World War II.

Tall and handsome, Lanny was a Daniel Boone look alike. At eighteen he now had all disciplinary rights over rebellious Enoch. Harsh and stern, he beat Enoch often at Anne's request. The beatings subsided some when Lanny married greedy Martha two years later.

Chad married Vanny, who kept him in line and sober most of the time. They built a sawmill at her insistence. Over Anne's protest, when Enoch was fourteen he quit school and went to work full-time for Chad at the mill. Merl also quit school and the boys were work partners for many years to come.

Enoch and Merl were wild bucks sowing their oats at every opportunity and frequently getting drunk and into fist fights with other teenage boys. What the future held for Enoch was anybody's guess. Were his problems a direct result of his environment? Was he cursed? If so, only God could save Enoch from the fate that awaited him as an adult. Could he change? Would he change? Only time would tell.

Merl, more level-headed and less insecure was not submissive to anyone. In control at all times, he was the ultimate manipulator with a secret deviate nature that most never saw. Enoch's insecurities blinded him to the truth about Merl's character.

Enoch and Merl both had one other thing in common--a troubled soul. Because of Enoch's obvious mental problems and Merl's manipulating head games their relationship was as fragile, dangerous, and volatile as nitroglycerine. Their friendship was the curse!

In 1950 after Merl and Enoch got into an argument with Chad and quit their jobs, they decided to work together in the logging woods. Merl was lazy. He preferred to tell those with whom he worked how the chore could best be done, while he watched. He and Enoch eked out a living. Though the earnings from selling logs were split between them, Enoch did most of the toil.

An unlikely pair, Merl the extrovert, and Enoch, a shy introvert. They were as different as pink and green. But both had opposite sides to their personalities that flipped like a coin when drunk.

Merl figured out exactly what buttons to push in order to manipulate Enoch for his own personal gain. Most often Enoch was the slave and Merl his master.

Enoch constantly second guessed his own decisions. Merl reassured him his decisions were right whether appropriate for the situation or not. Merl was Enoch's crutch. He had been since they were eleven.

Women worshiped Merl as if he were a sex god. He thought of himself in that vein, proud of his natural endowments. Others loathed Merl once they got to know him well, and called him a sociopath for he seemed to have no remorse when he took advantage of those less fortunate after he had won their trust.

Consuming rot-gut homebrew brought out the best and worst in both young men. Merl was an overly generous soul when he first started on a drinking binge, but that soon changed. Then became a mean-spirited son of a bitch with those who loved him.

When drunk, Enoch was ready to kick some butt as quickly as a warm breeze could change to cold when bad weather rolled in. Moonshine made them both crazy and belligerent, but Enoch was more aggressive with his fist when hopped up on liquor. Even Merl feared him then.

Merl had great ideas but could never follow through. He was becoming the ultimate manipulator, flem-flam man, con-artist, and skirt chaser. At age eighteen, he dabbled in gambling, and lost his pants. Seeing that wasn't going to make him rich, he came up with another scheme--he concocted, bottled herbal remedies, and sold moonshine. That didn't work either. In another county he pretended to be a traveling evangelist and held a brush-arbor revival. He played the role of a Pentecostal preacher but the offerings were too small. After that, he took the title of Father Shaman and claimed to have mystical powers because the spirits of Sitting Bull and Crazy Horse rested upon him. He said they were his spiritual guides and protectors. Mocker's and those he took advantage of said the spirit of Sitting Bull Crap rested upon him. He had stars in his eyes, and holes in his pockets. He'd try any get rich-quick scheme to get out of work.

In the mean time Enoch worked like a horse every day, skidding logs with an old team of mules he named Blaze and Mabel. Always, he shared his weekly earnings with Merl, whether he had helped or not.

At eighteen, Enoch a peculiar, shy man. Tall and strong with a light sunburned complexion and fine strawberry blond hair, he fidgeted, exaggerated facial expressions, and talked with his hands. His mood swings and bouts of depression hampered his social life. Relationships were a problem from childhood. His deepest thoughts were read on his face without him speaking a word. He couldn't take teasing. His sense of humor and pranks were sometimes on the cruel side, though he did try to have a lighter side in his personality. His fear of rejection held him back from connecting to others until he felt safe. His tone was harsh for self protection. He feared being taken advantage of, and often the look of insecurity and bewilderment shone in his steely blue yearning eyes.

The least of conflict stirred Enoch's anger to excess. His every emotion was to the extreme. Up and down his moods swung. The saintly angel and all was good and calm, then without warning he snapped, wild and crazy and all hell broke loose. For those around him, he was a emotional roller-coaster.

Generous to a fault, his choice of friends was questionable. His belief in God was strong, but he could curse with the best of the good ol' boys. He liked the women but never the strong domineering kind. He was better looking than all his brothers, built up like Jimmy Stewart with colorings and features like Robert Redford. Girls liked him at first, but lasting relationships were few. Frequently, Enoch called the whole world a chicken shit.

In 1952 when Merl was twenty, he took his parents and pregnant thirteen-year-old youngest sister, Della, down to Florida to harvest oranges. A pitiful sight, fat, unkempt, and big boned, Della babbled continually, wanting to be accepted while running her stubby fingers through her long brown stringy and dirty hair. She patted her large belly and talked to the unborn child while in public.

Before leaving Loafer's Glory, Bertha placed an ad in the *Missouri Star* newspaper to advertise for Della a husband. One caller came from across the state line.

With strawberry and tomato harvest at a close, Merl's family was making plans for the migratory trip. Enoch and Merl rode Blaze and Mabel out of the forest toward home as the Ozarks evening sun slowly began to dip behind the distant western hills.

Riding down the rugged logging way Merl took the lead as Enoch and Mabel brought up the rear trotting behind Blaze a few paces. Merl glanced back and shouted, "I'm going to Louisiana next week to pick up my pops. He's visiting grandma. Says she's in a bad way. Moms read the letter to us last night. Grandma's got breast cancer."

"Well, that's too bad. But she is old. Lived her life. Bet Pops Luke is taking it hard. Are you gonna be able to get your old beater truck to running?" Enoch asked.

"He's sad, all right. Moms will get him out of that once we get there. Done got the truck going again. Just need some new tires!" Merl shouted and turned with a pitiful pout, dropped his eyes and chin.

"Don't worry I'll help you out there. Go down to Poojam's store and tell him I sent you for tires. Have him to put them on your truck. I'll take care of the bill and you can pay me back later."

Merl grinned. "You're a real pal."

"That's what friends are for," Enoch said.

"We'll travel on to Florida after picking up Pops next week. You'll have to find another helper," Merl said.

"I know," Enoch said. "Think I'll go to Grant's and find work at the barrel mill."

"We just scratch with the chickens. Damn, wish I could figure an easier way to make a living," Merl said.

"Yep, that would be good. If you figure it out let me know. Hell, we're just two old ignorant mules. Should have tried harder in school but couldn't learn anything under ol' mean spirited Obey!"

Merl laughed. "But we had loads of fun skipping school. Life's too short not to have a frolic. I do what I wanted to do, when I want to do it! Nobody's gonna order Merl Judas around. One day I'll find the easy ride and pot of gold! Then the self righteous hoot snooty around here can kiss my rear."

Enoch scowled. "Good Luck! You won't find gold in Loafer's Glory unless it's slave labor, radical religion, and gossip. Just wood on your back and water in your eyes. Broke down by the time you're fifty. That's Loafer's Glory gold! Fool's gold!"

They turned the mules onto the main road a half mile from the Judas home. In the distance they saw a swarthy lanky man riding a tan and grey peacock spotted Appaloosa. Trailing behind was large red Shetland pony with pink ribbon bows tied to its blond tail and mane. They laughed hysterically as the man raised from his saddle and waved. "Howdy boys! Can you tell me where the Judas family lives?"

Merl chuckled and yelled back,"I'm a Judas!"

"Wait up boys, and let me ride with you a spell," he said.

Merl and Enoch waited as the man dress like a 1900's "dandy" trotted toward them. One of Chad's beat-up logging trucks passed and stirred the dust on the byway as they waited. The truck backfired and the Shetland began to buck.

"Calm down Pearly!" the stranger gruffly shouted.

As he drew near Enoch smirked. "Looks like he stepped out of a time warp."

"Reminds me of old photos of my grandparents," Merl said.

"Call me Booger!" the man said while trying not to stutter again and he shook their hands.

Enoch suspiciously asked, "What's your business here?"

"Booger Shooter is the name. Booger is my nickname. Albert Shooter the real name," he said and picked at his nose.

Enoch and Merl glanced at each other and chuckled.

"I come about the ad in the *Missouri Star*! Come to court a gal named Della," he stuttered as he tipped his bowler hat.

"I'm Della's brother," Merl said. "Follow us, we're headed that way now."

The men formed a line on the edge of the road with Booger bringing up the rear.

Enoch glanced back and watched Booger adjust his bow tie then pick at his large nose again. Clothed in a dark brown three-piece suit and white shirt the graying fifty-year-old stranger sweated profusely as the sultry evening summer heat blanketed them before the sun went down.

They rode into the Judas yard and tied the mule reins to a low hanging oak branch. "Moms, Della has a courter!" Merl shouted.

Bertha stepped onto the back stoop. Smiling and rolling a strand of hair on her index finger, she asked, "Who you be?"

Booger dismounted and removed his hat holding it close to his chest. "Booger Shooter! Albert the real name. I come to meet Della Judas," he said and reached into a saddle bag draped over the horse's haunches, pulling out a small package wrapped in gold foil paper with a red ribbon. "Are you her ma?"

"Yes, sir! I'm pretty Della's ma!"

"Well, then this here package is for you, Ms. Judas."

Bertha jumped off the porch, took the package, and tore into it immediately. "Thank you, Mr. Shooter."

He stuttered, "You're welcome, Ma'am!"

Smiling she shook his hand. "It's a pleasure to meet you, Mr. Shooter. Call me Bertha." She squealed when she pulled two pieces of candy from the package and popped them into her mouth. "Chocolate-coated cherry candies! Umm, so good!"

"I'm glad you like them," he said.

She nodded and took him by the arm. "Let's go inside and I'll introduce you to Della."

Enoch watched Della dart out the other door and run for the outhouse before they stepped inside. He heard Bertha say if they had known he was coming Della would have gotten all gussied up.

"Della, Honey, Mr. Shooter has answered the ad. You got a suitor! Come meet Albert."

Della shyly poked her head out the outhouse door and slowly walked back to the house. Pouting, she slugged along, in a soiled flour-sack skirt and dingy white blouse with ruffles down the front.

Enoch and Merl chuckled while sitting on the front porch listening to the conversation inside.

"I don't think Della wants any part of Bertha's match making or Mr. Shooter," Enoch said.

"Ah, she's nuts! She don't know what's good for her," Merl said as he reached under the stoop and pulled out a jug of moonshine. He popped the cork and downed a gulp, then handed the jug to Enoch.

"Ma sure wants to get shut of Della. She's in a family way you know," Merl whispered.

Enoch downed a swig. "Nope, didn't know that! Just thought she was fat," he whispered back.

"Well, she is! Don't know who the papa is," Merl said as he dropped his eyes to the ground and shuffled the dirt beneath his feet.

"Didn't know Della had a man friend? I never knew of her leaving the place," Enoch whispered and handed the jug back to Merl.

"Ma says she sneaked out of the house and got tied up with one of those Mexican migrant workers during strawberry harvest," Merl said. "Papa is long gone now!"

"Not so loud, they'll hear you inside," Enoch said.

During earlier generations the "dues" an exchange of property or goods, trading for a bride was an acceptable practice. By Enoch's time the traditional custom had lost its' importance as a means of expressing one's ability to provide for a wife. Though a few families persevered, practiced the ritual. The Judas clan kept the old way alive–Bertha. The men heard her ask the suitor for fifty dollars. But he declined, stating that Della was too fat and too young to be a wife, Della giggled. Enoch and Merl chuckled again and downed another swig of moonshine.

Bertha's sigh echoed more disappoint than the suitors stuttering refusal. She had sold away Della's oldest sister ten years earlier when Molly was only twelve. The sixty-five-year-old neighbor purchased her for one hundred dollars. Bertha was right proud of herself on that deal. But it was obvious that Booger wouldn't be Della's husband when he walked out of the house, glared at them, mounted his horse without saying a word, and led the red pony up the road from the direction he had come.

"Moms, where was that man from?" Merl asked as Bertha and Della stepped onto the porch and sat down beside them to finish off the box of chocolates.

"Gainesville! About a hundred miles from here in Missouri. Too bad. Looked like Booger Shooter had plenty of money. Bet Della could be happy with him," she said.

Most everyone in the community thought Della and Bertha were a little touched in the head.

Bertha stroked Della's hair. "The next suitor can have her for free! I shouldn't have asked for the dues. Della ain't that pretty," she said. "Not one penny! The next suitor could have her for free." Bertha sighed.

Della stopped giggling and patting her belly, hatefully glanced up at Merl. She began crying and ran for the outhouse again.

Bertha tried hard to get rid of her after the first suitor declined. Bertha altered her scheme and it became well known--her plan was to find a husband for Della in Florida since there were no takers in Loafer's Glory.

Merl mocked Della publically, saying she was crazy. He wanted her married off more than all the rest for she said she carried his little secret, and he had played with her peepee since she was four.

Merl met sixteen-year-old Lilly in the orange groves, and they married after a short courtship. A plain girl with short, mousey brown hair curled in ringlets, Lilly was kind hearted and quite intelligent. Her eyes were large and dark brown. She tugged on her earlobe when thinking intently and when pressured to speak. She compensated shyness with forced smiles. Sometimes her thin lips twitched before she spoke as though she were changing her mind before she got the first word out. Lilly fell desperately in love with Merl.

Merl's charismatic personality and good looks were magnetic. He matured to resemble Elvis Presley. When Elvis took America by storm, Merl pushed his brawny palm over his luxuriant glistening black hair every time the comparison was spoken. He worked continually to improve his Elvis mannerisms. He acquired the good ol' boy status even in far off counties. Women swooned over him.

His deep-blue sensuous eyes pierced the soul; a hard fellow to dislike. With an innocent, warm, boyish smile his constant ease of humor and calm base voice made him a pleasure to be around. He was thought of as a bit rebellious but level headed and kindhearted by some. The rest of his family were just labeled weird.

He gave money and groceries to the less fortunate as a public display but usually the money he had connived out of some other trusting soul. He was always eager to help a neighbor in need if he was noticed in the community for the deed. Children trusted him immensely because of the playful attention and gifts of sweets he showered upon them for no apparent reason.

A prankster and the life of the party, attention always focused on Merl. Artfully wooing those around him, Merl had learned to get his way early on in life. Skilled at seducing most everybody into feeling good about themselves, he was the ultimate manipulator. Lilly was unable to resist his charms and good looks.

Fantasies of making it big as a singer danced in his head, but he couldn't whistle a tune in a fruit jar. Insecurity led him to try and convince others he was intelligent and well educated and he did for a time. Having only a seventh-grade education, he was people smart and persuasive, the ultimate politician. He could sell the devil hot coals on an idea but was soon found out, although only after he had ripped off some trusting soul.

When the orange harvest was finished, Merl brought his naive teenage bride and family back to Loafer's Glory. They built a plank shack on his parents' property. His older brother, plodding Ely, and his homely, domineering wife Fanny also built a small house.

In Florida; Della gave birth to her illegitimate, retarded baby boy, Rafter. Proudly displayed him to all the Loafer's Glory neighbors. Della claimed that Rafter belonged to Merl. No one believed her.

Bertha intensified her search to find Della a husband. Eventually she settled for a half-wit ex-convict recently released from prison. Over the years they had three children together before he was incarcerated again for shooting at a neighbor. Della was never happy. Her story that Rafter belonged to Merl didn't change. Her cry for help was ignored.

While Merl was away in Florida twenty-year-old Enoch journeyed to Hamilton Illinois and took a job with the barrel mill where Grant also worked. He and another lumberjack labored together splitting logs into stave bolts.

Jeb and Enoch stood on either end of a five-foot oak log. Using axes and wedges to section the wood into triangular-shaped pieces they swung, one after the other. Timing was important. Enoch went powerfully down with his heavy steel axe head. His muscles bulged and sweat dripped from his sunburned brow as the blade crashed into the oak timber. Chopping sounds and the ring of steel against steel echoed through the wilderness as they hammered against the wedges with a heavy maul to rip the wood.

Enoch's axe embedded deeply into the log, slowing his timing. He tugged to release the bound axe-head. Jeb's timber-reaping tool become a lethal projectile. Enoch ducked. Too late. He suffered a deep wound to his skull directly above his forehead and between his eyes. Addled, he fell to the ground bleeding profusely. He groaned while grasping the bloody gaping wound.

Jeb stood unable to speak or act as the axe handle fell from his brawny hands.

Enoch crawled to his knees, wiped the blood from his eyes, and shouted, "Fool, don't just stand there and gawk! I'm hurt bad! Get me to the hospital!"

Jeb snapped out of his trance and ripped off his sweat-soaked shirt.

"Hurry Jeb, before I bleed to death!" Enoch cried.

After Jeb bound his head in the soiled shirt, he raise Enoch to his feet. They walked part of the way to the road. As Enoch weakened, Jeb dragged him along.

When Enoch became faint from loss of blood and could stand no longer, his head pounding painfully, he whispered calmly, "Carry me, Jeb. Hurry, I don't want to die."

With both men covered in Enoch's blood, Jeb frantically hoisted him over his shoulder, his voice trembling from fear and exhaustion. "Hang in there, Buddy! Hang in there! We'll make it." Jeb galloped huffing for every breath. He deposited Enoch on the truck-bed.

Delirious, sleepiness setting in, his head pounding with every beat of his heart, Enoch heard Jeb frantically fumbling around in the cab. Finding a tattered, sap-stained coat, he rolled and placed it under Enoch's head. Thirty minutes later Enoch was unconscious when they arrived at the hospital. Doctors were not certain he would live as they rushed him into the emergency room.

Miraculously, Enoch survived surgery, and the accident. He hallucinated for days. Thinking the doctors were enemy soldiers trying to kill him, he had to be restrained.

After the initial swelling in his brain subsided, he slowly began to gather his wits and the restraints were removed. Still recovering, he managed to get dressed and walk out of the hospital without being released. He left all of his belongings behind. His head yet bound in bloody dressings, he arrived at Anne's after a week of hitching rides.

His road to recovery was slow. Within three months he returned to work with his pal, Merl. They harvested timber for Chad's sawmill.

Though physically strong and able to hold a job, he wasn't well. Short-lived episodes of erratic behavior, intense anger, and irrational hallucinations, such as searching for Egyptian tombs in the hollows, caused his family and the community great concern. He was harmless, all bluster and yammer, benign unless drunk on moonshine. His personal safety was of great concern for all when he wen off his rockers this way.

As his condition improved and he regained more self control, he joined the Redwood Baptist church in an effort to try and curb his temper, thinking religion would help and God would chase away the demons that sometimes spoke lies inside his head.

Episodes of nonsense talk subsided the next year. The demons whispered and roared but he learned to fight them by quoting the scripture Anne had him memorize. His unpredictable infrequent babbles just changed from topics of Egyptian tombs in the hollows to the mark of the beast and other religious or military themes. The scar on his head faded, and was hardly noticeable when all his hair grew back. Nevertheless, he became obsessed with reading the Bible and quoted scripture constantly.

On occasion he referred to himself as the Navy Kid Captain Sailor. This terminology came about after the day he met Leve's husband Jake when they traveled from Amarillo to see Anne, the spring of 1953.

During World War II Jake had been a baker in the Navy. He addressed Enoch as Kid Brother upon their first meeting. After their introduction from then on, Enoch referred to himself as Navy Kid Captain Sailor just before a serious schizophrenic episode came upon him. Enoch had the highest regard for Jake.

For every incident in his life and in the lives of those around him, good or bad, he found reason to apply scripture. Then that changed to cursing again after a couple of years. Some days he was as sane as most and then would be totally out of touch with reality.

His personality had changed. Some attributed it to the accident, and others said it was the religion. Some said he was crazy all his life. Others believed he had inherited a form of schizophrenia. A few people believed his condition was the curse of the cow horn, but most folks thought the blow to his head with the axe caused his mental problems. Nonetheless he was labeled the crazy preacher and this became his covering for many years to come while his and Merl's friendship was on again and off again.

Whatever the case for his social and mental disabilities he didn't regularly drink homebrew the following year after the accident. The change was for the better, and not consuming moonshine produced less frequent spells.

His mental problems were masked by his religious zeal. Most everyone had religion in Loafer's Glory, and constantly quoting scriptures was commonplace. Community fears and rejection changed to respect and acceptance in religious circles. The church people called him nervous but a good preacher after the pastor allowed him to conduct a few services in his absence.

He became more open, friendly, and fought to control his anger. His renowned preaching in the community and popularity as a man of God spread to adjoining hillbilly counties. Encouraged by the church congregation, he was evangelizing on weekends and holding week end revivals all over the Ozarks.

During strawberry harvest in the spring of 1953, after Delena and Shawn returned to Loafer's Glory and purchased a home, he was elected assistant-pastor of the Redwood Free Will Baptist church. At Anne's disapproval Enoch chose the family's Baptist heritage as his religion. He was also dating the thirteen-year-old daughter of a bootlegger.

He despised the tongues and radical clothesline religion, preached hard against the Charismatic movements. He and Anne argued often.

Chapter Three

Delena and Anne harvested canning strawberries most of the afternoon and returned to the homestead. As she relaxed in the cool breeze on the swing in Anne's yard, Delena could hear Anne singing "Amazing Grace" inside the house. She slipped off her sneakers, let them drop to the grass, and kicked the ground again. The wooden tree swing hanging from a huge red oak in the front yard of the old home place flew back and forth faster.

The month before, she and Shawn returned from Washington state and purchased a home a mile down the road from Anne. Delena met Shawn nine years earlier when she moved to Washington State to harvest apples.

They had lived in the same hotel there. Delena, who looked like the glamorous Joan Crawford, got him in her sights as his strong build caught her eye while she gracefully descended down the staircase from the upstairs rooms. He stood in the lobby, tall, dark, and handsome in his navy blue business suit with a white shirt unbuttoned at the collar and no tie. Love at first sight she said. When he politely smiled and nodded, she melted.

Gazing into his dreamy blue bedroom-eyes, she decided to marry him. After a short courtship, she did. He was the man of her dreams. Happy could not explain the way her heart joyously sang ever day of their lives.

She raised the hot cup of coffee to her red painted lips and sipped. She remembered Anne's words from thirty years ago: "Jesus, if this baptism of the Holy Ghost is of you, and if it is real, let me have this walk in you with double portions," Anne had said and instantly began staggering like a drunk woman in their Baptist church while praising God in the unknown tongue.

Delena smiled at the memory. As the late afternoon spring breeze ruffled her short curled hair, she grimaced at the thought of Ma and Enoch continually arguing over church doctrine. He was shouting again in the house.

"Drop it, Enoch! Don't disrespect Ma!" she yelled through the open back door.

Inside the house their quarreling stopped as Anne stomped out with her Bible in hand and sat down beside Delena.

Scowling, she said, "That boy loves to argue more than anyone!"

Delena placed her arm around Anne and patted her back. "I know, Ma. He just isn't right. He gets stuck on one topic and runs in circles. He just doesn't know when to let it go."

"Poor little Enoch. What's he gonna do when I'm dead? No body will have the patients with him that he needs." Anne said.

"Well Ma, we have to trust God that someone will love him. And be there for him."

Anne nodded.

Enoch's mental problems were not as severe since he got the Baptist religion. Though they didn't agree with Baptist doctrine--once saved always saved--they were grateful he wasn't seeing people and things that weren't there anymore. Merl Judas was a destructive influence. He was a user but Enoch refused to dissolve the friendship naively hoping to convert him to Baptist. Scallywag Merl distressed Delena.

Openly vocal in expressing his thoughts that all Pentecostals were half a bubble off plumb, his religious stance troubled Delena. Why did he vehemently reject the Holy Ghost doctrine of Pentecostalism? After all, Enoch cut his teeth gnawing on the back of a Pentecostal church pew while Anne preached. Anne's hammering about the Holy Ghost had only made matters worse between them. She had sympathy for them both. Tensions were high, but Delena could do nothing except love them. God would have to work that out.

She had a run in with Enoch some weeks before. He said Ma mocked God and for a woman to preach was a shame according to Baptist doctrine. Delena fiercely defended Anne's pastoral and evangelistic ministry when Enoch started on a toot that day. He wasn't speaking to her now. She figured he'd come around when his anger subsided.

She was proud to know Anne was a trailblazer, strong willed, a woman ahead of her time, a woman of courage and tenacity. She remembered being nine years old the night Anne received the Baptism at their Baptist church.

"Ma, do you recall the night God filled you with the Holy Ghost?" Delena asked.

Anne smiled. "I sure do! The most glorious time in the Lord I had since salvation day when I was fourteen."

Delena giggled. "You know, Ma, we were all so dumbfounded and embarrassed! Except for you of course."

Anne laughed and then scowled. "Well, it was a new move of God in these hill. Most didn't know what to make of the Pentecostal experience at first."

Delena smiled. "You were caught up in the spirit! On the front steps of the church the deacons yelled at Pa, She lost her mind! Demons she got from being in them Holy Roller meeting!" Delena said.

She continued sipping strong coffee from the cup as the sun slowly began to dip beyond the horizon while she and Anne reminisced.

"I remember how anxiously Pa had loaded the family on the wagon, popped the mule's back with the reins, Get up there, he said as you went on praising God, seemingly in a trance while laid out in the back of the wagon."

Anne nodded. "God was blessing me good that night. I won't ever forget the experience though I don't recall a lot of what was happening around me. I just remember the Holy Ghost ministering to my hungry soul."

"Fear had gripped my heart watching you with the other kids encircling us as you spoke nonsense tongues! Pa didn't make matters any easier. He was just as concerned as me. The mule lugged the carriage slowly over the trail toward home, hauling our bewildered family. We genuinely didn't know what to make of this babble and shaking that had come over you, Ma," Delena said.

Anne grimaced. "I don't recall that. Just what happened when I came out of the Spirit that night."

"Pa had wanted to crawl under the church pew and hide in his embarrassment. His face was red as a pomegranate for the longest time but he said nothing until we got home. He beat you that night." She sighed. "That was the first time he ever lay a hand on you."

Anne bowed her head. "That was my first beating from Isaiah. Oh, he had shoved me a round a time or two before that but that was the first real beating."

"Well, that's the only thing I hold against Pa--his drunkenness and beatings of you, Ma! No man will ever beat me!"

"Don't hold that against your Pa. He was a good man. Demon liquor ruled him. Satan manifested in his drunkenness. He had been nipping moonshine before we got to church that night." Anne shook her graying head, "It was the liquor!"

"That wasn't the last beating!" Delena snarled as rage, hate, fear, and loving emotions surged forth in her soul one right after the other for Pa. Watery eyed she embraced Anne. "Ma, I'm so proud of you. You never gave up the faith. You are strong!" Delena smiled and kissed Anne on the cheek.

"I love you too, Honey," Anne said.

Ma's hellfire and brimstone messages frightened Enoch as a child. The messages frightened all of them. But to fear God was a good thing. Sometimes no one understood Enoch. He changed after he and Merl Judas became friends. Lost all respect for Ma, and those who saw after him. He was different, maybe the cow-horn curse had made him different, or perhaps Merl's influence, her siblings said. Even Ma sometimes believed his mental problems were the cow horn curse. They all feared him when he went off his rocker. As he had not known a father, Anne was everything to him despite their many quarrels. He had told her often that he loved Ma. But sometimes he acted as though he hated the entire family.

"Enoch has always been my problem child. Worse than the rest. He was rebellious all his youth and teen years. I thought he was going to drive me insane with worry. Being marked by the cow horn was bad enough. Perhaps the head and brain injury was recompense for the beating Isaiah gave Newton," Anne said. "This is my son, cursed of God." She sighed and dropped her head, wiping a tear from her eye.

Delena shivered at the mention of Newton's name and the incident near twenty-five years ago. She gazed up into the tree and watched a cardinal building a nest while trying to drown the thought from her mind.

The harsh living conditions, struggles, poverty, and years of labor in the fields had stolen Anne's beauty. At age fifty-eight, she was way old before her time, her Pentecostal bun now streaked with lines of gray. Tired, her health was failing.

Delena's eyes watered as she patted Anne on the back again.

"I don't fear dying, but leaving him alone. He needs someone understanding until he dies. Delena I don't think I'm going to live much longer. The thought of leaving Enoch alone in this world grieves me deeply," she said and took a deep breath.

"Ma, we have to trust God!" Delena said.

Anne nodded and smiled. "You're right--life's all in God's hands anyway. All I can do is pray."

Delena nodded.

Anne's holiness doctrines were as strict as ever. She stood and scowled. " You need to wash off the makeup and the red lipstick. It makes you look like a harlot!"

Delena sighed and rolled her eyes.

Delena condemned Enoch's attitude about women preachers and the tongues in defense of Ma. But she was hurt when Anne constantly scolded that she would bounce right into hell for wearing the makeup and shorter dresses. She sighed. Shawn approved. His opinion mattered more.

Anne glanced toward the old ramshackled house and said, "Well, I'm going back inside to work up some of the berries before church. You just whisper a little prayer that he doesn't start on me again." She clutched her Bible and strolled back inside.

Now in her early forties Delena had never completely recovered from being raped. Shawn allowed her to be in control of their relationship. She had to be in control, and appreciated him for his sensitivity toward her emotional needs.

The day before, she had seen Newton and his family on the Racoon Springs town square. Standing on the courthouse steps he held a small dark-complexioned boy on each hip. They didn't speak when she passed by, but their gazes locked and he shamefully turned his head at her loathing glares as she brushed by him.

He pretended not to know her when his pretty young wife asked, "Who is that? Probably another one of your old girlfriends."

Newton had dumped Sally and married a young teenage girl, tall and blond with steely blue eyes whose father pastored a small Pentecostal church in Newton county, sixty miles from Loafer's Glory. They made their home in Rooster Ridge. The couple couldn't have children so they had just adopted two small orphaned boys, ages three and four.

Some said Newton had changed. But Delena couldn't believe that story. Poor Sally was so distraught that she drank pure lye after he married, which killed her. They didn't find her body until a week later lying by the Goose tracks at the edge of the highway fourteen bridge where the train crossed the Buffalo. Badly bruised with several broken bones and contusions to her head, she wasn't dead after the fall. They said the lye finished her off. Law enforcement ruled her death a suicide. Delena suspected Newton had murdered her. As she passed by him that day she thought, Pa and Bill should of killed you. Poor Sally, she loved the bastard. Hopefully he'd treat this girl better.

Because of Shawn's good looks, wealth, and considerate nature Delena became the envy of many a single woman in the community. Deemed the religious rebel by local Pentecostal Christians in Loafer's Glory, some frowned on her because she married outside the faith and a darky to boot, as others secretly referred to him.

A devoted Catholic, Shawn tolerated her religious choice with reservations as she did the same for his lack of understanding the Pentecostal ways. Politely he expressed many times his feelings that Pentecostals had no respect for the house of God. She was grateful he wasn't radically harsh or forceful with her about anything. But he was Catholic and she wasn't about to change him, nor he, her. Delena said love is tolerant.

Deep hatred of organized religion rooted inside her heart after Newton betrayed her trust. She strayed far from the oppressive holiness doctrines. Her way of worship was her own. But her religion was still based in Pentecostalism. She called herself a Live Forever Latter Reign. She believed her body would never taste of death. She believed she would go through a metamorphosis like a butterfly but she would never die, or go to the grave.

Delena didn't like it when Shawn smirked at her beliefs when she got a little over zealous, but that was all and he'd politely change the subject at her frustration. How could she make him understand? Not many accepted her unconventional religious belief, though a few were beginning to fall under these teachings in small groups around the country.

Delena knew other religious folks labeled her nuts, a Jezebel. At that she responded with: "I'm not a murderer! Jezebel was a killer! I'm not!" The local church gossip about her had started. Heated and frothy rumor stewed in the mind pots, a putrid mingling of lies and truth that poisoned the good-hearted religious folks.

Man's doctrine, tossing the chamber pot, and one bucket of sewer in the cistern polluted the entire reservoir of life-giving liquid. Was she in a cult? She didn't think so. Latter Reign combined with her own personal twist concerning the doctrine of eternal life, a female-son-of-God.

Passers by regularly heard Anne's travailing prayers in the unknown tongue. For thirty years she continued to pray near the pond in warm weather. The community had mixed opinions about Anne and her religion too. Knowing Anne would not argue religious doctrine publically, some were quite vocal and insulting with her. Delena didn't like hearing her mother or the family put down because of their religion.

Enoch was the exception.

Trouble was on the horizon. Enoch was dating Ora, a thirteen-year-old girl from Rooster Ridge. Delena felt it in her gut. White trash, the girl came from stock of nothing but Indian darkeys and poor no counts. She cringed at the thought of him marrying her. Not so much that she was dark but she was the daughter of a bootlegger. After all, Delena's own great grandmother Liz was Black Dutch-Cherokee.

In 1950 a tree fell on uncle Bill. The falling-timber darn near crushed every bone in his body. He survived until January, '53 but wasn't much of a man afterward. No strength left. No good after the accident. He shouldn't have been in the woods anyway at sixty-eight years old. Moonshine destroyed another life. The accident wouldn't have happened if he'd have stayed out of the forest drunk. He was confined to his bed the last three years. Delena grimaced.

Poor May Bell, his wife, died a month later, just this past February. Worked herself to death tending to him those last two years. She died of a broken heart. He was a son of a bitch but May Bell loved him.

Jimmy died four years after Isaiah with Tuberculosis. Then Hanna died a year after Jimmy with TB. Enoch was the last baby she ever helped deliver. Delena smiled, Hanna sure liked the moonshine but thought no one knew she was a lush. Delena missed them.

Bill remained in the Klan to the end. He was there when they beat that dark-skinned Ora's daddy nearly to death in 1945. Now Enoch was dating her. If the girl only knew Enoch's own kin nearly killed her daddy, she'd have nothing to do with him.

Delena sat upright and squinted. Maybe she should tell Ora. Enoch didn't need a wife. What if he had children by her? They could pop out looking like a kinky-haired black jungle bunny. Folks rumored that Negro blood was in that wood pile. Blacks are all right in their place. God forbid! She wasn't prejudice, just practical.

Unless his mind got right and stayed right, black babies or white he didn't need any children. She was light enough to pass but darker than most other whites. What if their children turn out like the dark-skinned girl's slobbering momma Iris? God forbid! Pitiful Iris should never have married.

Running her fingers through her short curled hair Delena kicked the ground again, swinging faster. Anne had trusted the Lord to help keep the family together all these years. He had answered her prayers. Ma's entire life was built around her religion and children. She wanted all her children's lives to be as dedicated. She sighed. "I hope Enoch receives the Holy Ghost, then he will understand," she whispered into the wind.

As the last shades of orange and purple sunlight faded to night, Delena lifted her gaze through the open back door when Anne flipped on the porch light and called for her.

Enoch, in his '38 truck, was pulling out of the drive to meet Ora, his new sweetheart. She sighed. At least they weren't arguing.

She watched Anne checking to see her bun was still in place and pressing her thumb hard onto the page in her Bible to make certain she didn't lose the section. Standing inside the screen door cracked half open, Anne asked smiling, "Delena, are we going to revival tonight?"

Anne had no more spoken than Shawn drove up. Delena smiled, happy to see the love of her life, and overflowing with love for her aging, faith-filled ma. She stood, and slipped on her sneakers. Dangling the empty cup, she strolled across the grass toward the porch. "Yes, Ma. Let me wash up and change my dress, then we'll take you."

Part Four
The Bips
1940 to 1955
Ora's Turbulent Youth, Courtship, and Marriage

1999: A Letter To Saul From Ora.

My dear son, Saul:

I'm sorry if I made you hate me. I know I've done a lot of wrong things in my lifetime. Not lived a good life. Scared and poor most of my days. Just a baby myself when I had ya. Never had a childhood. I was too young I guess. Your father and I should never have married. If only your daddy had moved us away from that hell hole, Loafer's Glory. We should have left when we first married. Maybe we could have made it together. But it didn't happen that way.

Just wish I could start all over again. Now I'm too old and tired to deal with the past mistakes. Oh, the horror of it all. I was brainwashed or stupid. Both maybe? Uneducated, poor, and prideful. Had too much shame and responsibility as a kid. Maybe that's why rebellion set in?

I will always love you. Guess I'm as confused as this letter sounds. Hope we can be good friends even though I betrayed your trust, again. Just couldn't bare the shame of a court trial, and exposing all the scarred--opening old wounds. Yes, I lied.

Heard you are writing that book now. Hope you're kind to my character. Hey, remember your momma was a lady, a pretty lady. Just rebellious and ignorant. Maybe my story will stop some other naive young girls from making the same mistakes.

Love you always. Hope you can forgive me once again.

Your momma, Ora.

Saul's eyes watered when he read the letter. Poor wretched Momma, he thought. Sighing, he sat down and began to type. He mumbled, "Momma was my first best friend when I came into this world. She broke my heart. No! She murdered my soul! Where does she fit in my life? Does she belong at all? Her story is hardest to write. Such a contradiction of terms describe Momma."

Chapter One

The one-room plank shack in which Ora was born had a dirt floor. Originally built as a smokehouse, now it housed the poverty stricken family. After her arrival in 1940, her father Daniel laid rough boards on the earth inside.

Her older brother Joe was two the day she was born. Ora's mother Iris was quite intelligent, but her physical disability was unsparing. Afflicted at birth with palsy, Iris could hardly care for herself as she shook violently, slobbered continually, and walked with the help of a cane. She had the nasty habit of chawin' tobacco. The babies were inadequately nurtured.

Iris had married Daniel Bip when she was thirteen and gave birth to her first child the same year. Her refined English features endowed beauty to her trembling, slight form. Her eyes were large and bright green, and she wore her long, wavy, dark brown hair in a French bun. The body-length apron looped over her neck and tied in the back kept saliva and tobacco juice from soiling her plain clothing.

Ora's small-boned, ninety-pound Black Dutch-Cherokee father, Daniel, eighteen years Iris' senior and disabled with only one lung, was an alcoholic. What he lacked in body size was made up by his large, irregularly shaped nose. He dipped snuff and smelled strongly of Prince Albert. His skin was dark and swarthy; his eyes, small and black. His hair was coal black, straight and coarse as a horse's tail. He was an ugly little man by most standards.

Fiery, with a short temper when sober, Daniel drank a lot of moonshine whiskey to mellow his explosive temperament. He established his own illegal still in the woods behind his home that generated extra income. Working part-time as bootlegger, automobile mechanic, migrant worker, and farmhand when not drunk, he was petulant and suspicious in nature; the more rebellious seed in his family. As were they all.

They lived up the road from his Jesus Name Pentecostal holiness brother Tex, and sister-in-law Diana. Little Ora respected them. Diana was her second mother.

Diana, fair skinned, blond haired, and saintly, had the nature of an angel. Never speaking a harsh word about or against anyone, she lived her Christian religion and was truly forgiving, nonjudgmental, kind, and soft spoken.

Some thought she wasn't harsh enough and felt she let others take advantage of her sweet nature. Diana wasn't weak at all. Spending many hours on her knees to control her feelings and deeds, pleasing God her priority, her nature was generous above all Brush Creek residents. Shabbily dressed but clean, she wore the flour-sack attire and the Pentecostal bun.

Her calloused hands worked daily in the fields, caring for her children and home. Dutiful Diana found the time to help tend to Iris' little ones. If not for Diana, none of them would have survived early childhood. Iris simply could not care for her babies because of her constant violent shaking. But she continued to have them and Diana played a major role in raising them.

Tex was nearly exactly the opposite in personality and character to his brother Daniel. With a larger build, he was still small in comparison to the average Caucasian male. Dark without the yellow tint that Daniel had, Tex was relatively handsome and kind, considerate, and gentle natured with his wife and children. His shining black hair framed a perpetually joyous smile.

Most radical Oneness doctrine followers despised believers of the Trinity. Seldom did religious folks of different doctrinal beliefs fellowship together or become friends. Tex and Diana were Oneness and Anne was of the Trinity doctrine. These families became the exception to the rule as their friendship grew strong over the years while they worshiped together in house prayer-meetings and brush-arbor settings. They were tolerant and respectful of their religious differences. Though their individual beliefs were set in steel they found common ground.

Anne knew of Iris and Daniel but avoided contact with them. Since Daniel was a known bootlegger, she shunned the appearance of evil. She didn't meet Ora for several years.

Iris seemed to be perpetually pregnant. She gave birth to a set of premature stillborn twins with no midwife present in the winter of 1945. Malnourished herself when these babies came, she and Daniel did not know what to do. They did not want anyone to find out she was pregnant again, and had lost more babies. The doomed couple made a pact to tell no one about the miscarriage.

Iris held the two dead baby boys for a while. Then Daniel, their eldest son Joe, who was only seven, and five-year-old Ora pulled up loose planks from the shack floor. They dug a hole in the ground beneath the house to bury the newborns. Iris cried bitterly.

Iris' protective, domineering mother, Gladis and the community found out about this incident. Gladis was against the marriage from the beginning, and wanted Iris to move back home. Her many cousins were in thick with the Ku Klux Klan and local law enforcement. Motivated by revenge and racism against Daniel, the KKK took opportunity for violence in the belief they were doing God a service. The moonshine still, stillbirth, and illegal burial tipped the scales against Daniel. Daniel was hated by Iris' family.

Ora woke to the sound of horse hooves tromping about in the front yard and on the porch. The engine ping of an automobile and headlights glared through her bedroom window. Joe was sleeping on the floor across the room.

She shook him. "Get up, Joe. There are demons outside!" she whispered with a quiver in her voice.

They wrapped themselves in the tattered quilts they were lying on and ran to the window to see hooded men. Ghostly images were hoisting a large wooden cross high into the air at the edge of the yard.

The pungent smell of kerosene drifted through the cracks in the walls around the window as the cross was doused and lit. The flames roared high as the cross burned.

Men began to yell outside the front door, "Daniel Bip, come out or we'll burn you out!"

Ora and Joe ran toward Daniel and Iris and huddled close to them and the other young children.

Hooded men battered down the front door. Hate-filled voices spued scriptures as the sheeted devils dragged Daniel out of bed and into the yard. The siblings fearfully cried.

Iris screamed and whacked one intruder over the head with her cane as she slid out of bed. "I know that is you, cousin Elmer Don! Leave my Daniel alone! Leave us be! We did you no harm!" Iris shrieked.

Ora squealed as he shoved Iris back on the bed and watched them forcefully exit the house with pleading, struggling Daniel in hand.

Ora helped Iris walk onto the porch. They could do nothing. Joe angrily threw rocks and cursed the Klansmen as the horrified family watched helplessly while these men beat Daniel.

Brutally pulling him into the back of a rusted old pickup, the KKK drove away with him and the family continued their tearful screams.

Ora shivered in the biting cold as they heard him pleading with the attackers to stop the beating. She and Joe held tight to Iris' trembling body as Daniel's cries faded into the night.

Four hours later, the hooded KKK criminals dumped Daniel in the front yard. His face was unrecognizable. His right lung was collapsed after being punctured by a broken rib. Torn loose from the chest wall lining, it could not process the oxygen into his system properly. He lay there, bleeding, bruised, and gasping for every breath, as Ora and frightened loved ones struggled to help him to his feet and back into the old dilapidated shack. Daniel sat down on the bed and wiped her tears. "Pops, who were those men? Why did they do this?" Ora asked.

"One of them was a law man." Daniel groaned. "Hand me my jug, Joe."

Joe pulled the heavy moonshine crock from under the bed, popped the cork, and hoisted it to Daniel's trembling lips. Daniel swallowed and lay back on the bed.

Ora ran for a wet clean rag beside the wash pan. Returning she wiped away the blood from her father's face that had dried over his eyes.

Iris lay beside him. "One was cousin Elmer Don. He's been nothing but a bully all his life."

"But why, Pops!" Ora asked.

"They got angry over mechanic work I did on one of their cars." Daniel panted and turned to Joe. "Son, hand me the pistol on the wall."

Joe ran for the gun and tiptoed to gently lift it off the nail. "Here Pops!"

Daniel placed the gun under his pillow. "This will never happen again!" Daniel snarled. "I'll kill the bastards first!"

"I hate them, Pops! Give me the gun and I'll kill Elmer!" Ora shouted and burst into tears.

"No, Honey, this is between me and them," Daniel said.

"Maybe we should move!" Iris said.

"They done me some damage inside. If I make it through the night gotta go to the doc come morning. We'll talk about the move tomorrow. If I don't make it you take the children and get to hell out of the county!" He closed his eyes, and gasped. Trembling Iris squeezed his hand and cried.

From the day of the beating onwards, Daniel slept with a loaded pistol under his pillow and one hung over the door. He never went anywhere without ready access to one of his guns. No one was ever prosecuted.

Before Bill died in 1953 he got troubles off his chest. Delena said he repented of his evil ways. He gave a different reason for Daniel's beating from what Mr. Bip told his children. "The lazy drunken fool wouldn't work and provide for his family like he should have. These men had only intended to teach him a lesson. We thought we were doing God a service! Make him work to provide for his family. None of us intended to hurt him so badly! Was I wrong? If I was he wasn't the first. God's gotta do lots of forgivin' this old backsliding Baptist sinner. Maybe I'll make it to heaven? I hope so!" Bill died the day after he made his peace with God. But he never asked Daniel to forgive him.

Shortly after the beating both the Bip Families moved twenty miles to the community of Rooster Ridge. Iris conceived many more times over the next eight years. Some of the children were stillborn, and others were miscarried. But from that time on, she always managed to see a doctor or have a midwife present during the birthing process.

Chapter Two

Ora was old beyond her years at thirteen. She became woman of the house doing daily chores at age six when Diana taught her how to help with the younger siblings, prepare meals, and care for Iris. Ora took over household responsibilities as Diana's assistance became less. Her duties in the home increased drastically the older she got.

Living day to day was a struggle, with fear the greatest motivator. Ignorance and poverty were the standards in many families. Education was not even a dream for some children. Ora's family lived in the impoverished community of Rooster Ridge during the 1950's. She was illiterate, having attended school only one month in the third grade. Daniel made her quit. Iris needed her at home to help with the babies.

By the age of nine, Ora smoked cigarettes around a few accepting family members. Prince Albert roll-your-owns. She cursed like a strumpet, and dressed the holiness Pentecostal way to please her aunt Diana. Always hiding her vices from the religious, she had learned to be tough and how to fit in with those around her to survive. If they were religious, she acted religious. When around roughens, she conducted herself accordingly.

In 1953; Iris was twenty-eight and pregnant, again. This was her twelfth baby. Six had died during the pregnancies or birthing process. Ora dreaded having another infant in the home. Coming into puberty, Ora wanted more freedom to spend time with friends.

Her breasts began to develop before she turned thirteen in March. Her raven wavy hair laced about her feminine form to her hips and danced in the breeze when she worked in the fields.

To cover her fear of being rejected, her embarrassment over her shabby attire, and to be polite she smiled a lot. She smiled even at strangers, followed by a cheerful howdy or nod in greeting. With a dark olive complexion and large brown bedroom eyes, she was a beauty to behold. Some said it was the Cherokee, possibly Negro blood in her genes, a touch of the tar-brush that contributed to her exotic beauty. During strawberry harvest the men began to take notice.

The Bip family hitched a ride on the back of a logging truck for the twenty-mile trek to Loafer's Glory to pick the strawberry crop in May. Ora's whimsical cousin Fanny, thirty-eight, had given birth to her fifth child the week before. Needing help with domestic chores until she recovered after the birth of her baby girl, she asked Daniel to let Ora come stay.

While harvesting the berry field, Fanny said, "Daniel, ya just gotta let Ora help me out. Remember the Golden Rule! I promise to do right by ya and Ora if you let her stay."

Though Fanny's version of the rule was self-centered. Daniel agreed, under the condition that Diana or Gladis would help Iris.

When the day's work came to a close Ora's family set up housekeeping in a picker shed on old man Bonner's farm near the strawberry fields. 1953 brought a moderate harvest out of the fourteen hundred acres of berry fields. One-half million dollars were generated from more than seventy thousand crates of berries. The pickers got less than five cents per quart. The fastest and best field hands could harvest one hundred quarts in eight hours. Faster than most, Ora picked her day's wages and gave the money to Daniel.

The fields only produced a fifty percent yield that year because of a late frost. When the berry crop was in at the end of two weeks, Ora remained in Loafer's Glory with Fanny while her family caught a ride back to Rooster Ridge on another logging truck.

The uneducated hardworking families were bonded into a closely knit community and loosely connected to the people in surrounding villages. Her family custom was for young teenage girls to marry and begin raising children of their own by age fourteen. Looking forward to finding a husband, she wanted to get away from her parents and start her own life.

Times had changed in the past forty years. Some girls were marrying when they were older, and now couples looked to wed someone from a distant town to prevent inbreeding and lessen the chance of birthing dead or deformed babies. Some families were stricken with genetic diseases, Kings Disease, they called it, because first cousins had married and were raising children. Many of these families' babies died before age five. In earlier generations this practice was acceptable, but no longer. Anyone who married a first cousin in the 1950's was considered white trash and their children were shunned. Marriage of second cousins was okay. No inbreeding in Ora's family, and she wanted to keep it that way. Homely Fanny might be an inbred.

Ora's and Enoch's meeting wasn't by chance. Fanny was a drab woman with a small head, long neck, thin greasy-looking premature graying hair, a flat chest, extremely large hips, and long black hairs growing on her boney legs and ankles. Chad often shook his head and said of her, "She is so ugleeeee, the maggots crawl off the carne cart to avoid having to look at her when she passes."

The berry plants and other crops afforded shade from the hot sun for smaller wildlife. Beneath the plants rattlers or copperheads lay ready to kiss the picker on the hand or take a quick bite out of the leg. Fanny was like the snakes.

She, like most field laborers, relished wearing work boots. Her simple dresses were hand sewn and she created her own crude decorations of lace and darns to grace them. The printed material salvaged from the fifty-pound flour sack stitched together made the dresses and shirts for families, and had for decades. Styles hadn't changed much in twenty years, though dresses were a little shorter, striking mid-calf. Store-bought clothes were only worn by the women for church, weddings, and funerals.

Fanny was in style with the shorter attire. With her small crossed beady brown eyes and razor sharp long nose, crooked on the end, she looked like a witch. And her voice sounded like the calling of a crow. Frequently twitching her head and checking to make sure her bun was in place she repeated, "Praise the Lord," giving herself more time to think of what to say next during her conversations.

Doing her chores she hummed a gospel tune. She proudly thought of herself as a match maker, while arranging many young marriages in the community.

Fanny's husband Ely obeyed her every command and supported her match makings. He was a catch for Fanny. Ely wanted to be like Elvis. The poor soul, though the tried, just wasn't endowed with the natural genetics to be an Elvis look alike. He was more of a Gomer Pyle.

To Fanny's way of thinking a girl should marry and start a family as soon as she "became a woman." In Fanny's eyes, a girl who was fourteen and unmarried was a spinster, in need of serious intervention of a match maker. The match maker was of course Fanny. Sex before marriage didn't fit into her protocol. After all, she was a religious woman and had to be moral. Confused and ignorant in many ways, she claimed to be a Christian. Pentecostal Holiness was her choice and she wore the bun in public.

The Hotman and Judas families knew each other well. Their love-hate relationship included periods of shunning and back stabbing. Anne had strong reservations about Fanny's match making. She didn't approve of such with the younger girls. Anne was quite upset when Fanny married off her ten-year-old daughter Bela Judas to twenty-three-year old Benny Stant.

Ora listened to Fanny's advice and fell under her spell of misdirection. Fanny told her that Enoch and his family were hardworking people and fairly well-to-do compared to most of the other folks around

Loafer's Glory. She mentioned that Chad's sawmill was the source of income for many families, and the Hotman's crops were bountiful. Rumor had it that gold was on Hotman land.

Enoch's family was indeed hard working and financially secure compared to many others in the community. Their living conditions were better than most. However, he didn't come from a family actually having a lot of money. But to Fanny they were rich.

Fanny pressed Ora to think about developing a relationship with Enoch before she had ever seen him. "Ora, it's time you find yourself a man and start thinking about raising a family of your own," Fanny would say many times during Ora's stay that spring.

Ora agreed to meet this man called Enoch.

"Play hard to get! Flirt and roll your beautiful brown eyes and act shy when he talks to you," Fanny directed.

Ora giggled like the little girl she was as Fanny went on and told her about the birds and bees. With Fanny's help, a plan began to develop.

Fanny stuck her face over Ora's shoulder and whispered loudly, "Let him get close and stroke your long black hair. Let him kiss you with his tongue inside your mouth."

Ora turned her head in the other direction to avoid Fanny's foul breath, but she was beginning to dream of romance. Ora peeled potatoes for supper while Fanny began topping overripe strawberries for canning. Fanny sat and lurched zestfully backward and forward in cane bottom oak rocker on the other side of the room. She swung her crossed leg high every time the rocker rolled back. The baby slept on a floor-pallet near the open front door to keep cool.

Tiny droplets of salty sweat beaded on their brows when Fanny built a fire in the wood cookstove to prepare the evening meal, and boiled water for canning.

"Fan it's Merl, got more berries," a man yelled from the porch.

A lump knotted inside Ora's throat as she saw the young couple through the screen door. Her face turned bright red. Fanny yelled, "Come on in, children. You're just in time, I'm ready to can this batch."

Squirming in her seat, eyes downcast, Ora was afraid they had overheard what was being said. Glancing up and quickly lowering her face again she noticed Merl resembled that famous new Rock 'n Roll singer.

Fanny said, "Young ones, this is my cousin Ora. She is here to help me for a few days. Praise the Lord."

"How are ya," Ora greeted them.

"Thirsty now!" Merl answered as he poured two glasses of cider from the gallon jar on the table and handed one to Lilly. He glared lustfully into Ora's innocent eyes as he took a seat directly across from her.

His staring made her uncomfortable and she dropped the potato on the table and ran to check on baby Agnus.

As Ora returned to the table, Lilly stuttered, "Where do you live?"

"I come from Rooster Ridge to help cousin Fanny." Blushing shyly, she said, "Merl, did anyone ever tell ya that you look like Elvis?"

He touched his long sideburns, and pushed back his greasy coal black hair. "I've been told that a time or two," he said.

Pouring herself a cup of Cider, and flipping her stringy long hair back, Fanny said, "Praise the Lord! Daniel and Iris are her parents. Bless their poor souls."

"Ya pa is a little man and on the sickly side, ain't he, girl," Merl said.

"Pa and Ma, they both have lots of health problems. But I help them get along," Ora said.

"Ya pa needs to lay off the moonshine, life would treat him kinder. Praise the Lord," Fanny said.

"Ya poor ma. I don't know how she ever had so many kids. But you are right smart pretty!" Merl said and winked at Ora.

Ora blushed, lowering her gaze again.

Lilly punched Merl in the side, her lips trembling, and stuttered, "Stop flirting with that child!"

Ora giggled then so did Lilly.

"I'm gonna take Ora to Anne's prayer meetin' tonight and let her meet Enoch. Praise God, I think they'd make a dandy couple," Fanny said.

"That ol' Enoch was my best buddy in school. He is a squirrel. Some say he's nuts. The accident didn't do him no good," Merl said. "Darn near split his head in half with the axe, his partner did. I don't know how he survived!"

"Anne's praying! That's how he made it! No doubt," Fanny said. "But he is a hard worker! He could give a girl nice things. Sides, it's time for him to get away from his ma and start a family."

"Lilly is a gonna have my youngun. She ain't a showin' yet but she will be gettin' big soon," Merl said, as he lay his hand on her belly.

She slapped it off. "You shouldn't have told them so soon, Honey."

"Is this your first one? When is it due?" asked Ora.

Smiling, tugging her earlobe, Lilly replied "The first, about February."

Dimples piercing her cheeks, Ora said, "Babies are lots of work. But ain't that what life is for us all? Just work and stealing a bit of joy when ya can. But the babies are fun too, sometimes."

"My baby will finish high school and go on to college if I have any say in the matter. I want it to have a future. Migrant work is too hard and a body can't ever get ahead," Lilly said.

Starting to feel a kindred spirit for Lilly, Ora asked, "Where you from?"

"Florida."

"Did you get much book learnin'?" Ora asked.

"I finished ninth grade," Lilly answered with a smile.

Laying the potato and knife on the table Ora pushed her hair off of her face, gathering a loose ponytail. She dragged a pale blue satin ribbon from her apron pocket. With delicate, but calloused fingers she tied a knot around the hair at the base of her neck. "Wow, you are a lucky girl," Ora said. "I got some third grade. But I can read a little and do numbers and write my name. My brothers don't know how to do that. They aren't interested."

Lilly nodded. "Machines are taking over. My dad told me I had to learn the books to survive. He said one day migrant work and field hands to harvest cotton and the like will be a thing of the past. I think he's right."

Ora smiled, embarrassed again when Merl winked at her one more time. She blushed.

"Well, time to pick a few more berries," Merl said as he stood and gulped down the last of his cider.

Walking toward the front door making certain not to awaken sleeping Agnus, Lilly said, "It's really nice to meet you, Ora. I guess we'll be seeing you around for a while. Come have supper with me and Merl one night."

Merl smiled, wrapped his arm around Lilly, and ran his fingers through his hair. "You do that girl. We'll treat you in so many ways you are bound to like some of them." He winked yet again as they stepped off the porch into the yard.

Ora waved bye to them at the front door. "I'll probably do that before I go back to Rooster Ridge."

Ora continued to watch as he and Lilly sauntered back down the dirt road to the strawberry field.

Chapter Three

Enoch stood on the front porch smoking a roll-your-own. "Who ya got there with you, Fanny?" he asked, staring at Ora intently as they strolled off the dusty road into the yard.

"This is my cousin Ora from Rooster Ridge. She wanted to come to your ma's prayer meetin' tonight. Praise the Lord!"

Ora held her head down while peeking through hair that draped over the side of her face.

He winked.

She glowed. *He's not bad lookin'.*

Pulling a can of tobacco from his hip pocket and waving it in front of her and then shoving it back into his pocket, Enoch asked, "Wanta smoke?"

Timidly, "Sure," she replied.

Smirking, Fanny left the young couple to visit in the yard. Enoch opened the small can of Prince Albert Tobacco. Digging inside his shirt pocket, he flipped out an Ol' Country Boy cigarette paper. With a pinch of tobacco he rolled and licked it together. Striking a match on his pant's zipper, he lit the smoke and handed it to her. They blew rings that clouded over their heads as they visited and laughed.

Inside Enoch happily introduced Ora to Anne. She greeted her with a hug, a kiss on the cheek, and a joyous smile. She then gave each of them a tattered old song book and they sat in the corner of the living room floor. Other religious folks came in and sat. All the young people were scattered on the floors as the older ones took the chairs. About twenty people filled the house.

As the service progressed the Spirit came into their midst as a holy fog and filled the room. Ora felt it and smiled as Enoch watched her weeping hard under conviction. At first she was embarrassed that she couldn't control her crying especially in front of Enoch. As the presence of the Holy Spirit ministered to her soul her pride vanished. It didn't matter anymore what Enoch thought. This was between her and God. The Lord saved her soul.

She also received one extra blessing, the baptism of the Holy Ghost with the evidence of speaking in an unknown tongue. Afterward Enoch walked with her to Fanny's house, flashlight guiding their footsteps so not to step on a copperhead. He told her he didn't approve of the tongues but that was her choice.

She kissed him on the cheek at the front door as they said goodnight. When she went inside and shut the door behind her, she watched from a window as he strolled down the gravel road toward home. Happily he jumped into the air and she heard him mumble, "I'm going to marry this girl." She sighed, for now her relationship with God was more important. But Enoch and Fanny continued their persistence.

Ora listened to Fanny's advice and flirted with Enoch. She attended several meetings at Anne's over the next two weeks as she and Enoch soon became full-time sweethearts. The courtship continued for almost a year after she returned to her father's.

She was pleased her conversion helped Anne to accept their relationship. She knew the widow Hotman felt nothing but disdain for her mother and father. But Anne liked her. She was different from her folks. And, she had the Holy Ghost.

Her salvation experience rooted inside her heart. She knew it was real. She tried to live the holiness life for a time despite numerous stumbling blocks. Within six months, she returned to her old nature, drinking moonshine, smoking cigarettes, and cursing.

She wasn't about to hide these vices while putting on the pretend face to masquerade as a saint. She couldn't do that anymore. Now, she knew God was real. She felt she wasn't worthy of the love he had shown her the night of salvation. She feared God. To be a fake would insult him.

When not able to walk in the strict teachings of church holiness, shame and frustration set in, making for problems between her and Anne. A guilty Christian complex took hold in her heart.

Anne's stern glares and harsh tones when Ora failed to be holy made her feel hated. Considering all the circumstances she was accepted by Enoch's family, but his relationship with them had always been a love-hate one and that's the way it would be with her. Or so he had told her. He was labeled the village idiot by some because of his mental problems--the cow-horn curse, and blow of the axe, crazy Baptist preacher was mockingly his community branding outside religious circle. She resented that. He was no better or worse than all the rest in her mind. Though she didn't want to come under Enoch's public humiliation. Given time she would change how he was perceived by folks in Loafer's Glory. She'd show them all that they were wrong about them. He just needed lots of love.

She knew how to deal with rejection and persecution. She was strong. Being the bootlegger's daughter was worse. She could help him and he her. Pops moonshine production only lowered her social status in the rural society but she would rise above it. Her mother's affliction was considered a curse from God. Iris was shunned as a leper. Why couldn't people see Iris for the sweet person she was instead of judging her because of the disability? To judge was sin.

It didn't really matter how pretty or smart Ora was, the labels remained. They always remained! Even when one changed from light to dark, and vice versa, the family labels never washed off. As they had been that way for a hundred years, deep inside she knew the attitudes wouldn't change for her but naively she hoped.

Six months after their meeting she was having second thoughts about the relationship. She sensed the Hotman's felt they were better than her. Maybe she wasn't good enough for Enoch. It appeared his family didn't think so. In her heart of hearts she longed to leave the state. Move to a town where no one knew her, and start all over fleeing the past. She hoped if they married, Enoch would take her away from this place of sorrows. Her childhood was miserable because of the gossip and persecutions her family had suffered. Maybe she wasn't as strong as she thought.

Reconsidering, and anxious about her relationship with the Hotmans, her wandering eyes found an attraction toward Merl as he secretly made passes, flirting during her frequent visits to Loafer's Glory to be with Enoch. She was torn. The forbidden love of a married man or a semblance of stability with ostracized Enoch and his harsh-spoken people. Those were her choices because she was a shamed backslider, the bootleggers daughter. Who else would have her? She was pretty but her family roots were the curse. Many men wanted her to use. She wasn't a whore--a lady. Sometimes she wanted to be with Enoch and other times he repulsed her as she lusted for Merl. Enoch was safe.

She couldn't betray her best friend, Lilly. She couldn't break Enoch's heart. She hated Anne's self-righteous judgmental attitude and loathing of her family. She had no choices. She must choose one of two evils. She couldn't care for Moms the rest of her life. She wanted Merl, but she mustn't deceive Lilly. To pray through again was the hardest choice-- too many stumbling blocks. She covered her emotions of inferiority, anger, and confusion with smiling entreaties toward those around her, though secretly she loathed many. She continued trying to hide her desires for Merl, and warred in her spirit about the religious holiness. She'd never be able to live by those rules. She wasn't about to be a hypocrite. Gossip and slander were the worst sins. She wouldn't be guilty of carrying tales, or repeating hearsay. Even fools seemed wise with zipped lips.

When Lilly gave birth to a baby girl in February, Ora decided Merl would never be hers. She struggled to fight off her feelings as the infatuation of a silly inexperienced young woman. She had to dismiss them as only a secret fantasy. Her feelings for Merl couldn't be real.

Her torment ended two months before her fourteenth birthday in January of 1954 when Enoch asked her to marry him. Though her heart was truly with Merl, she said, "Yes."

Merl's advances intensified. She wouldn't break Lilly's heart. She had to marry Enoch. He was her way of escaping the environment at home and perhaps being married to him would quench her secret desires for

Merl. After all Enoch was good to her. He loved her and she loved him. Just not as much passion there as she felt for Merl. They would marry and leave Loafer's Glory or surely she would succumb to Merl's charms.

Chapter Four

Daniel held to the old traditions not allowing Enoch to marry Ora. The dues must be paid. Enoch's dead pickup needed work. Unable to haul logs he was short of cash. He'd get the money. No one would keep Ora from him.

Springtime growing season in 1954 brought the beginning of a journey down one of life's rocky roads for Enoch and Ora. Tired of caring for Iris, and the young ones, Ora wanted out immediately. They hitchhiked to Mountain View forty miles from Loafer's Glory and got papers for her father to sign. The same day they had blood drawn at the local health office. Ora never gave Daniel the papers. She knew he would not sign without the exchange of money. Money, Enoch didn't have. The money being a sign that Enoch could provide for her.

Three days later she and Enoch returned to Mountain View for test results. They were clean of sexually transmitted diseases. Ora was a virgin. She discounted the incident when she was nine by the town drunk, Elmer Don. In her mind, she was a virgin until she chose to be with a man.

Necking at every opportunity they spent the day milling around on the streets, desperately trying to figure a way to get Daniel to sign *before* he got the dues. Enoch would ask Chad for a loan to fix his truck. He had to get back to work. By noon, out of desperation, Ora forged Daniel's name to the consent forms.

As they sat on a bench in front of the courthouse she tossed her long hair off her slim shoulders, sighing she said, "There! I've done it!" Then she folded the document and handed it to Enoch.

He squirmed. Frowning Enoch whispered, "Ora we could get into lots of hot water over this. When your Pops finds out he'll shoot me."

She giggled. "If that be the case then I'll give you the finest funeral Loafer's Glory has ever seen."

Smiling he nodded. "I love you more than anyone in the world. I'd die for ya."

Whispering, she kissed him on the cheek, "Let's go get married! We'll worry about Pops later."

He nodded.

They hitched a ride on the back of a logging truck to Rooster Ridge. Arriving before dark they presented the papers to the Justice of the Peace. They were married in his living room.

"I now pronounce you husband and wife." Justice of Peace smiled and nodded. "You can kiss your new bride now," he said.

Enoch dropped his brim hat and raised Ora off the floor. They passionately kissed. Balding, stocky Justice of the Peace and his skinny wife chuckled when Enoch placed her on the floor again. Ora squealed with excitement, "Yes! Mrs. Enoch Hotman!" The easy part was over. Daniel lived a mile up the road.

Strolling toward Daniel's home dread engulfed them. They'd have to tell him. Daniel smiled from the front porch as they ambled off the road into the yard. Ora held Enoch's hand and placed her other arm around Daniel. Smiling she said, "Pops, I have something to confess."

Daniel glaring at Enoch and asked, "Have you got my Ora knocked up?"

Enoch squirmed. "No sir! I'm a preacher man. Wouldn't do such a thing before marriage."

Daniel sighed. "Good, I ain't ready to marry off my oldest daughter," he said.

Enoch glanced at Ora and dropped his gaze.

Ora kissed Daniel on the cheek. She asked, "Pops, what if I decided to marry Enoch real soon?" His eyes downcast as she waited for him to respond. Ora fidgeted when he didn't answer. She said, "I will you know," and she sighed. Still no answer. She asked, "Would that be okay if I love him?"

Daniel's eyes flitted from Enoch and then back to Ora. His forehead wrinkled. Then he raised one eyebrow. Suspiciously he asked, "Have you two been up to no good?"

Ora said, "No Pops, we did all the right things." Smiling, she flipped her hair back and asked, "Are you going to answer my question?"

Head down, Daniel silently scowling, then he raised his gaze. Smiling he said, "Son, if you loan me fifty bucks I'll sign the papers for you to marry Ora. That is if she loves you."

Ora was enthused, jumping about she hugged them both.

Daniel said, "You bring me the money and the papers and I'll sign them."

Realizing they didn't have the money at the moment, Ora's cheerfulness faded once again as she glanced up at frowning Enoch. She looked Daniel in the eyes as Enoch took a deep breath and sighed. She said, "Pops, we already got married! Enoch will bring you the money in a few

days."
    Daniel began to curse, angrily racing into the house he pulled a loaded gun from over the front door. Ora trembled fearfully and screamed, "Run Enoch!" she shouted.
    Enoch leaped off the porch with raging Daniel at his heels he ran for his life.
    Panting, Daniel yelled, "Don't ya ever come back, you thief!"
    Ora, pleading with Daniel. She yelled, "No! Pops, don't shoot my husband! I love him! Pops no! Stop, Pops you'll get winded. Come back!"
    Old man Bip had a temper, and at that Daniel trusted no one after the beating in 1945. He wanted the dues paid. Ora screamed to Enoch who was flat-footing-it as hard as he could go on up the road, "Get Pops the dues, Enoch," Ora shouted.
    Daniel turned around glaring at Ora. Gasping for his breath he strolled inside, hang the gun over the door, and pulled the moonshine crock from under the bed. Trembling he fought to pop the cork but was having difficulty getting it to break free.
    Tearfully, smiling Ora wiped her eyes and said, "Let me help ya, Pops."
    He downed a swig, laying back on the bed as his breathing began to ease he squinted, "Girl, I wanted better for you than this. I don't know about Enoch. Folks say he ain't right in the head," he said.
    Ora said, "Right enough for me Pops. I love him. Besides you married Moms when she was only thirteen. Haven't I got a right to a life of my own and some happiness?"
    Scowling, he said, "You ain't gonna marry this man. Your ma needs ya at home."
    She sighed and whined, "But Pops."
    He interrupted her and said, "Pipe down. They won't be any buts. I say no!" Grinning, he said, "Maybe later. The boy's gotta prove to me he will provide for you! He must pay the dues."
    At that hint of hope but still disappointed she kissed him on the forehead, then her gaze fell to the floor. It was the damn dues he wanted. He didn't care if she married, other than losing his slave, domestic laborer. He wanted the money. That was more important than her happiness.
    Ora wasn't allowed to leave the place. Daniel had the marriage annulled the next day. She pined away to be with Enoch and resentfully cared for her siblings and impaired mother.
    Her spirit was lifted a week later when Enoch's brother Lanny, and wife Martha pulled into the driveway. Had Enoch sent them? Had Anne? Her zeal was dampened during a heated conversation with Daniel

when they spoke their minds. If she and Enoch were fooling around--they said they didn't want sin in Enoch's life. He had to marry her. But if they weren't bedding down then they'd rather Daniel not sign. Enoch didn't need a wife.

Insulted, Ora smiled to hide her rage an embarrassment.

Daniel said, "What Enoch does is his business, none of your'. It will be *my* decision if Ora marries him."

Scowling Lanny turned to Martha and mumbled that Daniel was a nothing but lazy no-count sinner drunk. He wouldn't listen or cooperate.

Angry Daniel overheard the slur and grasping the gun from above the door. "Hit the road! You aren't welcome here," he yelled along with a few choice profanities. Ordering them to get out of his house, he was intent on shooting Lanny as the couple dashed for the jalopy, then speed away.

Nobody told Pops what to do. Nobody! Ora was surprised Pops hadn't shot them both. She thought, Lanny had gall! The nerve of the that bastard. Martha wasn't much better when self-righteous Lanny harshly spoke to them while Martha stood by smirking. The Bips weren't wretched sinner infidels, or white trash as the Hotmans implied. Just sinner Baptist, Bapti-costals, and poorer than most families. Pops was insulted, and now he might not ever sign. Hell, most everyone used the moonshine. Pops was just more open. She was a virgin. How dare Lanny bespeak otherwise! Pops had to defend her honor. This was another Hotman control issue. She'd be damned if any of Enoch's family would have their say over him when they married--if they wed.

Two weeks later on her birthday, Enoch drove his logging truck into the Bip yard. Ora had continued pleading with her parents to give them their blessing. She and Iris stood in the doorway watching, listening to the two men talk.

Pops and Enoch had a lot in common when it came to their religion. That was in her favor. Would Pops sign the papers? Both men had a hard time accepting the Pentecostal way of life. Neither was about to give up his tobacco or a shot of moonshine with the good ol' boys every now and then. That too was in her favor as they might turn out to be friends. But the money was most important. Did Enoch have the cash?

She had watched Enoch behind the pulpit, folks said he could preach down heaven with his hellfire and brimstone messages. Having the altars full at the end of a service with the congregation wailing in repentance. She smiled at the thought knowing that made him feel he had done it right. And the offering plate would subsidize their income. Maybe he'd be famous some day. She was glad he was just as determined to have her as his wife as he was at preaching a good sermon.

Enoch said, "I vow before God and you and Iris to give Ora a good home, to provide for her and any children we may have together. I'll work hard and give her a secure wonderful life."

Daniel asked, "Have you got the fifty dollar loan money with you?"

Enoch reached into his pocket, pulling out five ten dollar bills he placed them in Daniel's hand along with a new consent form. The dues were paid and they shared a shot of moonshine.

Daniel signed the papers as Ora ran out of the house and kissed Enoch while Iris wept and hobbled back inside.

Daniel would never repay the loan. That was their unspoken understanding, money to the parents of a bride being common with some Ozark's families, in the old tradition.

Chapter Five

Borrowing a dark blue skirt and jacket from her cousin Fanny, Ora dressed for the wedding one week later. Only having one menstrual cycle in her lifetime, and that happened the month before. Ora was content she had made the right decision. Fanny was elated.

Dogwood's and Redbud's blossoms painted the hills with happy hues of springtime that late March day of the wedding. Midmorning before the ceremony Enoch plunged into cold Big Creek scrubbing himself with a bar of Anne's homemade lye soap. He dressed in khaki pants and a white shirt. His clothes were stiff with the flour starch in which Anne had soaked them before ironing.

Anne was strongly opposed to this union, partly because the newlyweds would have to live with her, since they had no place of their own. And she didn't believe the marriage would work.

Ora's older brother, skinny Joe, picked him up at Anne's. Leaving a cloud of orange clay dust in the air they drove to Rooster Ridge, honking the horn and yelling out the car windows as they flew past Daniel's shack. Daniel and family joined them in Mountain View. Iris had to watch the ceremony from the truck cab where she cried throughout.

Married once again by the same Justice of the Peace on the court house steps. This time the union was official. Around sunset Joe drove the newlyweds to Loafer's Glory.

Enoch had Joe drop them off at a strawberry field a quarter of a mile away from Anne's. Once Joe was gone, they embrace on the hill overlooking the green berry patch, which was not quite ready for harvest. As dusk began to engulfed them they strolled to the berry shed located under a huge red oak tree at the edge of the field. Making certain no one was around they entered the shack. Enoch hoisted her up onto the counter top and stripped off her clothes.

"Stop! Stop! You're hurting me!" she whimpered. But he wouldn't stop until the marriage was consummated.

When the act was over, Enoch glared at weeping Ora. "There," he said, "I got what I wanted. You can go back to your pa now. It wasn't worth the fifty dollars."

Tearfully, Ora screamed "You sorry piece of hog crap!" Bounding to her feet she slapped his face.

Enoch simply walked out of the shed wearing a smug grin, and her hand print on his cheek as he zipped up his pants. She trailed along behind him buttoning her blouse, shivering in the chilly air and attempting to straighten her hair. Enoch just kept marching toward the road.

"You cold-hearted, friggin' ass-hole! Please don't do me this way!" she painfully yelled.

When he ignored her name calling and pleading, she picked up a rock and threw it for all she was worth, hitting him in the back of the head. "There, you a sorry, crazy polecat. You deserve worse!" She turned around, mumbling, and trotted down the dusty road in the direction of Rooster Ridge, hot tears of hurt and anger streaming down her face.

She heard him breathing heavily and the sound of jogging as she glanced behind her. She gasped for fear as Enoch was rushing to catch her. The first rays of silver moonlight and shadows of fading red sun at dusk mingled when he grabbed her arm and swung her around. She struggled to break free from his grip.

He shouted, "Don't you ever call me that, girl!" Then he backhanded her.

She fell to the ground and picked up another rock. "Ya hit me again and I'll kill ya!" she snorted.

He glared at her. "Don't ever call me crazy again!"

She was sobbing uncontrollably, pounding her fist in the dirt. "Why? Why have you done this to me?"

Enoch's demeanor changed from anger to sweetness as he gently helped her up off the ground. His eyes watered. "I had to know if you love me. Forgive me. I was mad at your Pops and couldn't get him out of my mind. But you made me mad. I don't like being called crazy. My family said that ever since I was born! Don't won't my wife to do the same."

She punched him in the gut. "You aren't gonna have a wife at all if you do me this way again. I ain't no punching bag. You gotta be gentle with me. Some cruel joke!"

He held her tight as she struggle to get free. "I love you more than my own life. Promise me you will never leave me. Forgive me. Pissed me off that I had to pay the dues. It just ain't right. You ain't no nigra slave. Most folks don't do that around here anymore."

Ora started to calm down, still resisting a bit. "You silly fool, I love ya, or I wouldn't have married ya. I won't call ya crazy if ya won't ever hit me again or play cruel head games with my love! Your right about the dues. But it was a loan! Now give me your word. No more hitting!"

"I promise. It wasn't worth fifty dollars. You are worth more than millions. Feel like I stole ya at that price."

Glaring, she said, " You hurt my feelings worse than the roughness and fisting. That wasn't love making. Don't know if I'll ever get over this. The money was a loan! I'm a lady! I expect you to treat me like one."

He laughed, while nodding. Her composure changed as she smiled and began to giggle. He said, "In the future I'll try and be more considerate."

"You fool! You damn well better do right by me." She sighed and then smiled.

He nodded.

All forgiven, they kissed, and in their embrace her hands became covered with blood from the wound on the back of his head. She trembled and cried out, "Oh my God, what have I done!"

"I'm okay, Honey. I'm a tough ol' boot," he said and laughed again.

She calmed and kissed him again. With their passions and tempers subsided, they strolled arm in arm to Anne's house.

Enoch and Ora were as different as the moonlight and sunlight that had mingled together for a few moments. Ora had experienced the first of his many mental episodes to come against her. Would their marriage last? Were they promise keepers, or would their time together be as brief as blended evening moon and sun light?

Chapter Six

The next few years were turbulent. The underlying animosity toward her by Enoch's family only worsened in ensuing months as the friendship between Ora's and Merl's family strengthened. The Hotmans labeled her Jezebel.

Merl's and Lilly's baby girl April was born in 1954. The couple had two more children over the next three years, as did the new Hotman family. During the next five years either Ora was pregnant or Lilly, or both.

When Ora was six months along in her pregnancy with their first child, Anne told her to stay away from Merl when Lilly or Enoch wasn't present. She said it didn't look good.

Being a stubborn sort, Ora didn't care how it looked. She continued to sneak out of the house, walk down the path to the outhouse, cross the fence, then trot down the cattle-trail to the pond in the hollow where Merl met her in the woods, knowing all the while Anne was watching.

She said they weren't having an affair. This was Ora's act of defiance to their loathing of her. She deliberately made this appear as giving them what they expected of her, after all she was Enoch's little darky harlot. So she says.

One cool day in October, Delena was visiting Anne when Ora excused herself politely and went outside. Anne asked Delena to accompany her to the barn. She said, "Come with me," while lifting a small-handled wicker basket off the kitchen floor. They stepped out the back door heading up the hill behind the house. Delena followed five paces behind as they chatted. The old plank barn stood on the hill three hundred feet from the homestead overlooking the pond where Ora and Merl often met.

As they approached the barn, Anne said, "She does this every day Merl refuses to work in the timber with Enoch. That boy needs to get a new helper. Merl Judas is lazy as sin."

Anne continued to grumble as they crawled up the ladder into the barn loft to check for chicken eggs in the hay. Suspiciously, Anne spied out the hay doors. "Come watch, Delena," she whispered.

They peeked out the open doors while hiding from view. There, at the edge of the woods, stood Merl. Ora ran to him. They embraced and trotted hand-in-hand into the bushes.

Anne turned to Delena. "I wonder if that baby she carries even belongs to Enoch. It's daddy may be ol' chicken-thief Merl. That heathen has been stealing my chickens at night. I saw him run off into the woods with my best laying hen. I wish I had never sold to Bertha Judas that piece of property." She sighed. "My poor Enoch got himself into something that is going to destroy him. That woman does not love him! I see her pining away, panting, and hankering for chicken-thief Merl."

Finding an egg in the hay behind her, Delena gently placed it in the basket with four others they had pulled from a nest. Scowling, Delena said, "Ma, you have got to tell Enoch. Merl isn't the friend he thinks he is."

Anne replied, "It's not like he doesn't already know! I've tried,

Honey. But he goes into a rage defending Merl. There is no reasoning with my baby boy. "Ora, stands up in church and gives out prophecies, then acts like this. It's a shame."

They crawled down out of the loft with a half-dozen fresh farm eggs and returned to the house. They placed the eggs in the fridge and sorted through the dried pintos on the dining room table for dirt and pebbles before cooking the beans. Ora arrived a few minutes later with an arm-load of fresh turnips she pulled from the garden to prepare for dinner.

Hatefully, Delena and Anne glared at Ora.

She glanced over at them smugly. "Can I help you, girls?"

Anne replied in a stern sad voice, "Don't you need to repent over something?"

Ora smiled through her disdain of Anne, the hurt, anger, and rejection. "Nothing more than all the rest in this God-forsaken community," she snapped.

Delena excused herself and politely told Anne goodbye. She ignored Ora with a cold shoulder as she stomped through the living room, made her way out the door, and strolled briskly toward home. Neither Ora nor Anne spoke another word to each other the rest of the afternoon.

As the sun began to set in the western autumn sky, the loud, battered, old logging truck pulled into the driveway. Ora met Enoch at the front door. She embraced him and welcomed him home. Anne rolled her eyes in disgust when they kissed while she placed the cat-head biscuit dough in the wood cookstove. At dinner, she complained that her chest was hurting and went to bed early.

Chapter Seven

Iris and Daniel were having marital problems since he could not care for her constant needs, the children, and hold a job. After Iris gave birth to Mick, Gladis who lived in Racoon Springs, moved Iris and the two youngest children, Mick, six weeks, and Irene, two, in with her to care for them herself. Daniel wasn't allowed to see Iris after that.

Daniel protested at first but gave up after he was threatened to not come around. They divorced. That autumn, he met short, pleasingly plump, graying Gert in the Bottoms while picking cotton near Grubbs Arkansas. They married and moved deeper into Stone County, twenty miles from Rooster Ridge.

Gert was his god-sent bride. Ora hated her, even though Daniel's life and the lives of the children remaining with him changed drastically for the better. Harsh-spoken but kindhearted Gert kept her new family clean and fed. The undisciplined children resented her presence when she made them mind.

Ora wasn't happy that her parents divorced. She venomously rejected Gert, never a kind word flowed out of her lips about the woman. Ora didn't have much good to say about anyone other than Merl. She was becoming obsessed with him. Wild fantasies of love danced in her head for Merl while hate ate at her soul for Gert and Anne.

Daniel asked Ora to care of her younger siblings as they wouldn't mind him or Gert. She agreed. Ora convinced Enoch it was time to find a place of their own so they could take in her brothers. Enoch couldn't turn them away. They rented a house next door to Delena and her husband, Shawn Zablan.

Enoch insisted the boys go to school. They weren't interested. Frustrated Enoch gave up. They were as stubborn as he was back when Anne tried to make him attend school. They'd get their comeuppance when they were grown. Wood on their backs and water in their eyes, Loafer's Glory gold.

Within a few weeks her three younger brothers, sneaky Aaron, small John, baby Pete, and older Joe moved back to Daniel's. They were never forced to attend school after that. Instead they worked in the fields with their parents as they continued bucking and rebelling against Gert's wishes. Daniel allowed them to do as they pleased.

Daniel had taught all his children how to play musical instruments, including Ora, and about hillbilly music. In that they found great interest and were home schooled. Ora says it wasn't as though they didn't have an education. They just couldn't read and write or figure numbers. They weren't stupid. They had attended the school of common sense. Making money was more important, better training. She had taught herself how to read and write a bit. She says she graduated with flying colors from the school of hard knocks, the head of her class. Though she secretly wished she could have gone to regular school to be with kids her age. The book learning wasn't that important. Ora and her siblings were all rebellious, and were not about to be ordered around by any grownup as they had no respect for most adult. They'd have to learn life's lessons the hard way or remain ignorant.

After one of their arguments Enoch bought Ora a used guitar as a peace offering. He asked her to learn gospel songs so she could help him out during his occasional revivals and brush arbor meetings. Pops Bip came to Enoch's meetings and played fiddle on occasion. He and Ora had Gospel bluegrass jam sessions, and the shouting-Baptist congregations liked that, so did Ora and Enoch.

Being a good hand at playing the fiddle, jig dancing, and folk singing, Daniel became friends with Jimmy Driftwood, who lived up the road in Timbo, Arkansas. They were members of the Rack 'n Sack Folklore Society. Jimmy's friendship bolstered Daniel's confidence, and Daniel was becoming a celebrity of sorts for his fiddle playing. That made Ora proud. Perhaps Jimmy could help her become a famous country music singer one day. People out of the county were beginning to appreciate Daniel for his talent--even showing him respect. That made Ora happy, along with the fact that he had stopped selling moonshine and wasn't drinking.

Though Ora and Enoch fought, both got along well with Shawn. They loved him because he always treated them with respect. Nevertheless, their loud vocal disagreements next door disturbed him on a daily basis. But he said nothing.

On the other hand, Delena was quite vocal. She stood in the yard on many occasions, yelling across the fence, "Quiet down over there! You two shouldn't air all your dirty laundry for the neighbors to hear."

Ora hatefully hollered back, "Enoch don't need your help! Mind your own business!" The brawling worsened.

One frosty wintery morning two months before the first baby was due, Delena's rooster began to crow. The sun was up, and at daybreak Ora slid out of bed. She strolled into the kitchen and prepared sweet chocolate gravy with cat-head biscuits and eggs for breakfast. Enoch staggered into the kitchen wearing boxer shorts, he sat at the table as she poured him coffee. Smiling she said, "Good morning sleep head."

Enoch growled, "What's so good about it?"

Ora, set the coffee pot back on the wood cookstove and placed her hand on her large belly. Joyfully she said, "The baby kicked!" She took Enoch's hand and placed it on her abdomen. "Feel that?" she asked.

Enoch sipped his coffee and quickly set the cup down. He shouted, "Damn it girl, that's hot enough to burn the hairs off my tongue!"

Ora giggled, "There again! Did you feel the kick?" she asked.

Enoch glanced up smirking, "Oh that! It's probably gas. Don't know how you can eat lemons, dill pickles and chocolate ice-cream at two in the morning. Yucky!" he said. Then he lay his ear on her stomach. Smiling he said, "Well I'll be! It is kicking."

Ora smiled and chuckled, "Honey, cravings are what the baby likes. Moms told me to eat what I hanker for, cause that's what the baby needs to grow," she said.

Enoch said, "Well, this baby's gonna be a contradiction of terms.

Sweet and sour!"

Laughing Ora said, "He'll come by it natural. I'm sweet and you're bitter."

Scowling Enoch said, "And what does Moms know? Hell she lost as many babies as survived. If it hadn't been for Diana none of you kids would have lived."

Ora held back her tears at his harsh words and pulled the pan of hot biscuits out of the oven. She used the pot rag so not to burn herself and popped one loose. Glaring she snorted, "Your breakfast is ready! Eat before it gets cold!" Then she tossed the biscuit onto his lap.

The hot bread burned his naked leg. Cursing, "Damn you!" he shouted, knocked the bread to the floor and jumped to his feet.

Ora folded her arms, smirking she said, "I'm sorry, Honey. I was aiming for your self-righteous face. I'm tired of you putting down my Moms and Pops."

Enoch stuck his finger in the steaming bowl of gravy and jerked it out. He smiled and licked off the sweet brown goo, then he strolled to the cupboard and opened a can of evaporated milk. Scowling he barked, "They're poor white trash!" He raised the can and said, "You know, I was going to dump the gravy on your head but it was too hot. So this can of milk will do!"

Ora turned to run out the back door. He leaped, grabbing her hair and held on while she screamed and struggled to get free. Laughing, he poured the milk on her head as he snorted, "I know you don't love me. You love Merl Judas. That's probably his little bastard you're carrying!"

Most every morning he'd awaken in a bad mood and they fought tit for tat, but she wouldn't be out done. Head games, one against the other. Was this a power struggle, or did they just hate each other?

She said she was keeping her distance from Merl, but daily confrontations with Enoch caused her to only fantasize about him ever so fondly. Her affections hadn't changed. Though her loyalties toward Lilly were slipping. They must leave the state.

Her game of "I Got You" with Anne had backfired, intensifying Enoch's jealousy. Now she was rejected by the Hotmans more than ever. The least hint of respect was deteriorating between the young couple. Ora's hopes for a life with Enoch were fleeting away with every altercation. She loved him in a twisted sense. He was her security but deep down she also despised him and hated his family because they had not loved her back when she tried to be accepted. Most all her fights with Enoch and his people were over Merl, or putdowns of Moms and Pops. Hotmans hatefully glared at her. They terrified her, but she wasn't about to let them know.

She was a fourteen-year-old child having a child, and these flawed Bip and Hotman individuals were her baby's people too. Ora often thought of these things during the pregnancy. Would they be as cruel to her baby?

She wiped the canned milk out of her hair as Enoch dressed for work. Doing the dishes she glanced out the kitchen window to find Shawn petting a starving stray hound dog. Smiling, he glanced up as she pecked on the window pane and waved. She loved sweet and kind Shawn. How did he ever get stuck with cantankerous Delena? He deserved better.

Their morning quarrel over, Enoch kissed her on the cheek and patted her belly, smiling he said, "I gotta go. You have a great day. By the way I'm gonna buy you a new wringer washer before the baby gets here. Don't want you havin' to wash dirty diapers on a scrub board."

She grinned and held him tight. "I love you Enoch. Though we fight. I love ya. You're a good provider," she said.

After he left for the day she finished washing the dishes and rubbed her protruding stomach with oil, hoping to prevent more stretch marks. Grimacing, she thought about the ancestor's blood that surged through the baby's veins. Native Americas, Negro slaves, European immigrants, outlaws, Christian Puritans, a combination of good and evil, talent, insanity, and genius were all there in the gene pool. Her baby that kicked and turned inside her belly was thoroughbred--all American. She smiled.

This was the legacy of a hundred years. The hotbed of cultural depravation, and third world type economic and social circumstance. Her infant would receive these humble beginnings for survival upon arrival in this backwoods hillbilly community of Loafer's Glory. How could she bring a child into this hell? But then it was heaven too when she felt loved and appreciated. Would the baby love her unconditionally? Would she love the child? Would the birthing be hard? Would her offspring be beautiful or ugly? Smiling she whispered, "Beautiful! If you're a girl I'll name you Jane. I like that name. But if you're a boy I'll call you Saul. He was a strong and might king."

She realized at this birth the families' saga would now continue with the next generation. Perhaps one of her children would write it all down. Maybe this baby when he grows up?

The baby could make the marriage work, and if Enoch would agree to move them away from his domineering judgmental siblings, and mother. She felt she had to get away from Merl.

Enoch said no. He was at the bottom of their pecking order. Seemed he enjoyed their put downs, didn't feel complete without their frequent verbal floggings, and their yanking out his tail feathers. Just like a flock chickens. She chuckled. No body was going to tell her what to do.

She wouldn't cow-down to them. She'd insult them right back! She was strong, a survivor. Her baby would be too.

Smiling she sighed, and waved at Shawn again, while wondering how many children she would bring into the world. Deciding, three or less. She wasn't going to be a baby factory like her poor crippled moms.

In late winter of 1955 their first born would arrive. Ora and Enoch hoped his life would be better. They and other relatives would share stories, folklore, and family history about the first and second generations with their offsprings. They both looked forward to that. Truly, they came from a land of extremes. This was the origins of pain and pleasure for them all. The people and the land told the stories of what had been, and how it was now. Lifestyles hadn't changed much for decades. Neither had the attitudes.

The ancestors were connected to them and those not yet created. All their lives were entwined. The past, and the predecessors were from where all present life came. Antiquity was inescapable. Maybe her baby would learn to read and write. Education would be a way of evacuation. Maybe he'd escape this shame based society, and its' poverty. Maybe he'd write a book about her/them someday. She'd have to learn to read better.

Scowling, she thought, repent for the forefathers or the curse would remain upon her children. They might never abscond the ignorance, poverty, and persecutions. But she'd do that tomorrow. The naive hopeful dreams of a young girl, a longing for that better portion--more prosperous easier life. That might never come to pass if she didn't repent.

She was already old before her time but still a child at heart. She wanted the freedom to have fun, to be a carefree kid. She glanced down at her stomach when the baby kicked again. That dream was snuffed.

She had experienced so little, never having a childhood. Ever since she could remember she had done nothing, other than to care for babies, her sick mother, and Pops. Now she would have one of her own. Well, at least she knew how to take care of a baby. They would be best of friends too.

Would her lust for Merl over rule her sense of reason? That would take away her security with Enoch. She was bound by the legacy of past generations, the iniquity of her forefathers, and the curse of Loafer's Glory Gold. Her mind longed, and body burned for Merl's touch. But that was taboo. Would she be able to restrain herself? Be moral!

She was practically illiterate though she wanted to learn, but didn't want a hateful teacher. The time and effort, cost money. She'd work at it by using what little knowledge she already had, and then apply that limited skill to reading news papers and old magazines. Numbers could come later. First she had to have give life.

The dishes finished and put away, she watched Shawn playing with that scrawny stray. She scowled. He could get the mange. She heard him laughing. Smiling, she spun around, and flipped her long hair over her slim shoulders while grabbing up the guitar as she sat at the table. She strummed, tilted her head and squinted. A new song she thought, as she worked on birthing a new melody.

Wondering maybe if her child was a girl when it kicked again. She'll be a famous movie star when she grows up. And if a boy, named Saul. Dr. Saul Hotman, or perhaps a teacher? He would write her story. She had an interesting life. My babies will make me proud someday. I can't give them much. But I will give them life. That is more.

She sighed. Maybe the iniquity of her forefathers wouldn't be visited upon the children. She smiled. Maybe their dreams would come true, and they would find love, security, and all the childhood happiness that she never knew. She'd try to meet their needs. There, that's right," she said when she hit the guitar cord she was searching for.

She stopped strumming. Smiling, she whispered, "God, give me a daughter."

END OF SECTION ONE

Segue

1999: A Letter From Jane To Saul

My dear brother, Saul:

Hope this letter finds you in good spirits. I was wondering how the manuscript is coming along. Has it progressed? When people read about you and me, some won't believe what we survived. When I think back on it now, I don't know how we ever came through all of that stuff with our brains intact.

I heard Merl Judas was gravely ill. Is that true? By the way how is our father doing? I was so glad he survived the lung cancer a few years ago. Well, hurry up and get "Section Two" finished. We'll be out in a few weeks during summer vacation, and I'd like to take a peek. If that would be all right with you. "Section Two" is our story isn't it?

Gotta take the boys to a ball game so I'll close.

Love Ya Always, Your Sister, Jane.

Saul stuffed the letter back into the envelope and dropped it on the desk top. He chuckled.

Jane still had her boys at home. Teenagers, those are the hard years for a parent. Dirty diapers were a breeze compared to the teens' hormone overloads, and peer pressures.

Their home was too quiet with all the children grown and gone. Now, only his wife Elisabeth, he, and the quiet, polite old folks, Enoch, Leve, and Jake, who needed twenty-four hour care. Seven bedrooms empty of children. Dolor seemed to invade the place as those who had helped to raise him were near death. Though the love was overpowering.

They had raised their son and two daughters, and opened their home to thirty-eight foster children over the years. They needed the break, but both were suffering from empty nest syndrome. Still silence, without the chatter and music of children would take some getting used to. The old folks who occupied every free moment when they weren't asleep needed the quiet. He glanced at the clock, two a.m. This was his writing time.

He smiled, looking forward to the weekend. The grandchildren livened up the place when they came to visit.

Jane's words had helped remove the writer's block. He sighed. Searching and shuffling through the stacks of notes and rewrites scattered around his desk. Frustrated he scratched his head, and looked again. To his left, there, finally he found the passages. Grabbed the pages, sat down, and turned on the computer. Grimacing he whispered, "Will I ever finish?"

He took a deep breath while running fingers through his hair, and leaning back, exhaled. The effort wasn't just about the characters or the history. He had a universal message, much more important. Inhumanity, abuse, and injustice were generational. But there was hope. Knowledge was the key to change. At that thought, contentment surged through his mind, knowing the cycles of abuse could be broken. He sighed, and whispered, "Thank you God."

He was a survivor.

Time to tell *his* story. Leaning back again while tapping a pen on the chair arm. In his mind he planned the next section. Where to go from here?

Two minutes later, bounding up right, and smiling. "This will work," he mumbled.

Brainstorming about the innocent voice of a young boy. Telling his own turbulent adventure of survival, through a child's eyes. The story wasn't over, it had only begun for Little Saul Hotman. "Saul's Memoir," a message to the world, NEVER BE SILENT about the abuse. A tremendous communiqué coming from the lowliest in modern society. The tiny uninhibited voice of an impoverished, violated, and desperate little boy. His lament would trumpet for the millions, their silent-victims' song. The tale of a world wide epidemic--abuse against the powerless, innocent stolen, and injustice. But a far more excellent story. Never despair. Little Saul Hotman, *his* inner-child would tell.

He sighed. Hoping he hadn't overwhelmed the manuscript with too many accounts of the forefathers. But he had especially selected each experience. The legacy of the past was crucial for the fullness of the work. Giving clear root images, reasons, background, and setting the plots for "Section Two." Family blessings and curses were generational. No, it wasn't overdone. The ancestors would stay.

He had made good on his promise to Delena to share their stories. Remembering that she often said we're an extension of the good and bad who walked the land before. He knew those were words of truth. In a sense that described what he was trying to show--the duality of human beings, and how every experience of the forefathers touched the lives of the descendent.

Putting it all together was the chore. Little Saul Hotman had to tell Jane's and his story in first person or it wouldn't have the impact of innocence. He'd have to break the literary rule, now. He questioned if this could be done successfully. Could he make the transition from third person to first person, segue smoothly, and go on to the finish? "Section Two" had to have the voice of a child.

Stopping for a moment as he glanced at Delena's picture hanging on the wall across the room. She was a beautiful young woman, back then. He thought about the last letter he had received from her two years before. Thank goodness he had kicked those two old wicked whores out of his house, treacherous sisters, Bitterness and Hatred. Don't get mad, get smart was what Delena had said. He smiled.

He had chosen wisdom, forgiveness, and not oppression. But Delena would never know. It was the organic brain disease. He sighed. She would never read his book, her stories. She couldn't even recognize him anymore. What a sad disease. "I will miss you always, and dedicate this work to you, Delena," he said while jerking back a tear. Then he sipped coffee from a large mug she had given him as a gift.

"Your strong spirit is woven throughout. You'll never be forgotten, Delena. You cantankerous old woman! I sure love you," he said while gazing up at the ceiling. Then he stood, stretched, and sat at his desk with pen in hand.

Concentrating on the writing, in first person point of view, he spoke, and wrote the line down....

For "Section Two," I will begin "Saul's Memoir" at birth.

He spoke again, thinking out-loud as he went back forty-five years, connecting to his inner-child. Memories and powerful emotions flooded his soul as he relived a time that was, long gone. He had to disconnect emotionally. Objectivity, and honesty were important for this sensitive subject. "Section One" was easier to share, that wasn't his story. He hadn't lived their lives. No deep emotional attachments to those accounts. Tho he felt the impact of the incidents on his flawed, and emotionally scarred relatives as they had a hand in raising him, and in that, his life was affected. He couldn't shut down from a flood of overwhelming bad energies, memories while writing "Section Two." He had to finish the manuscript. Someone desperate, somewhere, needed the hope found in these passages.

His mind over powered with melancholy-sweet images of his mother Ora, father Enoch, and Merl Judas. *I am born,* he boldly and defiantly wrote for the beginning of "Section Two."

The middle-aged man, Saul Hotman continued composing, day after day, until the passages were eternally pasted to the pages....

HOTMAN'S INNOCENCE
SECTION TWO
SAUL'S MEMOIR
(In First Person)

Part One
Family Chaos
1955 to 1960
Saul's Genesis Travail

Chapter One

I am born. Taking on darker features in our Cherokee gene pool, with the exception of dirty blond hair. From the beginning I am a distasteful sight for some. I do not look like a Hotman at birth. My momma Ora said family members gathered around her bed. Grandmother Anne politely asked them all to leave the room as she stroked Momma's forehead with a cool wet rag. They left, congregating in other parts of the house.

Plain dressed in an ankle length black skirt, and white blouse, Anne glaring suspiciously, positioned Momma's long dark-hair across the pillows. She lifted me out of her arms, examined me from head to toe, searching for Hotman traits. She sighed, and lay me back down next to Momma. "Well, girl, you've gone and done it! Ya got you a high-yellow brown-eyed Merl chicken there! You should be ashamed. You should repent!"

Momma turned to face the wall, biting her tongue to hold back vulgarities as rage bubbled in her guts. She knew my father Enoch's siblings were standing outside. Me, and this old religious hag are going to have it out one day, she thought. Realizing now was not the time, she held her peace. Agonizing, calling for Daddy, she said, "Honey, please ask everyone to come back tomorrow." Her cold dark-brown dagger eyes, glared back at Anne "I'm not feeling well," she said through clinched teeth.

Grimacing, Anne nervously checked her bun. "Well," she said and stormed out of the room.

Momma watched out a window as Anne angrily stomped up the road heading home. The north wind whistled through the cracks around the window facings where we were lying on the bed. She saw Anne pulling out a green wool scarf from her black coat pocket and tying it around her head. Tossing the ends over her shoulders she tramped on up the highway. Momma pulled the covers up over our heads. "I'll be glad when the old bitch is dead," she said seething. She breast-fed me, disappointed she sighed, then lovingly whispered, "Little Saul, I wish you *were* Merl's child. Why couldn't you be a girl? I wanted a girl. Seems I never get what I want. God always hands me the short end of the stick but I'll love you anyway." She sighed.

Momma said the delivery was hard. Her water broke days before I finally popped out of her baby-oven-pot. She said I damn near killed her as the pain felt like she squatted to pee and felling on a sharp burning stump, rammed up inside her forbidden zone. She was relieved when the labor and birthing process was over. She didn't hold a grudge but forgave me for all the travail I had put her through. Forgetting the pain that had been intense only moments before when the local country doctor placed me on her abdomen before cutting the umbilical cord. She vowed to never have sex again after that, but she wasn't true to her promise.

One-by-one family and visitors marched back into the room and gave their reserved congratulations. Momma knew they all suspected I belonged to Merl Judas. Momma said she was infatuated with Merl when she give birth to me. No way would she have broken Lilly's trust. She knew who I belonged to--I wasn't Merl's. She was glad when they were gone.

Other rumors had it that I belonged to Grandfather Daniel as I had inherited a smaller version of his large irregular shaped nose. Her fifteen-year-old young girl's heart was broken. She wanted me but also wished I had never been born. She knew the feelings were the same with other family members but their reasons were different.

Anne's heart-dropsy worsened after I was born. Her children insisted she see the local doctor. He placed her on a water pill to clear the fluid around her heart. This went against everything Anne believed. A guilty Christian complex had a hold on her for two years when she told her pastor about the pills. He pressed her to throw them away and trust the Lord alone. She did and the illness put her on her deathbed within a couple of weeks.

Anne lay dying. Gathered around her bed were the daughters she loved. She spoke softly to each one of them.

Momma stood clutching me in the doorway. Anne motioned for Momma to let her hold me. Daddy's sisters passed me from one to the other around the bed. They lay me next to Grandmother Anne. I beheld her face, wrinkled with age from a hard life, as she placed her leathery hand on my head. She held me in her arms and prayed over me under a surge of excited energy. She shouted in the unknown tongue. I was terrified. Not knowing to crawl away or stay, I squalled. That was my first memory of childhood.

I continued to cry as those around me wept bitterly. But Momma wasn't crying. She scowled. I also felt a peace and an unexplainable love flowing from Anne though she grimaced when I tried to crawl over her swollen abdomen toward Momma standing at the end of the bed. Anne struggled not to lose her gentle embrace around me as I squirmed. Love and hate filled the room, emanating from those around me. I didn't fully understand what was happening. My emotions were all mixed up, sad, wonderful, peaceful. And I was afraid.

Angrily, Momma scooped me off the bed as Anne continued to loudly pray. Anne reached for me as I was being pulled out of her arms. I reached back as Momma swished me out of the room.

I heard her praying still when Momma took me outside to console my frantic bawling. Anne died praying in the Holy Ghost. Then came silence.

Mournful yowls, like the sound of wounded animals broke the hush and cascaded from inside the house. My aunts and father wept over the loss of their beloved mother while Momma mumbled profanities.

Daddy stepped onto the front porch. Grief stricken, his face wrenched he moaned, "Ora, Ma is gone." He tried to hold back his tears.

"Well," she said, unconcerned. Momma held a grudge. Anne had tried to make a truce and asked forgiveness but Momma's heart was hard against her.

I could feel the tension between my parents and the coldness in Momma toward Dad that day. Daddy was crying. Great sadness seeped over the brim of his soul as he went back inside the house.

Momma did not try to console him. She whispered under her breath when he was no longer in sight, flipping her hair back and adjusting me on her hip, "A good riddance! The old battle axe is dead!"

Indignantly, she reached into her purse on the edge of the front porch and frantically fumbled for something. She grasped a pack of ready-made smokes and a fluid lighter. She shook down the pack, drew out a white cigarette with a brown filter. She lit up a Winston and tossed the pack and lighter on the porch beside her purse. A wreath of smoke laced around our heads as she puffed and exhaled while bouncing me on her hip. I continued to cry and hold my arms tight around her neck.

Chapter Two

When Anne died, she left the home-place to Daddy and Momma. We had lived there a few weeks before her death. Momma resentfully helped testy Delena to care for Grandmother Anne those last days. When Anne was gone, Momma was happy to have the home free and clear. At her insistence, Daddy bought her many nice things to furnish the place.

Daddy worked hard in the timber, sawmills, and fields to provide for us in those early years. He purchased a television and a new '57 Chevy with a white top and blue fins for Momma. He also purchased new furniture.

He was preaching more intensely after Anne's passing, holding brush-arbor revivals in summer. Despite his religious vigor, they continued to have their squabbles, predicaments always inflamed by Merl's flirtations. But for a time it seemed they would make the marriage work.

With Anne's passing Momma was liberated, and found more time to spend with the Judas family. Our families became very close over the next two years. Daddy, ignored the signs, believed her when she insisted nothing was going on between her and Merl, and the fighting stopped.

Nine months after Anne's death, a blood vessel burst in Shawn's brain and he died two days later from the cerebral hemorrhage. After applying for his life insurance and trying to take claim to all his other assets, Delena discovered he had deceived her for over a decade. Delena's overwhelming grief was intensified, then her love for him turned to hate. Shawn was a bigamist. He had a wife and five children in Hawaii whom he had abandoned years before. She had been his whore all those years! But at least he wasn't excommunicated from the Catholic church, and a black cloaked priest had given him the last rights at the Veterans Hospital in Little Rock when he died.

Everything went to his legal family in Hawaii. However, Shawn's first wife was kind enough to give Delena the home he purchased in Loafer's Glory. Bitter, her heart broken, she felt he had betrayed her trust as badly as the rapist Newton had. He was evil. She was his fool. She'd never get over his treachery.

Getting on with her life, she secured a loan and built a new restaurant next door to her home in Loafer's Glory. She now had a way to make a living and never again returned to the migrant worker fields.

Delena's Restaurant became the center of activity for the young people from miles around. Business boomed. She made a good living catering to the young folks flipping burgers, tossing fries, selling cigarettes, pop, and ice cream. The pinball machines and Juke Box brought a hefty profit every week.

Soon, competitors' stores, restaurant owners, and resentful community members falsely accused her of serving moonshine by the dipper full out of a galvanized water bucket she chilled in the pop tank. Although these accusations were unfounded, her business suffered. She learned to accept slander and gossip as a way of life.

For one good thing said about a neighbor, ten more had something bad to say. It was impossible to stop. Most folks liked to hear the down-and-dirty enhanced stories, whether true or not. She determined no one would run her off or ruin the business.

She hunted down some of the gossip mongers and threatened them with a slander law suit. That helped for a while but then she was labeled an uppity money-grubbing Jezebel. She really gave the neighbors something to gossip about when she commenced courting Saul, a dark-haired handsome gambler, fifteen years younger.

Chapter Three

Jane came along eighteen months after I was born, the same degrading suspicions were spoken about her genetic origins. Some said she belonged to Merl, too. Jane was especially dark but she looked like pretty long-legged Lou in the face. Except for the darker features she was a Hotman. "The prettiest baby girl in the country," customers in Delena's Restaurant often told Momma.

After Jane was born, Momma clothed her in store bought satin, lace and frilly little girls dresses. She now had her baby girl and my wardrobe changed to pants and boys attire. Jane got my hand-me-down feminine wardrobe as Daddy insisted that Momma stop pretending I was a baby girl. He said I wouldn't be natural if she kept it up. So from eighteen months on, I was Momma's boy.

I was four when our family stopped into Delena's Restaurant for ice cream cones during 1959's strawberry harvest. Proud to show off my new red sneakers, jeans and tee shirt we strolled inside. Merl and Lilly were there sipping on root beer floats as we took our regular booth in the corner. First thing Momma pulled out her coin purse and poked a nickel in the Juke Box. She punched up a snappy rock 'n roll tune.

Disapproving, Daddy frowned. He didn't like that kind of music.

Smiling at Daddy, she said, "Darn! I hit the wrong one. I meant to play Johnny Horton's new one." She sighed.

Jimmy Driftwood was now internationally famous for writing the country music hit "The Battle of New Orleans," recorded by Johnny Horton.

She said, "That Jimmy sure can write a song. Pops told me Rack'n Sack is making plans to get government money. They want to build a folk center in Mountain View. Pops and a hundred of his musician friends plan to drive a caravan to Washington D.C. one day. Perform for the President at the White House in the Rose Garden. Those powerful politicians are bound to like their music, a hoot-in-Annie on Capitol Hill! Jimmy thinks that will secure the federal funds. Could be lots new jobs when vacationers come to visit these hills. I bet with Jimmy being so famous Rack 'n Sack can get it done too."

Daddy dropped his gaze, "Jimmy's songs are better than that devil's music," he mumbled.

Merl took Lilly's hand and they boogied to the center of the restaurant floor.

Momma giggled as she watched them dance. Lilly's cancan poodle skirt swirled high, showing her thighs as they danced in their stylish 1950's attire, complete with bobby socks, black and white saddle shoes, blue-jeans, and penny loafers. He flipped her over his back and her white panties flashed before she landed on her feet again. Other young couples joined them on the dance floor. Momma tapped her foot and patted the Juke Box to the beat.

Daddy sat with Jane and me and mumbled, "Baptist don't dance!"

I turned, grinning, watching the joyous young adults.

Delena double dipped the ice cream cones from a large bucket in the freezer behind the counter and motioned for Momma. They brought us the ice cream, and Momma sat down facing us on the other side of the booth.

Delena frowned disgustedly at Merl. She walked over to him as he vulgarly shook the black bottom dance. Delena, sneaked upon him. Swinging back the broom, she heaved and let it go, hitting his rump with the straw broomhead.

Merl jumped a foot off the floor, doubled his fist, and turned around. He was ready to sock her. Scowling, he looked at Delena and his fist went limp. Shamelessly smiling, he pushed back his hair.

"There won't be any of that stuff here! Now, knock it off!" she said, shaking her finger in his face. "I'm not running a whore house! Go jump in Big Creek or sit down." She glared hatefully at Lilly. "And you should be ashamed of yourself."

Merl smugly chuckled, as blushing Lilly laughed along with everyone watching them. "We won't do it again," he said. Panting, they pulled two cokes out of the cooler and sat down in the booth beside us.

Jane and I licked our strawberry ice cream cones, snickering when Momma did with Lilly and Merl. They were whispering, poking fun at Delena. Jane and I didn't know what was so funny. But it had to be funny or they wouldn't be laughing, I thought. Delena's anger always frightened me. When she glared at us I stopped laughing.

Standing beside me on the seat, Jane payed her no mind but went on bouncing to the beat of the music, imitating the other young folks still dancing.

Daddy said little. Pouting, squirming in his seat, he sighed. I knew he was angry again when Momma and Merl ignored him after he tried to join in the conversations. Lilly was eventually left out of the discussion too, and she shrugged. Daddy nodded.

Delena just shook her head and contemptuously rolled her eyes.

She made every effort to keep her mouth cinched while wiping down the tables. She sighed and glared at Jane.

Daddy told Jane to stop squirming and she sat to finish her cone.

Delena hated Merl. She had told me so. I didn't know why. I didn't really understand the courtship dance. But I loved Merl, he was like a second daddy for me. He never yelled at Momma, and he always brought Jane and me candy when he came to visit our home. He made us laugh a lot. Sometimes he tickled us in a teasing way by rubbing his stiff whisker stubs on our tender faces and bellies when he had not shaven for a day. He perpetually played games and gave Jane and me lots of playful attention. I agreed with Momma, he was a great friend.

In comparisons, Daddy, was distant, not showing much affection to any of us. He was so serious and sad most of the time. But he never spanked me or Jane. Only Momma paddled us, or slapped our faces when we misbehaved. Merl did whip April sometimes. I never wanted him to whip me.

Merl placed his hand on Momma's knee. I didn't know he shouldn't be doing that. Momma giggled and I giggled.

She smiled, gazing into his deep-blue eyes.

Daddy angrily crawled out of the booth. "Keep your filthy hands off my wife!" His veins throbbed on his neck as he got into Merl's grimacing face.

Merl told him he meant nothing by the gesture.

Hatefully glaring at Momma, Lilly's lips trembled. "Let's go, Merl, we gotta check on April and Dotty. I'm sure Fanny has other things to do this afternoon than to babysit our girls."

Merl didn't resist. Slightly intimidated he stood. "You crazy fool, get out of my face!" He shoved Daddy back.

Shaking angrily, her hands on her hips, Delena said firmly "Get out and don't ever bring your stinking hide back in my restaurant!"

Jane and I were crying as Lilly and Merl left in a huff.

Furious Momma was red faced. She cursed Daddy and Delena.

Customers uncomfortably shot out of their seats and paid their bills, leaving cash by the register, not waiting for change as Delena, Momma, and Daddy continue to argue.

Grasping a broom handle tight Delena sashayed closer to Momma who was now standing by the front door. "You ol' harlot! Enoch should never have married you! You never have given a damn about him!"

Momma grabbed Jane and me and we raced for our '57 chevy, now two years old. During our swift flee we dropped our cones on the gravel parking lot. Jane wailed harder as Momma tossed us in the back seat and screamed for Daddy to take us home. "Get your crazy butt in this car now! We are going home!"

They got into the car and slammed the doors shut. Momma was cursing every breath. Daddy floored the gas peddle, and the back tires spun a great cloud of gravel-dust into the sultry spring air. They fought the entire mile drive to the house. Raging all the while, Momma hit Daddy in the face with her fist and pulled his hair.

Daddy back handed her. Wild eyed, he spat, "Shut your mouth, Jezebel! I'm gonna finish this when we get home. You won't be wanting any of that Merl Judas stuff when I'm through with you!"

When we arrived home, Momma ran for the house, Daddy hot on her heels. Jane screamed as we watched them racing across the yard. I tried to comfort Jane through my own tears as we crawled out of the back seat and toddled inside.

I hid Jane under her bed, and crept into the backroom where they were yelling. Thinking I could stop their fighting, I stepped between. Grinning from ear to ear, I said, "You kids kiss and make up."

They stopped arguing for a moment, looked at me, then each other, and chuckled before they resumed their brawling about Merl.

Daddy shouted, "This affair can't go on!"

"I'm not going on in an affair with Merl! Your old suspicious paranoid mother and domineering sisters started this crap!"

I wasn't sure, but I thought that was where the rides and elephants were. "Let's go!" I said.

They paused. "Go where son," Momma asked.

"To the affair where the rides are," I said. They might be arguing over whether or not to go. Obviously Daddy didn't want Merl to come along or he wouldn't be cursing him.

They looked at me, bewilderment on their faces, laughing.

I scowled. "Like uncle Joe told me."

Momma chuckled. "No son, that is a *fair*. An affair is when married couples kiss some other men or women they like a lot when they aren't married to them."

I didn't understand exactly but figured the two words sounded alike and I had misunderstood. So for Momma and Daddy to kiss each other was okay but not other men and women. We definitely wouldn't be going to a fair tho.

"Your crazy Daddy is accusing me of having an affair with Merl. Have you ever seen me kiss Merl?" she asked.

"No Momma! Never!"

Daddy back handed her, screaming "Don't be bringin' the kids into this. Don't be calling me crazy in front of my children!"

Placing her hand on her cheek, Momma wept. "You bastard! I'll kill ya if you hit me again!"

Trying to shove him away, I yelled, "I'll kill ya if you hit her again!"

Daddy shamefully stormed out of the house and drove away.

Chapter Four

A week after the incident at Delena's Restaurant, Daddy held a revival meeting at the Redwood Baptist church. He had been the pastor there for a year. The crowds overflowed the church building. Elders built a brush arbor outside in the parking lot. Services continued nightly for another week.

The last evening of the revival, Momma slipped out of the arbor during the middle of the service with Jane. She left me alone in my seat. When she returned thirty minutes later with Jane, she mocked Daddy's preaching under her breath. That made me angry. I couldn't figure what Daddy was doing wrong as she whispered, contemptuously, "You are making a fool of yourself. You are no preacher!"

I thought he was doing a great job as his gestures and emotions were exaggerated in the delivery and he shouted, "Praise the Lord!" and the congregation echoed his vocalizations.

By the end of strawberry harvest the hundreds of migrant workers were preparing to move on. Many had attended the arbor meetings. Dozens came and knelt in the sawdust around the rough plank benches the night the revival was coming to a close. Momma went to the front, and knelt down by Daddy's sister Tina's husband, Roscoe. He was a big man, tall and brawny, with eyes as blue as Leve's, a handsome man but an alcoholic. He came to the altar to give his heart to the Lord for the first time ever.

Roscoe shoved Momma. She fell on her side in the sawdust. Glaring angrily but she said nothing as Roscoe jumped and ran out of the brush arbor, cursing under his breath at every step. The people around Momma stared hatefully.

I stood on the podium platform mimicking Daddy's gestures as he preached a fiery sermon. I waved my hands, shook my fist, pointed my index finger, puckered my lips in an angry scowl, and shook my head. The commotion of sour-faced folks whispering and glaring at Momma as she raised herself brushing away the sawdust that clung to her plain dark-blue skirt and taking her seat again caught my eye. I echoed him when he said,

"Praise the Lord! Repent!"
I said, "Praise the Lord! Repent!"
People began to walk out of the arbor.

Daddy stopped his preaching and made me sit by Momma. Then he resumed again to close the service. He had not seen the incident. I thought he thought it was me making them leave as I pouted back to my seat. I thought, I didn't like uncle Roscoe anymore, he hurt my Momma.

After the service Daddy told Momma to keep a watch on us kids, and not to let me on the platform again. "Do you understand son?" he asked while driving us home.

I felt shamed, because he implied I made the people leave. But Roscoe was the bad guy. He caused the scene when he shoved Momma. I reached for Jane's hand, sitting next to me in the back seat. Pouting, almost in tears, I said, "Yes, Daddy."

Jane mumbled in the dark, "Saul in trouble."

Roscoe never came back to Daddy's church. The next week he visited with Daddy at home. I was hiding behind the big Red Oak in the front yard listening.

Daddy met him in the drive. Roscoe never killed the engine in his '49 Ford pickup. He spoke through the downed drive-side window. "Enoch, you got yourself a really cheap one there, you did! Did indeed! No reflection on your character but she put her hand in my pants at the altar." He paused. "Right there in front of God and everybody!" Sadly, he nodded. "No shame! Just no shame in that girl. I got me one too, the first time. Women like them leave a trail of sorrow everywhere they plant their feet. They have no heart. No shame! Sure am glad God saw fit to give me your sister Tina. Now there's a good woman."

Red faced, Daddy kicked the truck tire and beat his fist against the truck bed. "Damn that woman!"

"Hey, watch it! I know this log truck isn't much but it's all I have!" Roscoe growled.

Trying to calm himself Daddy breathed deeply. "Sorry Roscoe, she makes me so damn mad! I should never have married her." He sighed. "But I love her."

Now why did Momma put her hand's in his pants? She didn't have to check his diaper. Grown men don't wear diapers. I ran into the house to ask her why she did this.

Squatting to my eye level in the kitchen she pushed back her long hair and firmly held my shoulders. Angrily, she asked, "Who told those lies?"

"Uncle Roscoe," I said, pointing to the driveway.

She sighed and denied all the accusations. Glancing through the window she and I watched Roscoe drive away and Daddy angrily marching for the front door. Her hand shook as she patted me on the cheek, and her voice trembled, the hint of fear in her tone. "Now you run along outside and play. It's not true."

I heard Daddy asking her about the incident as I stood eavesdropping, outside the open backdoor. She denied all.

I believed her. She said it didn't happen. Daddy was raging about affairs the entire night. Why was he being so mean to Momma? She never kissed other men. Roscoe was a trouble maker. Why was Daddy constantly yelling at her about a fair? Thinking of booths and animal shows and rides, I questioned if maybe he wasn't crazy as I drifted off to sleep.

Community accusations continued, and later that week, Daddy was informed that someone had seen Momma and Merl in the parking lot on the other side of the church, having sex while he was preaching. What was sex? Momma and Daddy got into another verbal argument over Merl.

I worshiped Momma. She was the prettiest Momma in the world and I didn't understand why everyone seemed to always be picking on her. Daddy made me angry for yelling at her. I was beginning to hate the religious folks who said bad things about Momma. Accusing her of sex. What was that? One of those games adults played; bad, or it wouldn't have everybody in such an uproar.

Chapter Five

Momma's alleged hands-in-the-pant episode became a real problem as the rumor spread throughout the small communities seemingly overnight. Momma's infidelity gossips were floating around since before they married but this incident made matters much worse on the home front. I didn't believe she was a wicked girl. I never saw her kiss other men. But the situation at the altar with Momma and Roscoe brought our family much shame, and after that Daddy was too embarrassed and angry with her to pastor.

Social standards and expectations of the religious community required that he resign the church. He had to, to save face.

He had gotten away with smoking, and a shot of moonshine now and then as a sinning Baptist. But adultery by the pastor's wife! This was the big sin. Not tolerated! He couldn't face his sheep again for shame.

Daddy protected Momma from the humiliation of going before the board of deacons over this incident. He loved her deeply despite all the problems, and wouldn't put her through that. He went before the board alone and simply told them he resigned as pastor, refusing to answer any of their questions over the episode.

After that he put us through something worse--he forced us to discontinue fellowship with Merl's family. I thought he was surely crazy for doing this. Momma said he was delusional for believing the lies. He acted nuts when he was drunk. Momma kept telling me he was insane. I was sad. April Judas was my friend, and I missed her. Was Momma right? I agreed, Daddy *was* crazy.

Burning hate seared Daddy's insides, expressed through his short temper and wrinkled brow. At the mention of Merl's name the putrid rotten stanch of jealousy over Momma's affections washed over him. Any sane person fled his presence as he began to rage. Drunk on moonshine, he talked to me about a thing called divorce. But I didn't like the sound of that.

I over heard many comments that Momma was a bad girl. I didn't think she was bad except when she cursed Daddy. The pain was more than Daddy could bear. He cried a lot when he thought no one was watching. I cried too when he told me one day we all might live in different houses.

That week he gave up the church, and got drunk as Cooter Brown on Friday night. Feeling his jolly ol' moonshine spirits he drove me to Delena's Restaurant for a hamburger. Jane and Momma stayed at home.

When we arrived, I ran inside. Daddy staggered several paces behind me. I crawled onto a swivel stool in front of the counter. Grinning, while waving a dollar bill in Delena's face I said, "Daddy, and me wanta burger! Put lots of pickles on mine."

Delena wrote down the order as Daddy wobbled through the front doors. Slamming her receipt booklet on the counter and placing hands on hips she sneered, hatefully. "Enoch, I can't serve you drunk, you'll have to wait outside. I'll send Saul out with the burgers. You really need to go home and sleep it off." Smiling, she winked at me, and fuzzed my dark short hair with her hand.

My hair had changed colors, going from dirty blond, to dark brown with a slight red cast. Daddy said it was the color of his deceased uncle Jimmy's.

Dotting across my face an inch wide band. Freckles speckled over the bridge of my nose to the high cheek bones. Momma called them angel kisses. "Stop!" I said while grinning, and Delena quit.

Daddy smiled, threw his hands in the air, and swayed out the door.

When I got back into the car, he glared over at me. Smirkingly drunken slurred speech, he said, "The whole world is a chicken shit!"

I pulled a burger out of the bag and laid it on an old *Racoon Springs* newspaper beside him. I began wolfing down the other burger and sipped on a bottle of coke. With my mouth full I struggled to speak. "What's a chicken shit?"

He chuckled. "Chad's a mean chicken poo. Your Momma's a lyin' chicken poo! Merl not! He's hog shit! Delena is bossy chicken poo!"

I swallowed the half-chewed mouthful. "I know Daddy! But what is a chicken poo!"

Laughing hysterically, he shouted out the parked car's window "Chicken poo! Chicken poo! Chicken poo! The whole damn world is a pile of shit!"

"Daddy, you're drunk! Take me home to Momma!"

Laughingly, he said, "I'm poo, and you're a little chicken poo!"

I whined, "Daddy, take me home! You're crazy!"

"You really are a chicken poo brat. You love your Momma but you hate me. Everybody hates me!" he said, bowing his head over the steering wheel.

"I love ya, Daddy!" I said with a mouthful of food while reaching across the seat and patting him on the shoulder.

He raised his head happily. "Dookie! Dookie, Son! Like you find in Jane's diaper sometimes! But it comes from the chicken butt. The whole world is a chicken shit!"

Knowing the meaning of that word, I threw my burger on the newspaper beside his, shouting, "I am not chicken dookie! You might be a drunk chicken dookie but I am not dookie! Take me home to Momma!"

He drove us to the house, laughing while I pouted. Momma was right! Daddy was crazy, I thought, especially when he was drunk.

Chapter Six

A week later on a warm Friday morning Jane and I played with our toys in living room. The place had no running water. Momma had drawn buckets of rain water from the cistern near the back porch, and placed them on the wood cookstove, making ready for our baths and to wash dishes while preparing breakfast.

They sat having coffee across from each other at the kitchen table. In only green plaid boxer shorts, with a wash pan and a mirror in front of him, Daddy sharpened his razor on a wide leather strap. Then he carefully shaved his face, as he did every morning.

Momma stood up, her cleavage showing slightly through the new nighty he bought her on their wedding anniversary. She walked toward the wood cookstove behind Daddy.

He watched her slim brown form float past him. Like a ballerina in silk lace she carried herself with poise and grace. Politely she refilled his cup before refilling hers then placed the pot back on the stove. She kissed him on top of the head as she returned to her seat.

He smiled and went back to shaving. Momma stood, staring right through him. Glancing up from the mirror and stopping to sip his coffee, he asked, "What you got on your mind, Honey?"

Shaking her head while coming out of deep thought, she replied, "I'm taking the children with me to pick canning berries." She sat, sipping the steaming hot black coffee from the thin glass cup. Looking up from the mirror again to glare suspiciously at her, he said, "There are no more berries! You're using this as an excuse to meet him."

Her tender composure and smiling face changed to anger and a scowl. "Oh crap! Here we go again!"

Finishing shaving he tossed the razor into the wash pan full of hot soapy water on the table. Splash foamy leaped over the edges of the wash bowl. Water ran off the table onto the cracked and worn linoleum floor. He wiped the remaining shaving cream off of his smooth-shaven face with a clean hand towel while keeping his mouth shut in a tight line. Then he stood up, his oak-chair falling over backward on the floor with a crash. Shaking, red faced, he shouted, "Do you not have any shame?"

She tossed her hair back off her shoulders. "I hate you! You're crazy! This marriage is never going to work. I want a divorce!"

Pounding the kitchen table, he raged, "You've got to consider the children!"

"I do a hell of a lot more for these kids than you even *think* about."

"Saul will tell me the truth! I forbid you! I don't want you around Merl. I won't sign any divorce papers!" he growled back at her, motioning for me to come to his side.

I crawled off the sofa and ran to him, bright eyed, smiling. "What, Daddy?"

He glared at me and then hatefully looked up at Momma. "Have you seen your momma kissing Merl?" he asked.

"No, Daddy! Never!" I said, and raced to kiss Momma.

"Go in the livingroom and play with Jane," she said, and pushed me away.

Momma had never pushed me away before. Something was wrong. I ran to the sofa, trying not to cry, and sat with Jane who was playing with a small red-haired doll.

Sarcastically, contemptuously, rolling her eyes, Momma mumbled,

"I don't want you around Merl," she said mocking, yelling, "Go pray to your God like your momma did. He'll tell you the truth. He'll tell you this marriage was made in hell!"

Furiously he growled " Ma was right. You don't love me. I should have killed Merl years ago!"

"I tell you, I am not bedding down with Merl! He is just my friend. Much more than I can say for you. I'm not a loose woman! I'm a lady!" she shrieked beginning to cry.

Daddy turned around, his brow wrinkled as a silent tear rolled down his cheek, he checked on Jane and me in the living room. He turned back to her. "Saul and Jane don't need to hear this. Now, shut it up before I shut it up for you," he whispered.

Momma threw her hot cup of coffee across the table at him. Daddy ducked. It shattered into several tiny pieces on the floor beside the wood cooker.

Jane crawled from the other end of the sofa and huddled close to me for protection.

Enraged, Momma ran out the back door screaming, "Ya fool to listen to the gossip mongers!"

Daddy peered out the open back door. We could see Momma racing toward the barn, cursing every breath. I could see her from my perch on the sofa through the space between Daddy's long legs in the open outside doorway.

He wiped the hot coffee off his right shoulder with the same towel he used to clean his face of shaving cream. He drew up the half bowl of chocolate gravy left over from breakfast. Playfully peering at Jane and me, he winked, wearing a sinister grin, and out the back door he ran. He hurdled off the porch taking great strides toward Momma.

She was running wildly. The closer he got the louder she cursed. Like an Olympic sprinter with his six-foot and three inches of muscled frame and long legs, he ran in only his boxer shorts to intercept her fifty feet from the house.

Giggling, Jane and I hurried to the back porch to watch. Momma always looked so funny with food in her hair that Jane and I couldn't help but laugh, yet at the same time I hated him for doing her this way. Daddy had this thing about pouring gunk on Momma's head when they fought. We knew what was coming.

I remembered dumping chocolate gravy in Jane's hair when we got into an argument over a toy after breakfast several weeks before. Momma paddled me good. She made me promise not to ever do that again. She let Jane dump gravy on my head the next day. I cried for half an hour. Daddy, shouldn't be doing this. I'd dump gravy on his head when he was asleep, or tell Momma to.

They fell to the ground in the green pasture where Betsy, our milk cow, grazed on the tender green shoots of rye grass and fescue. "You will stop seeing him! You *will* obey me, Ora," he said as they struggled in the dew-covered grass. Daddy held her penned beneath him and dumped the warm bowl of gravy on her head. He laughed hysterically as she cursed and they continued to tussle.

Betsy strolled over toward them. She stuck her snout on Momma's head, sniffed, and rolled out her long wide tongue to lick the gravy. Daddy slapped Betsy on the snout. "Git!" he shouted.

She bawled and trotted off toward the hollow with her heavy teats swaying back and forth between her hind legs. He had hurt her feelings, now. The next day's milk would be bitter. Every time she got scolded she'd hide in the hollow, gourds grew there. Maybe Daddy would give the bitter, putrid milk to the hogs. I wasn't going to drink the rotten stuff again.

Laughing and crying Momma continued to fight. She cursed him even louder as he smeared the remaining gravy through her hair, to her waist. When she stopped struggling from exhaustion, he kissed her passionately on the lips and released her. She responded by whacking him upside the head with the empty glass gravy bowl.

He kissed her again and she surrendered to his affections, wrapping her arms around him in a gentle embrace.

Momma and Daddy fought like this, often blood coming from their blows to each other. Nevertheless, their quarrels always ended the same way. With a kiss and then everything was fine for several days until the next round. Most of the time Jane and I cried. But not this time. We were happy they had made up again, and there was no blood.

Laughing shamefully, Momma, wiped the excess gravy out of her hair after they returned to the house, embracing. Daddy finished dressing for work. He pulled on his faded, sap-stained overalls. His soft cotton, discolored shirt was tattered and a dingy green-white. He slipped on his gray socks and heavy worn work boots. Momma lit a cigarette as she swept up the broken cup in the floor.

As Daddy was leaving he said, frowning, "Stay away from Merl! I meant it, Ora."

Momma smiled, nodding. "Yes, Massa Enoch," she said while bowing before him. They chuckled and she kissed him again.

Jane and I ran to him, and he pecked us on the cheek, goodbye. He raced to the dilapidated '47 pummeled green logging truck parked in the drive. The banger had no muffler. The smashed passenger-door hung in place with bailing wire.

Two weeks earlier, the truck had rolled over on its side. Daddy had missed a curve on a steep hill after he and Momma's older brother Joe had loaded logs on the back. The laden truck's left front tire slipped off the edge of the road after hitting a bump. Daddy had tried to throw it out of gear and pull the emergency, but the break failed. He threw open the door and bailed-out just as the unmanageable vehicle began to career down the mountain side through a section of new growth timber. The truck rolled backwards, struck a tree flipped over three times as it descended down the hillside into the hollow and landed on the snaking logging road from where it had just been driven. Joe had jumped out of the passenger door at the same time Daddy abandoned the cab, yelling for him to get out. The runaway truck came to a stop after landing on all four tires in the road below. The mules barely got out of the way as they were hobbled and eating their daily ration of oats below when the accident happened. Joe sprained his ankles when he exited the truck. He could hardly walk but he limped back down the steep way and helped Daddy check on the mules and truck. Daddy forced open the hood with a crowbar and checked the engine. Every thing was intact there. Though the bent driver's side door was half way up the hill leaning against a tree. He and Joe sat down inside the truck and Daddy turned the ignition. Boom, she fired up at the first turn of the key and they drove home. Daddy reload the harvested logs dumped in the process the next day with no helper other than his mules, Blaze and Mabel.

Joe, now recovered, would return to work in the woods this morning. He and Daddy teamed up together months before, since Merl kept having to take several days off work to attend to personal business, so he said. Daddy said Merl was lazy and he had to have a helper even then because Merl was not dependable anymore. Disassociating from Merl wasn't a great loss for Daddy on the job.

Daddy said he was through with ol' lazy Merl. The windows in our living room rattled when he started the motor, and drove off.

When he was gone, Momma pitched the broom onto the back porch, and mumbled under her breath, "Slim chance, you jerk."

Chapter Seven

I found my self angry a lot when Daddy made the accusations that Momma was having an affair even though I didn't know exactly what that was. It had something to do with kissing and touching. Sometimes I couldn't tell if they were play fighting or if this was for real. My life was confusing, frightening, and a little insecure. Especially, now that I understood the word divorce.

She cleaned off the table of dirty breakfast dishes and washed them in an enamel dishpan, and then dumped the dirty water out the back door. Filling the dish pan again with warm water she gave Jane and me a sponge bath while we stood on the kitchen table.

Momma checked all our parts high and low, between and in the dark places for ticks as she scrubbed us with lye soap and a rough wash rag. When we were clean, she lifted Jane and me off the table and we stood on the floor naked while she buffed us dry with a rough clean towel.

Momma heated more water and washed her long wavy hair. She vigorously scrubbed herself in the privacy of their bedroom while Jane and I ran naked through every room in the plank house. The strong, sweet smell of perfume drifted through the air after Momma gave herself a liberal spraying.

With our baths finished, her hair neatly combed and drying, she dressed Jane and me in clean, fresh-smelling line-dried clothes. After loading us into our '57 Chevy, she started the engine and cranked up the static, fuzzy sounding, a.m. radio to a rock 'n roll station. Momma began to sing, and backed out of the long drive to the main road. Our hair swirled in the warm breeze rushing through the rolled down windows. Elvis Presley singing "Hound Dog" vibrated through our bodies as we sped down the highway.

I rolling my eyes at her with disapproval, frowning. Daddy called this the Devil's music. "Where we goin' Momma?"

"To the Bonner field to pick canning berries," she said.

Momma, did, indeed, drive us to the strawberry patch, but berries were not what was on her mind. I knew no berries were left to be picked in this field. Other local families had already taken the best and cleaned the vines, bare. We were there only the week before and found no fruit then. The berry harvest was now over. Perhaps we'd go to another field. "But Momma, the berries are all gone," I said.

She parked on the road next to the patch and left the radio on. Another Elvis Presley tune, "Heartbreak Hotel," was playing. Off in the distance at the edge of the field stood a man. I thought he was Merl Judas. Smiling as she opened the door and got out of the car, she said, "You kids wait here, and behave yourselves. I won"t be long."

Momma galloped across the empty berry field, her hair bouncing with every stride as she made her way toward Merl. Waiting, his arms unfurled, and she fell into his embrace. Watching them share a long, passionate kiss, I thought, Daddy's suspicions were correct.

She was kissing another man. I had to tell Daddy. As I curiously observed, I was hit with a sudden wave of nausea. Fearful angry tears rolled down my cheeks, and I wailed hysterically. The word divorce pounded in my mind. My crying upset Jane and she howled. In my anger, I lay on the car horn.

We screamed so loud that Momma heard us from the field over the annoying blast of the horn and the blaring music coming from the radio. She and Merl ran back to the car to see what was the matter.

Aggravated, her piercing brown eyes glared at me. I knew that look very well. Would she paddle me? No! She slapped my hands off the horn switch. Realizing that neither of us was hurt, she scolded us for making such a fuss. We stopped crying.

Resentfully, I watched her hug Merl goodbye. This didn't feel right. I'm not so sure I liked Merl anymore. I didn't want him kissing Momma. Daddy wasn't crazy after all.

She got into the car to drive us back home. I kept quiet, angry, thinking it was as everyone had said, as Daddy had said. I stood up in the seat and turned to look out the back glass as we drove away. Merl was waving. Momma was smiling.

What was that word? Oh yes, I remembered, affair.

Entranced in the music as she drove, Momma flipped through the stations to find another song and lit up a cigarette.

Sick to my stomach I did not speak to her for most of the five-mile drive back to our house. But when she pulled off the main highway onto the dirt road that lead to our place, almost in tears, I said, "I'm gonna tell Daddy."

Enraged, she tossed her burning smoke out the car window saying nothing for a moment her dagger eyes cut to my soul. Elvis' "Don't Be Cruel" began to play when she tried to convince me the scene I had just observed was not what I thought it was. She explained that she and Merl were only good friends, nothing more. "You shouldn't be kissing Merl!" I said, "Not on the lips, Momma! Daddy told me so!"

"Child, don't you get smart with me! I'll slap you right now!"

"Why are you lying to me? Daddy, says only married folks kiss on the lips."

Again, in a firm voice, she denied what I had seen and demanded I say nothing. In her frustration she tuned to a different radio station. She shouted over the blare of the radio, "We're not talking about this anymore!"

I felt the overwhelming urge to vomit. Just as she was turning onto our long, gravel driveway, I cried, "Momma, stop the car, I'm gonna puke!"

She nodded, frustrated. "Let me park the car! You can wait two minutes."

But I couldn't wait. Desperate with nausea, I opened the passenger door, intending only to hang my head outside so I wouldn't mess up the car. But soon as I pulled the handle the door swung completely open and yanked me out of my seat. I found myself hanging with my head and chest suspended over the gravel roadway that whizzed by beneath me.

She screamed, panic stricken. "Saul, don't open the door! Shut the door! Oh, Baby!"

"Momma, help me!" I pleaded while struggling to hang onto the door latch and fought to keep my feet and legs inside the car. She screamed again, and let go of the steering wheel as she tried to grab me. I felt her hand touch the tail of my shirt just as my legs were dragged out of the car. But she couldn't hold me. I clung to the door handle with all my might and tried to pull my feet up under my body. But it was a futile effort.

The door swung back toward the car. Now my upper body was wedged between the moving car chassis and the half-open door. Unable to hold my legs up any longer, I let them fall. They bounced along the road bed and I watched as rocks ripped into them, tearing off the flesh. My arms grew weak. My hands slipped off the door handle and I tumbled to the ground.

I landed flat on my back with my head in a cactus bed alongside the driveway. My eyes opened just in time to see the rear tire spin over the top of my left ankle.

In her confusion and horror, Momma had hit the gas instead of the brakes. The blood, skin, and flesh flew through the air behind the back tire as it ripped away all the soft tissue while crushing bone. Road dirt and tiny pebbles were ground into the open wound.

Momma very nearly crashed into the side of the house, stopping only two feet from impact. I could hear Jane screaming in the back seat. Frightened eyes in her wrenched face, watched me through the back glass as she pulled at her dark brown hair.

Momma frantically jumped out and ran to my side, sobbing uncontrollably. "Oh, baby, I am so sorry." Her hot tears splashed into my eyes and on my face, mingling with mine. Her tears became my tears. This would not be the last time our tears mingled together.

My anger with her was gone, only empathy for her grieving heart surged through my young mind. I didn't like to see Momma cry.

She asked was I in pain. I told her I wasn't. And, indeed, I felt no pain. Only a warmth, and a sense of perfect peace all around me. My love for Momma intensified as she cried hysterically over me. I cried, wanting to comfort her.

Sobbing painfully, she bellowed in her terror and grief, "This is all my fault! God's recompense!"

The accident was not her fault, but not understanding that word recompense I ignored it. "No Momma, it is *my* fault. I opened the door," I said wanting to comfort her.

Momma loaded me into the car and wrapped my injured leg in Jane's new Easter coat, which happened to still be in the backseat. Jane had worn it to Easter Sunday church services weeks before. As I watched it being soaked with my blood, I knew she would never wear it again. Jane and Momma continued to wail.

The radio played. We shrilled and howled. Momma, shaking so badly she couldn't drive fast, made it to Mary's our nearest neighbor, a half mile away.

Chapter Eight

Mary Jones, fifteen years older than my mother, was Momma's best friend, second to Lilly, and she played the piano during church services. She had six stair-step children of her own who often came to our house to visit. Sometimes she babysat Jane and me and we stayed overnight. I had a crush on her eldest daughter Sally. All of Mary's children were at the Baptizing Hole for a cold swim this morning, leaving Mary alone at home.

Cutting the wheels too sharply, Momma, missed the turn. The Chevy jumped the ditch, sending us bouncing inside as the car came to an abrupt stop. She leaped out yelling, "Help me! Help me!" Her long hair tossed from side to side as she ran for the front door. She pounded the door. "Mary! Mary! Mary! My baby is dying!" she screamed while hot tears streamed down her cheeks.

Mary bolted wide eyed out of the house with white sticky bread dough on her hands and a half-skirt apron around her waist.

Mamma grabbed Mary's arm and they raced across the yard to the car half in the ditch.

She raised her face to the sky, anguishing, "I can't drive! Oh God, don't let my baby die!"

Wiping dough off her hands onto the apron, Mary said, "He is not going to die!" as she hoisted me out with her stocky arms and placed me in the front seat of her black '53 Plymouth. The smell of warm yeast dough drifted up into my nostrils from her hands and apron as my bloody leg swiped against her soiled covering. On any other day Mary would let me sample one of her hot fresh buttered rolls. The scent of yeast was so strong I could almost taste one. But my stomach churned and the smell repulsed me.

Smiling, she whispered, "Don't be afraid, Honey. Your momma and I are going to get you to Doc Anderson. He will stop the bleeding. God is not going let you die."

I nodded.

Momma put Jane in the back seat when Mary dashed inside the house for her car keys. Momma slithered into the front passenger seat next to me and shuffled me into her lap. She squeezed Jane's bloody Easter jacket tight around my ankle, and a red-stream flooded onto the floorboard, splashing onto Momma's white cloth tennis shoes. My blood coated her hands.

Mary sprinted out of the house, lunged into the driver's seat. We flew toward the local country hospital. Mary's eyes watered as she drove. She grimaced, holding back her tears, and quoted scripture all the way. *"And when I passed by thee, and saw thee polluted in thine own blood, I said unto thee when thou wast in thy blood, Live; yea, I said unto thee when thou wast in thy blood, Live, Ezekiel 16:6,"* she said believing the stop blood scripture.

As the car zoomed around the winding hills, I beheld a lagoon of my blood on the rubber mat beneath our feet rolling back and forth around every sharp curve. Momma's bawling saddened me to tears again.

Momma continued wailing as she held me in the front seat. Jane cried too. Momma cried harder when Jane tried to comfort us by reaching over the back of the seat to kiss us through her fright. Salty tear drops gyrated down Momma's face and permeated onto my shirt. "Don't cry Momma." I pleaded.

Calming some, she asked, "Oh baby, is it hurting badly?" I shook my head. "Then why are you crying?"

"Because it hurts me to see you crying so hard," I said. We both chuckled. She stroked my forehead and bellowed like a newborn calf when I began drifting off to sleep in her arms from the expenditure of blood.

Her panic screams unnerved me. I awakened and immediately fell to sleep again.

By the time we drove the six miles from Loafer's Glory to Racoon Springs, I was drunk from the loss of blood. I awoke as Momma hoisted me into her arms, and carried me inside the small hospital. Reeling and weak, I desperately tried to keep my arms around her neck when she lay me on the emergency room table. Jane and Mary remained in the waiting room. A nurse forced Momma to step out of the emergency area into the waiting room with Jane and Mary.

"Don't leave me, Momma," I whimpered.

Nervously wrenching her hands together, she cried, "I'll be right outside, Honey." They slammed the heavy wooden door in her face.

Unexpectedly, the doctor slapped a nasty smelling rag over my nose and mouth. I couldn't breathe and threw it off while fighting with the nurse's soft hands when she put it back to smother me again. I had never smelled anything so horrible in all my life. Jane's soiled diapers could not even begin to compare. The nurse penned down my arms and the doctor pressed the rag back over my face. Determined to get away I struggled. My muffled screams turned to whimpers as I tried to holler at the ancient gray-headed doctor. "I hate you! Leave me alone!" I mumbled, thinking he is going to kill me.

The middle-aged nurse with luminous red hair under her cap compassionately said, "Don't struggle, Sweety. Just try to relax. We aren't going to hurt you."

I squirmed even more to get away from her grasp and the pungent odor. Then everything slowly faded away.

I awakened, still smelling the ether, and groggy, I heard Doc Anderson's concerned voice in the distance as Momma held me in her arms. "Ms. Hotman, we stopped the bleeding, the bandages will need to be changed in a couple of days, so bring him back. His leg is broken in eleven places," he said.

Feeling safe in Momma's arms, I dozed off to sleep again.

Chapter Nine

The next thing I knew I was at home lying on the sofa. A crowd of friends and relatives gathered around me. My ankle numb, but I felt no pain except for when Momma yanked some of the cactus prickles out of my scalp with the tweezers. I whined for her to stop and she did, then kissed me on the forehead smiling, her eyes bloodshot and puffy from constant crying.

I was happy to see everyone except for Merl's mother who claimed to be the local witch. She looked like one too. Seventy-years-old with wrinkled swarthy skin, her black eyes seemed to cut right through to the soul with evil. She and Momma kept glancing at each other as though they shared a secret. I knew the secret--Merl. Daddy told me her heart was dark with wickedness and blasphemies against the Lord. She frightened me. I didn't want her around. I was afraid she and Merl would take my momma away from me.

Jane and I had heard her cursing her family many times. She only lived a quarter mile down the road from our house, and Merl was there a lot. His house was only a few hundred yards from hers. I never ventured into Bertha's yard on our many visits at Merl's home. Too many stories abounded about her being a mean witch. I was afraid of her. Had she cast the spell on me to make Momma hate us and love Merl?

I was overjoyed having most of the visitors who came expressing their concern and offering help. I wanted the Judas witch Bertha to leave. She didn't stay long, and I was glad when she left.

Retarded Rafter, now six, came with his grandmother Bertha. Rafter was Merl's baby sister Della's boy, who had him out of wedlock in Florida. She was said to be retarded too. Retarded and crazy were a lot alike. But crazy was worse, especially like when Daddy was drunk.

Della didn't come to see me that afternoon. I was glad she stayed away. She always smelled strong of sour pee. Delena said Della was nasty, nasty as could be. Being around her gave me the hee bee jee bees. I was glad she didn't come.

Rafter brought me a small dart board he found on the side of the road. I held the dirty piece of cardboard. For some reason I cherished this gift. I felt pity for Rafter though I could hardly stand to be in the same room with him because he smelled of sour pee like his momma. I thanked him with a grin. As he held my hand, he smiled. I visited with those I trusted for a few minutes before once again descended back into unconsciousness.

Evening fell and my fever rose to one-hundred-five degrees.

Chad went directly from the sawmill to chat with Doc Anderson. Since Doc Anderson told him I probably needed to see a specialist, he drove to the house, to tell my parents to make sure my fever didn't rise. If it did, they were to get me to the hospital in Little Rock immediately. He knew they didn't have any cash on hand. He was concerned I wouldn't get the care I needed. He smelled of tobacco smoke, soured wood, and sawdust.

He always smelled that way. He examined me as Momma and Daddy watched. "You best get this boy to a hospital emergency room now, or you will bury him this time tomorrow!"

Chad was right. I could have died. This would not be the last time in my life he'd take charge for my welfare.

He knew what the face of death from wounds in battle looked like. Though feared and despised for his harshness and blunt manner, his word was always respected as law by everyone in the family. Intimidated by his harsh manner, Momma resented him intently. She wasn't alone. Tenderness buried under his strident image that most never saw. But I felt it and saw his hidden weakness on many occasions. There was kindness behind his scowl.

Chad positioned me in his car while Momma gathered wet towels, ice, and packed an overnight bag, then we drove to the Baptist hospital in Little Rock, a hundred-mile trip from my home. Chad gave the hospital one hundred dollars to admit me since Momma hardly had money for a coke.

Daddy stayed behind, and made arrangements for someone to care for Jane. The next day he arrived at the hospital in our blood stained '57 Chevy. He brought Momma extra clothing and cigarettes. Daddy had to return home the same evening. He wanted to stay, but he had overextended his credit with the new car and furniture. He labored as many hours a day as possible or we could lose everything.

I awoke in the hospital to overhear them arguing about the affair, again. Momma stuck to her deceptions in denial. She informed Daddy that he was a madman for believing lies and gossip. She said she had not seen Merl in weeks other than to wave at Lilly when she drove by their house.

He wanted to believe her. He was hypnotized by his love for her.

But I knew she was a liar. I drifted off to sleep again.

The next day, I awoke to discover gnawing needles and snaking tubes stuck into my arms. Copperheads! I thought, and shivered while dazed. No, doctors' torture tools? Are needles actually red wasp stingers? Two glass bottles filled with red hung on a rack at the foot of my bed. Uncle Joe, stuck his head inside the room. Pointing to the bottles of blood, he said smiling, "Saul, that will make you strong like me. That's my blood dripping into your body." I nodded and he waved bye. Good. Now, though small, I'd be as powerful as Uncle Joe.

"Momma!" A nurse came in and told me I was in the hospital in Little Rock so the doctors could make me better. Momma had gone to get something to eat and she would be right back. Okay. I fell asleep.

When I awoke, a stocky handsome man dressed in a dark-blue pinstripe suit peering into my face, calling my name.

"Saul, can you wake up and talk to me?" he asked tickling me tenderly in the ribs.

I stared into his large brown eyes. Mamma was with him. This doctor had ruddy cheeks from being in the sun. His short dark brown hair was highlighted with sparkles of gray in his long side burns. He combed it neatly back. I liked his big pearly white teeth when he smiled. He made me feel safe when he cheerfully spoke about the up-coming surgery and the reasons for all the tubes and bottles attached to my arms. He calmed our fears. His breath was like mint candy and he wore a lite and spicy man's cologne. I never knew a man could smell as sweet as a woman but in a strong way.

He ruffled the hair on my head and tapped me on the chin with his right index finger. "You're a courageous, bright boy. I'm going to have my wife come visit you after surgery," he said. We smiled at each other.

"She will probably bring you something special for your bravery," he said.

Thrilled, I asked, "A new set of toy soldiers?"

"Is that what you want?"

I nodded.

Momma kissed me on the forehead and they left the room. I fell asleep dreaming the promise of new toys.

I awakened in the operating room. My arms and legs were strapped to the table and my head was restrained. The needles and tubes were still in my arms, and Momma was there at my side. The doctor, now dressed in surgical green scrubs, leaned over and told me that I had a staph infection in my left ankle. He said they were going to do everything they could to save it, but if they couldn't, they may have to amputate and give me an artificial leg. The infection was spreading rapidly.

I peered up at him. "Save it," I said. Everyone in surgery chuckled, including me. By now I felt as though Doctor Nix and I were buddies.

Smiling, he said, "We'll do our best." Then I heard him tell Momma that because of my age and weakened state, they could not give me enough anaesthesia to put me completely out. He said he wouldn't even start the anaesthesia unless I began to feel a lot of pain. He turned back to me. "You are going to have to be very brave," he said. I nodded, and the nurse tied the surgical mask over his face.

I could feel vibrations as the knife scraped against my broken leg bone, but remarkably, no pain. (The nerves were probably damaged, or I was in shock, or perhaps the Lord helped me?) I never knew for certain why I felt no pain.

When he finished cleaning the wounded area, he leaned over me again. "Well, you're one brave little man," he said. "We've got the first part done. But we aren't finished yet." He then explained that they were going to take skin from my right thigh and graft to the exposed bone on my ankle. The doctor asked if I was ready. I nodded.

I felt the first incision, excruciating pain as his scalpel cut into the skin of my thigh. I grunted once and then no more pain. All I felt was the perfect peace I had experienced when the accident occurred. Momma was crying silently. Heavy crystal-colored tears streamed down her face again as she held my hand and stroked my arm strapped to the operating table. I smiled at her and she wiped away her tears. "Don't cry, Momma," I said.

She kissed me on the forehead and smiled through her sorrow. Warmth and peace blanketed me, and I simply fell asleep.

I awakened in my room after the surgery to find Momma and Daddy smoking cigarettes and arguing again over Merl. Momma had on her pretty baby-blue party dress. She looked like she stepped out of a band box, resembling pictures I had seen of famous female country music singers in magazines. Momma reached over and turned on the radio beside my bed. The sound of soft country music filled the room.

Angrily, she cursed Daddy and told him to leave.

Raging, cursing Merl, he crushed the fire off the cigarette butt into the ashtray beside my bed. He stormed out of the room. "Go to hell with Merl," he yelled. He never returned to the hospital until the day I went home.

A few minutes later Merl came in. He must have been hiding, waiting for Daddy to leave. They shut the door. I pretended to be asleep. They embraced and kissed passionately. Sharing a cigarette together they talked about how much they loved one another and Momma's plans to divorce Daddy. They finished the cigarette and crushed the butt into the ashtray. Grief overpowered me.

I couldn't take anymore, and once again I began to scream.

"Son, it's gonna to be okay," she said, racing with Merl to my bedside and then stroking my head. Momma cried with me. But we were crying for different reasons.

At first Merl glared down, then his expression changed and he kindly patting me on the chest, grinning, "Your one tough soldier, Son," Merl said.

"I'm not your son! Don't call me that! Don't touch me!" I shouted as I picked up his large hand and tossed it off my chest.

He scowled and took a seat on the other side of the room.

Momma frowned. "Don't be rude to Merl!" she growled as I turned my face to the wall, crying hysterically again.

I wanted him to leave. But he didn't. When my squalling didn't run him off, I simply stopped crying and told them I wanted to go back to sleep. I decided then that I could never trust Momma again. One day she would leave Daddy, Jane, and me for Merl. They stepped outside and when they were gone, I really did cry because of a broken heart.

189

The antics of my poor, uneducated, dysfunctional family did not go unnoticed by hospital personnel. Momma left me alone for hours and was off somewhere in town with Merl as the days rolled by. Merl came to visit her at least twice a week. Many times they kissed and flirted in front of the nurses. Some of the staff rolled their eyes, knowing he was my mother's lover and not my daddy.

The days turned into weeks and Daddy never came to see me. I missed Jane and I wanted to go home. I wanted my father. I was in the hospital for over a month.

Some of the hospital staff thought Merl *was* my father.

"Your Momma and Daddy really love you a lot. Your daddy looks like Elvis Presley," some said.

"He's *not* my daddy! He's our chicken-thief neighbor, Merl!" I yelled. Some of the nurses didn't know how to react so they said nothing and left the room. Others apologized quickly. Some got watery eyes.

Two days after surgery Doctor Nix's wife Tina did come visit me. She was a high-class woman about thirty years old. Diminutive and fat with frosted blond hair in a page boy cut with bangs, she dressed in the finest of fashion and wore a large diamond, a ruby, and other rings with precious stones, one on every finger. I never once saw a run in her nylons. Her makeup was not over done and her high-dollar high heels made her wiggle when she walked two inches taller. She brought candy and toy soldiers and little cars small enough for me to play with while being confined to the bed. I liked her at first but when she started asking me about coming to live with her and the doctor after the first week she made me mad.

I was losing my momma and this lady wanted to take her place before she was gone. It hurt too badly to think about. She tried to read to me but I got board with that. I told her to take her books home and make up a story. To me that would be more fun and I could help her if she got stuck. She didn't read to me anymore.

Scowling, I said, "Mrs. Doctor, I already have a momma! I won't leave her. We'll all come live with you," I said, thinking about all the nice toys she had brought to me.

She laughed loudly, and my anger quickly fled while she continued to try and develop a trusting relationship between us. Mrs. Nix visited most every day. She consistently brought me new toys. I gladly accepted the gifts. We made up many make-believe stories. I incorporated my toy soldiers and cars and they played out the scenes on my pillow.

I enjoyed the company while Momma was away somewhere in town with Merl.

Mrs. Nix never did win my heart as the son she wanted. Even with all her kindness, rewards, wealth, and polish my heart belonged to Momma. Nothing she did could have redirected my loyalties from Momma to her. Dr. Nix and his wife had wanted to adopt me.

Doctor Nix realized the seriousness of my degrading, deteriorating family life and the impoverished environment where I lived. He asked and pleaded with Momma to allow him to adopt me many times and on the day Daddy arrived at the hospital to take me home he asked one last time. I could hear them talking outside the door of my room.

"Your boy is special. He is a very intelligent child. He is so brave. My wife and I would like to have him as our own. I'm forty years old and we can't have children."

"I know. Maybe someday he will grow up to be a doctor or lawyer," Daddy said.

"Would you consider allowing us to adopt him?" asked Doctor Nix.

"Absolutely not! I have already given you my answer many times before," responded Momma.

"If you ever change your minds give me a call. My wife and I could give him a good life," he said with hope still in his voice.

I did not want Momma to give me away. I knew Daddy wouldn't. She might. I didn't trust her. Had she already sold me to these educated strangers?

Daddy snapped, "Is he ready to go home?"

The doctor gave them instructions for my care. Two nurses lifted me out of bed and placed me in a wheelchair. They then rolled me out of the hospital and loaded me into the front seat of the '57 Chevy. I was going home. Momma had not sold me and the Doctor wouldn't be adopting me. I determined that I had to fix my parents' marriage. Was I partly responsible for all the fighting? Was this part of Bertha's curse? But at least they didn't get rid of me in this dreadful place called a hospital.

The car smelled of death where the blood-soaked carpet had soured and Momma was unable to remove it all after the accident. Daddy got behind the wheel and shut his door. Smiling, I held his arm tightly in the front seat.

Momma stuck her head in through the passenger-window. "Jane is in Merl's car with John and Pete (mother's younger brothers). I am going to ride with them."

Grimacing, his fist pounding the steering wheel. "I'll be a coon's behind if you will! You go get Jane and let's go home."

Rolling her eyes defiantly she said, "I will ride with whom I please. I've been locked up in this hospital all this time with your son. I am tired and on an edge. I don't need this now. Go climb a tree!" She stormed across the parking lot and crawled into Merl's dark-green '53 Chevy where Jane was screaming for her.

"Well, Son, I guess that settled that," Daddy said with an embarrassed chuckle.

I hugged him. "Let's go home, Daddy."

We pulled out of the parking lot that hot afternoon in July for two-hour drive back to Loafer's Glory. Momma, Jane, and the others followed us in Merl's car.

Chapter Ten

In the months that followed, during my long recovery, my mother and father came to an uneasy truce. Momma conceived for a third time in the spring of 1959 and Daddy suspicioned she carried Merl's baby. She started to show the week I came home from the hospital.

He told her to get rid of the pregnancy. Malevolent forces were all around us. Fear and anger was concentrated in my family. Wicked phantoms seemed to be pushing Momma to have an illegal abortion. He told her about a Negro woman who lived in the back-alley slums of Little Rock. One of his older sisters had used her years ago when she got into trouble before marriage.

"She can fix this problem," he said.

"It's your baby!" Momma cried.

"Even so, we don't need it now!"

"I won't kill my baby!"

"Why not? You, pert near killed Saul! I guess it must be Merl's or you wouldn't be so intent on keeping the thing!"

Momma wept bitterly while changing the bandages on my wounded legs in the living room.

The veins in Daddy's neck throbbed, and he continued to rage.

"Kiss and make up," I whimpered in the midst of their yelling.

During the days of my recovery I felt no severe physical pain. I actually can remember very little pain. But the itching in the wounds as they healed was extremely uncomfortable. I was constantly being scolded for rolling up tissue paper and running it under the bandages to scratch the never-ceasing itches. The enduring pain was in my broken heart because of Momma's infidelities with Merl. I can only imagine the lust in her heart must have been as overpowering as the itching in my wounds.

Eventually they did kiss and make up. Momma finally persuaded Daddy that she and Merl had never had an affair. She promised to never speak to Merl or go around him unless Daddy or one of his siblings was with them.

An uneasy peace invaded the house during the remainder of my recovery and the gestation months of Momma's pregnancy. She gave birth to my brother Bobby in November of 1959. Bobby looked exactly like Daddy. My wounds and bones were completely healed shortly after his birth, But I had forgotten how to walk.

Momma eyed me one day, her determined gaze stealing my helplessness as she dragged me off the sofa and forced me to try and walk. "Saul, the doctor says you should have been walking two months ago." Momma said.

"I'm afraid, Momma."

Smiling she said, "Now son, you can do this. Momma will help ya. Oops I meant *you*." Lilly's friendship inspired Momma to try and speak properly. She had taught her to watch her tongue and get rid of some of the hick slang.

She placed my feet on the floor in front of the sofa where I had been lying. I was moaning hysterically and resisting with all my strength not to get off the couch. I hadn't walked in six months. I was afraid to put any weight on my weak left leg.

Momma yanked me off the seat and held me upright with my legs dangling to the floor. I bucked in fear that she would let go and I would crumple. Gently, she coached me to position a trifle of pressure on my feet and legs. Surprisingly I was standing all by myself. Though my legs were weak and shaking I stood. My tears turned to laughter.

Momma let go of my hands and walked three feet away from me. Squatting eye level to look me square in the face, she reach out and motioned for me to come to her.

Trembling fearfully, I asked, "Do you promise to catch me if I start to fall?"

Smiling, a tear rolled down her cheek. "Yes, Saul, Momma is right here to catch you."

I took one step toward her. Both of us laughed with joy when I took my second step and she scooted backward away from me again. Now she cried tears of joy. On the third step I fabricated a fall to let her intercept me. She did. My trust escalated.

I was glad Momma and Daddy were getting along and now I had a new baby brother to help look after. This motivated me to walk again, real fast. Within a month Jane and I were running naked through the house after our baths again and I'd walk to the barn early every morning to help Daddy milk Betsy before he went to work in the log woods. When we returned to the house, Momma, had sweet chocolate gravy, cat-head biscuits, homemade strawberry jam, eggs, and bacon waiting on the table for breakfast. We were a family again.

Chapter Eleven

After the accident, I developed an allergy to strawberries; they became the forbidden fruit. Merl and his family had not been in our lives for months, not since the day I came home from the hospital. When Merl dropped off Momma, Jane, and my young uncles that afternoon, he made himself scarce.

Merl was Momma's forbidden fruit. She didn't seek him out again for months, but I could feel her heart pine for him. I never really knew what motivated them to break off the affair. I have always suspected perhaps because of guilt or godly conviction inside Momma. I also speculated that she felt trapped in an unhappy marriage with three small children but had no skills to provide for us if she left Daddy. I never knew the true reason.

In October of 1959 Lilly gave birth to Merl's third child, Amos. I could not compel myself to tell Daddy I had seen Momma and Merl kissing. I loved both my parents. If I told, the fighting would have only gotten worse. The day Amos was born, Momma was sad. She didn't play her music or sing her songs and pick on the guitar in the evening. She hardly spoke all day and stared into the distance as if in a trance.

Daddy wanted to evangelize some in the surrounding communities and small churches but none wanted him because of the gossip about Momma's unfaithfulness, and the times he had made a public ass of himself while hopped-up on moonshine. As a result he had to this point altogether quit preaching. Folks no longer had any confidence in him as a minister of the gospel. Nevertheless, he was preparing sermons and preached again his hellfire and brimstone messages with a renewed vigor and assurance shortly after Bobby was born. His preaching engagements were limited to our home. He practiced new sermons on the attentive congregation consisting of Jane and me in the hope a door would be opened soon. He wanted to pastor. He said that was his calling.

With Momma and Daddy not fighting, life was good. I hoped he'd pastor again someday. In his renewed faith, Daddy felt he had misjudged Merl and Momma. He wanted their forgiveness. I think it was because Bobby looked just like Daddy. In a gesture of goodwill Daddy asked Merl to work with him again in the logging woods.

Merl agreed.

No doubt in my mind: Daddy's reasoning ability was getting worse because of the head injury several years before. Momma questioned everything he said and did, saying he was insane. She told me about the accident that happened to Daddy after I came home from the hospital. Now, I too, felt I could not trust Daddy's reasoning. With Momma's influence I was losing respect for Daddy. I was beginning to believe he was crazy like everyone said when he renewed the friendship with the Judas family. I told him I didn't want "Chicken Thief Merl" around us, but never explained my reasons. Both my parents scolded me for calling Merl names. I dreaded what I sensed was about to become of the situation because of Daddy's irrational decision for us to associate with Merl again. I wanted to tell him about Momma kissing Merl but dared not for fear they would divorce. My loyalties were torn between the two of them.

Daddy was crazy and I felt safe with Momma. Momma loved Merl and I felt threatened so then I felt safe with Daddy. Both of them wanted my loyalties. I dared not tell either of them my fears for losing their individual love for me. I wanted Merl to simply go away.

During the coming months Daddy's erratic behaviors worsened and he began to hallucinate frequently. This was the beginning of the soon to be end for my family unit.

On the verge of a nervous breakdown, Daddy's delusional spells frightened me. Even as a child, I knew something was wrong. Alcohol consumption worsened his problems. He frequently broke into nonsensical speech, repeating the same phrases over and over.

One day as we were driving he began to say, "No, no, howdy, howdy." His being out-of-touch only lasted for a few seconds, but I cringed in fear. Shouted from the backseat as he ran off the shoulder of the road, "Daddy! Daddy! What's wrong!"

Momma punched him in the side. "Knock it off, you crazy fool! You're scaring the children!" He snapped back to reality and swerved onto the highway again.

Terrified, Jane held tight to my arm the remainder of the trip home.

Momma compelled Daddy to sell the '57 Chevy. She said it haunted her after the accident. Daddy was now fearful of driving. He sold the car and purchased for Momma a '48 rattletrap. Using the extra money to help buy a new logging truck, he and Merl went in together on the vehicle as a business venture. This was his way of showing Momma that he trusted her once again, and an effort to redeem his friendship with Merl. Nervous Daddy trembled when he drove and as a result Merl did most of the truck driving.

When Bobby was a couple of months on, Daddy said he and Merl needed to work closer to train service. They'd get a better price for the ties. Daddy bought a track of timber near Slegiman, Missouri. Merl's clan and my parents decided we'd move to Missouri and harvest the trees. Together they rented a large house there. Momma brought all our new furniture.

Two months after the relocate, Daddy, Merl, Joe, and the others ate breakfast together as usual. The men left for work and Momma took Jane, Bobby, and me to the laundry mat. Returning home, Momma unloaded the wicker basket, putting away our clean clothes. I noticed all the Judas children's toys were missing. Lilly and her three kids were gone.

Bewildered, and missing April, I asked, "Momma where did Lilly and April go?"

Smiling she said, "Oh she probably took them out to get a coke."

I scowled. "No Momma, all their toys are gone, even April's bike."

Frowning, Momma scolded, "Saul stop making up stories. Her bike is in the back yard." Then she strolled to the door, sticking her head out, "Well, it is gone!" she happily said then turning and racing to Merl and Lilly's bedroom. She checked Lilly's closet. Her clothes were gone too. Momma glowed. Laughing joyously she fell backward onto Merl's bed. "Thank you, God," she said while wiping a tear from the corner of her eye.

Why Lilly had left us? Maybe she caught Momma and Merl kissing again? No! They didn't do that anymore! Maybe they were? If I had only told Daddy about them kissing. But I doubt any knowledge of the sort would have changed what was to be. His mental illness worsened as every day passed. Delusional indifference, and denial because of his love for Momma kept him under the cursed friendship with Merl. We were being deceived and manipulated by Momma and Merl. Daddy was weak emotionally, Momma and Merl were his crutch. Why couldn't Daddy stop their attraction, the affair, the kissing?

Lilly must have discovered the truth. Why didn't she tell Daddy? He was unpredictable in a jealous rage he might kill Merl, maybe Momma. Was Lilly right to keep the secret? I would never tell. Their kissing affair was in the past. They didn't do that anymore. Why did Lilly abandon us? Were they kissing again?

After Lilly left, Merl remained in the house to help Daddy and Joe in the timber. I continued to keep my mouth shut, hoping Momma's and Merl's kissing affair was over forever. They told Daddy that Lilly gotten homesick for her parents and returned to Florida. She would be back.

I suspected they were lying. What I didn't know was that the flames of passion between Merl and Momma had rekindled. Their desires slowly began to roar again as a destructive blaze in the lives of those who truly loved them. Their lust would not be quenched this time.

Daddy brought Blaze and Mabel to Slegiman. Mabel had labored hard for Daddy several years. Gentle as could be, she was medium tan in color with a white star on her forehead. Though she stood fifteen hands high and was massive in size compared to small children, Jane and I had no fear of her. Sometimes, we groomed and fed the mules with Daddy's help. Blaze and Mabel were part of our family.

Mabel developed a strange sickness. The country veterinarian told Daddy about the mule's seizure condition. He said she needed to be put down. Daddy didn't have the heart to kill her. Of course that decision was partly influenced by Jane's and my squalling the day he took her into the woods and was going to put a bullet in her head. To our delight he came leading her back to the house. We ran out into the yard and hugged her massive legs.

Daddy just shook is head, sadly. "Saul, I'll let her live a little longer but the vet says she is only going to get worse. You know one day I will have to put her down. I'm doing this just for you and Jane but one day you will wake up and she will be gone. It's for the best you know. I don't want her to suffer. You children are going to have to learn not to be so selfish."

"But Daddy, You can't shoot Mabel! She's part of us. She belongs here. Please don't ever shoot her," I begged.

"Son, she'll have to be put down. But for now I won't," he said.

"But you must promise!" I shouted.

He nodded,

Daddy's eyes were bloodshot from where he had been crying. When he went inside and told Momma he couldn't shoot Mabel, Jane and I heard her cursing him again.

Mabel worked hard, but sometimes, as she pulled her load of logs out of the forest she would fall to the ground on her side as though asleep. Five minutes later she'd get to her feet again and finish dragging her burden of timbers up the hill. In Missouri the condition worsened. The seizures began with episodes once a month the year before. After Lilly left, the seizures increased to three times a week.

The Blue Goose tracks ran through the property where Daddy purchased the timber. On a cold windy work day in February, 1960 Merl hitched Mabel to a load at the bottom of a hollow. As the train passed in the distance, halfway up the hill Mabel flopped motionless to the ground. Merl cursed and kick her, beat her with a whip and rocks. She couldn't move. She didn't flinch. Merl stomped over the few yards and asked Joe for gasoline. Joe said he assumed Merl wanted the gas for his chainsaw.

"Joe, I need some gas. That lazy Mabel won't move again," he said.

"Give her a few minutes and she'll be okay," Joe said and he went back to running his chainsaw.

Merl carried Joe's gas can over to Mabel. Joe had no idea what Merl was about to do. He never suspected as Daddy and he focused their attentions on cutting trees, vibrations and roar of the chainsaws' buzz blocked out the scene unfolding behind them. When Joe's oak timber fell to the ground with a shattering pound he turned around and saw black smoke rising over Mabel in the distance. The smell of burning hair and gasoline was strong. Joe shut off his saw and ran toward the sick mule, now ablaze. Yelling at Daddy to bring water from the truck bed at the top of the hill, he hastened to smother the three foot flames. Joe took off his coat and beat at the blazing hot fire as it leaped into the air off motionless Mabel's hinder parts.

"Hurry, Enoch! Gotta have water! This brut set her on fire!" Joe yelled as he continued to fight the blazes on the haunches of the burning mule.

Daddy came running in a panic, and dumped the five-gallon thermos of ice cold drinking water on Mabel. Joe continued to garrote the flames with his coat. After tossing the water Daddy lunged for Merl, hitting him in the head with the empty thermos can. Merl backed off in fear.

"You crazy devil! What is the matter with you? You've killed Mabel!" Daddy raged, at Merl. "Get out of my sight!" He shouted and shoved him back.

Merl ambled up the hill to the truck with no remorse. He opened a bottle of coke and whizzed it down in three large gulps while screaming back, defiantly, "I did you a favor. The old bawd wouldn't pull her loads anymore. She should have been put down a year ago." He chuckled.

Joe's coat was ruined by the time the fire was snuffed. Moments later Mabel awoke and struggled to her feet. As she was trained without coaching, she pulled the huge log hooked in the harness behind her up the hill to the truck.

Mabel was burned badly, the hairs gone from her hinder parts, tail, and legs. Her privates were seared with second-and third-degree burns. Merl had soaked a rag with gasoline and shoved it into an orifice, doused her with a good cup of petroleum, and set her on fire in his impatient cruelty and rage. He was determined she would pull the load on his command.

Almost in tears, Joe unhitched Mabel. He used Blaze to help hoist the log onto the truck. Mabel panted heavily, snorted, and heehawed in pain continually. Frustrated, Joe sent Merl on his way to the mill with the load of logs. He examined Mabel closely. Wrinkling his brow, he shook his head. "That damn Merl, I otter kill the bastard!" he seethed. He patted Mabel on the neck and spoke gently to try and calm her.

Daddy collapsed to his knees behind a tree, weeping, shaking, praying, and cursing. When Merl was gone with the logs, Joe trotted back down the hillside. Daddy was wailing uncontrollably.

Joe placed his hand on his shoulder. "I'm sorry, buddy. Ya, gotta get him out of your life. He'll be your ruin," Joe said.

Defeated, "I know. Gotta, find another hand to help. Ora will have a fit," Daddy said.

Frowning, Joe said, "Ya made a bad mistake puttin' his name on the truck. He's stealing ya blind. He ain't good for ya and my sister."

Pounding his fist against the tree, Daddy said, "My life, been hard all my life. He ain't no different from most others. The whole damn world is a chicken shit!" Daddy said.

"I'm goin' back to Arkansas. I'll kill the monster if I have to be around him much longer," Joe said. "You gonna have to get another mule. Mabel is done in. We gotta put her down or sell her if we can and get another. Blaze is too old to work it all."

Daddy looked up the hill at Mabel shaking and snorting. Silent tears streaming down his face. "We'll sell her or trade. Can't bring my self to put her down. Don't tell Saul and Jane! Ottar set Merl's butt on fire! I'll make the bastard get us a new team. Blaze gotta go too. Just too old. I should shoot her, but I promised the kids I wouldn't. Can't lie to my babies. But I need to put her down, " he said while trembling, lowering his face in his hands. "No! No! Howdy! Howdy! Captain, captain! I'm a navy kid captain sailor. NO! No! Howdy!" Daddy mumbled and cried uncontrollably as he began to tell Joe of the abuse suffered during his life at the hands of those he had trusted. He told of the beatings inflicted by wire as a child and showed the scars on his legs. He shared the grief in his heart, knowing Momma didn't love him. He told how he thought Merl was his friend but had broken his trust. He shared with Joe his troubles and shook while slipping in and out of fear and rage. Banging his head against the tree, he said, "They say they are innocent but I know they are liars! I know they are messing around! I just know it! NO! NO! Howdy! Captain! Captain!"

Joe yelled at him to snap out of it. Daddy took several deep breaths and they walked back up the hill when Merl arrived with the empty truck. The men loaded their tools and the mules on the logger vehicle. They returned to the house. Daddy and Joe said nothing as Merl preached to Daddy about what they must do and told Daddy to give him the money to buy another team of mules. Daddy handed Merl the money and he shut-up his bitching.

Daddy fell into a silent depression for several days, refusing to work or get out of bed. Momma harangued him. "You're a lazy, crazy jerk. You aren't much a man or husband. Merl can work circles around you. You shouldn't have been such an insufferable sissy hitting Merl in the head over ol' lazy Mabel. You and that mule are just alike. Merl should have poured gasoline on your ass and set you ablaze too. Ain't no man gonna hide in the bed and cry like a baby over an old sick mule. Get up and go make us a living!"

He refused to get out of the bed and go to work for the next week. Merl got rid of Blaze and Mabel and purchased two younger mules. Momma and Merl took charge deciding we would move to New Glarus, Wisconsin where Ely and Fanny lived, and worked. Merl and Daddy would work in the timber there. Daddy resisted and informed them he had money invested, and the timber must first be harvested in Slegiman. Merl submitted to Daddy's commands. He wouldn't have but Daddy had the bank roll, though it was small.

The men returned to work on the track of timber where Merl set Mabel ablaze. In late March tensions heightened for all the men and Momma. None of them getting along. The Blue Goose whistle screams echoed with mechanical blues sounds the irritation, frustration, and the power struggle going on between Momma, Daddy and Merl. Blue Goose's tracks were about to run out. Her days were coming to a close and so were the control issues with the adults. Daddy received word that the rail line was shutting down and Joe told Daddy that he would be leaving to return to Arkansas by the end of the month.

Joe's brow wrinkled with concern, he said, "Cover your backside, Merl is up too no good. He's gonna take ya for all ya got."

Momma told Daddy they would be moving to New Glarus with or without him come April. Merl had good reasons for wanting to leave the area. Momma knew. My father would soon discover. Merl was stealing items from the neighbors. He had traded Blaze and Mabel with the promise of cash later for the new mules, while pocketing the money Daddy gave him. The owner wanted beast of burden back, and threatened to turn Merl into the law if he didn't return the animals or pay up.

Daddy's mental state was worsening. Momma's disgust and

loathing of Daddy was now spreading toward her children. Her raging foul language revealed her heart's desire. She wanted free of her Hotmans.

Part Two
1960 to 1962
The Family Breakup, Crimes, Monsters, and Hope in the Midst of Despair

Chapter One

The trio's last day in the woods together in Slegiman a large gray timber wolf meandered in to the work camp. Though probably harmless the beast frightened the men.

Joe seized a rock the size of a softball. He threw it for all he was worth and hit the canine. The animal yelped, then flopped to the ground, dead from the blow. Daddy was amazed.

Daddy returned to Rooster Ridge with Joe over the weekend. Momma and Merl remained behind in Missouri. He boasted to folks at the old breeding ground about little Joe's bravery.

Joe, now twenty-two, remained in Arkansas to court his new girlfriend, fourteen-year-old pretty and petite Rebecca. Daddy hitchhiked alone back to Slegiman the next day.

Momma and Merl were kissing ceaselessly while Daddy was in Arkansas. That's why Lilly relinquished her marriage, and fled with the children? My insides were in knots when he returned. Was I ever glad to see him! They stopped after he arrived. Momma and Merl didn't know I had sneaked around and spied on them. But I couldn't bring myself to tell Daddy about the disgusting kisses.

The next day after breakfast, Daddy wanted to pack the furniture on the truck and return Momma's new housekeeping goods to the old homestead in Arkansas, or take it with us to Wisconsin and then return for the mules. Momma and Merl would have no part of it.

"You, crazy fool! We gotta go *now*!" Momma shouted in her usual hateful tone when speaking to Daddy.

"We need the mules to work. Don't need this ol' furniture. It won't put food on the table," Merl said.

Red faced, the veins on his neck throbbing Daddy said, "But I still owe for the furniture. We gotta take it back or take it with us."

Momma and Merl discounted Daddy's reasoning again. Daddy conceded, but he was a very unhappy man. The men loaded the mules onto the truck.

Momma tossed a few of our clothes into orange crates and set them next to the cab on the truck bed in front of the mules. Daddy, Jane, Bobby, Momma, Merl, and I all squeezed into the cab. Merl drove the big white rig

We headed for New Glarus.

Defeated, on the verge of tears, Daddy continued to harp about the new furniture my mother was throwing away and they were leaving behind. He didn't understand the rush.

Momma also insisted we leave her old rattletrap car in the front yard of the rent house. She said it wouldn't make the trip. Momma sat by Merl holding five-month-old-Bobby. Jane stood in the seat next to Daddy on the passenger side and I sat by Momma.

They both yelled at Daddy as though he were a moron. Even at five years old it didn't make sense to me to be leaving the new furniture behind. But I said nothing as I crawled into Daddy's lap to comfort him.

On April fools day 1960, we made the trek to New Glarus, Wisconsin, where Daddy and Merl had a new job skidding logs out of the National Forest near town. But this move was no silly joke for my family. We were the fools, the butt of one of life's harsh realities.

The adults around Jane and me were lost in a fiery confusing deceitful web of lies, poverty, fear, ignorance, and lust. The situation complicated by Daddy's mental illness was on the verge of an explosive eruption.

Soon crimes began happening that would affect our lives forever. Daddy should never have allowed Momma and Merl to rule over him. We rented a large farmhouse on the outskirts of the village.

In New Glarus our new landlord brought over two beds until we could afford our own. The turn-of-the-century Victorian-style house with tall white columns had four bedrooms upstairs and two downstairs. The place was owned by a dairy farmer and a herd of fifty or more milk cows roamed the fields surrounding the house. Beyond the back pasture was a dense woods and our dump for garbage.

With no heat and temperatures continuing to dip into the twenties outside the atmosphere was as cold at night as Momma's heart toward Daddy. We had no coal for the basement furnace while going without electricity for the first week. However, we did have indoor plumbing, which was new to me. I thought the people who owned the house were rich because only wealthy folks had indoor plumbing and running water in our area of Arkansas. The only commodes I had ever seen were in gas stations and hospitals.

Momma got angry with me when I was playing in the bathroom. "Stop frolicking in the water!" She swatted me on the behind. I giggled and flung sprinkles off the ends of my fingers into her face. Her demeanor changed quickly as she laughed and fuzzed my hair. Rolling her eyes, and pulling her locks back, then letting it fall to her hips again she giggled. "You silly boy. You're right, this is to be happy about." Drawing her lustrous mane under her nostrils, she sniffed, frowning. " Pue wee! Guess I need to wash this mop." She grinned. "Running water is certainly going to make life easier. Bobby's dirty diapers! My hair, your baths, clothes," she said and tickled me.

I flushed the toilet again. With a swat on the behind she forced me to quit flushing, wasting water. "Now, Saul, I told you to stop!" She strolled into the kitchen. "Come out of the bathroom now!"

I had pushed her as far as she would go. I'd best mind or I'd get it good. I ran into the empty kitchen thinking the water was wonderful and did a hand spring landing on my butt. "Ouch!"

Momma glared at me and shook her head. "Simmer down, Son. This isn't a barn!"

I smiled while jumping to my feet. "I won't do it again, Momma."

"You best not!" she said while opening the empty cabinet doors over the kitchen sink searching for something, while I sneaked into the restroom again. I was looking forward to a warm bath in the huge bear-claw-footed tub. But that had to wait until the electric was turned on. No hot water.

Momma, Daddy, Jane, and Bobby shared one of the upstairs bedrooms. Merl wanted me to stay with him down the hall. Momma had no reason not to trust him. After all, she was his lover.

Daddy resisted the idea though. He wanted to keep our family together. Momma overruled Daddy and I wound up bunking with Merl. I was the largest child and with no space for five of us in one bed, I reluctantly submitted to sleeping in Merl's.

On our first night in the house, Merl and I stripped to our under clothing and crawled between the cold bed sheets. To stay warm in the briskness I pulled the heavy handmade quilts Anne had left us over my head and snuggled close to him.

He spoke to me in gentle comforting tones and wrapped his large muscular arm over my shoulder and held my back close to his hearty chest. I had been shivering from the cold, but now I felt safe and cozy even though I didn't like Merl kissing on Momma but he sure was toasty and it felt so good having his body heat against my goose-bumped legs and arms.

A week passed. I was beginning to think that Merl wasn't such a bad guy. If my parents did separate, he might be my new dad. The second week we went through the usual routine of me shivering and Merl pulling me close with his arm draped over my chest. Then he changed. Merl broke my trust as he began to rub his rough hands on my chest and belly while speaking kindly. He patted my bottom and leg. Then suddenly his hand was in my under clothes. He was fondling me.

Horrified, I couldn't breathe. I couldn't move. I couldn't speak. What was happening? Why was he touching me there? No one had ever touched me there liked that before. That didn't feel right! Stop! Stop! Don't touch me! This was my forbidden zone.

I wanted to cry out for Daddy but had no air in my lungs to move over the vocal cords. I simply froze. Out of sheer terror I stopped breathing altogether. Then Merl placed my hand on his private parts. I blacked out from absolute panic.

The next morning I couldn't find my underpants. Naked and alone in the bed, I was sore, spots of blood were on the sheets and I felt dirty. I could only remember pieces of what had happened, but I knew something horrible had taken place. I was still trembling. Merl was mean to me last night! I didn't like him anymore! Did he touch Momma that way? No! She wouldn't let him touch her pee pee! That was why Lilly left him! He hurt her too, maybe? He did this to me because he knew I didn't want him kissing Momma! I wanted their kissing affair to stop! He hated me! That was why he did this to me! Della said he played with her pee pee. No one believed her. Why would he do that? She told and the Judas family said she was crazy. No one believed her. They wouldn't believe me either. I don't want to be labeled nuts. That's what will happen if I tell.

Should I tell Momma? No! She would only ridicule me like she did Daddy. She would call me a liar while she defended Merl. Just like the Judas family did Della. Daddy was losing his mind. Momma said he was the village idiot. Stupid or not, he would help me if he could. What could he do? Merl was stronger than Daddy these days. Daddy was smoking and not eating. He was losing weight, and if they fight Daddy was sure to lose. Maybe he didn't mean to hurt me. Was this normal? Daddy never touched my pee pee that way. Why did he put my hands on him. I didn't want to. Merl was mean. He was the son of a devil. What was that word? Oh yes, son of a bitch, or was it witch? That too!

All these thoughts ran through my mind in a few seconds. I would sleep in the room with Momma and Daddy from now on, even if I had to sleep on the cold floor or under the bed. I forced myself to move and search for my clothes. Relieved to find my pants, I fearfully sighed and quickly slipped them on. But my search for underclothing was futile. I never found my underwear, never!

After sliding my pants on nausea overpowered me as I ran to the bathroom to vomit. I cleaned myself in the cold tap water. Just then Momma walked in. She admired herself in the mirror, picking at hair framing her face and pinched her cheeks. She saw that I had vomited. Concerned, softly, she asked, "Are you queasy, Son?"

I told her I was only sick to my stomach. She thought I was coming down with a virus and tried to send me back to bed. But I refused. No way was I going into that room! I wanted to go home, to Arkansas. I wanted to get away from Merl. I was terrified of him! I thought he was the cause of all our troubles. I wanted him to go away! How do you kill a devil?

He and Daddy had left before sunup to work in the woods I dreaded the thought of Merl coming in at sundown. I spent the day quietly hanging around the house. I washed myself frequently in the restroom. I felt dirty, but couldn't seem to wash it away with soap and water. By late afternoon the bleeding stopped. The pain continued. The physical anguish could not compare to the emotional turmoil eating me up inside.

Momma finally scolded me and told me to stop playing in the water.

I looked after my younger sister the rest of the day while Momma worked to make the cold, empty house resemble a home by cleaning it and hanging some ragged curtains she found in the attic.

The only furniture was a player piano in the living room that had been there when we moved in, two beds upstairs, and a dining room table. A couple of chairs were given to us by another neighbor earlier the same week. Bobby played on a pallet of Anne's quilts. Jane napped beside him and I huddled close for warmth. I could not sleep. Momma's heart was as cold as the empty room. I blamed her but said nothing.

I didn't know what had happened to me was rape by a pedophile. In my mind he was just being mean to me. Not knowing what sex was made understanding how he hurt me difficult. The pain, fear, and shame were all there but not the understanding. The word affair concerning Merl's and Momma's relationship I only connected as kissing and that was wrong. She was to only kiss Daddy and her kissing Merl in itself was turmoil enough. Kissing and touching pee pees were not connected acts. Sex was a word I didn't understand.

That night I threw a fit at bedtime and refused to share sleeping quarters with Merl. Merl glared at me as if warning not to tell. Momma threatened to paddle me unless I did as she said.

I wanted to blurt it out, but who would believe a five-year-old child? What would I be shouting? Merl hurt me! He hurt my pee pee and bottom. Then he would deny it, calling me nuts like his sister Della. They would laugh and Momma would spank me for lying. After all, I had gotten myself into the situation by agreeing to stay with Merl days before. Merl might kill me. Maybe it was my fault? Had I made him angry? What did he do to me? I didn't understand.

Merl abused me again and did threatened to kill Momma, Daddy, Bobby, and Jane if I ever told. Lying there, night after night under those heavy handmade quilts that Anne had left us, I could feel her prayers somehow. Daddy said many times, Ma was in heaven with Jesus. "Son, you be a good boy and we will all be together in heaven someday. Ma sure loved Jesus. He helped her out of lots of troubles when I was a boy." Merl was going to kill me and I'd go to be with her. Maybe she could hear prayer since she was an angel now. Maybe angels could rescue me from Merl.

I assured myself that Grandma could see me and she would tell Jesus to come help me. Daddy told me Jesus was a help in time of trouble. My imagination and hope in a higher power sustained me though the nights of evil. Coming from a religious community, even though I was only five, I tried to believe there was an all powerful God. I had no one else to turn to.

Chapter Two

I thought Buddy could actually understand what I was saying. That week Buddy and I buried ourselves in an iglu of hay and fell asleep. I was awakened by the sound of one of the mules braying. I peaked through the crack in the loft floor to see Merl doing ugly sexual things with one of the mares. Buddy and I didn't make a sound. I lay in the hay, motionless, until Merl left.

When I knew the coast was clear Buddy and I crawled down from the loft and ran to the basement. No place was safe from his grasp. I thought, I will hide but he will find me! No living creature was safe with Merl around. Buddy and I crept to the back of the coal bin, where I hunkered down holding Buddy tight in my arms and softly cried.

Fearful for my life and the lives of my family members, I endured this netherworld on earth every night for six weeks. Relief finally came one rainy Saturday afternoon near the end of May. The men could not work in the rain. Daddy was in the barn sharpening chainsaws. He brushed down the mules and gave them each a bail of hay, a bag of oats, and fresh water to drink. When he returned to the house one hour later looking for Momma. I told him Momma and Merl had gone into the basement to clean up the coal bin and the area around the furnace. Suspiciously frowning, Daddy crept downstairs.

I heard Momma shrieking and calling Daddy bad names.

She screamed, "You crazy sneaking son of a bitch!"

Flying up the staircase, scowling Daddy stormed out of the basement, silent tears of hurt and anger gyrating down his cheeks. He mumbled, "Messing with my best friend. I am a fool! Why didn't I listen to

Ma? Intercourse!"

I thought, Momma and Merl having intercourse down there? Is that like kissing? Furiously, Daddy ran out of the house, slammed the door, and walked briskly to town.

I'm sure he would have driven away despite his fear of driving, but the only vehicle he could drive was the new logging truck he and Merl had purchased together before we left Arkansas. And Merl had the keys. But now Daddy knew about the kissing! Maybe now he would take us far away from Merl. I knew their marriage was over and we would live in different homes, just as Daddy had told me might happen the year before.

Daddy was gone for three days. He rented a motel room in town. During those three days Momma shared Merl's bed and we children were placed in a separate bedroom together. We huddled and cried ourselves to sleep every night.

We had electricity now, but no coal for heat. Though still cool at night, the adults decided warm weather was at hand and not to waste their money on coal.

Daddy returned after three days, defeated. Humbly he asked Merl to drive him, Jane, and me to South Bend, Indiana. Daddy's tall pretty blond sister Lou, her four children, and husband Martin live there. Daddy decided Martin had plenty of drywall work, and he wouldn't have a problem signing on with one of Martin's crews. He gave Merl his half of the truck. We left my six-month-old brother Bobby with Momma. We also left my Buddy.

Jane had her own secrets of terror from New Glarus when we arrived in South Bend, but I wouldn't know about her molestations for some time to come. She too fearfully kept her mouth shut! Jane was three and one half years old.

I didn't know if Jesus had heard me or not. But Buddy could, and now Buddy was gone. I would not see him, my mother, or Bobby for the next three months, though relieved to be away from Merl, I missed them already.

I thought Jesus actually seemed like the story of Santa Clause. Was he real? Daddy often said there was a narrow line between the truth and insanity concerning spiritual subjects. I didn't know what he was talking about. I wanted to believe Jesus would help me keep my family and that he did exist. Daddy called that faith and belief in Jesus, but folks said Daddy was crazy. Maybe faith was imagination, believing lies?

Momma said she believed in Jesus. Though angrily she cursed Jesus name when fighting with Daddy. Everyone around me said they
believed in Him except for Merl. They also said they believed in Santa. I knew Santa Clause wasn't real. I had my reservations about this Jesus. I thought, and hoped he surely did exist. But the professing Christians around

me certainly didn't walk the talk. They just believed in Him. I guess that made them sinner Baptist. Merl said there was no God. What did that make him?

    Stories about my grandmother Anne caused me to believe she was a holy saint, maybe an angel. But Momma hated her. I thought she hated Jesus too, though she said she didn't. Momma said He was her personal savior. She said she loved Jesus. Maybe her love for Jesus was kinda like the love-hate she felt for Daddy. Momma contradicted herself and said God was love, then she gave Him the first name Damn. She confused me. To curse Him and Daddy was love? I knew what love was. I loved Momma, Daddy, Jane, Bobby, and Buddy. I wasn't about to cuss them. Love was kind and didn't call anyone ugly names to hurt their feelings. Momma and Merl hurt everyone's feelings.

    Daddy's people cherished Anne's memory. They canonized her after she died. Though Daddy never understood her tongues and hated the antics in the Pentecostal experience he said Ma had something from God that was beyond his reasoning. Maybe the tongues were real.

    Delena said angels talked in tongues. That was the language spoken in heaven--if it existed. A few people on earth spoke that dialect, though not understanding the words that flowed out of their mouths. Delena said only a select group of two or three in any congregation understood the meanings of this babbling tongue. I certainly didn't. Daddy said devils talked in tongues too. Grandma couldn't be a devil. When we moved to South Bend I continued hoping she would help me if she were an angel now. Maybe her tongues could cast a good spell on us and fix my family.

    I had heard Pentecostals call sinner Baptist, hypocrites. Some said Momma was a sinner Baptist Pentecostal Jezebel and Daddy was the crazy preacher. Did this make them hypocrites? Was that the same as crazy? What's a hypocrite? Merl wasn't a hypocrite. He was a devil.

Chapter Three

    Lou, a tall slender blonde, with long model legs in her mid-thirties was a polished, upper-middle-class businesswoman. She wore the latest in fashion attire, high heels, and matching accessories. Diamond rings adorned her fingers, and she wore sparkly ear bobs and light makeup, bright red lipstick with the hint of rouge to match on her cheeks. Her bottled platinum-blond hair was worn in the beehive. Lou kept the books for Martin's drywall business. She had no idea what Jane and I had been through and we were not about to tell. Not even each other.

Jane was spotting blood in her panties when we arrived at Lou's house. She screamed hysterically when Lou tried to bathe and dress her. Hyper-active, high-strung Lou couldn't understand why the child made such a fuss. Lou thought the tiny bit of blood from Jane's rectum was nothing serious, that perhaps Jane had scratched herself. The bleeding stopped after a few days and she thought nothing more of the problems as Jane began to trust her when she was bathed and dressed.

In August the summer of 1960, Momma called Lou. She wanted Daddy to bring us back to her. Two and a half months had passed since the separation. She and Bobby were alone. Merl had gone to Florida to patch up his marriage with Lilly, abandoning Momma.

Against his better judgement, but driven by his love for Momma, Bobby, Jane and me, Daddy borrowed Martin's new Chevy Impala and returned us to Momma.

Few words were spoken between them as Daddy unloaded our clothes, which were packed in brown paper grocery sacks, from the trunk of the car and carried them into the big white house there in Wisconsin. He held nine-month-old Bobby for a few minutes then kissed him goodbye. Bobby had grown a lot over the past three months. So had my dog Buddy. I was overjoyed to see them both. Sadly, Daddy passed Bobby back to Momma, hugging Jane and me goodbye. "I love you kids. Now mind your Momma," he said, and drove away.

I was happy Daddy had overcome his fear of driving. Martin taught him how to finish drywall and he was making more money than ever before, but his heart was broken over Momma. My heart longed for him to stay with us as he drove out of sight, returning to Indiana.

We stayed there with Momma for one week. She had no job and food was running out. The twenty dollars Daddy had given her before he left didn't last long. So Momma borrowed money from our landlord to make the trip back to Rooster Ridge, Arkansas to see her father, Daniel. She took Buddy to a neighbor for them to keep until we returned. I cried. I had been so happy to see him, but now we were leaving him behind again and I didn't know when we would return, if ever.

Momma stacked quilts on top of the rear floorboards of her beat up '50 Ford until they were even with the backseat. Jane, Bobby, and I slept there comfortably while she drove. At one point during the trip I awoke and saw tears rolling down her cheeks. I tried to comfort her as best a five-year-old could.

The day was cloudy, and rain fell for most of the long drive.

The constant rhythmic clunk, splash, and squeaking noises of windshield wipers flapping during a heavy down pour was overpowered by the sound of Momma moaning in the front seat as she drove. Her painful sobbing awakened me. Momma's crying broke my heart. She was weeping uncontrollably while trying to hold back her groans of anguish. I crawled over the seat and sat down beside her. I patted her on the leg and looked up. "Momma, why you crying?"

She sniffled, and wiped her face with a clean white handkerchief. She sighed, and took a deep breath. "I'm okay, Saul. You wouldn't understand if I told you," she said while searching for her cigarettes on the dash. The pack had slid to the passenger side and I handed them to her. "Thank you, Son," she said as she pulled one out of the pack, lit it, and beginning to smoke, her tears subsided.

"You're welcome, Momma. Why were you crying?" I asked again.

Shaking her head, she sniffled. "Baby, adult stuff is too complicated for you to understand. Now you don't worry. Momma is fine."

I knew Momma wasn't fine. "Do you miss Daddy?"

She frowned. "No, it's over between us. But I do miss Merl. I love him!" she cried.

Sadly, I leaned my head against her side. "Are you and Daddy getting a divorce?"

She sighed. "Yes, Saul. He is crazy! I can't take it anymore."

"Daddy says you and me and Merl are chicken dookie." I snarled. "He's crazy, Momma!"

She giggled.

"I don't like Merl, Momma. He's mean to me."

She rolled her eyes like she did when Daddy said something crazy. "Oh, you silly boy! Merl loves you! Where on earth did you ever get such a thought!" She scowled. "Probably from your lunatic daddy! Merl is a good man and he says he loves me. Maybe one day he will come back to me and he will be your new daddy," she said as she began to sob again.

I couldn't tell her. I decided I would never tell her. She would tell Merl, then he would deny and call me a liar and then kill us all. No! I'd never tell her. Momma was more nuts than Daddy. I didn't want Merl to be my daddy! I couldn't understand why she wanted to be with the monster. She always vehemently defended Merl. I couldn't change her mind.

"God will work it out, Momma. Daddy says He is help in trouble," I said wanting to comfort her and myself. I stood in the seat, hugged her neck, and kissed her on the cheek.

She grimaced while patting me on the leg. "We'll be all right, now you crawl into the back and go to sleep. We'll be in Arkansas soon," she said, sniffling and wiping the tears from her eyes again.

I crawled into the back thinking maybe Momma was going to meet Merl. I wanted to go back to Indiana. I wanted Daddy! I silently cried. I wished Momma didn't love Merl. She loved Merl more than Daddy, Jane, Bobby, and me. What I thought in the hospital was going to come true. I fell asleep.

Right around the town of Springdale, Arkansas, the clunker overheated when the water pump quit. After paying for the car to be repaired, she was flat broke. Not having enough gas in our tank to drive the additional two-hundred miles to Daniel's place, Momma tried to call one of her uncles who lived in Springdale but his telephone was disconnected. So she called Chad and asked him to wire her some money. She led him to believe we would be moving back to Loafer's Glory.

Chad told her that all of my father's family had pitched in and remodeled the old homestead. They had put new sheetrock on the walls and linoleum on the floors. Chad told her they would help her raise us kids if she came back there to live. She agreed, and Chad agreed to wire her fifty dollars (a good sum in those days).

Momma picked up the money at a Western Union office in Springdale a few days later, never intending to ever return to Loafer's Glory. She loathed Daddy's siblings.

Bean harvest was going on at full tilt in the fields around Springdale at the time. We joined the locals and migrant workers there to make a little money until we received the cash from Chad. We had no place to stay, and nothing to eat. Momma said we'd sleep in the car near the fields over night, then she parked under a broad shade Oak close to the patches.

Momma got out of the car and approached the foreman as I toddled behind at her heels. He gave her a bushel basket. Smiling he bent down ruffled my hair with his large hand and asked, "Little fella, you want a basket?"

I nodded.

Momma smiled. She said, "Use your manners Saul."

Grinning, I said, "Thank you," as he handed me a basket half the size of hers.

He nodded, pointing to the rows wanting us to pick.

We strolled to the place, and set down our baskets. Momma glanced over her shoulder as she trotted back toward the car. "Saul you stay here and start picking. I'll get Jane and Bobby," she said.

"Okay Momma!" I yelled.

The next row over we met a stocky handsome woman named Ginger. About thirty, Ginger had three children. Her youngest, Nina, was ten, blond, and pleasingly plump, the next, Violet, twelve, was tall, husky with light brown hair and piercing blue eyes, and the eldest, a boy named Robert was fourteen, robust and handsome with coal black hair and dark tan skin. Jane and I tried to befriend them, but the children didn't want much to do with us.

Robert glared at us and mumbled, "Not another one!" He sighed, and scowling Violet nodded. Nina stuck her tongue out at Jane and me when we waved.

Grinning, I said, "Howdy!" When they didn't respond with a friendly greeting, I crossed my eyes, crinkled up my nose and stuck my tongue out.

Momma took one of Anne's handmade quilts out of the back seat and made Bobby a pallet in between the bean rows where we were picking. She dragged the pallet behind us as we picked our way to the end of the rows. The women talked as they worked.

Ginger had a bass voice with broad shoulders and light brown hair, cut short and curled to her shoulders. In some ways her features reminded me of our good neighbor Mary back in Loafer's Glory. Yet, there was something about her that was quite different.

Perhaps that was why Momma took to her so quickly. She looked like Mary. She seemed to be kind hearted and generous. She had brought milk for her children in an ice chest, and she gave some to Momma for Bobby's bottle. She also shared their sandwiches with us. When Ginger found out we had nowhere to stay the night, she invited us to her house.

Though I was thankful for the food and a place to sleep other than the car, the friendship that seemed to be blossoming between Momma and Ginger gave me a strange, confusing feeling. I didn't understand why Ginger kept touching Momma's hands and rubbing up against her as they squatted picking beans. They weren't interested in the bean harvest but rather happily conversed.

Momma turned her head to see if anyone was watching. I scrutinized their every move and hung onto each word they spoke. Momma seemed a bit embarrassed as she rolled her eyes and blushed while I gawked. She quickly brushed off Ginger's hand from her leg and frowned. Then she turned to me and smiled, giggling with Ginger. Something was wrong with this situation from the beginning, but I did not understand what it was.

Two days later, Momma and Ginger conspired to set Momma up to go "out" with a local, married businessman. Momma put on her prettiest baby-blue chiffon dress. She looked like an angel. She painted her lips bright red, which she had never done before. She put on thick makeup and rogue. She curled her hair, and perfumed herself with a sickening sweet cologne Ginger gave her.

I had never known Momma to be extravagant in the application of her beauty aides other than perfume. Diana's holiness background forbid the use of such things. Momma had always used a little makeup sparingly out of respect for Diana's teachings but now Momma, backsliding, a greased monkey slipping on ice. When the man arrived Momma took Jane and left with him, leaving me behind. I cried for the entire four hours she was gone.

When they returned, Jane was wearing a beautiful, new, pale pink dress and new black-patten-leather slippers. Momma stood in the yard and kissed the man goodbye. Her suitor, a short stocky man with thinning light brown hair, fifty and a pot belly and thick black-rimed glasses, was ugly. I wanted to run out in the yard and hit him when Momma let him feel her up and he slurped, suckey face with his lips pooched forward like a huge carp's mouth. My guts rumbled with anger. Another affair? I didn't want her to kiss anyone but Daddy. I ran for the restroom to vomit.

That same evening I overheard Momma and Ginger talking in their bedroom while I eavesdropped outside the closed door. Momma had gotten money from this man for her time with him. The man wanted another date, and Momma decided to oblige him.

I burst into the bedroom crying and begging her not to do this. She scolded me for crashing into the room without knocking first, then she tried to tell me I had misunderstood.

I remembered Daddy telling me women who get paid for their time with men are Jezebels. She was lying! The money lay in a neat stack on the bed in front of them. She said it was the money Chad had sent. I knew better. I had overheard. Oddly enough, she did not see him again.

By the end of the week Momma finally received the money Chad had sent us. I went with her to the Western Union office. When she got back into the car I asked, "Momma, did Chad send you more money?"

She sheepishly, stuttered, "Ah, yes, he said the fifty wasn't enough."
I believed her.

On a hot sultry Sunday afternoon she told Ginger that we were leaving, so the two women decided we'd drive to the lake before we had to go.

When we arrived Robert and his sisters unloaded the picnic baskets from the trunk of Ginger's black '56 chevy and they spread a quilt on the shaded beach a few feet from the water's edge near a large white oak.

Ginger and Momma strolled toward the pier's edge out into the deep part of the lake, where the waves splashed against the support beams underneath. Ginger kept trying to hold Momma's hand but she resisted.

Suspicious of this woman, I followed close behind. Ginger began to cry and tell Momma that she was in love with her and could not live without her. Momma was gentle but firm in her refusal as she explained she had to leave. Ginger began to cry hysterically, reaching to touch Momma as she continually pulled away.

"Ora, Honey, we can have a good life together. We can help each other raise our kids and we won't have to worry about some sorry man breaking our hearts. Please stay! Please!" Ginger begged.

Momma held back the tears. "Ginger, I thank you for all the help and your offer is tempting but we have to go." Momma motioned for me to go back to the picnic quilt.

I wasn't about to leave. I didn't like Ginger and had to make sure Momma would go and if she didn't I planned to push Ginger in the lake.

Watery eyed, Momma said, "I'm the wife of a minister. What I have done is wrong. I have ruined my life and probably the lives of my children. Now I am pregnant by a man who is not my husband. I love Merl, but he left me and went back to his own wife and children. I have to go to my daddy's. Gotta decide what to do with my life. But don't worry, Ginger, we will always be friends."

Ginger continued to sob, begging Momma to stay. When she saw that Momma was resolute in her decision, Ginger finally agreed to take us back to the house.

As Momma packed our things, she noticed a cigarette had burned a hole in her pretty baby-blue dress. She glanced at me, shamefully frowning as if to say I will never do this again. She nodded, grimaced, and then took the dress and threw it into the trash. She fell to her knees in front of me and wrapped her arms tight around my chest. "I love you Saul," she said and kissed me on the cheek.

I smiled. "I love you too Momma!" I said, relieved that Momma wasn't going to play the Jezebel again. Though I wasn't sure exactly what was a Jezebel. But lots of folks called her that, and I knew it had something to do with kissing men other than my daddy. What was that word? Oh yes, affair.

Daddy told me women who get paid for their time with men are criminals. So I knew what Momma did was against the law. I knew it and so did she. Nevertheless, she justified her actions as an act of desperation to take care of us. Even so, the fruits of sin fell all around her, for she had indeed shamed herself in the eyes of many and ruined any future of a life with my father again. It didn't matter. She never loved Daddy. He was just her way out.

He bought her for fifty dollars and she resented that. She never truly loved him and she was glad to be free of him. I loved them both and wanted them together.

Ginger and her children left the house after we returned from the lake. She said she could not bear to see us go. We loaded up our things and went to Daniel's home in Rooster Ridge.

Chapter Four

Despite her promise to Chad, Momma never did return to Loafer's Glory to live. She had made her choices. Now, she would live with them.

Daniel never sold his place in Rooster Ridge. After he and Gert married they rented a home near Timbo. Returning to Rooster Ridge two and three times a year they stayed at the old home place to visit friends in the neighborhood, and during strawberry harvest. When we arrived they were preparing to travel for the cotton harvest around Grubbs.

Joe married his fourteen-year-old sweetheart two months after he returned to Arkansas from Slegiman. They built a one-room shack down the road from Daniel's homestead. I could hardly wait to see Uncle Joe and meet my new aunt.

We stayed at Daniel's house for about two weeks. Daniel was sick with a rotten chronic cough, and his strong bad breath smelled of rancid meat. His lungs were infected. Gert was worried. She thought the affliction might be contagious, possibly Tuberculosis.

A grouch, Daniel glared at me over meals as I stared at him. The loud annoying slurping noise as he sucked the coffee off the edge of the saucer while holding it to his face was grating on my nerves. His black-dagger eyes frightened me as he scowled every time I ate.

Jane's and my loud playful laughter and running through the house put Daniel on edge. He said nothing about wanting us to leave but Momma took Jane, Bobby, and me to Joe's house after Gert asked her to get us away from Daniel. Gert was genuinely concerned for our health as well as Daniel's.

Joe and Rebecca now married less than three months. Joe had no schooling. He could not even print his name, but knew how to deal with people, lots of common sense.

Rebecca was naturally beautiful, rosy cheeks, tall and slim with long golden-brown wavy hair to her hips. Her spirit was angelic as she showered us with smiles and kindness. Unfortunately, Rebecca's incurable ear infections left her fatigued and dizzy most of the time. She couldn't keep up with Jane and me as we were inquisitive, getting into cupboards and boxes of personal items, pictures and their important papers. We wore her out.

I was special to scrawny, laughing, smiling Joe. Partly because he had donated blood after the accident, and I was his *first* nephew. To Joe that made me more like a son as his own blood now flowed in my veins.

Momma was gone six days. We didn't know where she was. With the cotton harvest coming on Joe and Rebecca were planning to move to Denton Island. They'd work the fields of white while stooping over from sun up to dusk. Laden with heavy cotton sacks strapped on their backs, two feet wide by eight and twelve feet long, packed with the days pickings they would drag the harvest out of the fields. Two full sacks, three, and maybe four for the day, then on to the weight scales. That was the days pay. The money saved by Thanksgiving would keep them through winter. Three children were too much for Rebecca to handle during harvest. They couldn't afford to keep us. She called Chad to have Daddy come and get us.

Two days later Daddy pulled into the yard in a brand new '61 Pontiac Bonneville. It shone like a polished black agate in the autumn sunshine. He had bought it the week before. Jealous Joe's eyes gleamed with envy as he strolled outside and saw the new car. Sarcastically, Joe said, "Ya must have found a South Bend goldmine."

Daddy said, "Nope, wages are better but I still work my tail off."

Momma had arrived the night before. She was inside packing our clothes in the same brown grocery bags that Daddy had when we left South Bend. When she finished, Daddy and Joe strolled indoors.

Rebecca insisted that she and Joe purchase bologna and bread for sandwiches. As their beater Studebaker truck rolled away heading for the local country store it left behind a cloud of dust and oil smoke.

Momma and Daddy alternated between calm discussion and raging arguments. He placed me on his lap. She pulled Jane onto her lap and they sat on the edge of the bed where Bobby was lying with his bottle. They both cried and discussed getting back together.

"Ora, I forgive you. I don't want our home busted up. Please come with us to Indiana. We'll start all over. I love you. I can't live without you," he said. Then he reached for her hand.

She scowled and jerked back. "Don't touch me! Enoch, I'd give anything if that were possible. But too many harsh words and lies have flowed under this bridge. To forgive and forget all is only a fantasy. The truth is I simply don't love you anymore. I haven't for a long time. Don't guess I ever did. I've always loved Merl!"

Daddy sobbed. "Honey, please don't. You'll regret this decision many years from now. Please, reconsider." He cried uncontrollably while placing his hands over his face.

I put my arm around his shoulder. "Don't cry Daddy, I love you."
Momma scolded, "Hush! Act like a man!"
Daddy flew into a rage, red faced he shouted profanities about Merl.
Desperate to put an end to their quarrels. I sighed. Smiling, I took Daddy's and Momma's hands putting them together on my lap. "You kids stop fighting," I said. "Kiss and make up."
Cooled the heat of emotions for the moment, but soon they went back to fighting. There was no reasoning with Momma. She was resolute. Defeated Daddy gave up as usual. Silently he hoisted Jane and me onto his hips, and carried us out.
We held the sacks containing our few clothes. Once in the car, Momma tearfully hugged Jane and me, then she raced for the shanty. Jane and I watched her sobbing bitterly as she stood at the door of the shack observing us pull out of the drive. We continued waving goodbye through the rear window until the new automobile drove us out of sight. Once again we had left Momma and Bobby behind. We would now stay with Daddy's cousin, Hatty, and her family in Landis, Arkansas.
Merl returned to Momma that day. He was waiting for her at Daniel's. Though they despised him. Daniel loved Momma. Gert said Momma was foolish if not stupid. They tolerated his presence only for Momma's sake. The afternoon we left, Momma took Bobby to an elderly babysitter's house down the road from Joe's and Rebecca's place. She asked her to keep him for a couple of hours while she grocery shopped. She never returned. She abandoned Bobby and went to Florida to start a new life with Merl and his son, Rambo, whom she now carried in her womb.
The elderly sitter called Daddy's sister, Sonny, after two weeks with no sign of Momma. Pretty Sonny, took Bobby to raise along with her own three children as if he were one of hers.
We drove past the Red Wood Baptist church. Daddy shamefully held his head down. Jane played with her red-haired doll as I crawled over the seat and stood beside him. "Don't cry, Daddy. God will send an angel someday and fix our family," I said as I kissed him on the cheek.
He chuckled and put his arm around me. "You're the only angel I need," he said. "Your momma used to look like an angel in the blue dress I bought her."
"I know! But she kissed a man in Springdale and burned a whole in it with a cigarette. Momma threw her pretty party dress away when left there." I slid down and sat next to him, laying my head against his side.
Daddy winced. Neither of us spoke again for the remainder of the trip, both knowing we would never again be a family.

Chapter Five

When Daddy left us with his cousin Hatty, he and my mother's cousin Eddie, drove to southeast Texas to work in the logging woods. Eddie at twenty-two was a devoted Pentecostal Jesus Name Holiness believer, though he did sneak around and dip the snuff and take a chaw of tobacco every now and then. Being wiry made him and his short fat wife Lawanda seem unmatched.

Lawanda was eighteen and domineering, vulgar mouthed, and had a voracious appetite for sweets and coke. She wore round green ear bobs, cheap costume jewelry, and bright red lipstick. Her glistening coal black wavy hair parted in the middle hung to her shoulders. Sometimes she made the trip to Texas with Daddy and Eddie. She was a Baptist, and enjoyed being argumentative with Eddie over church doctrine, especially the clothesline religion, and the topic of once saved always saved by grace. Hatty smirked at her antics with Eddie when they dropped by with Daddy to see Jane and me in between trips.

The first day at Hatty's, she told Jane and me nursery rhymes, and I imagined Eddie and Lawanda when she shared the story about Jack Sprat and his fat wife.

Hatty understood our situation. She was raised in the Masonic Home Orphanage in Batesville before she returned to Loafer's Glory when she was eighteen and married her husband Derk. She knew firsthand what we were experiencing....Hatty at thirty-five was a large-boned handsome woman. She spoke with slurred speech caused from a stroke years earlier. Her motor skills were not impaired other than just being slow. Intelligent, cheerful, kind, and extremely demonstrative with her five stair-step children, she was no less attentive, and loving with Jane and me.

Derk reminded me of grandfather Daniel. They had the same build and colorings, but completely different personalities. His booming bass gravelly voice coming out of his small dark form just didn't seem to fit. He smiled a lot, never giving himself over to anger or fits of rage. He had a father's heart for Jane and me.

Jane was bleeding again and needed medical treatment. Hatty became quite concerned and told Daddy about the problem on several occasions. Daddy's alcoholism worsened as he drank on a daily basis, and Jane never got the treatment she needed.

The men were gone two weeks and sometimes a month at a time before they returned to Landis. Eddie's home was in Rooster Ridge where Daddy bought moonshine after dropping him off. The hooch being more important he drove directly to Rooster Ridge to buy bootleg whiskey. Then he'd return to our old home place in Loafer's Glory for another drunken weekend by himself. After two days rest from their jobs, they drove back to Texas.

Daddy's depression deepened as he continued to drink. His episodes of erratic behavior and nonsensical speech came and went during the coming months. When Daddy came home he often wouldn't put forth the effort or time to see us, only checking in with Hatty after we were asleep. Stopping by for a few minutes to visit Jane and me on occasion before returning to Texas, and usually tipsy. He stayed drunk a lot during the first year after the separation.

We spent late summer and autumn through Thanksgiving with cousin Hatty, her husband Derk, and their five children. Derk's and Hatty's children were older than Jane and me, but they helped us feel we belonged with them. What was theirs was ours. Hatty insisted they share. Nevertheless, she didn't have to be forceful as they were gracious, good-hearted people. This family lived the Golden Rule: Do unto others as you would have them do unto you. Her version of the rule wasn't like Fanny's.

Momma said her cousin Fanny reminded her of a turkey-chicken. She wasn't able to determine what her bred, or her attitudes. Fake Fanny said one thing but did another. Momma didn't trust her. She hated herself for listening to Fanny's advice and marrying Daddy. Fanny was selfish, and had never paid Pops for her help with Agnus before she and Daddy married. Fanny's version of the Golden Rule was a joke. But Hatty's wasn't. Momma loved Hatty and so did Daddy, and Jane. Fanny was a different subject.

I had heard about Fanny and her split personality but could not recall ever meeting her since Momma stayed her distance after I was born. Hatty's Golden Rule was genuine. I was as confused about this Fanny as I was the separation. Though Momma did love Fanny she had no respect for her. I had no desire to come in contact with this woman Fanny. I was glad Hatty's Golden Rule wasn't fake. Whatever that was.

I was a year younger than Hatty's youngest son, John. He too lived by the Golden Rule, being considerate of Jane's and my feelings. He and I played daily with their Red Bone and Blue Tick 'coon hounds. Derk liked to run his dogs almost every night.

Hatty served roasted racoon the next evening after he'd bring home a kill. My taste buds were never given the opportunity to savor 'coon as my imagination ran wild, and the cooked beast resembled a skinned cat–just couldn't stomach the sight. Beans and cornbread were the trusty staple at every meal. From those bowls was where I found my portion.

When John, six and a little bigger than me, got off the school bus we played in dog houses. The four hounds loved the attention. John laughed a plenty and we wrestled having great fun with the pooches. Covered in canine slobber from head to toe and sometimes dog feces on our shoes when Hatty called us to dinner--not to mention the Arkansas Spotted Dog Ticks that embed themselves into our belly buttons, head, legs, and arm pits. Hatty cleaned us up and checked our bodies for ticks before we could eat. That was the rule.

I detested being given a sponge bath every day. Hatty heated an enameled dishpan full of cistern water on the potbelly stove in the living room. Water was hot when we came in from playing outside. After she bathed us we slipped on clean clothes and sat down to eat. We took turns asking the blessing.

The older ones tried to buck up against Hatty's rules sometimes. She'd say, scowling, "I'll tell your Pa!" That was the end of that.... The love and respect for others displayed in the character of this poor Arkansas family was a blessing. They had something that all the money in the world cannot buy: A family, love, and security. I wanted to live with them forever..

But before Christmas, Hatty and Derk took us to Sonny because they did not have the extra money for Jane and me during the holidays. They didn't want us to feel left out. We wouldn't see Daddy again until after Christmas.

Sonny and her husband Dan were poor, but they shared what little they had with us. Dan, a short handsome man, combed back his light brown hair like Elvis Presley. He was friendly sort, but a lady's man. His gambling and fooling around with other women caused family problems. But they kept their arguments confined to the privacy of their bedroom while trying never to expose us children to their marital disagreements.

Christmas came and went. Sonny said that Santa left me a small red race car, and Jane a set of paper dolls. I knew she had put them under the tree, but Jane believed her. The gifts were slim for all in the house. Snow fell heavily leaving a foot after Christmas. We made snow men. Sonny prepared hot coco and a large dishpan of snow-cream every day until the snow began to melt the next week.

After New Year, I began to cough. It wasn't horribly bad at first, but changing weather, and lack of food and rest made me sick with fever, and the cough became chronic. Had I caught Daniel's coughing disease? Gert had told me his condition might be contagious. I wanted no more hospitals. I was afraid Sonny would take me to the doctor or tell Daddy if he ever came back to us. I did my best to suppress my coughing and tried not to complain when I felt bad. But Sonny knew I was getting sick.

When Daddy returned from Texas in mid-February, Aunt Sonny

told him to take me to a doctor. I trembled at the thought of another hospital. But she quickly changed the subject to Bobby and I was relieved. She had bonded to Bobby, and he to her. Motivated by a mother's love, she asked Daddy to let her keep him.

Daddy worried letting Bobby go, but he couldn't drag a one-year-old around the country as he sought work. He already had his hands full with Jane and me. He didn't wish to return to South Bend and drywall finishing. Liking the out of doors he chose working in timber again. He'd take Jane and me with him when he returned. That way he wouldn't have to make so many trips. Daddy reasoned this would be best for Bobby until we were settled again.

Sonny said there was something wrong with a woman who throws away her children. It wasn't natural! Dan felt he couldn't afford to raise another child, but he reluctantly accepted Bobby because Sonny intently coveted him. Jane and I returned with Daddy to Texas. Once again we left Bobby behind.

Had Momma thrown us away? No! She left us to Daddy. I didn't know she had abandoned Bobby.

We moved to the swamplands outside of Spurger, near the Neches River. Total population was 120 people--and as many cats and hound dogs. Daddy worked in the swamp forest close to the river cutting trees for the nearby paper mill. Eddie and an old man named Mr. Roberts, who attended the same small Pentecostal church, Eddie attended in Spurger, also worked with Daddy. Mr. Roberts, a scruff skinny whiskered man, was a hard laborer.

They loaded the short logs on Mr. Robert's flatbed truck and drove them twelve miles to the paper mill. Dad, Jane, and I lived with Mr. Roberts and his tenderhearted wife, who reminded me of Gert, my step-grandmother. Dad paid them room and board. Mrs. Roberts cared for Jane and me during the day while the men worked.

This turned out to be a worrisome time for Daddy. The swamp environment was not for the fainthearted. In dangerous working conditions, the men waded up to their knees in swamp water during the rainy season, crossing low places in the pine forest and scrub oaks to fell twenty to thirty foot tall trees into the muck.

The dry season wasn't so bad. Though mosquitos were a constant nuisance. The men also had to be watchful of cottonmouth snakes, timber rattlers, and copperheads. They were told to look out for alligators as well, but they never happened on one. Aggressive wild hogs occupied the forest and kept the men on continual watch. The hogs were crossbred between native Red Razorbacks and escaped domestic pigs from local farms. They were large like the domestic animals and mean like the Razorbacks. Some purebred smaller Red Razorbacks still foraging in the woods. The men's worst fear was getting tangled up with a herd of wild pigs or a sow with a litter of piglets. Some of the larger boars had tusks, four inches long, and they were razor sharp, true to their name.

One sunny warm afternoon in mid-March, Eddie finished working for the day and was heading back to his truck when he heard a rustling in the undergrowth alongside the muddy logging road behind him. He stopped, thinking maybe my father was trying to play a prank on him. He set down his chainsaw and threw a broken tree limb into the moving bushes. A shrieking squeal rang out. He had hit a wild Razorback boar!

Eddie flat-footed it as hard as he could back to his pickup. The hog was less than ten feet from him by the time he jumped into the back of the truck. That was as fast as he had ever run in his entire life. He was safe in the back of the truck, but the hog wouldn't leave.

Eddie yelled and waved his arms to try and frighten it, but this only aggravated the pig even more. Finally, Eddie decided to take a different approach and lie down motionless in the truck box. After a few minutes the hog finally ran back into the undergrowth.

Daddy and Mr. Roberts finished for the day and strode out of the forest to find Eddie's chainsaw lying on the road ahead of them. They carried it back to the truck where Eddie had shut himself inside.

That was it for Eddie. He had all of the Spurger swamps he wanted. Eddie and his obese wife packed their things and returned to Rooster Ridge.

Daddy laughed for a week every time he thought of Eddie's fear and disgust when they found him that afternoon locked in the truck. I was glad when Daddy's spirits were jovial for those times were seldom.

Chapter Six

Daddy embarked upon a new relationship with a beautiful woman in Texas. I was elated! Now I'll have a real momma again.

Virginia had a striking resemblance to Momma. But Momma was prettier. She was divorced and had a two-year-old son of her own. Daddy wanted this to work, hoping to find a wife to help raise us kids and someone to truly love him.

Shuffled around often in the last several months, Jane became frightfully attached to Daddy, she screamed every time he got out of her sight. Some days he took her to the woods with him and she rode his hip as he tried to work.

Daddy cried a lot too. He worried and continued to grieve over the loss of his marriage. Concern about the welfare of his children tormented him. He knew he could not raise us alone and hold down a job. He was drowning his sorrows in the bottle. He had to have help. Virginia fit the bill.

One rainy night he and Virginia took me out on a date with them. Jane stayed with Mrs. Roberts.

Missing my own mother desperately, I looked into Virginia's eyes. "Miss Virginia, will you be my new momma?" I asked.

Virginia squirmed in the seat. Fiddling with the ends of her long beautiful hair, she cleared her throat and gazed out the car window. There was dead silence as Daddy continued to drive. My question just hung there in the thick, humid air. Sadly, she took a deep breath, and patted me on the head, then she smiled and said nothing. Virginia liked Daddy, but after this night she no longer wanted to see him. It was my fault. I shouldn't have asked the question so soon.

Daddy was drunk again as he sipped on his beers before driving Virginia home. He was talking nonsense and weaving over the road. He pulled off the paved highway onto the gravel lane leading to Virginia's house. Nearly running the car into the muddy ditch he gunned the engine and swerved to the center of the byway.

Trembling with anger and fear she yelled, "Stop the damn car! I'd rather walk than to ride with a drunk!"

He kept driving, mumbling, "No! No! Howdy! Howdy! No! I'm a Navy Kid Captain Sailor!"

Horrified, Virginia reached for the keys in the ignition. He grasped her hand, and forcefully held it on his leg as she stretched in front of me standing between them on the front seat.

Wild-eyed, he said as he let go of the steering wheel to pat her hand, "I love you Ora, Honey."

Virginia cried, "You damn maniac, stop the car! Now!"

At her screams and the car veering out of control he let go of her hand and slammed on the brake. The car fish-tailed, sliding to a fast stop and we lurched forward. I fell over into Virginia's lap.

Virginia, badly shaken, helped me to my feet again. I slid down and sat close to her. "It's Okay, Virginia. Daddy does that some times. But he is fine now." I held her hand. She yanked it away, and clutched tight to her purse straps while breathing heavily as silent rage and fear churned inside her widened eyes. Silvery moonlight beamed through the passenger window and I could see her face turn bright red. We sat in the car on the side of the country road three miles from her house. Daddy stepped out to relieve himself in the ditch. I was embarrassed by my father's crude behavior in front of my potential new mom.

Calming some, she sighed. "You, poor-child! No wonder your momma left him," she whispered, looking around behind us out the back glass into the silver-dark. "I hope my brother comes this way. It's about time for him to get off work. I'll ride with him the rest of the way if he comes by." But that didn't happen.

Fearful, that she didn't like me anymore, and dread of losing her, I asked, "Miss Virginia, are ya gonna marry my Daddy? I think you will be a good momma!"

She turned her head. "Oh sheesh!"

Daddy slid into the driver's seat and apologized. He told us he wouldn't drink anymore. He drove Virginia home. Walking her to the front door, I heard them arguing, but they kissed goodnight and she went inside. Daddy staggered back to the car. He got in and said, "The whole world is a chicken shit. She dumped me, too. I don't want to live."

"Well Daddy, you are a chicken dookie when you're drunk!" I giggled and he laughed with me.

True to his word, Daddy fell into an inescapable depression after this night and lingered in bed for a week. He stayed drunk perpetually. A few days later he was sawing down a large oak tree, when slipped in the mud the saw kicked back into his right leg below the knee. It ripped out a half-inch gash and sawed into his shin bone before he managed to shove it away.

Daddy bleeding profusely, Mr. Roberts glanced up from his work fifty feet away, ran to him, frantically took off his shirt and wrapped the wound in a tourniquet. They hobbled out of the woods and Mr. Roberts drove Daddy to Woodville for medical attention.

The doctor who sewed up the leg told Daddy that he was a very lucky man. He also told him not to return to the swamp until the wound was healed to prevent infection. "I've had all of the Spurger woods I want in one lifetime," Daddy replied while making plans to leave Texas.

To incite matters, the damp, rainy weather caused respiratory problems for me. I was coughing up a tiny bit of blood and the congestion in my chest made breathing difficult. I hated hospitals. I never wanted to ever go back to another one. I liked Doc Nix but not the hospital so I tried to hide the illness as long as I could.

On Thursday of the week Dad was injured, he got his paycheck, thanked the Roberts for their hospitality, and started off with us on the long drive to Arkansas. Before we pulled away Mrs. Roberts stuck her head inside the driver's window and told Dad that I needed medical attention for my horrible cough. She told him Jane was leaving blood in her panties and she couldn't tell what the problem was but she needed to see a doctor too.

Daddy assured her he would get us to a physician, then we rolled out of the driveway heading for Loafer's Glory.

We drove all night. I stood in the front seat beside Daddy. He fell asleep at the wheel and the Pontiac careened off the road once, nearly crashing into a tree as he missed a curve. I talked to keep him awake. I told him I would not let him fall asleep anymore, and I did exactly that.

However, he nodded off several times before dawn and lay his head on his arm out the car window in the cool, March night air. The cold wind didn't wake him. Dreadfully frightened, I wanted to go to sleep myself, but did not dare. I begged Daddy to pull off the highway and take a nap. He refused. Many times during the long drive I shook him or pulled his hair to wake him up. The car swerved often to the shoulder of the narrow Ozarks routes.

We finally arrived at Sonny's at dawn without a major accident. I was relieved and exhausted. The cock began to crow and the first rays of morning sunlight stabbed through the scattered clouds. Perched on the roof of the outhouse, the old Road Island Red rooster sang his morning song while a whippoorwill echoed from in a nearby Red Oak tree. Smoke bellowed up from the chimney on Sonny's house and into the cool, blue, morning sky. The lights blinked on one by one in every room of the old plank shack.

We knocked on the front door. Jane was sleeping in Daddy's arms. All I wanted was food and sleep. Wheezing, I struggled to keep from coughing. I didn't want Sonny to know I was sick. She was sure to send me to the hospital.

Sonny welcomed us in. After a sumptuous breakfast of chocolate gravy and homemade cat-head biscuits, Sonny gave me cough syrup and aspirin and put me to bed on the sofa near the wood stove in the living room. Jane and Daddy fell asleep in a rocker across the room.

I woke in the afternoon to the sound of Bobby crying and Hank, five(Sonny's youngest son), playing with his battery-operated puppy he'd gotten for a Christmas present. The puppy caused me to miss Buddy again. Hank and I were buddies but he was younger than me and I always had to take the lead and show him the rules of our games. He didn't like me bossing him.

Sonny's eldest girl, pretty blond Janice, twelve, and ruddy-faced Derk had caught the big yellow school bus after breakfast. I was fascinate by the sound of their voices as both spoke with a rasp. They sounded much older than some adults when they would speak because of the fullness of their voices.

Daddy was gone. Would he come back to get us? Had he gone to the bootlegger's again to get more moonshine whiskey? I hated booze! What liquor did to my dad. I disdained his ignorant drunkenness. Having a drunk daddy was better than no daddy at all.

He didn't return for a week. No one knew where he was. While he was gone, Sonny let us stay with Chad and his four children. Lance, the oldest son, was on his way to college the next fall on a basketball scholarship. Randy was sixteen. All he had on his mind was girls and cars. Bossy Danna, thirteen and the only girl, no one could do anything to please her. Stan, only a couple of months older than me, was as bossy as Danna. They all had blue eyes and blond hair with freckles. Danna's hair had a strawberry cast.

Stan was fun to play with if we did what he said. That got old fast. When Stan was tired of playing, he simply didn't want us around anymore. He was a Dennis the Menis type, but with a cruel selfishness in his manner. We shared his room at night, though he didn't want *me* in the house.

Our last night there he yelled for me to get out. But Aunt Vanny told him I *would* sleep on the bottom bunk. Face to face, he politely smiled and agreed to obey her. Vanny took Jane by the hand and led her down the hall to Danna's room. She said, "Jane you should stay with us forever. Danna needs a little sister."

Whimpering Jane said, "Nooooo! I live with my Daddy and brother Saul."

Vanny sighed. She said, "Danna, help Jane get ready for bed."

Danna said, "Okay Momma," and I heard the door to Danna's room slam shut.

When Vanny strolled toward the kitchen and was out of hearing range, Stan glared at me. "Your ol' crazy daddy and cheap, white trash momma don't have nothin' but white trash kids," he said. "You're nothing but pond slime, and I don't want you here." Jane's okay cause Momma and Danna say so. No body in my house loves you or wants you! Daddy's gonna get rid of you for me!"

Loathing for him washed over me, but I swallowed the lump in my throat and held back my tears. I thought for a second, and then mumbled, "And *you're* chicken dookie!" Wanting to hurt him, yet knowing his parents would protect him. Fighting was not an option. This was their home. Why didn't he like me? I wasn't my parents. What was white trash? It must be like the garbage dump down the hill from their home. Maybe it was because I wasn't a girl, the reason they all hated me?

I wanted Stan to be my friend, though he wanted no part of it. He shoved me down on the bottom bunk. "You're only here because Mamma says so for tonight. I want you out of my room tomorrow!"

Biting my tongue I crawled under the covers. Stan climbed up to the top bunk. He had hurt my feelings. Be brave! Never let them know. Crying silently with my head under the blanket, listening to Vanny and Chad whispering in the next room I drifted off to sleep.

I awoke to the hum of the diesel motors turning the huge, circular saws at Chad's mill a few hundred feet from the house. The blades squealed mournfully as they ripped through the giant, White Oak logs. The noise was grinding on my nerves. My nostrils burned from the pungent smell of burnt diesel, fresh sawdust, and soured wood that filled the air. Dust billowed across the yard as the first banged-up logging truck rolled past the house with a load of fresh timber. My eyes watered from the acrid fumes and dust.

Coughing uncontrollably for a couple of minutes after awakening. A spot of blood soiled my pillow. I flipped the cushion over to hide the stain. Not wanting breakfast, and I asked Vanny to take Jane and me back to Sonny's house.

Vanny said goodbye to her children as Randy packed them in the car. Once they were gone, cold distant silent Vanny loaded Jane and me into her vehicle and motored us back to Sonny's. I didn't think she was unhappy to see us go, anymore than we were to be leaving.

Spending as much time as possible with little Bobby when we returned, I realized somehow he now belonged with Sonny. I didn't know where Jane and I fit anymore. What was to become of us? We were not wanted by most of our relatives. The ones who did want us had too many children of their own to afford taking in two more.

The night before, I had heard Chad and Vanny confiding in each other about an orphanage, and some woman named Leve. They were trying to decide what would be best for Jane and me if Daddy broke down under the stress and grief. The thought of a ragamuffin home horrified me.

To our surprise Daddy came back, clean-shaven and sober that evening. He held Jane and me in his lap on the rocker and told us we would go back to Indiana. He'd work for Martin again taping drywall.

The dread of an orphanage lifted.

Almost a year ago, Lou and Martin were good to us when we stayed there the first time. Though Lou was grouchy, she made it a point to hug and cuddle and laugh with us every evening at bedtime. In those moments all was forgiven. I couldn't hold a grudge against her.

The thought of this move was comforting. Lou's and Martin's children, our cousins accepted us. They weren't hateful like Stan, and I looked forward to being with them again.

Don was rowdy and spoiled but fun to play with. He wasn't belligerent, or cruel and he didn't make fun of Daddy or pin ugly labels on my family. He liked sharing his toys and I liked his company.

Patsy giggled a lot and made all satisfactory marks on her report card. She could read, and liked reading stories to us. Maybe I'd go to school there? Patsy could help me learn how to read.

Alvin, tall and dark headed, was thirteen an a bit rebellious, sneaky, and always coming up with fun games of tag and hide and go seek with the neighborhood kids. Jimmy, sixteen, just thought about girls. He wasn't any fun.

Lou would be temporary Mother for us again. Jane and I got along well with Patsy and Don before, we felt safe there but Lou was strict. She griped incessantly about the least of things. We'd just have to live with that. It was okay because we knew she loved us. Other than that, great anticipation and happiness about the relocation kept my spirits high until bedtime.

Best of all--Daddy would be with us every evening after work.

Early the next morning Sonny and Bobby were up to see us off. She cried while kissing our cheeks, and then waved to us from the front door as we drove out of sight. I crawled over the seat and sat next to Daddy.

"Daddy?" I asked.

He glanced down at me. "Yes, Son, what is it?"

"Where did you go?"

"Fishing," he replied as he ruffled my hair and we laughed.

I didn't believe him, but didn't question him any further. He and Momma might be trying to work things out. I knew that was probably just my imagination. But the thought was my deepest desire.

Chapter Seven

I was six when we arrived at Lou's. Daddy returned to work for Martin and I attended kindergarten. Jane stayed home with Lou.

First thing, Lou went out and bought us new clothes. The second day she took Jane and me to the doctor. I was okay, other than my chronic cold symptoms. The doctor gave me cough syrup and pills for the respiratory infection.

Jane wasn't so lucky. Months earlier I had told Momma, "Jane's poop shoot is falling out when she goes potty." Momma laughed at me and seemed unconcerned.

Mrs. Roberts and our other care givers had told Daddy about Jane's condition. I had told him. Nevertheless, no one took the initiative to get Jane the help she needed other than Lou.

Daddy worked all the time. Frequently his mind slipped in and out of two different worlds. Momma had been preoccupied with her obsession for Merl. Momma's concern for her children wasn't strong enough to notice the seriousness of Jane's condition. Her lack of money to pay a doctor for his services was a big issue. Jane just never got the medical attention she needed until Lou had us checked out. Lou had money to pay the doctor, Momma didn't. Daddy's mind didn't focus on the immediate needs of his offspring. He was lost in his own world of torment and sorrow.

The doctor acted funny when I began crying as he told me to take off my pants, and he examined my pee pee. I was afraid. Was he like Merl? My innocence had already been stolen. What was he going to do? How was he going to hurt me? Merl was the giver of pleasure and pain. Was this doctor too?

I thought he was going to do to me what Merl did. Embarrassed, I didn't want Lou to watch. I hated her for bringing me to this man. "I hate you!" I yelled as he held my penis between his fingers and it tingled with pleasure, erect. The pain was next, I thought. Then he whacked the head with a flip of his forefinger. That wasn't the kind of pain I was expecting. I bawled.

The doctor said nothing as he glanced up at me with a scowl and turned to Lou who was trying to calm Jane as she began crying with me.

He walked toward the sink and turned on the water. "You can put your nephew's clothes back on him now."

I was confused. Was that all? He didn't hurt me. He just embarrassed me. I was violated. I didn't like him. Why did he play with my peepee? I was pleased that was all he did. I was glad it was over. I was grateful he didn't play with my bottom. I felt dirty, powerless. Was I like other children? Was this normal? Were all children touched the way Merl touched me? I didn't want his pleasure or your pain. I didn't want him touching me, I was a child. I couldn't comprehend such things. I was innocent. I was ignorant. I was vulnerable. What were those strange monstrous emotions Merl stirred inside of me? My feelings were mixed with rage, hate, anger, fear, and pleasure. I didn't want Merl touching me! I was a child! I was innocent! I felt dirty. Merl was the adult, he was to be my protector. Love me! Help me understand what happened. I was a leper. Yes, I was unclean, soiled goods. Merl Judas, your touch made me feel guilty and filthy. I loved you. I hated you! I hated me! I would never trust again. Merl had taken all my self-esteem. I would look at all adults with loathing and mis-trust. Merl should never have touched me that way. I would never be the same again because of his crimes against me. Why did you do this to me,

Merl Judas? Daddy didn't. He was my friend. Perhaps crazy was easier to trust. He didn't hurt me. But I was ashamed. People made fun of him. I was his son. The son of the village idiot. I refused to wear the labels. My heart cried, I was not white trash as Stan says. But crazy was better than dirty and mean like Merl. I wanted my daddy.

Grimacing, the doctor washed his hands and shook his head, looking me square in the face again from across the room. I thought he was going to ask a question as Lou helped me slip on my pants again while trying to calm my crying. Jane continued to whimper on the other side of the room. Lou smiled and chuckled. "Saul! Stop making such a fuss. The doctor didn't hurt you. He just wanted to make sure you are healthy."

I shrieked louder. Jane frightfully bellowed too. Lou's brow wrinkled. "Now, hush before I give you something to really cry about!" She slapped my leg. "Shut up Jane!"

I was experiencing extreme nausea. I didn't allow myself to vomit. I wanted to go home. I wanted Daddy! The doctor was annoyed. "Never mind," he said while tossing a brown paper towel into the trash can next to the examination table where Jane sat, softly whimpering.

I stopped crying as Lou pulled down Jane's panties for the doctor to examine her. I had to protect her. I would kick them! Jane and I would run out of this place! No! Not Jane! He was gonna hurt her peepee. I was afraid. What was he going to do to her? I was too small to protect her. They would kill us. Why did Lou bring us to this place of pain and sadness? I wept silently as the doctor continued to examine Jane.

Jane screamed and fought like a wild tiger! Crying uncontrollably she yelled, "Noooo! She moaned. "Noooo, please don't do that."

Finished, he shook his head, looked at Jane, then glanced at me. He turned back to Lou. "Your niece has a growth and pocket of infection on her rectum. We will have to do minor surgery. She must have fallen on something. Have you not noticed blood in her stool? This growth probably drops down and is visible when she has a bowel movement."

I was relieved. He didn't hurt Jane. I didn't want Jane hurt like I was hurt by Merl. This doctor man wasn't a bad guy. He was going to fix Jane's poop shoot like Doc Nix fixed my leg. Surgery was the word I remember. That was bad but it fixed people. Jane would have surgery on her bottom. He was a good guy. Maybe we could trust him. Maybe?

Lou nodded. "Not really, doctor. They came to stay with me for a couple of months last summer and I noticed some blood then but it stopped and I didn't think anymore about it. I thought she had scratched herself."

"We'll schedule her for surgery tomorrow," he said.

Jane and I never wanted to see another doctor after that. Back then

I guess people just didn't talk about ugly secrets in the family. Apparently Merl had damaged Jane's rectum. It was corrected with surgery. Jane recovered quickly. I didn't know that sexual abuse was the reason for her surgery until later. If he would have asked, we would never have told. I didn't know what sex was. I thought what Merl did was just being mean.

Chapter Eight

Lou and Martin fought constantly. Martin was an alcoholic. He thought nothing of sharing a bottle with his children. Offering the booze to me, but I declined every time. I had seen enough drunkenness, wanting no part of the beer or whiskey. His youngest son, Don, nine months younger than me, loved the stuff.

Lou dressed Don and me as twins. Though we were as different as light and dark. In fact he was husky, a cotton top with pale skin tones, and rosy cheeks. I was a bean pole and had dark olive complexion with brown hair. We certainly didn't look like relatives.

Lou didn't know that Martin would take Don and me to kindergarten each morning, then make me go into the classroom, while taking Don on the job with him to spend the day. Don sipped on his dad's beers the day long. Martin picked me up at school in the afternoons and I was to lie, pretending that Don was in class all day. This went on for weeks.

The last week of school at the end of May, I let it slip one afternoon when talking to Pasty. Lou overheard. She and Martin got into a loud, cursing argument. Martin grabbed Don and tossed him in the car. They drove away and were gone for three days. Martin had a girlfriend on the side and spent a lot of time with her after that. He was hardly ever home.

Lou cried incessantly. If I had only kept my mouth shut! She was angry and short-tempered. No one could please her. She could spank hard and did so frequently. To that point in my youth no one whipped me as hard as Lou. Daddy never paddled us, though Momma often threatened to. But it was never more than a swat on behinds and hands. We children walked on eggshells. Afraid we'd displease Lou and she'd pull out the belt.

The end of May rolled around and school was out for summer. Daddy fell off his drywall stilts and broke his shoulder. He was unable to work for many weeks. In early June, Lou, us children, and Daddy piled into her new station wagon and drove to Loafer's Glory for vacation.

After arriving at Delena's house no more than twenty minutes when

Daddy began to cry uncontrollably. He said his head hurt, the awful pain in his body felt like someone had beat him with a baseball bat. He ran out of the house and said he had to see a doctor. He sped down the highway around the winding curves in Lou's car to Doc Anderson in Racoon Springs.

The next time I saw Daddy, he was a patient in the Arkansas State Hospital for the Mentally Ill. The lunatic asylum. Daddy was not crazy. He does not belong here, I thought as two strong male Licensed Psychiatric Technician Nurses dressed in white guided us through the maze of breeze ways and corridors to the visiting area marked off in one corner of the dining room. We sat at the tables as one nurse poured the adults coffee and the other went for Daddy who was locked up in another part of the hospital.

Delena sipped her coffee and set the paper cup on the long table. She turned and watched as several patients marched in and lined up along the wall on the other side of the room. "Look there in the lunch line," Delena said with a smirk.

"What?" Lou asked as she clutched tight to her red purse that matched her high heels and pleated skirt. She turned to look behind her.

We gazed across the large dinning hall to the other side of the cafeteria where patients from Unit One were lining up for their noon meal.

"Well, I'll be damn!" Chad said while slapping his large hands on his knees and chuckling.

Delena and Lou tried to hold back their laughter as they watched a husky red-faced bald man fumble with a ladies sanitary napkin wrapped around his neck.

I didn't know what it was. It made me angry that they were making sport of the man. Now they would make fun of my Daddy since he lived here with these strange people. I didn't see the humor. I thought the man had a white bandage around his neck. A tall male nurse noticed the commotion and promptly relieved the patient of the article, tossing it in the trash behind the kitchen counter. The patient just turned his back toward us and banged his head against the wall.

Daddy stepped into the visiting area escorted by the other stern-faced male nurse.

He didn't seem any worse than when he and Momma fought. He was sad, browbeaten, like after their fights. My heart broke. Not that he was sad but that he was locked up.

Someone across the room squealed, and Daddy blushed, embarrassed. We watched as a skinny man stole another patient's dinner roll. He ran to the corner of the room, and began wolfing it down. The other patient, with cold empty brown eyes, frowned angrily, then calmly walked over holding a carton of milk. With a full bass voice, he asked, "Would you like some milk with my roll?"

The other timidly nodded. At that he promptly opened and dumped the milk carton on his head. "There, you damn thief! Enjoy my roll and milk!" He punched the other patient hunkered in the corner.

The nurses ran to the scene and dragged the aggressor out of the building as he kicked and yelled.

Nervously, "Enoch, are we safe? What if one of those people, notice us." Lou pauses, placing her hand high on her chest, fearfully. "And, you know," she whispered.

Daddy said, "They lock up the violent one in Rogers Hall across the street. These guys are pretty much harmless."

"Hell, that didn't look harmless to me!" Chad scoffed.

Daddy bowed his head. "I should never have checked myself in this place."

Jane and I crawled into his lap. I wanted to cry but I wouldn't let myself. "I love you, Daddy," I said as I kissed him on the cheek.

Jane did too. "I love you, Daddy."

Daddy raised his head smiling and hugged us tight.

His doctor, a large-boned tall man with salt-and-pepper hair, dressed in a black business suit, stepped into the room and told us Daddy was going to be all right. The separation had triggered a severe depression. Daddy had asked him to come and talk to us. I learned Daddy was having something called a nervous breakdown because of all that had happened between him and my mother. In addition he had some brain damage from a blow to his head.

After the doctor left we walked outside and sat at a picnic table under a huge oak. The hospital grounds gave me the creeps. I felt ashamed and embarrassed that my own father was in this place. Two men were kissing, three tables down from us.

Shocked, his eyes popping nearly out of his head, Chad yelled, "Look at those friggin' queers!"

Queer? What was that? They were touching each other like Momma and Ginger had touched that day in the fields. What did this mean? I was confused. Was Momma a queer? What was a queer?

Another patient was pulling tiny imaginary things out of thin air and poking them into his shirt pocket. Three men walked around glassy eyed, hopped up on medication, and were begging for money to buy cokes. Some approached us to mooch cigarettes. Chad pulled out a pack and Daddy shook his head.

Chad caught the signal. "Sorry boys I only have enough for me today."

One jolly soul jumped on top of a table and began singing off key, trying to act like Elvis. That one reminded me of Merl. We saw other patients there who were much worse off than Daddy. They frightened me, and I wanted to take Daddy out of that dreadful place. But I couldn't save him. I cried as the nurses led him away when it was time for us to leave.

Now, was just Jane and me. A great sadness came over me as Lou drove us back to Loafer's Glory without Daddy.

"Poor, Enoch, that damn whore did this to him!" Delena seethed as she applied more lipstick in the small compact mirror she pulled from her purse. Jane and I sat on either side of her in the back seat and said nothing while we listened to the adults' conversation.

Chad lit a cigarette. "Hell Delena, the boy's been sick all his life. He ain't ever been right."

Lou fiddled with her hair while glancing in the rear-view mirror as she drove. "Ma always said he wasn't right. It's the cow-horn curse, ya know."

Jane and I were overcome with grief and shame. She crawled over Delena's lap and snuggled close to me. We slept the remainder of the trip back to Loafer's Glory.

We stayed with Delena and I visited with Bobby and other relatives in the area. After a week we returned to South Bend without Daddy. He remained in the hospital several more weeks and underwent electric shock treatments, thirty-three in all. But they didn't help. The treatments only made his condition worsen.

Chapter Nine

Back in South Bend Martin was waiting when we arrived. He missed Daddy too. Daddy became so proficient at his job that Martin had put him in charge of the crew working on show homes in the new building additions of town. Now those days were gone forever. The bankers and relators liked Daddy's work when they toured the houses he had finished, and consistently gave Martin the money he needed for future projects.

Martin did care about Jane and me. He was good with children, playful, and happy, but ignorant of the effects of alcohol on us. He thought it was cute when Don staggered and acted silly when drunk. He would regret his ignorance years later.

One evening Martin drove Don and me to see his mother, Bonnie, who lived in a mobile home park Martin owned. He provided his mother with a free house after she moved from Loafer's Glory. She hugged Don and Martin. He gave her $200. But she demanded an extra $180. Martin bowed his head in shame, browbeaten, but promised to bring her more the following evening.

Bonnie, a fat, harsh-spoken blunt woman in her mid-sixties, didn't care whose feelings she hurt. She wore her long graying hair in the holiness roll around the top of her head like a doughnut.

"That ol' woman you are married to is going to take you for everything you have if you don't get rid of her," Bonnie said then looked at me with a scowl. "What's this? Are you running an orphanage and taking in all the woman's foundling kin folks and their kids too? You need to get rid of him! You have enough kids of your own–if their yours. Take care of your own and your poor old sick mother, Son. You don't need this added responsibility! Besides, he's probably the reason you don't have the money to help your poor ol' mother!"

Red faced, Martin glanced down at me and rolled his eyes.

I smiled.

He smiled back and winked.

I winked back.

He told her he'd be back with the money tomorrow. I decided not to come along the next time. She didn't like me but Martin loved me. Embarrassed by Bonnie's insults and knowing she had hurt my feelings, he bought me a bike the following week.

August whirled around. Martin and Lou were fighting endlessly. He stayed drunk and the children were out of hand. Lou was constantly angry. The second week of August Lou said Jane and I needed to be closer to Daddy for more frequent visits. We needed to be there for him if ever he got out of the hospital. She loaded our things into the station wagon, along with my bike, and drove us to Delena's.

I suspected her true reasons were to dump Jane and me. She just didn't want the responsibility. Maybe Bonnie had something to do with this dumping? Perhaps Martin didn't want us after all? Lou's marital problems kept her grieved and stressed.

Delena had married a gambler fifteen years younger that summer after we returned to South Bend the first time. Saul was his name, just like me. If only for that reason I liked him from the start.

Delena ran the restaurant from sunup to eleven p.m. while Jane and I spent a lot of time with Saul. His gentle nature bestowed a genuine love and affection for us, hugging us and telling silly jokes and giggling with us. I grew to love him. Saul, at thirty-three was husky, with a dark olive complexion, coal black hair greased back, and piercing blue eyes. His large bright smile, jovial laughter, and protectiveness made us feel loved. Every night at nine o'clock he took us from the restaurant to the house next door and put us to bed. Faithfully he told a bedtime story and tucked us in. Then he stayed until we dozed off. To Jane and me this was heaven. In the past year Momma and Daddy left us to live with ten different families. Now we felt we were wanted and safe for the first time in a long while.

I enrolled in first grade at Racoon Springs Elementary school. Not having the social skills to truly interact with other children my age other than my cousins, I didn't make many friends, and the six mile bus ride frightened me, especially when the older students got a little rowdy at the back of the bus. I sat behind the burley bus driver, feeling safer there.

The first weekend after school started I found out the reason why Lilly left us in Slegiman, Missouri. That Saturday she dropped by to visit Delena at the restaurant with her and Merl's oldest daughter April and their two younger ones. They sat the counter eating hamburgers when Jane and I came running indoors. I didn't recognize them at first as I spied pretty blond April, now eight, sipping on a bottle coke with peanuts floating around inside. She looked grown up now, being taller and talking with the adults at the counter.

Lilly slid off her stool smiling as she came racing to the doorway and gave Jane and me a hug. We pulled back.

Smiling, she sadly asked, "You don't remember me?"

We nodded.

"I'm Lilly! And this is April." She pointed to the counter.

Glaring for a moment, then we happily realized who she was and threw our arms around her.

"How are you babies doing?" she asked while embracing us.

We smiled. "Fine," we said in unison.

"Come and have a soda with us, this will be better than old times." She took us by the hand and hoisted us onto the stools next to April. Glancing across the room to check on her younger children asleep in the booth.

April smiled. "Hi Saul! Hi Jane!" She waved and went back to sipping her pop. Other customers paid their bills and then it was just us and Delena.

"Can they have a soda?" Lilly asked Delena.

Delena smiled and nodded then opened two six-ounce cokes and set them on the counter as Lilly began to share with Delena why she left Merl.

She said, "The weather had turned exceptionally warm the week before I left Slegiman. Merl says he is hot at about two a.m. and takes a quilt to lay on in the kitchen floor in front of the open back door. I didn't think anything of it until a few minutes later I heard Ora get out of bed and shuffle toward the kitchen. I heard her and Merl whispering. I waited thinking she would go back to bed soon. But she didn't. Thirty minutes later I heard soft giggling and moaning noises. I suspected they were rotten deceivers, so I crawled out of bed and sneaked into the kitchen doorway and caught Ora and Merl in the act together. Rage rushed over me."

She banged her fist against the counter. Then continued after downing a sip of her soda, "All the gossip was true. They were lying on a quilt in the kitchen floor in front of the open back door." She leaned forward and whispered into Delena's ear, "Having intercourse."

She cleared her throat and glanced over at us children to see if we heard. I did but I didn't understand that word.

We smiled.

Relieved, Lilly nervously yanked on her earlobes and commenced conversing with Delena again in whispers loud enough for us to hear. Scowling Delena sighed. "I could have told you that! It's been going on for years. Shortly after you married him. Ma caught them meeting down by the pond many times," Delena whispered.

Lilly sipped her coke then continued, "I didn't give them the opportunity to explain. There was no explaining. They never knew I had seen them together. I only regret that I never told Enoch."

Her lips trembled, her eyes were watery. "I gathered my children and drove to my parents' home in Florida when everyone else was gone." She motioned for Delena to lean closer over the bar as she whispered, "Merl molested April in Loafer's Glory before he and Enoch moved us all to Missouri! Damn that son of a bitch!" She banged her fist against the counter. She whispering into Delena's ear again, "He got to April for the past four years! I never knew! I want to kill him!"

I heard but didn't understand.

April blushed and tearfully scowled at Lilly, slid off her stool and ran outside. "Momma, don't tell! He'll kill me! You embarrassed me! You promised not to tell! I want to go home!"

Lilly shamefully glanced up at Delena. "Don't tell anyone. Please!"

Delena stared in bewilderment at Lilly then April then Jane and me.

She nodded.

The younger Judas' sleeping in the booth awakened as Lilly hoisted them into her arms and left the restaurant. April continued crying as they piled into their car and drove off. She had come back to Loafer's Glory to court Mr. Bronze, a neighbor up the road. After a few short weeks she and her children returned to Florida. Eventually she married Mr. Bronze and they permanently relocated to Ohio.

We never saw them again.

One sunny, warm Saturday in early October of 1961, Jane and I were playing in Aunt Delena's yard. I was giving Jane's "Chatty Kathy" doll a ride in the bike basket when a yellow and white '58 Mercury pulled into the parking lot by the café near the front of the house. A tall, thin, beautiful woman with slicked back raven hair and dark sunglasses got out of the car. Wearing white peddle-pusher pants, and sandals, the woman walked over and sat down in the yard swing.

She Smiled. "Hi Saul. Hi Jane. Do you know who I am?"

Jane and I peered at her and shook our heads.

"Why, I'm your mother," she said and patted the seat. "Come over here and sit with me and let's talk."

I looked at her apprehensively for a moment. "You are not my momma, lady!"

She smiled and took off her dark glasses. "Don't you remember me?"

I thought I did. But her hair was pulled back real tight in a ponytail and I had never seen Momma wear her hair that way. This woman had relatively short hair. Momma's hair had always been very long, right down to her hips. My momma wore dresses and skirts to please her aunt Diana's holiness teachings. If this was my momma and she was wearing pants and had cut her hair, she would go to hell.

Despite our misgivings, Jane and I sat down beside her on the swing. The woman asked us if we wanted to go with her to Racoon Springs to get an ice cream cone. I said, "Delena has plenty of ice cream in the restaurant and she will give us some."

When I jumped up to run into the restaurant, she grabbed my arm and pulled me back into the seat. She said, "I liked the strawberry ice cream in town."

I said, "I have to ask Delena before we go anywhere."

She said, "Delena wouldn't mind if we go without telling her. After all, I am your mother."

The woman finally convinced us to get into the car. We were wearing only shorts, tee shirts, and were barefoot. That was okay. We would only be gone a few minutes.

The woman put Jane in the front seat by Merl's twenty-eight-year-old nephew Jeb, who sat behind the steering wheel. Jeb was the younger image of his dad Ely except that he inherited Fanny's witch nose. The woman then put me beside Jane, and squeezed in beside us, slammed her door, and locked it.

She shrieked, "Put it to the floor, Jeb. Let's get to fuck out of Arkansas!"

Jeb spun the back tires in the graveled parking lot and headed out onto the highway. "Guess we showed those domineering crazy bastards!" he said.

"Fight, Jane! This isn't our momma. She's stealing us. Kick, hit, and bite!"

Jane and I did just that. Jane bit Jeb's ear and he nearly ran off the road. I grabbed the woman's ponytail and pulled as hard as I could and held on. The woman turned around and slapped me and I let go. Then she grabbed Jane and threw her in the back seat. Jane was still pulling Jeb's hair. The woman slapped her hand and made her let go. I started kicking the woman with my bare feet and hitting her and Jeb with my fist, to no avail. All Jane and I could do was cry. We had been kidnaped by our own mother. We hardly knew her anymore. We had once again been taken from safety and into the arms of strangers and evil.

On the straight stretches Jeb ran the Mercury as hard as she would go. He only slowed enough to squeal the tires and lean into the sharp Ozarks mountains' curves. He sped through St. Joe, Pindall, Western Grove, Valley Springs, Harrison, then across the state line into Missouri. After an hour Jeb finally slowed down. He and Momma relaxed.

Jane and I continued crying. She was in the back seat alone and I was in the front between Jeb and the mean woman. I wanted to crawl into the back with Jane but they wouldn't let me.

We stopped at a drive-in restaurant in Branson, Missouri and ordered strawberry ice cream cones. I threw mine in her lap and soiled her white peddle-pushers. She had forgotten I was allergic to strawberries. Jane saw what I did and followed suit by throwing her cone into the back of Jeb's head. The woman threatened to paddle us. One at a time they cleaned themselves in the restroom. They never left us alone.

I didn't want to believe this woman was my mother. Jane and I referred to her as "Hey Lady."

We drove through Missouri and into Illinois. Late in the evening when we stopped at another restaurant. There, standing outside the ordering window flirting with the young teenage waitress, was Merl. Now I had no doubt this was my momma. But I continued to call her "Hey Lady."

Merl came to the car and slid into the backseat with Jane.

"Oh no! It's you again!" Jane began to cry and scream and asked if she could get into the front seat.

Momma told her to stop whining. Scowling, she turned around and looked at Jane. "Merl, isn't going to hurt you! Now stop your fuckin' whining!" Turning back to Jeb, she said, "I'm so glad we stole my kids away from those crazy mother fuckers!"

"Hey Lady!" I said and tugged on her blouse.

She glanced down smiling."What, Saul?"

"What is that name you called them and said to Jane?" I asked.

"What?" she asked.

"What's a mother fucker, lady!" I asked not knowing the meaning of the word and having never heard Momma or Daddy use it before.

The adults all roared with laughter. Jane and I began to cry again.

Trying to wipe the smirk off her face Momma looked down at me again. "Son, that's a bad word. You don't need to know the meaning." She chuckled and mussed my hair. Then she playfully tickled me in the ribs to make me stop crying. I did and so did Jane. But soon Jane was whining again.

Merl did hurt Jane. As we drove over the next three hours Jane continued to whimper from time to time and told Merl to stop. It was dark in the back seat. I just thought she was crying, not knowing I wasn't the only one Merl had molested. Merl fondled her in the backseat for the entire trip. She was only five-years-old.

Late that night we rented a motel room. The next morning Momma and Merl left to go get food. Jeb was in the shower. I picked up the telephone and told the motel operator I wanted to talk to Delena in Loafer's Glory. She asked if I knew the number. I didn't. But I told her that a woman who claimed to be my mother had kidnaped Jane and me and I wanted to go home.

Momma and Merl walked in. Momma yanked the telephone out of my hand and told the operator I was just playing. She hung up. Momma yelled at Jeb to get out of the shower and into the car. Jeb hopped out of the bathroom, quickly strapped on his artificial leg, threw on his clothes, and limped out the motel door with his uncombed hair dripping wet. Momma and Merl tossed us into the car and sped out of town.

We drove for two hours until we came to a small, dark green house surrounded by fields of tall drying stalks of popcorn plants. After Momma, Jane, and I got out of the car, Merl and Jeb drove away. I didn't like being with Momma. This woman was now a stranger. Nevertheless, I was glad that the two of them were gone.

We were alone for two weeks. The weather was getting cold. Jane and I still had no shoes and only the clothes on our backs. Momma washed out our shorts and tops at night after we went to bed.

One cool morning I ventured outside, crossed the barbed-wire fence, and explored the popcorn field. I pulled the largest ear I could find off a drying stalk nearest the house, crawled back under the fence, and took the cob of grain to Momma. She put it in the window directly in the morning sunlight and left it dry there for a week.

The day before we departed, Momma shucked the kernels off the cob and popped the corn for Jane and me. By that time Jane and I had accepted the fact that we might never see Delena again. Our only security now was in this woman, who looked and acted a little like the mother we had once known. But now Momma had a hardness about her I was not accustomed to.

The next morning Merl returned in his dark-green '53 Chevy. A noxious cloud of dread engulfed me as we got into his car and drove to the nearest town. We stopped at a shoe store and Momma and Merl took me inside but made Jane stay in the car. Momma found a pair of black patent leather dress shoes for Jane and handed them to Merl. She told him to see if they would fit Jane.

Merl was gone a long time.

Momma had me try on several pairs before she decided on red tennis shoes from a sale rack. I deplored them. She then went to the door and yelled at Merl, who was in the back seat with Jane. Jane was kicking at him and screaming.

"Do the shoes fit?" Momma asked, seemingly unfazed by Jane's antics.

Poking his head out the back car door, smiling, he replied, "Just fine."

Momma payed for both pairs. When we left the store and slid into the car, she scolded Jane for making such a fuss. Jane had another secret to add to her list of traumatic childhood memories. Merl had raped her again.

We drove several more hours arriving as the sun was setting at the big white rental house in Wisconsin where we had lived before. Cold brisk winds whipped from the north when we got out. The temperature wasn't below freezing, yet the wind chill cut to the bone on my skinny naked legs. I shivered, and pointed toward a large dog in the yard.

The woman grinned. "That's Buddy, Saul," she said.

Amazed and a little fearful I said, "But he is so big!"

He was now a full grown Collie. Overjoyed to see him but reserved because of his size. Timidly, I called his name. He whined. "Buddy it's Saul! Don't you remember me?" He wagged his tail, came closer, and sniffed me up and down. He remembered and began running circles, leaping onto my chest, and knocked me to the ground while happily barking, wagging his tail, and licking my face.

Jane crawled out of the backseat and came running to pet Buddy. He licked her on the face and she began to cry. He then focused his attentions on me and we wrestled. If I'd had a tail it would have been wagging too.

"You boys can play later, right now you need to get into warmer clothes. Let's go in," she said as she took my hand and pulled me from the ground.

Jane grabbed my arm, sniffling, and held tight. Buddy growling at Merl when he reached to pick up Jane and she screamed for Momma. Letting go of Jane's hand he kicked Buddy's gut, knocking the dog off his feet. Seething, Merl mumbled, "Damn dog. I'll teach you to bristle at me."

Buddy whimpered as he followed close behind us to the front door, and lay down on the porch when we walked inside. I wanted to kick Merl. Scowling I took a deep breath and sighed. Once again we're at his mercy.

The house was warm. Someone had finally purchased coal for the furnace. Merl's older brother goofy Ely and his homely wife Fanny, who now rented the house, were there.

Jeb, their eldest son pulled down his pants to remove his artificial right leg. He rolled off a stomp sock soiled with tiny spots of blood and yellow fluid.

His leg had been shot up in the Korean War and amputated mid-thigh. The wooden limb didn't fit right and had irritated the end of his stump.

Wanda, Jeb's young wife applied ointment from a green bottle to the open sores and blisters. She then placed a clean stump sock over the end as he cringed.

Ugly Fanny and Ely sat beside them on the living room sofa listening intently to a fervent hellfire and brimstone radio preacher. My eyes bugged out. I had never seen such an unattractive woman. She was as homely as Uncle Chad had said. Then she spoke. Her screeching voice was grating on my nerves.

Scowling Fanny squawked, "We've been expecting you children. Now you behave yourselves while your under my roof."

Jane and I nodded.

Pretty Wanda sat on the sofa next to Fanny. Wanda, only twenty-two, admired her bee hive hair style in a mirror. She dressed in the drab Pentecostal holiness clothing like Fanny. Her dark hair clashed against her pale white pious face. Ely's other daughters, Angel, thirteen, and retarded Agnus eight, and their rowdy son Donny, seven, were there.

Everything about that house had changed. It had furniture, it was warm, and the smell of fresh baked bread drifted from the oven. Across the room thirteen-year-old dark curly haired Angel held a six-month-old baby. He looked a little like my brother Bobby at that age.

Momma held Jane and me by the hand, and lead us to the baby.

246

Smiling happily she said, "This is your brother, Rambo. Merl is going to be your new dad, too."

We didn't say a word. I scowled.

Merl strolled over. Hugging Jane and me real tight. When he kissed us, I pulled away.

Jane escaped his deceitful embrace and held tight to Momma's leg while hiding behind her. I thought what a fake. He wants everyone here to believe he is a good guy. "He doesn't love you, Momma," I mumbled under my breath.

No one heard or understood my muttering. Moving away from Merl and hoping the child belonged to my daddy, I motioned Jane to come closer to Rambo. One foot away, we peered down into his face. Sure enough as far as I could tell he belonged to Merl. He had Merl's ears that were distinguishable by the long fat lobes on the ends and Merl's thick plump lower lip. My half-brother.

The same afternoon Fanny gave me Donny's old castaway clothes. Donny, a year older than me smiled when I put them on. The garments he had outgrown fit just fine.

We hadn't met before. Fanny and Ely moved to Wisconsin from Loafer's Glory after my leg was injured. I knew they lived up the road but before this day I couldn't recall ever seeing any of them, except for Merl.

Donny and I became friends right away. So did Jane and Agnus. Agnus was two years older than me but was developmentally delayed and closer to our age mentally.

Fanny was well known for her match making. She boasted about getting Momma and Daddy together--though disappointed that my parents marriage wasn't working. In the living room when supper was almost ready Fanny cornered Momma and Merl as they necked on the sofa. Like a pissed off Turkey-Chicken rooster she flogged them good, screeching, "Ora, you should have stayed with Enoch! Divorce and adultery are sin. You and Merl both are goin' to hell if you don't repent! I pray over my matches. God wants you with Enoch! Praise the Lord!"

Momma's killer eyes turned into flamethrowers of silent rage as she bounced to her feet and flouted off into the kitchen, poured a cup of coffee while mumbling profanities, and stepped onto the porch. Smirking Merl followed her and they shared a smoke.

Fanny stuck her head out the door. "Shame on the both of you. Now you got a little bastard Judas baby because of your selfishness. The both of you should repent and go back to your mates. Neither of you have any shame!"

They ignored her preaching as they sat on the steps and shared the coffee.

But Fanny continued speaking her mind, and bragged about the successful unions she had instigated. Then she told them that she'd find Angel a husband next year. All of her daughters were still with their mate. She went on boasting.

Fanny had made it clear she didn't approve of Momma and Merl's behavior. At that I took a real liking to this strange ugly woman.

Hen-pecked Ely always went with Fanny's opinion. He stuck his head out the door to put in his two-bits. "You should listen to Fanny's advice," he said.

Momma and Merl snickered.

Fanny and Ely loved Merl. They would not turn him or us out of their home. This situation became a witch's brew for disaster.

Chapter Ten

Wisconsin's autumn Indian-summer lingered during the first couple of weeks after our arrival. One sunny afternoon, Merl put on his scant leopard-design swimming trunks and flaunted himself on the porch as Momma happily had him posing with Rambo. First the right side then the left, Momma snapped the pictures as he postured, modeling like a body builder while sucking in his paunch and flexing his arm and leg muscles. He was aroused and the skimpy tight bathing suit bulged. Momma giggled.

Annoyed, Fanny asked me to help her gather the last apples of the season from the orchard about 200 feet from the house. I dragged a five-gallon bucket almost as big as me down the hill. Fanny followed close behind, mumbling under her breath. She scowled. "They're gonna split hell wide open!" She angrily stomped forward while fiddling with her bun.

I was gathering apples off the ground. Fanny threw a few into my bucket and continued to mumble. Then she hid behind the largest apple tree and peeked around the side at Merl and Momma.

"This is terrible, shameful!" she said. She shook herself, then went back to staring at Merl. She moaned while rubbing her breast against the tree as she gawked, entranced, lusting for her brother-in-law. She shook herself again. "How vulgar!"

What does that mean? Sounds like vulture--something is rotten?

I thought she was getting a thrill out of watching, or was jealous of Momma. I couldn't quite put my finger on what made me think this, but perhaps it was because she was so ugly compared to Momma. Merl certainly was better looking than Ely. She couldn't take her eyes off of him. Forcing herself to look away, she was immediately captivated again. The temptation to not turn away--too meaty. I didn't understand it was a sexual thing, but I thought she wanted to kiss Merl, have a kissing affair. Her competition was great--Momma.

I laughed. "Well Fanny," I said, "if it is so bad, stop staring!"

With a beat-red face, she snapped at me, "Child, don't back-talk your elders."

"I'm not back-talkin' you, Fanny. Just don't look if it upsets you—or excites you!"

She broke off an apple tree switch and whelped my legs ten or twelve times. "Stop that back-talk!" she scolded.

I bawled as tiny droplets of blood oozed from the whelps on my legs. Fanny, my hope of comfort? Religious holiness Pentecostal, she wanted Momma and Daddy back together. Maybe that way she could have Merl for herself? Something about her demeanor told me she really didn't like Merl. She was confused. Was this temptation? He wasn't religious. Maybe that was it. She was restrained in the chains of her religion but Momma and Merl lived out their fantasy. Perhaps what I saw was temptation and jealousy. I was too young to understand.

I thought Fanny was a godly woman. She wore her hair in the bun and never used makeup or jewelry. She prayed in tongues, too. Nevertheless, after that day I had lost any respect for her.

In coming days, I would see her make Agnus crawl into a burlap feed sack. Then Fanny tied the top closed and beat Agnus with a belt while the girl was bound. She whipped all her children this way over the years. She said they couldn't run from her until the punishment was over.

"Spare the rod and spoil the child! Praise the Lord," she often said.

Needless to say, we younger ones were never in danger of being spared or spoiled.

Starved for attention Fanny did the strangest things. In the barn by accident she scratched her leg on a nail. Then intentionally caused more bleeding by squeezing the open wound. Refusing to wipe the clotted blood off her limb that ran down from the knee to her ankle. Instead she let the red plasma dry and wore it for two weeks. When anyone came to visit, she made a point to draw their attention to the wound.

"Look now, what I have done to myself," she would whine in a pitiful voice while swinging her foot high above her knee.

Fanny was peculiar but something about her seemed to be more noble and moral than the rest of her family. Perhaps because her presence was so forceful as she said Praise the Lord when ending every other sentence. Maybe it was her domineering character, self assurance, and confidence in her beliefs and the way she religiously conducted herself while hammering all of us with scriptures. None of us wanted to make God mad. I perceived Fanny as an expert on the subject since she spoke in the tongues when she prayed. I was fascinated by the tongue talkers. Any tongue talkers.

Soon after our arrival Merl was up to his old tricks. One day he secretly made a pass at Angel, his thirteen-year-old niece. Angel told Ely and he confronted Merl. Fanny went through the roof and made Merl get out of the house. Momma defended Merl, but he tucked his tail and rented a motel room in town and stayed drunk.

He and Momma fought over his drinking. Tensions were running high in the household. About a week after Merl made a pass at Angel, Ely and Fanny moved their family to Bellville and rented another house. None of us knew Merl had got to Agnus already, and Jane again. They wouldn't tell. Momma and Merl fought continually when he immediately moved back in. Merl's drinking grew worse as he frequently stayed out all night in the bars. When he visited the local prostitutes Momma's rage exploded, but she calmed down, reconciled herself to his immoral passions. She said she hoped she'd be his only desire. She'd have to try a little harder to please him.

Merl's other women were routine but Momma wasn't about to give up and once took my jar of pennies buying gasoline for the car to hunt him down. In the parking lot of the tavern I watched her beg him to come back home.

He refused, and took his new girlfriend down to Florida. He told Momma the trip was to his children. I suspect he also left to escape his brother Ely's wrath. So Momma, Jane, Rambo, my dog Buddy, and I were left alone in the big white house with no furniture again. After Merl left Momma managed to get a job at the Frito Lay company, and she eventually purchased used furniture at a junk store in New Glarus.

Chapter Eleven

I was calling Momma, Momma again, only because she forced me to, shortly after Thanksgiving when Merl was in Florida. She told me to stop playing on the staircase. I wasn't going to mind her.

"Hey Lady! I don't have to listen to you. My momma is dead. You are a mean witch who stole me from Delena and Saul and I hate you!"

She grabbed me and busted my posterior with her hand several times and shook me violently. Through my screams of terror, hate, and pain she too cried and yelled at me. "I'm your mother! You will call me Mom or Momma or Mother. There will be no more of this Hey Lady crap!"

"Hey Lady! You're not my momma!" I screamed through defiant tears. She spanked me again.

Jane ran up the staircase tearfully screaming and hit her. "You ol stealin' witch, leave my brother alone!"

Momma commenced spanking Jane. "Stop! Momma! Stop!" I shouted at the top of my lungs.

She broke into sorrowful sobs and crumpled to the staircase steps. Momma held us in her arms and wept louder than Jane's and my howls. We huddled together there for the longest time. Again our tears mingled together and became one as they had the day of the accident a few years before. Now I cried not for myself, but because of Momma's broken heart. From then on I called her Momma.

Jane and I were glad Merl was gone. He told me often how stupid and ugly I was and then beat me with a belt when he got frustrated that I couldn't understand simple arithmetic homework. Terrified of him, Jane withdrew into a shell. But we were playful children again when he was gone. The low self-esteem and hidden rage he helped to create within me remained even after he left. I began aggressively acting out against those around me.

Momma was so sad without Merl that sometimes I wanted him to come back to just make her smile again. But I felt guilty for Momma's sake in that her joy with Merl was my pain, and her sorrow was my joy when he was gone.

Snow fell a lot that winter in New Glarus. A foot covered the ground before school dismissed for the Christmas holidays. Buddy had come up missing. I had not seen him since Thanksgiving. He was my only friend except for Jane and I terribly longed for him.

The loss of Buddy hit me doubly hard because I was having a tough time at school. The boys called me names and wouldn't let me play with them. They made fun of my clothes and unkempt appearance. Because we were so poor, Momma made me wear girls' green mittens with feminine designs stitched on the back. I hated them, but they were the only mittens I had to keep my hands warm at recess. The other boys pounded me with snowballs and called me "sissy."

I didn't know what a sissy really was while thinking it must be a bad thing since none of my classmates liked me. They provoked me to near tears, but I wasn't going to give them the privilege of knowing. I had a better plan.

One afternoon before Christmas break I challenged them all to a snowball fight, six of them against me. They agreed to give me time to make snowballs first since I had to fight so many people. Recess came and I went to make my stand on one end of the concrete playground. The six boys stood thirty feet away at the other end of the playground where the snow had been banked up by the school snowplow. I dug down through the snow until I found the edge of the concrete slab. Then I uncovered gravels the size of quarters. I grabbed a handful of these rocks and began to pack snow around each one until I had made a dozen.

The bullies begin to yell.
"Wimp!"
"Sissy!"
"Pussy!"
"You ready? Time's up."
"I'm ready!" I yelled.

I stood and let them hit me with most of their snowballs. When they called a time-out to make more, I charged and released my secret weapons with deadly accuracy. I hit two of the boys in the head, one in the neck, and the others in the hands and legs. All six bullies were in tears by the time I finished. Laughing, I said, "What's wrong pussy cat sissies! Can't take a little snowball in the face? Meow!" I yelled while painfully wanting them to be my friends. "Don't call me names anymore."

The teacher came running. Blood oozed down one of the bully's face where a rock had torn his flesh. It didn't take the teacher long to put two and two together. She sentenced me to spend recesses in the classroom reading during the rest of the semester while the other children went outside to play. That was okay by me. I couldn't read, but I liked the pictures. And I wouldn't be outside in the cold where the bullies could bother me. The teacher accused me of being the troublemaker that day, but I was only defending myself and treating them the way they treated me. As Fanny said, it was the golden rule: *Do unto others as you would have them do unto you.* I just gave them what they wanted. Just like they did unto me. Fanny was right--the Golden Rule sure did make you feel good.

My aggressions increased in the coming weeks. The parents of the bullies caused such a fuss the principle asked Momma to transfer me to a different school, which she did in January after classes resumed.

I was excited about the new start, though it didn't take long for me to realize bullies were at that school as well. But they didn't mess with me for very long. I became too forceful and efficient in exacting revenge.

Momma, gave Jane and me a sock filled with fruit, candy, and nuts for our Christmas gift. We had to share. Hoping Buddy would return soon. I saved some candy to divide with him, hiding it underneath the old scroll player piano.

Angel came to babysit us over the holidays during school break. Merl wasn't around and she was safe or Fanny would not have allowed her to come. I grew to love dear sweet Angel. She was so kind and loving. I thought she liked coming to babysit because Fanny didn't allow dancing. With no adults around she'd crank up the am radio to a rock in' roll station and we'd do the twist along with a few other steps she tried to teach Jane and me as we giggled.

I was in charge of looking after my younger siblings when Angel went home each afternoon and while Momma prepared meals, which made me feel grown up. And so did the twisting with our teenage baby sitter.

My chronic cough returned. Sick, I ran a low-grade fever every day. On New Years day Merl reappeared, and Angel abruptly stopped coming to the house. I missed her as much as Buddy. They were my only friends except for Jane.

Merl had not messed with me sexually again. For this I was immensely grateful. I did not know he had been messing with the other children, except for the incident with Angel. I wasn't sure what was a pass. Maybe it had something to do with kissing? Touching forbidden zone?

He came back to Momma unexpectedly that January. They verbally fought for a week then he told her he was leaving again, returning to Florida to be near his children.

Before he was gone, he shaved my head bald as an egg because I had gotten into his hair grease and gobbed the stuff on my hair to slick it back like Elvis Presley. All the other children in school made fun of my skinhead when I returned to classes.

A pretty dark-haired girl who sat right in front of my desk constantly whispered, seething derogatory remarks and flipped her long braids in my face. I thought she was gorgeous and wanted her to be my friend. Disappointed when she rebuffed my every entreaty for friendship. Snubbing, as if she were better. I asked politely for her to stop. Ignoring my pleas, she intensified her annoying assaults and mocks. I'd had enough! Late Friday afternoon during art class when we were using India ink to outline pictures we had colored with crayon, Vicki smugly slung back her braid one more time, then giggled. My eye burned where it poked.

Why was she doing this? I managed to control my anger enough to reach forward and gently take hold of her right braid. I shoved it into the bottle of ink then threw the ink-soaked braid against her back. Her white blouse was ruined. I grinned!

Scowling Vicki turned around and snorted, "You nasty bald flea, don't touch me!"

I smiled. " Keep your braids off my desk," I said and went back to coloring.

The teacher told us to put away our art supplies and gather our things to leave for the day. I smirked inside, knowing that Vicki hadn't noticed what I had done. The teacher didn't know either, and no one else had seen it. It was the perfect crime, so I thought. I beamed all the way home.

My pride over the act ended Monday when Vicki's mother arrived and talked to the teacher. Her mother was a pretty-faced fat woman with burned bottle-blond curly hair. While they were talking, Vicki turned around and gave me a dirty look.

"My mother is going to make your mother buy me a new blouse and coat!" she seethed.

Once Vicki's mom was gone, the teacher, Mrs Angely, took me into the hallway and explained I had ruined Vicki's blouse. Short Mrs. Angely was all business in her brown skirt suit and jacket. She scowled a lot. Her page-boy graying hair was neatly plastered to her head stiff as a board with hair spray. Frowning angrily she said, "Saul, this wasn't very nice. You ruined her new blouse and coat. Why did you do this?"

I answered smiling, "She wouldn't stop slapping me in the face with her braids, and she ruined my picture."

Mrs. Angely scowled. "But why did you poke her braid in the ink?"

"I didn't! She did it! It was an accident! I warned her this would happen."

She placed her hands on her hips, frowning sternly. "Young man, you are a liar! You did this on purpose, just to be mean! Now I want you to march right in that classroom and apologize to Vicky in front of the entire class."

"I won't do it! I'm not sorry and you can't make me tell another lie!" I shouted while secretly thinking and planning I'd cut off Vicki's braids if she slapped me one more time. My anger with Mrs. Angely would be taken out in revenge against Vicky because she started this and got me into trouble.

Mrs. Angely grabbed my ear. I was squirming on my tippy toes when we marched back into the room. "Children, Saul has something he wants to say to you!" She let go and sat at her desk grimacing.

I stood in front of all my classmates--the one place I did not want to be. They all hated me! I hated them. I wanted my Daddy! I wanted to go back to Delena. I faked my lower lip pooched out and said sadly, "Teacher says for me to say I am sorry!" I pretended to bow my head in shame.

"Now apologize to Vicky!" she said.

"I'm sorry, Vicky. I won't ever put your hair in the ink again. I promise."

"Vicky, do you accept Saul's apology?"

Sweetly, innocently smiling, Vicky said, "Yes Ma'am."

Mrs. Angely stood shaking her index finger at me. "Take your seat Saul! We won't have anymore trouble out of you or you'll be in the principal's office. Do you understand?"

I nodded.

My head dropped sadly. "Yes, Mam," I said while taking my seat again.

Vicki behaved herself for most of that morning. In the afternoon we had art class again. About midway through Mrs. Angely was called to the principal's office and she had to leave us unattended. Vicki took advantage of her absence by slapping me in the face with her braids and then laughing about it.

We just happened to be using scissors in art class. Without hesitation, I calmly grabbed Vicki's right braid and held on tight close to the back of her head as she struggled and screamed to get away. Then I hacked at the braid with my dull school scissors while the other children laughed. They whispered at us to stop before we all got into trouble. Mrs. Angely, who must have heard the commotion, ran back into the room and saw Vicki howling and frantically struggle to get free from my grip. I saw Mrs. Angely, but I wasn't going to let go until I had cut off at least one of Vicki's braids. But the scissors were too dull and I only managed to cut off half the braid about six inches from the back of Vicki's head before Mrs. Angely seized the scissors from my hands and made me sit down in my seat.

Vicki was crying hysterically. "My mother will get you for this!" she shrieked.

I sneered. "Oh yeah? Next time I'll bring a razor and shave your entire head like Merl shaved mine! Then I'll shave your Momma's fuzzy bleached head!"

I was in big trouble now. At that point the tall muscular principal walked in and grabbed me out of my seat. The rest of the class hatefully glared and snickered as Mrs. Angely tried to comfort Vicki while I was led out of the classroom.

He pulled as I resisted while strolling the hallway toward his office. There, he jerked out the paddle and gave me three swats. Then we sat at his desk. He asked what had happened. I explained my reasons. He scowled, nodded and meandered toward the next room. I heard him talking on the phone. When he was finished, he said Momma was coming.

Heading home, she was angry but when I told my version of the story she began to laugh. She said if I had problems with the other kids to go talk to the principal from now on. She couldn't afford to miss work.

In school the next day Vickie's hair was cut short. Mrs. Angely moved her to the front of the class near the teacher's desk. Now we were on opposite ends of the room. I was at the back of the classroom isolated from all the other children. I had to wear the dunce hat. No one was allowed to speak to, or play with me the rest of the week. That wasn't a punishment. For them to say nothing was better than being called names. None of them wanted my companionship anyway, so I wasn't missing out on anything there either. Little did I realize when we went home that Friday after school it would be the last time I would ever see any of them. I wouldn't miss them. That weekend a major storm blew in.

Chapter Twelve

The snow fell heavily into the next week. A foot snow white already covered the ground. Then a couple more harsh blizzards dumped an additional good two feet, along with several more inches between the major storms. The snow seemed to fall continually through the holidays past New Year's and into 1962. After one whiteout at the end of February, a snow drift reached some twenty-five feet up the peak of the barn and covered the rooster-shaped weather vane. When the snows finally stopped, accumulations were over the top of my head. School was dismissed for several days as a result.

By the time the roads were clear enough to go back to school, I got chicken pox. I had no more got over the pox when the weather turned cold again and we got another eighteen inches of snow.

With the stress of having to face the bullies lifted, the pox sores fading, and Merl gone, I was feeling much better. Time to enjoy the snow days. The mounds of white were an inconvenience for the adults, but I loved it. I wasn't looking forward to going back to school, but I need not have worried. Momma was making plans to move back to Arkansas shortly where she was going to file for divorce from Daddy. She planned to marry Merl someday. She hoped he'd come back to her.

Momma did not want Merl to drink and she was even more upset about the other women. They had fought about his affairs and the excessive drinking and he wound up leaving us for good in Wisconsin. So he said. I was glad. Momma did not believe the accusations made against Merl by Angel and Ely. She defended him to the bitter end. But I knew they had to be true for I had my own dirty little secrets concerning Merl. I think privately she knew of his pedophile fetishes and perversions but could not admit to herself that the man she loved had these problems. To live in denial was easier than to face the cold hard truth. If she approached the problems head on and confronted him she would have lost him forever. To admit he had these demons would have meant she had chosen the wrong man again. She wasn't about to give him up. Not now! She had forsaken all to have his deceitful embraces and kisses. He was her god.

Chapter Thirteen

Only days before we left New Glarus, Jane and I bundled up against the cold in heavy clothing and went out to play in the melting snow. We had snowball fights and built snowmen like all children do. We even found a virgin snowdrift and fell into it to make snow angels. To feel normal for a little while was wonderful.

While Jane and I were shaking the snow off each other, I looked down the long drive toward the main highway. I couldn't believe my eyes. In the distance I could see what looked like my dog Buddy coming toward us. I was overjoyed. Gone nearly three months and I had been worried sick about him. As he drew closer a finger of dread began to play with my insides. Something was plainly wrong with Buddy. He staggered as he trotted up the drive toward our house. When he came closer, I could see froth spray out of his mouth as he shook his head. Catching sight of us, first he growled, then whimpered, and finally moaned. Then he stopped and let out a ferocious bark.

Part of me wanted to run and meet him at the edge of the yard, but I held back out of fear. Buddy began to run faster toward us through the deep snow, leaving a trail of foaming froth in his tracks. When he came within twenty feet, he arched his back and his fur bristled around his face. He snarled.

"Buddy, my puppy, you've come home," I said, my voice shaking.

He whined like a puppy and wagged his tail. He snarled again, and whined as if confused. He sat down on his haunches. I took two steps toward him. He raised, his teeth shining as he crouched for a jump. I glanced behind me with horror-stricken eyes. Jane was about six feet behind me. What could I do to protect us? Nothing! We could not move fast enough in the deep, wet snow to get back to the house.. We were at Buddy's mercy.

Momma was inside, but I was afraid to call her for fear of rousing the dog's anger. Daddy had said that Jesus was a help in trouble. Everybody said that. Now was time to put this statement to the test. I remembered Ely and Fanny telling me to pray when I needed God's help. Fanny prayed in tongues. I didn't know that language. But in my heart, mind, and every fibre of who I was, I prayed like I had never prayed before. But I was careful to keep quiet lest I agitate the dog any further.

I heard the soft distant sound of horn music. Momma must have the radio on. It was the sound of a trumpet. Horrified, we had no escape. Fearfully trying to believe God would hear me, I looked up to the sky and whispered my prayer again. Just then a beam of light, about eight feet in diameter, stabbed through the clouds and shone around Buddy. An angel descended down the beam of light and grabbed Buddy by the scruff of the neck with a massive hand and held him still. He must have been ten feet tall and was clad in what looked like medieval armor. I knew Buddy couldn't escape his grip as I stood motionless, not able to fully understand what I was witnessing. Was this an Angel? God? Daddy said we all had a guardian angel. That was who he was! I was no longer afraid. Peace surrounded us, radiating from the strong heavenly presence of my Guardian Angel.

The angel spoke into my mind. He said to turn around and walk to my sister, take her hand, and *walk,* not run, into the house. Without a pause, I did exactly as he instructed. When we were safe inside and I had bolted the back door, I looked through the window hoping to see him again. He nodded and released Buddy from his grasp.

I smiled. I wanted him to stay. But to my disappointment he ascended back into the heavens through the light. The light followed him up into the clouds. He was gone as suddenly as he had appeared. I was sad. I wanted Momma to see him. She wouldn't believe me.

Buddy lurched for the back porch and leaped against the window. He snarled and growled, barking ferociously as he attempted to get into the house. Slimy froth was smeared over the glass.

The commotion brought Momma running. Terrified, she shrieked, "Oh my God, Buddy has rabies!" She nervously pulled the blind on the door window and made us go into a different part of the house. She closed the kitchen door that opened into the living room just in case Buddy was able to break through. Then she used the crank telephone mounted on the wall. With two long cranks and a short she called a neighbor and asked him to come and shoot Buddy.

In a few minutes things got very quiet at the back door. I looked out the living room window and saw Buddy stumble around the side of the house and head back toward the main highway. Jane and I cried. Buddy would soon be dead. I didn't want the neighbor to shoot him. But I also knew he was out of his mind. He had frightened me. He was no longer my Buddy. There was no hope for him. Why hadn't the angel helped him? I didn't understand. I didn't want him shot. But Jane and I were safe.

Taking Momma's trembling hand as we stood there watching Buddy swagger away from the house, I said, "Momma, he couldn't hurt us."

Her voice shaking, she squatted to my eye level. "Oh but, Son, he could have torn you to bits, and gave you rabies!" Her eyes watery, she pulled us close.

Smiling, I said, "No, Momma! The angel held him tight so Jane and I could come inside!" I said.

Her brow wrinkled and she tossed her hair back from her shoulders. She gave me a questioning look, eyebrows raised. "Saul, don't lie to Momma! You didn't see and angel!"

"Yes I did! I'm not lying! He had a shield and a sword and he wore a pleated skirt made from brass colored strips of metal!" I shouted.

She questioned me thoroughly and kept telling me not to lie. But my story never changed. I told her the truth.

She patted me on the head, and chuckled. "Angels do protect little children. Maybe you saw one after all."

I don't think Momma ever believed me about the angel, my Guardian Angel. But I never forgot that day. In my innocence from that time on I trusted with assurance that God could hear my prayers.

A few days after Buddy was shot and killed, Momma decided we'd return to Arkansas where she'd divorce Daddy. We left New Glarus to stay with her parents in Rooster Ridge, Arkansas.

Step-grandmother Gert despised Merl and she knew the "devil" would be slithering back into Momma's life. The only word Daniel used when referring to Merl was devil. He was glad the devil had left us. But he also knew Momma would welcome him with open arms if he showed up on the doorstep with his bag of tricks and sweet talk.

Daniel and Gert didn't want Merl around Pete, my mother's eleven-year-old younger brother. After a day or two it was obvious they didn't want us there either. In a heated argument Momma defended Merl. She refused to accept the truth about him.

Motivated by rage she moved us down the road to Joe's and Rebecca's abandoned honeymooner's shack. They had moved to Michigan where Joe was learning the drywall trade. Their shack had a tin roof and its walls were made of rough oak lumber. Holes were cut into three walls where windows should have been, but instead of glass the holes had a clear plastic tacked over them. The floor was also made of rough oak planks. Gaping cracks between the floorboards were wide enough for me to stick my fingers through. This shack became our home until the summer.

It was cold in Arkansas when we arrived on Momma's birthday in March of 1962(this was the year Stone County Arkansas was the second poorest of all counties in the lower forty-eight states). The day we moved into the shed dank chill ripped exposed skin with frostbite when the winds bellowed from the north through the hills and hollows The last blast of winter was upon us, spitting tiny snow flakes. Two days later, we drove to a local dumping ground two miles from our shanty.

Rummaged through the junk and garbage to find anything that might make our life more comfortable. I wore a ragged dirty coat three sizes too large. It was a gift from Pete. Slipping on a pair of old holey socks over my small hands and fingers to try and keep them warm, I helped dig through the rubbish.

I couldn't force myself wear the green girl's mittens one more time. I told Momma I didn't know where they were, had thrown them in the trash dump not far behind the white house in Wisconsin. Being cold and having frostbitten fingers was better than being laughed at by all the boys in school.

Momma found old clothes, dishes, and a broken table. Only one of the legs was missing. But the most valuable prizes were rusted stove pipes and a burned-out King wood-heater. Momma gathered an arms load of rags to use for grease lamps since we had no electricity.

We dumped our treasure into the '50 Ford car trunk. Returning to the shack, we gathered flat field rocks near the woods. Laying them on the floor under a window made a hearth for the stove. The heater's bottom had burned completely out. But the upper parts of the stove were intact and functional. We placed the rusted stove on the flat rocks and then poured five gallons of sand inside the corroded firebox. We then placed smaller rocks around the outside edges to keep it from moving and to prevent the sand from sliding out of the rim around the bottom.

The next day Pete brought scrap pieces of tin roofing. He helped install the rusted pipes by cut a hole in one piece of tin that was nailed over a window. The flu pipe was run out the hole. Pete placed tin inside and around the walls of the heater and on top of the sand. We built a fire. Now the drafty shack was warmer. The sides of the heater and pipes turned cherry red as the hot fire roared.

With no damper to control the blaze, the fire danced, thundering hot. There was no stopping it. The shack air was sweltering. Rambo cried. Jane sweated. I was comfortable. Momma's grimacing face was wet from perspiration when she opened the stove door and doused it with a bucket of water. Scalding steam and fiery smoke gushed into the room. Blistering water, wet ashes, and sand oozed down through the rocks and dripped through the cracks in the floor onto the ground under the house. I could hear the dying coals sizzle as they futilely struggled to stay alive. Momma had killed the toasty fire. I frowned.

I wouldn't have cared if the house had burned down--at least I was warm for the first time in three days! Nevertheless, she had to put the fire out. To stir my frustrations further she used the bucket of drinking water I had lugged up the hill from the spring in the hollow behind our new home earlier in the day. I had to fetch another pail before dark--in the cold. We would have to sleep one more night--in the cold until she could buy a pipe damper the next day.

The shed already had a bed and wood cookstove belonging to Joe and Rebecca. Momma cranked up the fire in the cookstove but it burned only an hour then the night chill set in again.

Jane, Rambo, and Momma shared the bed. I slept on a pallet of Anne's quilts in the drafty floor. It was horribly frigid. My weak lungs became infected quickly.

To make matters worse a neighbor had given Momma a gallon bucket of hog lard to be used in making grease lamps for light at night. Which she did. Smothering in the room filled with grease smoke I lay on the floor and placed my head near a crack to breathe cold fresh air drifting up from under the house. I coughed a lot and wheezed.

I was sick, smothering and short winded most of the time. Some days were worse than others. Momma accused me of faking to get out of doing chores and going to school. My condition improved a little when the weather warmed.

Momma enrolled me in Rooster Ridge school shortly after we arrived. My problems with the other kids followed all the way to Arkansas. Chronic coughing and low-grade fevers were a good excuse to stay home because I didn't fit in. Sometimes I faked being sick, especially after I shared my angel experience with classmates. They laughed in disbelief while nicknaming me the Angel Boy. I didn't like being called Angel Boy or sissy. I decided to never talk about my Guardian Angel ever again. Even Momma didn't believe me.

I was far behind academically. The sadness, and loneliness at times was unbearable. Rejection and I were well acquainted.

No reason existed to go to school. I couldn't learn anyway. Knowing how to figure numbers or read and write wasn't important. After all, none of Momma's brothers except for Pete could read and they got along quite well.

Tired of being sick, I didn't know how to get better. None of the adults saw to it that I got professional medical attention other than them poking an aspirin down my throat when I ran fever. Sadness ruled my life. My lack of social graces, learning disability, and the constant bullying by classmates made attending school quite an unpleasant experience.

Momma got government relief in the form of a box of commodities delivered to the shed once a month by welfare workers. Someone had reported Momma for neglect and abuse of us children that spring. Many afternoons she made us hide in the woods behind the house, fearing the state workers would come take us away. While hiding out, we gathered bundles of twigs and broken tree limbs for the night fire. With the fading sun we returned to the shed, built fires, and Momma prepared supper from the commodity foods. They even brought us powered milk--a real treat.

Within days of our return to Arkansas, Merl came back. Momma was happy again and I was happy for her that she wasn't sad, but Merl's presence only increased my gloom.

Within a week of his return, Momma saw her attorney to discuss the divorce. She was hoping to receive some back child support from Daddy. I looked forward to that. I was too embarrassed to eat the free lunches at school. I stayed on the playground at lunch time but Momma never knew this. Once in a while she gave me a nickel or a dime and I'd buy candy at the country store across the road from the school during lunch hour. Momma said many mornings that she wished she could share more money but she just didn't have it.

Constantly berating my father, and fearful he would kidnap us if he found out we were back in Arkansas Momma wouldn't allow us out of her sight except for school. She loved us. Though she had as many problems as my daddy. Hers were just different. She didn't talk nonsense but she was obsessed with a man that was mean to her and us. She worshiped Merl Judas. He was on her mind constantly. She often said, "I would lay down on a bed of hot coals and let him walk on me to keep him from burning his feet." I wished she could have those same feelings of love and respect for my daddy. But she didn't and I was learning to accept the fact that she hated Daddy. She was paranoia in a sense, suspicious and fearful, always.

A contradiction in terms, Merl was as sweet as candy, loving and kind, but these facets of his personality always preceded the flip side of his nature when he turned into the selfish bastard from hell. He was the giver of pleasure and pain for all of us.

Momma took Rambo into the attorney's office and tried to pass him off as my baby brother Bobby who was now living with Sonny in Loafer's Glory. She told the attorney she had custody of the three children all this time and she wanted the back child support. The lawyer had no idea Rambo was her illegitimate son by Merl. However the attorney did make a comment about how small the child was for his age.

She had tried to initiate the divorce proceedings some months before but had no money to pay the legal cost. Now the final paper work was filled out and a court date was set. Merl had given her the money to retain the attorney. She thought soon she would be free of ol' crazy Enoch (as she often referred to him) forever.

During the strawberry harvest in mid-May she went to court. That evening she was very sad but would not talk about it around Jane and me. Later I found out the Judge could not grant her a divorce because Daddy was back in the mental hospital again. Sonny had shown up in court that day and the Judge gave temporary custody of Bobby to Sonny until Daddy could attend court. Momma's attorney was upset with her because she had deceived him by pretending Rambo was Bobby and for lying to him about other issues concerning her divorce and the separation. He dropped her as a client.

That same afternoon Momma's Aunt Diana and Uncle Tex came to visit. They pulled into the yard in their black '50 GMC pickup. Momma held Rambo on her hip and greeted them. Smiling, happily, she said, "Come on in. I'll put on a pot of coffee."

She was overjoyed to see them. Diana, wore her holiness flour-sack green attire and matching cloth sunbonnet. Tex wore a new pair of bib overalls and pale blue shirt. They stood on the front step as Momma towered over them in the doorway.

"Honey, we can't stay but just a minute. I need to talk to you," Diana said. She stuck her head inside and saw me sitting on the bed with Jane playing with our toys. She fiddle with her bun and then waved at Jane and me. Merl had gone to town to buy cigarettes. "Hi Saul and Jane, you sure have some nice toys."

We smiled and went back to playing, but I listened.

Slightly panicked, Momma asked, "What's wrong? Has something happened to Moms or Pops?"

"No, I just don't want the children to hear," Diana said.

"Okay, let's go to the truck," Momma said as she stepped out the door, and they walked back to the vehicle.

Curiously, I dropped my car on the bed and ran for the door to listen. I hated it when adults excluded me from these conversations.

"Ora, Honey, you know I love you," she said as she embraced Momma and kissed her on the cheek.

Tex hugged Momma too and patted her on the back as Rambo began to whine. Tex spat his chaw of tobacco on the ground. "I love you too," he said.

"Ora, you know I have loved you like my own daughters. I did all I could to help your poor momma raise you kids. I've done my best to teach you right. You know that! But I am concerned about you, Dear Heart." She scowled. "Merl Judas is not good for you or your children. I know you and Enoch will never be able to mend the fences now that you have this little one," she said as she smiled and tickled Rambo in the ribs.

He giggled.

"Frowning harshly, Momma snapped, "What's on your mind?"

Diana said, "You shouldn't be living like this. You need to pray and ask God to help you get your life right again. This is wrong, Ora! Aside from the adultery, I can't put my finger on the evil I sense, but I know it is here and it is going to destroy your life."

"Well, that's my business and none of yours!" Momma shouted.

Diana shook her finger in Momma's face. "Now Ora, don't get in a huff. I love you or I wouldn't be here."

Fidgeting, Momma sighed as she hoisted Rambo higher up on her hip. Then she smiled. "Merl and I are getting married as soon as the divorces are final. He is divorcing Lilly this month too."

Frowning sadly, Diana said, "Ora, Merl is no good, and if you don't get away from him and do right you will hear the cries of your babies upon your deathbed."

Diana was the most dedicated and kind-hearted Christian I had ever known. Merl was the only person I ever heard her openly speak ill of. I thought she was right. Why was Momma not listening? Why was Momma so angry? Diana loved Momma! Should I tell her my secret before she married Merl?

"Just leave!" Momma shouted while turning and racing back to the house in tears. "I never want to see you again. I love Merl! I always have! I never loved Enoch! This is my life and I'll live it how I damn well please! It's none of your business! Leave!"

"But it's God's business! I love you!" Diana shouted sobbing as she and Tex crawled back into the truck. He nodded and grimaced when he started the engine. Diana pulled a handkerchief from her purse and wiped her eyes as they drove out of the yard.

Momma lay on the bed and wept bitterly. Jane and I tried to comfort her as we all huddled close. I handed her a handkerchief from out of a box of clothes under the bed. "Don't cry, Momma. We'll have a good life with Merl. I just know it," I said, wanting to make her feel better. I hoped my words would come true. I didn't want Momma to cry anymore.

Merl tried to cheer her up that evening. They talked a lot, kissing and hugging. Merl caressed and kissed on Jane, Rambo, and me too. He assured us that he loved us and we were going to be a happy family. I wanted to believe him. After all he hadn't touched us in an ugly mean way since his return.

He'd brought Jane and me a huge grocery sack full of chocolate candies the day he came back into our lives weeks earlier. We were now finishing off the bag of goodies. My baby teeth rotting and my front teeth were missing.

They made plans to move.

Chapter Fourteen

When the strawberry harvest was over in May, we relocated to the outskirts of Springdale to pick beans and steal turkeys. One day Momma's old friend Ginger and her children were harvesting in the same field as us, no more than thirty feet away. Ginger appeared to have a new woman friend now, and both Momma and Ginger pretended they didn't know each other. They didn't speak a word to one another.

Waving and smiling, I shouted, "How ya doin'?"

Ginger pretended not to hear me.

Her children hatefully glared at Jane and me. I heard Robert tell the others, smirking, "There is that squalling brat. He is such a momma's boy. A real sissy!"

They laughed at me and I reached down and snatched up a rock.

Momma frowned. "Saul, put it down!" she mumbled.

I dropped the rock.

"Pay them no mind, Son. Robert is just a bully. He'll get his come-up-ins one day," she said.

Almost in tears but not wanting them to see me cry, I carried my bean basket several feet up the rows ahead of them so I couldn't hear what they were saying. My feelings seemed to always be getting hurt. I wanted Daddy, but all I had was Merl. "I ain't no Momma's Boy! I'll be the best chicken thief there is! I'm not a Momma's Boy!" I mumbled while yanking the long green bean pods off the plants and tossing them into the basket. What was a Momma's Boy? Maybe a Momma's boy loved his Momma? What was wrong with that? Maybe he was a sissy? But I wasn't sure what a sissy was either. I just knew it must be a bad thing. No body called Merl a sissy. Momma said he is a real man, not crazy like my daddy. I'd try to be like Merl since he was good to us now.

We never lacked for poultry products in Springdale. Merl took me with him at least twice a week to steal chickens and turkeys from one of the big farms located a couple of miles from our house in the rural community of Lowell. Always fearful that we would get caught, I watched as he used wire cutters and snipped a hole in the tall fence for us to crawl through during our evening excursions to raid the chicken and turkey houses.

I was too short winded to catch the birds but I sure could hold them once Merl handed them to me. I shimmed through the fence hole dragging the frightened birds firmly in my grasp. Before leaving, Merl folded back the cut fence and wired the opening shut so it wouldn't be noticed.

I held the squawking, flopping birds, one in each hand, by their feet upside down. They beat me with their wings in a futile effort to escape. I stood there behind the car anxiously waiting to leave as Merl loaded them into an orange crate in the trunk. Then we'd head back to the house under the cover of dark with headlights off until we got a distance from the poultry farm.

Back home Momma was boiling water. I wrung off the bird's heads with my bare hands. Though I didn't like killing anything, the thought of fried chicken on the dinner table was more powerful that my compassion. Once the heads were wrenched off the bodies took off flying across the yard, or they flopped to the ground and ran with blood spewing from the open necks. I carried the dead birds inside to Momma.

She submerged them under scalding hot water for a few minutes, then pulled them out and placed the fowl in a large dish pan. We stepped around to the back of the shack and plucked feathers. The blistering wet chicken feathers stunk worse than dookie.

Merl gutted the kill. Momma deep fried or baked the chickens and turkeys we stole. We ate heartily after raiding the chicken houses. Though I felt guilty for stealing, a weasel.

I was happy in Springdale for a couple of months but soon our nightmare commenced again. Late in the night Merl came into the bedroom where Jane and I slept. He had his way with us. This became a ritual for the next month. I wanted to kill him when he messed with Jane as she cried and he muffled her screams with whispering threats and slammed his large brawny hand over her small mouth and face.

I loved him when he was good to us. I tried to love him for Momma's sake but I couldn't understand why he was so mean to us. He could be kind and shower us with candy, sweet words, and tender hugs. Confusion, shame, and fear were our closest companions. Momma was going to marry Merl. That made him my daddy. I loved, and hated Merl.

Chapter Fifteen

Migrating to the Bottoms that autumn, we harvested cotton. I was seven when we took up residence in the shanty on the cotton plantation at Denton Island. There the molestation became worse. Now Merl became physically violent with Momma. The sexual abuse was a nightly horror. His frequent fisting and beltings during drunken stupors insured our submissions. We were growing numb from fear, knowing what to expect but it didn't stop the pain. We went on living, keeping our mouths shut, enduring the shame. The sexual abuse was bad for me, but worse for Jane. I could do nothing to protect her. Jane and I, helpless, survive until he finished then returned to Momma's bed. Afterward, soft cries and whispers, blocking the obscene acts from our minds until the next time.

On many occasions when drunk, Merl told Momma he was leaving. He'd drive away. Momma bellowed all the while he was gone. He disappeared for two days in October. Momma's bawling broke my heart. I couldn't bear her anguish any longer. I knelt beside her and prayed for God to send him back to her.

Two hours later he drove into the yard with a grocery sack full of candy. He was sober. Momma rejoiced as she ran to greet him and fell into his arms. Fear and loathing surged through me. Why did I pray for him to return? But Momma was happy and she was more important than Jane and me. Her happiness was all that mattered. I guess I truly was a Momma's boy.

Merl was provoked easily, and slapping Momma around seemed to be a game for him. We knew the rules--he was in complete control. He beat Jane and me with his leather belt if we didn't produce what he expected of us in the fields. We suffered from malnutrition. Food being scarce some evenings Momma prepared one box of macaroni and cheese out of a box. Jane, Rambo, and I got a small portion each. She would have nothing to eat. A cigarette had to be sufficient to suppress her appetite. Merl got the rest.

Whining at the dinner table I said, "Momma, why does Merl get the whole bowl and we only get a couple of bites? I'm still hungry!" I enviously watched Merl scarfing down the mound of food on his plate. He reminded me of a greedy hog at a slop-bin, especially when he was drunk.

Scowling harshly she said, "Saul, stop your bickering! Merl provides for us. He needs his energy to work. When you can pick as much cotton as him then you will get the large portion." I bowed my head in shame.

After many days with little food and no money Rambo only had sugar water in his bottle. Feeling no dishonor I begged other migrant worker families in the camp for a slice of bread or sausage bit from a can. This was how Jane and I kept from starving that fall in Denton Island. Momma, Jane, Rambo, and I were hungry while Merl ate his fill of what we had and spent the meager wages on cheap wine. His carnal pleasures, the booze, and smokes were more important than us.

The Sunday week before Halloween evening when the closest neighbors were away at the Baptist church in Grubbs, I stole one of their laying hens. I wrenched off the struggling and squawking chicken's head and brought the bloody fowl into the house for mother to cook.

She scolded me for stealing and Merl beat me. But Merl had taught me how to steal chickens. Now this was wrong?

Merl instructed me to steal from enemies--the wealthy and strangers--but not from family friends. However, Merl consumed the largest portions after Momma cooked.

I was intimidated to keep my mouth shut about this to the neighbors and lie to the end if ever questioned about the missing hen. I had only wanted to help feed my hungry siblings. Jane and I got the legs, wings, and back pieces. I picked at the neck bone to scrap every morsel.

It was ineffable to expect six and seven-year-old children to work like adults long days in the cotton fields. The cotton sack Jane and I pulled through the rows of snow white tufts became a burden beyond our combined physical strengths before we could fill it, Merl had to drag it along as we continued to stuff cotton into the opening.

I abhorred picking in the early mornings. In warmer weather if there was no frost, the morning dew soaked our clothes as the leafs from the plants dripped the night catch of moisture droplets.

I could not recall ever seeing a black person in my lifetime before we arrived in Denton Island. As we worked the fields one afternoon a new family of migrants moved into the shed. Their images were distant as smoke spewed from the metal stovepipe poking through the tin roof of their shanty. The sweet appetizing aroma of bacon drifted across the way into my nostrils. My mouth watered for the taste of only one slice. I determined I would visit our new neighbors when picking was done for the day and mooch a slice and maybe a biscuit to share with Jane and Rambo. As the day went on we heard hymns drifting over from the distant field. Soulful singing of workers but I couldn't see anyone. By late afternoon I saw a black family picking cotton in our field as they continued their delightful harmonies. In my ignorance and fascination I asked Merl what kind of people they were.

"Those are booger men!" He chuckled.

Daddy had jokingly told me the booger men would get me if I misbehaved. They didn't look like the monsters I had imagined.

Merl said, "They are the devil's boogers! Head hunters! If you don't pick your quota this afternoon, I'll hand you over to them. They eat little boys and girls who misbehave."

In our horror Jane and I continued to glance at the black pickers a hundred feet from us in the field. We hastened our pace as we picked. Terrified not only of the black people but of Merl's threat, we stripped the cotton stalks of green boles encasement pods, leaves, and stems, quickly ramming them into the sack and then covering it with a layer of only cotton tufts. I was thinking this would increase the weight in our sack. We had to be careful not to let Merl see, who was working ahead of us in the adjacent row.

The day finished and Merl dragged our heavy sack to the weight scales and they dumped it into the gigantic wagon. When he saw the leaves and trash fall out of the sack, he distracted the foreman by offering him a chaw of tobacco.

The foreman declined his offer and said he was docking the weight because of the trash in the sack. As he was paying Merl the day's wages, the black family pulled their sacks out of the field to the weight scales. Scowling, Merl shouted, "You're gonna be dinner for them niggers tonight!"

I knew for certain Jane and I were going to get a flogging if we got to the house. *If* we got to the house! The black people were coming! No! No! Jane and I began to cry in horror. I grabbed her hand and we ran as hard as we could to the picker shed. I was wheezing and gasping for every breath as we hid under the porch until Momma and Merl came to the house and made us crawl out. We refused until they laughingly assured us we would not be handed over to the head hunters. Jane and I squirmed out from under the porch. Merl grabbed me and beat my behind with his rough hand for putting trash inside the cotton sack.

With his face rage contorted, he shouted, "Boy, you're just lazy! Stop that wheezing your puttin' on." Then he started in on Jane, whaling her with his brawny hand. Momma turned her back on us and went inside. I pleaded with him to leave Jane alone and told him it was all my fault. He beat me again.

Jane and I sat on the porch until after dark watching the black people's shack, fearfully curious as we dried our tears. We really didn't know what to make of them. They acted like people but they looked so different.

The black family built a bonfire behind their shanty facing ours. They played guitars, harmonica, and sang gospel hymns. Jane and I were entranced. I was beginning to believe maybe these creatures were not booger men after all. After our small ration of food for dinner, we returned to spying on our new neighbors.

Momma brought us a cup of coffee to share, as we sat on the porch in the dank evening air. Merl was inside getting drunk, again.

"Momma if they're the devil's booger men, then why are they singing praises to Jesus?" I asked.

She sat down beside us, rolled herself a smoke, and lit it, tossing a large kitchen match onto the black soil at the edge of the porch. A wreath of tobacco smoke swirled around our heads when she exhaled. Jane and I took a sip of the coffee and then Momma took a sip from her cup.

Taking the rubber-band from her ponytail and letting her hair fall to her shoulders she chuckled. She said, "Honey, they ain't devils or boogers! They're just poor folks like us trying to make a living. Their skin is black because their people came from a land far away from here. Their great grandparents were brought here bound in chains on slave ships and sold to white men to work the fields and do the white man's chores. They were slaves in this country for hundreds of years, until President Abe Lincoln and the Civil War freed them."

I sighed, relieved. "Where is this land they came from?" I asked.

"Africa! I heard their skin is black cause the sun is so hot there, they are all born that way so they don't burn in the hot sun." She sighed. Whispering she said, "Besides, you kids and me and Merl got a touch of the tar brush in our blood too. That's what I was told. Don't know it be true or not but that is something we gotta hide even if it be true."

Big eyed with fright I said, "But Momma, Merl told me they are the booger men! They eat bad white children after wringing off their heads like a chicken. He said they save the head as trophies. I'm, afraid!" Jane and I snuggled close to her.

With a stern look she responded by rolling her eyes and scowling, speaking firmly and harsh, loud enough for Merl to hear inside the shack. "Merl lied to you kids, Baby! They are just poor migrant workers like us. Their skin just happens to be black. They ain't gonna hurt you. Because they are black, they work on the other side of the fields and the white trash works on the opposite side. Truth be known ain't no migrant worker, fruit tramp, thought too highly of. We are called poor white trash by the rich folks. Now you kids don't worry your minds one bit more." She stood, smiling. "It's about bedtime. We got a lot of picking to do to get this crop in. Ya need your rest. Finish your coffee and come on to bed when I call ya."

We hugged and she walked back into the shed. With a sharp tongue I heard her tell Merl not to scare us. He slapped her and laughed. Rambo began to cry, and she ran to him.

Smirking, Merl stuck his head out the back door. "Boo!" he said.

Jane and I jumped out of our skins. I dropped the coffee cup onto the ground. Luckily, it didn't break or that would have been a rump warming from Merl before bedtime. Momma called us inside.

I picked up the cup, skipped into the house and placed it in an enameled dish pan. Momma ruffled our dark hair and kissed us on the foreheads as Jane and I headed to our bed.

We pulled Anne's quilts over our heads.

Merl stood glaring, propped against the door facing inside our bedroom, smoking a roll-your-own. The dim kerosene lamp in the other room wasn't bright enough to light his face, and he looked black. I thought, you're the devil's booger, as I peeked out from under the covers.

"Ya didn't need that coffee anyway, Son! Children who drink coffee will turn black before they are grown. That's what happened to some of them Negroes you been watching all day. Yep, sure enough, coffee will turn a kid black and he'll stay that way!" He laughed sinisterly.

I didn't know whether to believe Momma or Merl. But Merl used this excuse from then on to not allow Jane and me to have evening coffee with Momma.

Chapter Sixteen

I learned the meaning of hate, racism, persecutions of the poor, ignorance and illiteracy in Denton Island. I scorned the cotton. When the harvest was in, I loathed the school, my teacher, and classmates. But most of all I grew to abhor Merl more and more every day as I watched him rape six-year-old Jane night after night. His lies and beatings stirred terror in our hearts daily. We were helpless, innocent and ignorant children, unable to defend ourselves.

Watching Momma slowly grow very ill only added to my sorrows. She was lethargic part of the time. She had cancer but didn't know and I never knew until I was grown. Realizing she was sick, I could do nothing to help but try to behave, tend to my younger siblings, and be kind to her.

Cotton harvest was almost finished. I had already started school. The plantation owner purchased a new diesel-powered cotton picker and informed all the migrant workers he wouldn't need our help any longer. I watched him drive the new machine over the last few rows behind our shack one Sunday afternoon. The roaring contraption, a giant vacuum cleaner as it sucked the white balls of fluff out of the hard, open bowl in which the cotton was encased. The roar reminded me of aunt Lou's vacuum, louder though.

The noisy apparatus didn't pick cotton as humans did. It left strings and torn cotton balls on the plant and some fell wasting on the ground. This new invention actually sucked some leaves into the bailer trailer at the back of the machine. It probably harvested only three-quarters of the cotton. Even so, I could tell from this brief demonstration that our cotton-picking days were over. I was glad though. I sensed that somehow our nightmare with Merl was about to come to an end, too. I silently prayed every night for Merl to be gone.

Momma and Merl were concerned for jobs. They discussed options, having to learn another trade or get work in a canning factory, sawmill or chicken processing plant. They didn't know what to do. Both were practically illiterate.

Momma had enrolled me in the Grubbs school the last week of October. Since Denton Island community was too small to afford a school of its own, the school bus picked me up for classes every weekday morning that late fall. The ride took about one hour each way. I had the same troubles in class and with my peers, again. I didn't care if I learned anything or not. Part of me just wanted to die from shame every morning when I forced myself to get on the bus and tolerated the cruelty of mocking, giggles, and derogatory remarks. I kept my anger intact while watching out the window pretending to be somewhere else. Death wasn't my true desire. I wanted the pain to go away.

I smelled bad, and wore tattered dirty clothes. Other children made sport of me, name calling. Merl had shaved my head again when I got covered in lice that fall and I was once again a skinny skin head. This time I wasn't alone. Merl had also whacked off most of Jane's hair. If Momma hadn't pleaded with him to leave at least a couple of inches she would have been a burr head too. My self-esteem did not exist.

Momma and Merl decided to stay there for the winter after the rich plantation owner gave them permission to remain in the migrant workers' shack rent free. The black folks moved away. I missed their nightly singing and family laughter that echoed across the field to our shed. At one point, Jane and I apprehensively considered asking them to take us in, until we discussed the possibility. I thought life with them might be better if they weren't the devil's boogers. But I wasn't sure. The one thing we did know for certain was that they sure cooked savory smelling meals. No! They're cannibals. That was the smell of roasting kids. We decided not to take the chance.

November cold north winds chilled to the bone. Inside the drafty shanty I couldn't get warm. Didn't matter how many clothes I put on. The low-grade fevers kept me drained.

Merl attempted to find odd jobs to see us through, until spring planting. I fantasized about my mom and dad getting back together and remembered the days when life was good before Momma left Daddy for Merl. It was the only way I could cope with the abuse, hunger, and rejection.

One cold night a week before Thanksgiving, Merl did his dirty deed, then left us alone in our bed to silently cry ourselves to sleep. As I lay there, I remembered my guardian angel and how he had saved us from rabid Buddy. I heard Daddy's voice in my mind telling me again that Jesus helped those in trouble. I patted Anne's quilt tight around my body and thought perhaps she was watching and would tell Jesus to help us again. Daddy always said that Anne and Jesus were best of friends. I felt the same unexplainable peace that was present that day my guardian Angel appeared. This was the same peace I had experienced when I fell out of the moving car a few years earlier. I prayed for Jesus for help. Get us away from Merl. This time after my prayer I felt an assurance, more so than before, that God had heard and He would answer it. My hope was in Jesus if he existed. Despite any doubts I may have had an unexplainable joy surged through my heart after that prayer and I reached over to comfort Jane.

The next morning I stood outside by the back porch when I felt that peace again, became bold as a lion cub. Walked up to Merl and told him I was going to tell my mom and dad what he was doing to us. Though I didn't know it was sex. I just knew he inflicted pain, and shame.

Merl flew into a rage, grabbing my arm he thrashed with his strong, rough hand on my back and bottom. Then he shook me violently. "Your dad is crazy. What is he going to do about it? Your mother loves me! She'll never believe you. Besides, if you tell, I will kill all of you!"

"My angel won't let you kill me!" I shouted as tears streamed down my cheeks. I pulled out my shirt tail wiped my face and blew my nose, then tucked it back inside my tattered pants. Choking back my tears, mustering a stern look, and I glared at him.

He laughed hysterically, and I spit in his face. As the spittle ran off his wrinkled brow and dripped from the end of his nose he backhanded me across the yard. My nose and mouth were bleeding when Momma came to the back door.

Frowning, timidly, she asked, "What's going on here?"

Merl looked at me venomously, scowling as he ran his forearm over his face and wiped the spit on his shirt sleeve. His blue eyes were torches of hate as the blood rushed to his face, making red lines in the whites of his eyes while the veins in his neck pulsated to every beat of his heart. Puffing from exertion, he vainly ran his fist through his black hair. "Tell her boy!" he shouted.

I looked at Momma, defeated, on the verge of tears again. "Nothing," I said while shamefully dropping my head.

Merl told Momma I had been back-talking him and he spank me.

"Damn angel my ass!"

Glaring at Merl she opened the screen door. She said, "Saul, come inside." Momma couldn't protect us from him. She couldn't save herself.

Momma placed a rag, cool and wet on my cheek and wiped away the red-plasma as I sat at the kitchen table. I coughed up a dab of blood as I gasped to catch my breath. Momma compassionately stroked my hair as she told me to spit it on the rag.

I could see the sorrow, fear in her brown eyes as they watered and her hands trembled. Does she know Merl is hurting our pee pees? Does she know how mean he really is? Why does she stay with him? Why doesn't she go back to Daddy? Daddy won't be mean to Rambo. Momma, why do you love Merl? I despise him. I will never love him again! I want to tell you Momma but he will kill us all if I tell! I remained silent and grinned at Momma.

She smiled. "Look there, your front teeth are coming back," she said while placing her hand under my chin. "Son you shouldn't tell people you saw an angel. They'll say you are as crazy as your Daddy."

I giggled. Those who didn't believe in angels were the crazy ones.

Momma's quiet tears and shaking shouted volumes of fear but she said nothing that might arouse the wrath of the beast again. After wiping my face clean, she kissed me on the forehead. "You'll be fine, Saul. Obey Merl and this won't happen again," she said, smiling.

I nodded, smiling as Merl stepped inside. "I'm sorry, Merl. I won't spit on you again. I promise," I said. I actually felt quite smug but wasn't about to let him know my true feelings. I think he knew I wasn't sorry as he rolled his eyes and walked into the adjoining room. Grimacing, he flopped down on the old car seat in the livingroom that served as a sofa and reached for the green bottle of cheap wine lying underneath. He turned the bottle up and gulped down several large swallows then loudly belched. Leaning to one side, he farted.

The same afternoon we had dinner with the neighbors. The Joneses were God-fearing, Baptist people. Merl had helped them kill and dress-out a hog the week before. They had not given Merl any of the meat for pay, yet. Today we would feast on ham, cracklin' corn bread, sweet potatoes, cat-head biscuits, and homemade white gravy. Always hungry, we looked forward to the coming meal with great anticipation. Merl was a little tipsy when we loaded into the car.

Mr. Jones, a short stocky man with orange-red curly hair that he cut close to his head, was about forty-five years old. He walked with a slight limp. Mrs. Jones was a foot taller than her husband with strong Native American features, about the same age, and wore long straight black hair that hung down past her shoulders. She dressed in men's blue jeans and a plaid flannel shirt. Both of them talked with a funny accent.

When we arrived and went inside, kindhearted Mr. Jones saw the cut on my lip and the bruises on my face. He smelled the wine on Merl's breath, and shook his head while glancing at his wife. He stared into my eyes. "What happened to you?" he asked.

I glanced up at Merl. He scowled. "I was chasing a possum out the backdoor when I tripped over a stack of wadded-up cotton sacks and fell off the porch," I said.

Mr. Jones nodded.

"Oh really?" Mrs. Jones mumbled as she scowled at Momma. I could tell Mrs. Jones didn't buy the story. Mr. Jones stared at me with sad sympathetic eyes. I knew he didn't believe me either as they suspiciously watched Jane and me while pulling the chairs back from the dinning room table loaded with fresh cooked food. Mrs. Jones pointed to the restroom. Jane and I took the cue and went into the bathroom to wash our hands.

"They don't believe me, Jane," I whispered.

"Merl will whip ya again if they say anything to him," she whispered.

I sighed.

The Joneses had moved to Denton Island from some northeastern part of the United States when Mr. Jones became permanently disable after an accident on his job. The cost of living was cheaper in Arkansas and they were able to survive on his pension easily and in comfort. All of their children were grown and no longer in the home.

We sat down to the table for dinner. Mr. Jones offered grace before we ate. I bowed my head, too, and prayed silently for God to get Jane and me away from Merl. Nothing was left in me but fear and hate for him. Mr. Jones' prayer was short, but it felt like eternity. The food smelled so good, all I wanted was to gorge myself. When he finally finished, I filled my plate and began wolfing down the food like a hungry hound. Momma scowled and told me to use my manners. I slowed down a bit.

About mid-way through the meal, Merl excused himself to take Jane to the restroom. Moments later we heard Jane ask him to stop. She was crying. Pleading with him not to hurt her again. Then her voice grew muffled--he had put his hand over her face.

I suspected this would happen. Merl liked to take chances with getting caught. He often molested Jane in public restrooms or in the car when he thought no one was watching. (Who knows what goes on in the mind of a pedophile?)

Angrily, Mr. Jones ran to the restroom door and tried to get inside. But Merl had locked the door. Mr. Jones yelled at Merl, demanding that he open the door. But Merl acted as though he couldn't unlock it, so Mr. Jones kicked it open and burst into the restroom just as Merl was zipping up his pants. It was obvious what had taken place as Jane wiggled free from Merl's grasp and pulled up her panties.

Furiously, Mr. Jones shouted at Merl to get out of his house. Frightened and sniffling, Jane ran over and held onto my arm at the dinner table. I put my finger across my lips. I was afraid Merl would kill us and the Joneses if she did.

Momma stood, frowning. Panic stricken for Merl's safety she ran to his side. Merl and the Joneses had been friends and neighbors for months. Merl was the ultimate manipulator, but Mr. Jones was no longer deceived. For the first time in my life I saw fear on Merl's face as the color drained and he began stuttering a whopper in his defense. While Momma tried to drag him toward the front door she motioned for Jane and me to run for the car.

The veins in Mr. Jones' neck began to bulge and throb. His face turned flame-red, matching his western shirt. Yelling, shaking, Mr. Jones mustered restraint in his rage by doubling his fist and holding his arms tight against his sides to keep from hurting Merl.

Angrily frowning, Mrs. Jones calmly stepped toward the cabinet near the kitchen sink. She opened a drawer and pulled out a handgun. Pointing it directly at Merl's head from across the room, for a moment Mrs. Jones didn't say a word.

Seeing the gun, horror wrenched Momma's face as she tugged harder at Merl's arm. Her voice fearfully trembling, she mumbled, "Let's go Merl."

Smiling sinisterly, Mrs. Jones coldly stared at Merl. "You sack of hog crap! I should blow your sorry ass to kingdom come!"

Mr. Jones shouted in a voice that quavered from anger, "You will pay for this evil! God has prepared a lake of hellfire for the wicked like you." He turned to Momma. "How could you allow this beast to do such horrible things to your children?" Momma didn't answer. "I'm calling the sheriff," Mr. Jones said. "I pray to God, He will deliver these children out of your home and into safety. Now get out! Before I kill you both here and now!"

Merl raised his fist and threatened to hit Mr. Jones. "I'll knock your religious head into the floor! No bastard talks to me that way and gets away with it!"

Not flinching, Mrs. Jones cocked the pistol. Momma forcefully pulled at Merl's arm while pleading for him to get in the car. Dragging him out of the house she scooped up Rambo to her skinny hip, pausing only to yell at Jane and me to get into the car one more time. I grabbed a cat-head biscuit off the table and ran out the door holding on to Jane's hand.

"You children do not have to leave," Mrs. Jones cried.

"Thanks for the food," I said as I slid into the backseat.

At that point, our only emotional security was Momma. Besides, by that time Jane and I had become almost numb to Merl's daily abuse. I wanted to stay with the Joneses, but if we did Merl might kill Momma and Daddy, then come back to kill us. He might even kill Bobby in Loafer's Glory. He'd told me he wouldn't kill Rambo because he was a Judas, belonged to him. When he told me that the week before, I knew he didn't love Jane or me. Now it was okay for me to resent him. I wasn't a killer but I wouldn't have minded if someone else had murdered Merl for me at that moment.

Just a child, I didn't feel that I was in a position to choose with whom I would live. Our spirits had been broken by Merl's brute physical, mental, and sexual abuse and by Momma's passive cruelty. Though I had begun to fearfully rebel against him some.

Mrs. Jones was crying in her doorway as Merl sped out of their driveway. Mr. Jones was shaking his fist in the air. I really wanted to thank them for standing up to Merl, but knew I would never get the chance. Were they angels in disguise?

Momma and Merl stopped at our pickers' shack a half mile down the road. Momma ran inside and grabbed a few of our clothes and threw them into paper bags. Three bags in all. Then we drove the hundred miles to Loafer's Glory where Momma abandoned us at a neighbor's house close to Chad's place.

The week before Momma abandoned us, she told me she was pregnant with her second child by Merl. Little did I know that I would not meet him or see Momma again until the child was almost fourteen. Years later I found out that the cancer made the pregnancy extremely difficult. Momma only weighed seventy pounds six months into the pregnancy. She nearly died when forced to have an emergency hysterectomy at six months because the cancer in her uterus would have killed her and the baby. The baby was three months early. It was rough going for them both.

Eventually, Momma recovered. My baby half-brother Jacob survived. He was her fifth child. She was only twenty-two years old.

Over the years Momma, Rambo, and little Jacob suffered much abuse at Merl's hands. But Jane and I were free of him forever.

Part Three
A New Life
1962 to 1964
The Separation

Chapter One

The neighbor with whom Momma abandoned Jane and me was Merl's mother. A cantankerous elderly biddy with mousey gray stringy hair, she bragged that she was a witch with supernatural powers. I thought she was an ignorant, domineering old woman who was selfish, and half cracked in the head. In the back of my mind I still believed she had cast a spell on Momma. Needless to say I did not like her. The feeling was mutual.

Momma told Jane and me she would be gone in the morning. She was leaving us to our father, and she would go away with Merl and Rambo to start a new life. It would be better for all of us this way.

Holding back her tears, firmly, Momma said, "Son, you must be brave. Be strong, and take care of Jane always!"

I whimpered, "But Momma, you can't leave us."

She kissed us good night and said, "Hush now, be a man. Be brave. Jane needs you. You have to be strong! I will love you always. But this is best for you and Jane. Now go to sleep."

The next morning when we awakened Bertha was on the telephone talking to Chad. I heard her say, "Your crazy brother's wife was here with my son and they have run off and left these kids with me. I am too old to raise kids that aren't mine. You need to come get them."

I peeked around the corner into the kitchen while leaning off the edge of the bed as Bertha continued to talk to Chad. There she was as usual, the ends of her hair tucked in her mouth nervously gnawing and slicking her gray strands with spit.

An hour later Chad arrived and he loaded our brown paper grocery bags of clothes into the trunk of his car. Daddy saw us getting into Chad's car an eighth of a mile up the road while he was walking to the store. Every morning before he went to work he strolled a mile from the old homestead down the road to the local store for his morning cup of coffee. As we pulled out of the drive Daddy began to run behind the car, yelling for Chad to stop.

Chad ignored him. He drove us to our cousin Poojam's general store in Loafer's Glory across from Delena's abandoned restaurant. Delena and Saul had divorced, and she moved to Amarillo where she could be close to Leve. Jane and I wanted to see Delena but she was gone and her house was empty, the yard grown up with tall grass and weeds.

We went inside Poojam's Store and Chad bought us a bottle of Coke to share. Daddy came running into the parking lot. We ran outside and hugged him. He was huffing for every breath, bright eyed and grinning. We were elated to be together again, except for Chad. I saw him scowling through the window panes that covered the store front.

Daddy was now working for Chad and living at the old homestead. Daddy picked us up and carried us inside the store. He put us down in front of the checkout counter. Happily smiling, Daddy said, "I will take my children home with me now to raise." Joyfully, Jane and I sighed, and hugged his legs.

Chad's demeanor changed from tight-lipped satisfaction at the sight of our reunion to rage as he scowled again and banged his brawny fist against the checkout counter. Breathing heavily he kicked the side of the pop tank. "I don't think so! You can't even take care of yourself! These kids need a home. I'm going to have them placed in an orphanage!"

Daddy's blue eyes filled with tears and his face became fire red. "These are my kids. *I* say what happens to them! I am going to raise my children!"

Chad doubled his fist and began to punch Daddy. He was much stronger but Daddy continued to fight until Chad grabbed his head and beat it against a steel post in the center of the store that aided roof support.

Jane and I screamed at them to stop fighting through our tears. Customers backed away. The two toppled a small shelf of bakery goods, sending them sprawling over the floor.

Chad kneed Daddy in the gut, then the groin, and continued to bang his head against the steel post. "You ol' crazy fool! You haven't got any say!" he said while smashing Daddy's face into the steel post again. "You don't have brains enough to make this decision!" he yelled again and rammed Daddy's head against the post one more time.

Blood ran down my father's face from a long gash above his eyebrow and out his nose. Chad shoved Daddy in the final defeat against a counter. "Get your miserable mindless rump to the mill! There's work to do!"

Great shame surfaced on his face as he bowed his head. His face twisted trying to hold back his tears, flitting his eyes timidly, shamefully toward me to see if I were watching. He sighed and threw his arms in the air, defeated. Then a wild crazy look of confusion came over him as his eyelids fluttered and his eye balls shifted from side to side then rolled back inside his head showing only the whites. "No! No! Howdy! Howdy! If you don't believe in the American flag you ain't nothing but a whore!" He shook his head and was himself again as the wild look faded. He ran for the back door covering his face with his knuckle-skinned hands. Humiliated, he bolted out, leaving a sprinkling of his blood behind on the concrete floor. All the while Jane and I continued to cry.

Chad's lip was bleeding. Daddy had got in one good blow. I was glad as I resentfully watched Chad drag his shirt sleeve across his face to wipe away the blood. I wanted to bust Chad over the head with my bottle of Coke, which would only make matters worse for Jane and me, but hate rose up in me against Chad.

Jane and I did not see Daddy again while we lived with Chad and Vanny through Thanksgiving ,Christmas, and until New Years Eve. Chad called Leve Christmas night and told her to come get us by the first of the year or we were going into a ragamuffin home. He seemed to take pleasure in speaking these harsh words over the telephone in my presence as he hatefully glared at me. Fear gripped my heart, but I had to be brave. I had to take care of Jane always. Bossy Stan, Chad's youngest son's attitude toward Jane and me had not changed since our last visit eighteen months earlier. We were still the unwanted white trash that had invaded his domain and he didn't want me sharing his room again. I was ready to leave their house, orphanage or not!

I believe Momma abandoned us out of love and concern for our safety and also to protect Merl. I never believed she left us because of hate. She could not feed us. I believe she knew of the sexual abuse all along that we endured. Abandoning Jane and me was an act of love on her part. This was probably the best of her few options. She hated herself, not Jane and me. We were victims of our environment. Evil in others, poverty, ignorance, Daddy's mental illness, all the harsh circumstances were contributing factors to the demise of my family and destruction of our parents. Intense love and hate mingled in all of our lives. Shame and fear ruled the day as Jane and I continued in our struggle to survive.

Chapter Two

Leve, tall and pretty, picked us up on New Year's Day, 1963. We sat close to her protective presence on a Continental Trailways passenger bus as we made the trip to Amarillo. At forty-five years old, she was five nine and had high cheek bones, lean with black hair, a ravishing woman. Her eyes were so deep a blue as to shadow dark violet in color. She reminded me of perhaps an older, larger-framed, darker-complexioned Elizabeth Taylor. Neither Jane nor I could recall ever seeing her before, but we could see right off that she was very kind. She made every effort to calm our fears while holding our hands constantly or placing one of us on her lap to watch the miles swirl bye out the bus window as we made the trek to our new home on the plains of Texas. She never left our sides, except for restroom breaks.

People in the bus station at Oklahoma City and Amarillo and on the buses we rode were friendly, smiling and chatting. They didn't gossip and scowl and call me names like on the school bus in Denton Island. No one was mean to anyone else. If everyone in Amarillo was this friendly I would like this place. I might even like school and be able to make some friends.

We arrived at their home on 100 North Lamar street at two a.m. the next morning. I had never seen a street light before. I could play in the yard after dark and not have to worry about stepping on an unseen copperhead! The house sat on the corner where two paved streets intersected. Two street lamps, one shined in the front yard and the other lit the side and backyard. This would be a great place to ride a bike with paved roads and concrete sidewalks. The house was square like all the others rowed on the street but a dull gray in the dim light.

I dreaded walking inside. Who was this man Jake that Leve said was her husband? Would he hurt us like Merl? Was he crazy like Daddy? Was he a drunk like Lou's husband Martin? Did he have girlfriends on the side to make Leve sad and angry like Martin and Sonny's husband Dan who was raising Bobby? Leve unlocked the front door. I sighed and drew in a deep breath, shuddering at meeting possibly another monster.

He was sleeping in the bedroom and Leve didn't wake him. We would meet him in the morning. I sighed in relief. He probably wouldn't like us. He'd be like all the rest. We'd be thrown out or dumped or kidnaped before six months was up.

She ran a tub of warm water and Jane and I took baths. Then we were off to bed in the other room, all three of us. Jane huddled close to Leve and I took the outside edge next to Jane.

I awakened the next morning to the aromas of sweet bacon frying and fresh coffee drifting into our bedroom. Leve wasn't there. The house was warm and comfortable when I crawled out of the bed. I awakened Jane and we quietly toddled into the living room and timidly sat down on the sofa close to each other watching a husky bald man quickly wolfing down a large plate of eggs, bacon, and toast in the connecting dinning room. He didn't see us as he faced the opposite direction.

Our mouths watered while our stomachs burned and growled for just one taste. But we weren't about to ask. Momma always made us wait for Merl to finish breakfast then we got what was left, if anything.

Happily humming, Leve wearing a half-skirt apron tied around her blue silky flowered print dress, her shoulder-length black hair with tiny streaks of gray pulled back in a pony tail stepped out of the kitchen with two plates filled with eggs, bacon, cat-head biscuits and gravy. She sat them on the table next to Jake when she saw us and smiled. We smiled back. That man sure could eat a lot.

"Are you children hungry?" she asked.

We nodded. Jake turned around, smiled and nodded.

"Don't be shy. Come and take a seat. But first wash your hands," she said.

We ran for the bathroom and hastily washed our hands. Giggling, Jane said, "Did you see the man? He hasn't got any hair on his head. He's a burr head like you, Saul,"

I flipped water off my fingers into her face. "I know, he is as ugly as me."

"I wonder if we will get to eat til we're full?" Jane asked.

"I don't know but if we can't I'll steal some later and hide it," I said.

We wiped the smiles off our faces, walked back into the dinning room and took our seats as Leve directed. Then she placed the two huge plates of food in front of Jane and me. I could not believe my eyes!

We started wolfing down our breakfast before Leve introduced us to Jake. I crammed a huge spoon full in my mouth.

Smiling, she said as she placed her large but refined hands with long fingers on our heads, "Children, this is your uncle Jake. Jake this is Saul and this is Jane."

Smiling, my mouth full and trying to keep my lips together so nothing would fall out, I said, "Howdy! Jake!"

"Hi," Jane whispered with a mouth full of food.

He nodded.

I never recalled meeting a bald man before Jake. He was bald as an egg with a paunch of a belly hanging over his belt line. His muscles were firm and his large calloused hands were strong. Something in his big brown eyes that told me he was a good man. His brown eyes reminded me of the kindness I saw in Buddy's eyes before he went rabid. His focused intelligent air as he glanced over to read the partially folded newspaper beside his plate as he sipped on another cup of coffee caused me to believe that he was smart too!

Jane and I gobbled down the food he provided for us that first morning and frequently glanced up at him to see if he was watching us. He wasn't, just reading and eating. He was thinking, I could tell from the way the expressions changed on his face unconsciously. His kind face with calm stable demeanor gave me peace. I felt we were wanted here. I just knew I was gonna like him.

His voice was bass and kind as he sighed and pushed back his empty plate. "Leve, please bring the coffee pot and set it on the table. Have another cup with me before I leave. Okay?"

Leve sauntered out of the kitchen with a clear glass pot right off the gas burner filled with hot coffee still gurgling up and perking into the top. She set the pot on the table next to Jake and pulled a chair out beside me, took off her half apron draping it over the back of the chair, sat down and had breakfast with us.

"This is good!" I mumbled, and swallowed.

Jake unfolded the morning newspaper, glanced at Leve, and smiled. She smiled back.

Calmly, grinning, he said, "Now you kids eat all you want. There's more in the kitchen."

Leve enrolled me in second grade at Summit Elementary school in Amarillo. Jane was enrolled in first grade. My new teacher, Mrs. Jones, and the principal, Mr Hardin, were given no medical or school records. Leve told him about Jane's and my backgrounds and they told Leve not to expect either of us to pass that year.

No one expected much of me academically. But something about this new town made Jane and me feel safe. Even most of the strangers were nicer to us. These were city folks. They used more manners and everybody didn't know everybody else. The other kids at school were even nice to me, at first.

I didn't know how to read or write, although I could print my name with my left hand. The teacher thought I should be right-handed and told me to always use my right hand when I did any work for her class.

The other children attempted to help me learn and adjust during the first couple of weeks. But soon the newness of this challenge wore off and classmates got frustrated because I could not comprehend the materials. Most of them began to ignore me or make fun of me, except for one. Short and stocky with curly dark hair, Alvin became my best friend. By the second week I was beginning to think perhaps they too were chicken dookie, like those in Wisconsin.

During the two years prior to December 31, 1962, when Leve journeyed some six hundred miles from her home in Texas to bring Jane and me to live with her, we had lived with eleven different families. Probably more, although the twelve, standout most vividly. It would take some time for Jane and me to feel safe and be able to trust again.

Daddy's other sister, Delena, lived up the street from Leve, and was now with yet another husband Ricky. Her marriage to Saul only lasted six months. I liked Saul much better than bald, fat, gruff Ricky. But he was gone so I'd have to get to know Ricky better.

On Saturday the third week after we arrived, Delena walked the eight blocks to Leve's house. I asked her what had happened to Saul.

She explained that Saul had taken to drinking and gambling in their house, and she refused to have that behavior in her home. As she had often raged and got her way as a young girl, she did the same her last evening with Saul. She told me all about that night while we sat on Leve's sofa sipping cokes from six-ounce glass bottles. My attention bounced back and forth while watching *Felix The Cat* cartoons on an old tall black and white cabinet RCA television set. Jane and I poured a bag of peanuts in our pop as Delena continued to tell her story. She knew we loved Saul.

Folding her arms, she said, "He brought every drunk in the county in my home while I worked in the restaurant. There they sat getting drunk on moonshine, gambling, smoking, and laughing until day break. Night after night he did this after your Momma kidnaped you kids from us. He missed you guys really bad. He'd sleep all day and stay up all night!" She rolled her eyes and scowled. "Well, I wasn't about to live like that! I came in after closing the restaurant. There they sat, everyone of them drunk as Cooter Brown. Ol' bald fat Buck Ives lay passed out on my kitchen floor covered in his own vomit. I was mad as a hornet. My house was a mess and it really ticked me off when Saul asked me to fix sandwiches and coffee for his sloppy guest. I picked up a heavy ashtray and commenced cold cocking them on the back of their heads, running them out of the house! I did!"

She laughed and we giggled and tried to suck the peanuts out of the bottom of our empty pop bottles. "I wasn't real popular that night. I made Saul drag Buck out into the yard then I whacked *him* with the ashtray, and locked him out. The next morning he was asleep in the lawn chair as I pitched his clothes in the yard and told him to beat it! That was the end of that marriage. Damn drunks! I won't put up with what Ma took off Pa!"

She had hoped to reform his sinful ways but her hopes backfired when he wouldn't cooperate. So she divorced Saul. A month later she sold her home in Loafer's Glory and the restaurant to Chad and Vanny, then used the money to move to Amarillo.

Being barren Delena was envious that Leve had two children and she had none. Leve was also barren and rejoiced to have us as her own.

Delena was jealously determined to win at least one of us. After all, she had been our parent for a few months two years earlier, she considered herself our momma too. By the end of January Delena convinced Leve and peace-loving bald Jake to let her raise Jane. Jake gave in, not wanting to deal with Delena's temperamental raging, nagging, and pleading.

His nine-month-old son from a former marriage had died twenty-six years before. Four years later he met and married Leve after he was discharged from the Navy at the end of World War II. Jake always wanted a son. Now he had one!

The adults secretly conspired to separate us. Delena and Ricky had only been married eight months. Near fifty, with a large nose, bright blue eyes, bald on top and white short hair bowled around the lower part of his head, he never had children though he had been married three times before.

Jane and I walked home from school the day they made the decision. We knew nothing about their agreement. The never-ceasing Texas plains' winds drove cold February winter air up under our new coats. Jane played with her red ear muffs, neck scarf, and mittens, pulling them off and on to admire them then shoving her small hands into her new gray tweed knee-length winter coat. I adjusted down the ear flaps on my black fake leather cap and snapped the top on the matching pilot jacket Jake had bought for me the week we arrived.

We were proud of our new coats but our other clothing was shabby. Leve promised to take us shopping when the weather warmed up a bit. Since we'd have to ride the city bus while Jake drove to work in their '61 pale green Chevy Impala, she didn't want us to stand in the cold waiting for the buses.

The shiny car set right in front of our comfortable warm pretty new home. I was thrilled to see it every day when I arrived home from school. I was proud of the nice surroundings.

The motorcar looked brand new and I could hardly wait to take a ride with Jake. He had told me we'd go to the barber shop when my hair grew a bit more. He promised no burs! I'd never been to a barber shop before. I didn't know what to expect.

The neighborhood children were older than Jane and me and most of their parents' drove beat-up old jalopies. They thought Jake and Leve and now Jane and me were rich. But they didn't begrudge and happily looked out for us as Leve requested. We were in the center of a group of about eight children as we skipped down the street chasing a monstrous dried tumbleweed. When we came into Leve's yard we told our new friends good-bye and they strolled on down the street toward their houses.

Smiling, Delena held the brown paper sack of Jane's clothes, waiting for us while shivering on the front porch. Something was wrong. Delena was never there when we came home from school. Why was she out in the cold? What was up? Why did she have Jane's clothes sack.

She took Jane by the hand. "Sweety," she said, "you're going home to live with me."

Those were fighting words! I have to protect Jane, always! Raging, I yelled, "You are not taking Jane anywhere."

Delena smiled sweetly while swinging Jane's hands as they stepped off the porch. Jane commenced resisting and moaning while reaching for me as Delena dragged her along. "Now, Son, it's best for all of us." She scowled. " Stop it Jane!"

Crying, Jane screamed, "But I don't want to go. I don't want to leave Saul!"

Frowning angrily, I said, "I hate you! You will not take Jane from me!"

Jane screeched and struggled to break away from Delena's grasp.

I threw my books in Delena's face and grabbed Jane's hand. She managed to jerk free and we ran down the street yelling to the neighbor children to help us. Panic stricken, I hollered to the top of my lungs, "They're kidnaping Jane!"

The children leaped into action. "We'll hide you. Follow us!" they said and came running toward us as Delena sluggishly trotted behind on our heels.

Delena had gotten fat. Fifty years old and quite out of shape, she puffed as she chased after us. We ran out of the yard and down an alley lined with trash cans. She panted, and paused to catch her breath as she called after us, "Honey, come back! It's for the best. I'll give you a good home. I'll be a good mother! You can visit Saul on weekends."

But we weren't about to stop. We ran for our lives as the other children knocked over trash cans in Delena's path when she came running after us again. At the end of the alley, Jane and I ran up the street to the next alley. Our hands clinched tight together, I dragged her as she trailed behind. I was wheezing and coughing.

The other children caught up with us a block away. "The old lady gave up and walked back to the house," they said, panting to catch their breaths too.

Jane sniffled. I grabbed her arm and said, "Stop crying or they might come find us. My hacking will tell them where we are," I whispered in-between coughs. "I'll distract them, lead them off in the opposite direction."

Two of the older boys picked up Jane and dropped her inside a neighbor's trash can and placed the lid on top. Swallowing the lump of grief in my throat and wiping a tear from my eye, I said, "Be brave! Stop crying! I'LL come back at dark and we will run away. We'll hitchhike to Indiana, Aunt Lou's house. No one is going to take you from me. No one will separate us! I will look out for you always."

Jane sniffled, "But I'm scared Saul. It stinks down here. I'm cold and I don't like the dark." she said and cried.

"Hush! Do you want them to find you?"

Jane whimpered, "Be brave, sh," she said and was silent.

My coughing eased a bit, and I strolled the long way around to the house, and skipped into the yard from the opposite direction where Jane was hiding. I saw Delena on the porch and angrily yelled, "You old fat hag! You'll never take Jane from me!"

Husky Jake ran out and grabbed me. He was crying, dragging me kicking and screaming into the house. Frowning, he forcefully sat me down in a chair and held on as Delena and Leve walked through the front door. "Where did you kids hide Jane?" he asked.

I squirmed frantically to break free from his grasp. "You devil! I'll die before I'll tell you!" I yelled.

Leve calmly sauntered into the room and squatted to my eye level. "Now Saul, calm down. No one is going to hurt you or Jane. Tell us where she is. It's not like she'll live hundreds of miles away. You'll get to see her," she said as she reached for a napkin on the table and wiped the lump of dark blood off my chin I'd just coughed up.

Continuing to struggle I yelled, "Get out of my face, you ol' cow! You're like all the others! The whole world is chicken shit!"

She stood and brushed her shoulder length curled-hair back from her face. Calmly, not even fazed by my name calling she looked at grimacing Jake and wild-eyed frustrated Delena who was now also standing over me. "She can't be far," Leve said, sighing as she and Delena walked out the front door. "That child is coughing up blood. Gotta get him to a doctor!"

"No more doctors!" I mumbled.

She and Delena each wandered down a different alley. I broke free and dashed for the open threshold. Jake's belt swung, caught my right ankle and fouled the escape. I fell sprawling in the doorway. Glancing up, I saw Delena dart down the alley where Jane was hiding. Coming up behind her were our protectors, the neighborhood children.

Brokenhearted Jake bawled as he scooped me off the floor. Bear hugged on his lap, desperate to flee, I bellowed, coughed, and violently thrashed about.

My efforts were futile. Silent tears streamed out of his large brown eyes onto my head as he held me tight and rocked, whispering in my ear, "It's okay, Saul. No one is going to hurt you and Jane."

I could hear Delena brawling at the neighborhood kids as they pelted her with dirt clods. "You hooligans! Damn brats! Stop that! Don't you know this is best for Jane and Saul!"

The children finally gave up when Delena heard Jane sniffling and removed the barrel lid. Jane screamed. When I heard that scream, I knew Jane would be gone from me forever. I promised Momma, always. But I couldn't keep my vow. Jane was taken away from me like everyone and everything else I had ever loved. Then all went silent.

Delena hoisted Jane out of the trash barrel and ambled up the street to what would now be her new home eight blocks from where I lived. I could see them through the open front door. They're strolling up the sidewalk a half block away. Jane began wailing again and continued to struggle while trying to break free from Delena's grasp. Crying Delena barked, "Stop!"

The cold north wind whipped into the house through the open door. I wanted to run after them but exhaustion set in, my fight was gone. I simply sobbed, defeated, as pretty Leve walked back inside, smiling, and slammed the door shut.

During recess at school from the play ground I could see Jane through the window panes in her classroom. We weren't allowed to spend time together. Some days she'd jump up from her desk and run to the windows to wave but her teacher always dragged her back to her seat.

We were kept apart for almost six months. The adults decided we'd adjust to the separation more quickly this way. It was hard at first, a great loss, for Jane was my life; my only connection to who I was and where I came from. The last of my family was gone. It was just me now, alone with strangers.

Chapter Three

The week after Jane was taken away, Leve decided to buy me new clothes. We walked a few blocks to the local city bus stop. Boarding the public transit she dropped two tokens into the change collector. This bus was almost the size of the Trailways we had ridden into Amarillo some weeks earlier though the seats weren't nearly as comfortable.

Never before had I seen so many strangers, all in one place. I kept thinking maybe the next city block might clear the crowd when we turned the corner strolling on the sidewalks of Polk Street. I held tight to Leve's hand fearful I'd get lost in the sea of pedestrians. I smiled at the people we met passing , hoping if any bad bullies were in the bunch they'd go on bye.

"Howdy! Hi! Good morning! How are ya!" I said to everyone, just as Momma had taught. Some of the folks carried solemn ignoring faces set in concrete. Others stared and some chuckled or cracked a smile while returning my greeting. Other children on the street with their parents giggled and some just rolled their eyes like those at Rooster Ridge

School when I told them about my angel. One stuck his tongue out at me. That wasn't nice. What had I done wrong? That wasn't very friendly. So I tried a little harder to get them to crack a smile by smiling twice as big, which inflicted a tinge of pain in my face muscles as they stretched their limits. I was determined to make as many friends as possible in this new place.

Leve shook my hand and arm violently. We stopped in the middle of the sidewalk. She bent down to make eye contact, placing her hands on my shoulders. "Stop it, Saul! You are drawing attention to us," she whispered.

I was only trying to be polite. We strolled half a block and sat on a bus stop bench.

"Saul, it's okay to smile and be friendly but don't you think you are over doing it a bit?"

I didn't.

She sighed. "Well you are. Try not to draw attention to yourself on the city streets. Now let's play invisible the rest of the afternoon. I'd bet you'd make more friends if you didn't try so hard."

I smiled, liking that idea.

She patted me on the back. "It may take a little longer for others to warm up to you but it will be because they want to be with you for who you are. Now, stop the fake smile!" She smiled. "Okay?"

I happily grinned, and nodded. Nevertheless, I couldn't be rude and threw in a happy "Howdy" to the sadder-looking folks. Some gave me weird bewildered looks and went back to their invisible robot mode avoiding making eye contact. With our shopping finished we headed back to the bus stop for the ride home.

I had seen several black folks in town but said nothing to Leve other than to squeeze her hand a little tighter as we went our way in the shops. As we took our seats near the back of the bus to leave, the driver shut the door and started to drive off, when someone yelled from outside, "Stop! Please wait!"

The driver stopped and opened the door. Onto the bus bounced a panting, heavy-set black woman with strong African features. Wide-eyed and trembling, I wanted to speak but nothing came out as I huddled close to Leve and held tight to her coat sleeve. All I could think of was what Merl had told me in the cotton fields. I suspiciously watched her.

She dropped her token into the change collector, then strolled toward the back of the bus under heavy labored breathing from her dash. Black people eat mean white children! They save their heads for trophies! Merl said so. The closer she got, the more she smiled and showed her large white teeth. My heart pounded in my throat. I struggled to swallow the lump of nothing that cut off my breathing. Finally I could no longer camouflage my fear and pretend to be invisible. Should I smile back or hide? Terror stricken, I jumped into Leve's lap and knocked our bags off the seat into the bus isle just as she was about to reach our seat.

Grimacing, Leve asked, "What's wrong with you, Son?"

The black woman bent over and picked up our sacks without saying a word and set them on the bench across the isle. She smiled again and took the seat directly behind us. I am going to wet my pants, I thought as I continued to tremble.

Harshly, Leve asked, "Saul, what is wrong?" She then turned to the black woman. "Hello," she said.

The smiling woman nodded.

"Thank you for picking up the packages," Leve said.

The woman nodded again.

I was squirming, clinging to Leve, terrified, and couldn't understand why she was talking to her. Would Leve hand me over to her? Was this a set up? Jane? No, surely not! Delena wouldn't be so cruel.

Leve scowled. "What is wrong with you? Stop it now! Sit back on your side of the seat!"

I wasn't about to move one inch. No air would pass over my vocal cords. I simply pointed at the woman behind us and faintly mumbled, "The devil's booger!"

Leve scolded me so the woman could hear. "Saul! You hush your mouth! I'll paddle you here and now! Don't you call her names! You apologize this minute!" Embarrassed, she turned and smiled at the lady.

The woman nodded.

Momma had told me the truth. Humiliated, I wanted to crawl under my seat. Like a mouse I squeaked, "I'm sorry." Thank goodness it was only my imagination running away with itself. Jane was okay with Delena. Delena loved her. I sighed. Negroes aren't "devil's boogers."

The black woman nodded as she turned from my stares and smirked while gazing out the bus window onto the passing street. I continued to gawk. No longer afraid I wanted to touch her to see if the black would come off on my hand like the stove black polish on Grandfather Daniel's potbelly wood heater.

Showing all her teeth she turned smiling, and winked then went back to looking out the window. Fascinated by her dark skin and kinky hair I continued to ogle.

When we got home, Leve asked why I had been so rude. I explained Merl had said black people eat bad white children.

She laughed and spoke the truth. Until then, I never knew "nigger" was derogatory. Thought that was black people's race. I didn't like being called white trash or sissy. After Leve explained, I surmised being called a nigger was just as painful. Good thing too. The first black children arrived at our all-white school the next year. Some kids called blacks, niggers. Like a knife stabbing into my heart, when I saw the hurt. They were brave! They were heros, courageous. Desegregation laws were implemented nationwide, forced bussing programs in other towns across the country. All black schools closed in Amarillo, and those students were integrated. Children reacted to situations by what they were taught. Leve said ignorance was cruel, tolerance more precious than gold. I agreed.

Chapter Four

One cold morning I awoke, and after dressing, strolled into the livingroom. I thought, it was going to be like every school day. Leve began singing happy birthday when I marched in. Why was she doing this? Thought, I'd heard that song before. Didn't know for sure, or that I was eight, today. There on a small table by the telephone set a miniature stature of Mickey Mouse and a matching wrist watch. I hadn't learned how to tell time, yet. The watch was pretty but useless as far as I was concerned. Nevertheless, I wanted the Mickey statue.
I asked, "Whose toy? "
She said, "Son that's your birthday prize."
I was dumbfounded. "Why are you giving this to me?"
She said, "It's to celebrate your birthday."
I did not know people gave gifts on birthdays, only Christmas. "Why?" I asked.
Leve's heart sank, her eyes watered as she realizing I had never celebrated a birthday or knew when my day was. I could not ever remember receiving a gift for the past occasions. Momma would just say today is your birthday, and you're so many years old starting today. No gifts. Nothing special. Birthdays had never been important. They were like any other day.
Leve came closer, embracing me she said, "Son, this is *your* special day. It will be your day to celebrate, every year. A celebration of *you*, for being the wonderful little boy you are, and the man you will grow up to be. This is the day your momma gave birth to you eight years ago."
"But why are you giving me a gift?" I asked.

"Because you're special to me, and I love you," she said.

At that moment something happened inside my heart. The ice melted. I felt love and trust for her--an adult. Her simple caring expressions, and the small gift had softened the hardness. She loved me just the way I was. Her love was real. The kindness she bestowed ministered to my broken self-esteem.

I began bonding to Leve. Little building blocks of having a normal life were stacked one on top the other day after day during the first year I lived in their home.

School was a struggle because I could hardly write my name, nor say the ABC"s. I was stuck in second grade not because I belonged there but because of my age. Education was not a priority for Momma. She had not seen to it that I attend classes on a regular basis. Being malnourished during the past two years hindered concentration. I had numerous physical, social, and emotional problems to overcome. But I was determined I would learn and make friends while attending this new school. With Leve's support that desire was on it's way to becoming a reality.

Mrs. Jones wore her light brown hair streaked with strands of gray in a page boy. She was stern and got frustrated with me quite often because I had such a hard time comprehending the simple lessons. She assigned Alvin, the smartest boy in class, to be my buddy for the week. We had great fun playing at recess during those first few weeks. Alvin, a new friend was the greatest support a child could have after separating from a close sibling.

While we sat on the teeter totter one afternoon right before Easter break, he gently told me about God's plan of salvation. In a way that I could understand, sorta. Later Alvin's father came into the classroom and took him out of studies an hour early. Alvin and his family were traveling to Kansas for the holidays to visit family while his father tried out for a pastor's job with a Church of Christ there.

I returned to school after Easter break, looking forward to hearing about Alvin's trip. But Alvin's desk was empty. When classes were dismissed that afternoon I asked Mrs. Jones if Alvin was sick and when he'd reappear.

She sat me down beside her desk and somberly, with watering eyes, said that Alvin was in heaven now and he wouldn't be coming back. His entire family had been killed in a horrible car wreck before they ever got to Kansas. It had happened the day his dad had picked him up at school.

So, Alvin was with my grandmother Anne, and Buddy. I was very sad, but to know he was with Jesus now made it a little easier to deal with. Alvin was a Christian and a friend. He accepted me with all my flaws and shortcomings. The winter and spring of 1963 had filled my heart with great sorrow, once again.

Every evening before Jack got off work, Leve held me on her lap reading from a book she had purchased at a junk sale. I cried a lot those first few months. Not interested. Leve was persistent! Eventually I got interested in the story. Memorized the thing by heart, as she made the learning a fun game we'd play. All the while she helped me to feel safe for the first time in a long time.

I had felt secure once or twice in the past--when we lived with Delena and Saul, and when Momma held me in her arms just after the accident.

Benjamin Bea, a first grade reader, about a little boy and his dog and his new friends in a new town. The boy in the book kinda reminded me of myself. Leve taught me how to read from that book. "Benjamin Bea" became my hero. I wanted to be just like him.

Leve showered her affections and stuffed my guts with nutritious foods. Insisting I snack in-between meals, as though I were a fating hog to try and put some weight on my thirty-five-pound lanky skeleton. Those first six months after Jane was gone was a period of mother and son bonding between Leve and me. I learned to trust again because of her kindness, attention, patience, and unconditional love. She helped me to believe that I wasn't a bad kid. She taught me how to express human kindness again. Her love took away part of my fears and insecurities. Bonding with Jake would come later. He would be more difficult.

Chapter Five

Pretty Barbara Love was a girl in my class on whom I had a crush from the start. I found my first childhood sweetheart. It was love at first sight. She took a shine to me after the first month when I began sharing my graham crackers with her during milk break every morning.

Barb wore her long medium-brown hair in pig tail braids, just like Vicky had back in Wisconsin. But Barb was sweet and courteous. We sat beside each other at every opportunity during school. She helped me a lot in my schoolwork and threatened to sock the other boys who picked at me if they didn't shut up. She was the prettiest girl in class, and the other boys were jealous. They teased about my having a girlfriend, but that sort of teasing I didn't mind. I finally sorta understood what a sissy was and I didn't like being called that name!

Barb seemed grown up, because she wore makeup and a little lipstick. None of the other girls used the stuff. They were a bit jealous that Barb's mom allowed her to wear the grown-up glamor girl aides. Some of them didn't want to play with her. Said she looked cheap. What ever that meant.

One religious girl in class, Sally, who wore long blond hair and long dresses hurt Barb's feelings when we were playing at recess. No one wanted to be around Sally because she was so religious and hateful. A razor had never touched Sally's head. Scowling, she said, "My momma says any girl who cuts her hair and wears makeup is a Jezebel! Barbara Love, you're goin' to hell!"

Barb cried.

I whispered to Barb, "Pay her no mind, she is just a chicken dookie!" Then I stuck my tongue out at Sally and flapped my hands over my ears. "Oh, yeah! And your momma is stupid chicken dookie just like you!"

Barb stopped crying, giggled, wiping her eyes and smearing the makeup on her face. We went back to playing on the merry go round. Sally ran for the teacher. I looked at Barb, frowning. "Sally is a tattle tell," I said and pointed at Mrs. Jones strolling toward us. She forced me stay inside again during recess the next day and Barb had to wash the makeup off. I liked her makeup, she reminded me of the ballerina doll that spun 'round and 'round on Leve's music box. But it looked more like a Halloween mask when smeared. I wasn't about to tell her that. The next day she wore it to school again. The teacher said nothing. Sally scowled the day long.

Barb lived only two blocks up the street from my house, and let me carry her books home every day. One Thursday afternoon in the spring of 1963, we hurried through our studies then ran out to play chase, skip rope, and catch with a soccer ball. When Leve called us in to have dinner, we ate quickly and carried our cookies and milk outside.

A few days earlier, Jake had brought home a huge refrigerator box. It was all mine. He worked at a trucking line loading freight onto big semi-trucks. That's where he got the box. It was in the back yard, and I had placed old sofa cushions inside to make seats. I had also stolen one of Leve's candles for stormy weather and placed it in a coffee can.

The sun was going down as we crawled into the box, lit the candle, ate our cookies, and drank our milk. Then we held hands. Barb told me she loved me. No girl had ever told me that before other than Momma and my aunts. I had a funny feeling inside like I had never had before. But it was a great feeling. I thought I had to pee.

"Kiss me!" Barb said, closed her eyes, and pooched out her lips.

I turned ten shades of red and mumbled, "I don't know how to kiss like that, on the lips." That's the way I saw Momma and Daddy then Merl kissing.

She pulled me close, and put her arms around my neck. Then she kissed me on the cheek. "I'll teach you," she said.

Indeed she did. She kissed me on the lips. I really liked that. Then she kissed me again and again. She giggled and pointed. "Sorry Saul, my lipstick got all over your face," she said and tried to wipe it off with her bare hands.

Barb's mother called from down the street for her to come home. I didn't want her to go. I asked her to stay a little longer while planning to walk her home shortly after dark with Jake's big flashlight. We blew out the candle and crawled out of the box. Leve and Barb's mother were visiting in the yard under the street lamp light.

Barb ran and hugged her mother. "Mom, I want to stay the night with Saul."

Her mother and Leve began to laugh. Barb's mother, a short skinny lady with cropped straight light brown hair struggled to hold back her laughter as she looked at my face covered with smeared lipstick. "No Honey, you have to go to school tomorrow."

Barb said, "But can I stay with him tomorrow night? We have such fun together, and I love Saul."

Now the two women were really smirking at each other. "No Honey, not tomorrow either."

She frowned almost in tears and whined, "But why, Mom? You just gotta let us. Can Saul come spend the night with me?"

Barb's mother and Leve began laughing hysterically. Barb cried. I was starting to feel quite embarrassed. Why was Barb making such a fuss? Divorced Mrs. Love already said no! We couldn't play all night! I had spent the night with my cousins but had never had a guest in my house. Why was she so intent on staying with me? My childhood wasn't normal and I was deprived of the usual experiences children had with friends. I didn't want her to spend the night now. She was acting like a baby. Stop crying, Barb. Your momma says no!

"Please, Mom! Please?" Barb shrieked.

Barb's mother worked hard to muster a straight face as she placed her hands on her hips. "Honey, little girls and little boys don't spend the night together. Only married people do that."

Barb grabbed my hand and pulled me ten feet to stand directly in front of Mrs. Love. "Then let's go to the marrying place," she said. Barb was determined to get her way.

Leve and Mrs. Love giggled. Leve walked over, grasped my hand,

and led me toward the front door. "You have a nice evening, Mrs. Love," she said as she looked down again and tried to hold back her laughter.

Mrs. Love seized and dragged the resisting, screaming Barb by the hand and made her go home. Barb wailed uncontrollably as though some great love had died.

The next morning Leve sat down beside me at breakfast after Jake had gone to work. Smiling, she talked about "the birds and the bees."

Disgusting! I didn't want to hear all that "peepee" stuff. No wonder Barb's mom didn't want us to stay the night together. Though I had seen Jane raped repeatedly, and I had been molested, I didn't understand that was sex! I had just thought Merl was being mean, and hurting us.

The reality of what had happened to Jane and me hit home hard and I wanted to vomit. I pushed my plate back. Jane was going to have a baby by Merl! I couldn't tell Leve! Merl would find us and kill us if I told! Jane was to small to have a big belly and give birth to a baby. Would I have a baby? I was too embarrassed to ask, and Merl would kill her, all of us.

Frowning, I asked, "Do they always have a baby?"

"No Honey, just when the blood is present. It starts when the girls are teenagers. Boy's don't have the blood," she said.

I was relieved to hear the word teenager. Jane wasn't pregnant! I couldn't get pregnant! Yes, I am calming.

Smiling, she said, "It's okay for you to kiss a girl but don't play with her peepee." she said.

I felt dirty, wanted to hide. Sorrowful emotions almost as filthy as after Merl hurt us because of the memories that flooded my mind but I kept our secrets. Barbara and I hadn't even thought about our peepees. Why did adults have to make everything so complicated and dirty?

Barb's mom told her about the birds and the bees the same morning, and it was just as disgusting for Barb. We discussed what we had learned one afternoon when I took fig bars and a bouquet of Iris blooms to her house. I was a courtin'. I guess I was in love, but we didn't kiss much after that and she quit wearing the makeup to school. We certainly had no interest in each other's peepees.

Barb and her mother moved to Colorado the next summer. I had many more little girlfriends in the coming years, but I'll never forget Barb or that first sweetheart kiss in childhood. She liked me when I needed a friend most in my life. She too was there for me when Jane was taken away.

Part Four
1963 to 1964
Acceptance, Adjustments, Accomplishments, and Miracles

Chapter One

By the time school was out that first year I had been in numerous fights with the other kids because they were tantalizing with degrading remarks while making fun of me for being so skinny.

Leve said, "Sticks and stone may break your bones but words can't hurt you Saul."

She was wrong. The words did hurt. They broke my heart. I was provoked to anger frequently.

Leve said, "Gotta let their insults run off like water on a ducks back." I tried but it still hurt.

The teacher thought I was a troublemaker. Because of this, she didn't allow me to go out of the classroom at recess during the last two weeks of school. She didn't want any more fights. I think she was also genuinely concerned for my health. My respiratory problems had worsened. But even though I was sickly and small, I would never back down from a fight, despite the fact that I got beat up by the bullies most of the time. Needless to say, I failed second grade that year, although I did learn some things.

My health improved during summer. One week after classes were dismissed I went into the hospital and had my tonsils removed. The doctor told Leve my lungs were scarred badly from all the previous untreated infections. He told her my tonsils were the most inflamed he had ever seen. If they didn't come out I would be in a wheelchair by the time I was twenty-one and probably dead by age thirty. Leve agreed to the surgery.

The doctor found that chronic swelling and infection had pushed other glands in my neck out of place. He did corrective surgery stitching them into their proper location after removing the tonsils. The procedure took much longer than anyone expected and under anaesthesia I stopped breathing. The operating team worked frantically to energize my lungs in those few critical moments.

Leve immediately fell to her knees in the waiting room and cried out to the Lord to intervene. Later she said that right then I resumed breathing. I remained in the hospital an additional five days.

Though my lungs did not drain properly because of the scar tissue, my health continued to improve during the remainder of the summer. I grew one full inch and gained fifteen pounds. However, I was still skinny.

That summer I learned a myriad of tough survival skills from my rough new childhood friends on our poor side of the tracks in Amarillo. They looked out for me but I had a few encounters with neighborhood bullies on my own. Soon commit to memory--to run as hard as I could from the bigger, stronger ones. The running helped to keep my lungs clear of old mucous. Besides, I grew tired of getting beaten up.

Leve and Jake were thankful to have me in their lives as I was for them. Their support and love helped to build my self confidence. I was grateful to have a good home and to be wanted by those around me even though I missed Jane. Over the next several months I was slowly making friends and getting along with most of my peers. I knew by the end of summer that I was wanted. The stress of being castaway again was fleeting. My bonding to Jake and Leve wouldn't replace my love for Momma and Daddy. I longed for them occasionally, though the pain of losing my parents wasn't as sever as it had been when we arrived in Amarillo.

Still I hadn't *completely* overcome my fear of being abandoned. My new friends helped to make the adjustment period easier. Especially the family that lived next door. Darla was a year older than me with beautiful, long-wavy, light-reddish-brown locks that draped down her back to her hips, a tomboy with an angel's face. Her older brothers, husky Chester, fourteen, and ornery Harry, sixteen became my closest companions in the neighborhood. They took me under their wings like older siblings. Without their help and protection I would never have made the adjustment so quickly.

Two weeks before school started at the end of that first summer, the neighborhood children and I were ambling near the edge of our community at a place called Wild Horse Lake. It only held water during the rainy seasons. At that time of year the bottom was, covered in green tumbleweeds, and Johnson Grass. A low place in the surrounding terrain, Wild Horse Lake was a reminder for me of the large dried up hog ponds before a good rain back in Arkansas, though much larger. A train track ran along one side of the lake. Half a mile away hobos camped out under Route 66 bridge crossing over the tracks. They found shelter there while waiting to catch a free ride on a slowing freight. On occasions the bums wondered into our neighborhood knocking door to door and begged for food. I was sternly told not to give them handouts.

I wasn't obedient. Remembering the days when I had begged in Denton Island, I'd sneak some a morsel, a sandwich now and then when Leve and Jake happened to be out of the house. They caught me one day passing food out the back door to a scruffy graying black hobo. They scowled but let him have the meal. When he was on his way, they warned me of the dangers. The fear of destitute strangers that Jake and Leve instilled within me that day became much stronger than my empathy. No more charity.

Jake told me to be careful around the lake and never speak to the hobos if they happened by there. I wasn't allowed to go to the lake alone after that. Jake said on the shores of Wild Horse Lake was where the frontiersmen and cowboys established the town of Amarillo. Once a wild west life giving water hole. Dried up now because of modern progress. During springtime rains, the small remains of a once large oasis filled to the tracks. Eight foot deep in the middle, but the water evaporated during summer. Her wilderness glory was gone, but for a few short weeks the lake let our community know she had not forgotten her days of untamed splendor. I fantasized that I was a cowboy while riding my stick-horse at the lake's edge. Pretending to be a wagon train master, roping wild horses, and buffalo hunting as I played with my new friends. The older kids laughed but I was having great fun.

August 1963's visit, was the last time I'd desire to return to Wild Horse Lake. My companions, and I saw on the dry bottom hundreds of baby snakes. About fifteen children with me that day. We ranged in age from eight to fifteen years and I was the youngest. Running home we collected one-gallon lard buckets with lids and dashed back to catch serpents. Why were we doing this? What was I going to do with a bucket full of snakes? I didn't know. But it seemed like a fun thing to do since the other kids were so excited about them. I had to show no fear to fit in with the older children. This was peer pressure?

I snatched up six demons, as big around as a pencil and eight inches long, and tossed them into my bucket. Then I saw a grand snake about eighteen inches long and as big around as a quarter for most of its body length. The head was the size of a fifty-cent piece. Without fear, too ignorant to know the possible consequences of what I was handling and thinking it was a harmless water snake since only poison serpents existed in Arkansas and not Texas cities. I grabbed the fleeing devil by the tail and quickly slung him into my bucket head-first then slapped the lid on tight. I was proud; I had caught the largest viper of all. The older kids were going to keep their slithering reptiles and use them in science projects at school that fall. I'd just keep mine as pets.

At home I took Leve's number-two washtub out of the storage shed and filled it with water. Since my new pets were water snakes, I'd give them a place to swim while they were in my care. Once the tub was full, I opened the lid and dumped them.

Immediately, the largest viper swam to the edge of the tub and began to strike at the bucket. It slithered out, onto the ground and began to chase me around the yard. It was within three feet of my bare feet when I noticed a piece of plank lying under a window on the ground next to the house. I grabbed the board as I ran past and slammed it flat over the snake's back about three inches behind its head. The wiggling reptile fought to free itself, but I held the slat fast. I was safe for the time being, but couldn't let go. The viper repeatedly shot venom on the surface of the board as its fangs extended, embedding into the wood. This was not a harmless water snake! I didn't know what kind it was but it definitely wasn't harmless. The angry beast struggled violently to get away. I would surely be bitten if I released the binding pressure.

Just then dark-haired, pimpled Harry was strolling down the street, one of my neighbor protectors. He noticed I was in trouble and asked what I was doing. Panting and scowling, "This chicken dookie snake is trying to bite me!" I yelled.

Coming closer and examining the thrashing monster, he grinned. Harry said, "Hold the board taut ! I'll be right back," then he dashed for his house next door. Moments later he brought back a large fruit jar with a lid, a small can of ether and a rag. "Don't let go," he said as he set the jar on the ground, folded the rag, and applied ether onto the cloth.

The smell reminded me of the times I stayed in the hospitals. Harry dashed for another smaller slat from behind our storage shed and placed the end of it at the back of the striking serpent's head. Then he laid the rag over the viper's face and sprinkled more ether. Soon, the snake stopped violently flailing about. I didn't know if it was dead or asleep. But I didn't care, as long as it couldn't bite or come after me again. Harry proudly grinned and put the limp reptile in the fruit jar. I took a deep breath.

My heart pounding fearfully, I sighed. Relieved that was over. My voice quivering, I said, "Thanks, Harry!" He had saved my life.

He screwed the lid on tight, held the glass jar up into the light, and patted me on the back. "Did he bite you?" he asked.

Still panting from exhaustion, I said, "No! Thanks to you," and hugged him.

Scowling, he stepped way. "Glad you're all right! But don't hug me. What if someone sees? They'll think we're both queers!"

I remembered Chad using that word when those two men were kissing in the mental hospital. Does that mean crazy? No! Something else, kissing, and hugging, maybe? Embarrassed, eyes downcast as I realized the meaning, I said, "Sorry, I didn't know."

He smiled while admiring the paralyzed snake. "Well, you do now! Glad you aren't hurt. Can I keep him?"

I nodded and he ruffled my hair, turned, and walked across the yard to his house. I decided right then and there, I did not want any more vipers for pets.

Was I a queer? Merl touched me but I didn't want him to. No! I wasn't a queer. I didn't want to. Chicken thief Merl was a queer! He and Momma were the crazy ones, more so than Daddy. They should have been the nuts I went to see at the lunatic asylum. Not Daddy. Fanny and Ely should be locked up too. They made me hate myself and ashamed of my father. Daddy was a good man. They were evil. They belonged in prison. Angrily I shook my head to toss the bad memories out and focused on getting rid of the other serpents. Would I ever forget? The memories were too painful.

I was beginning to relate to the older kids, most of them accepted me. Made friends of many adults easily but with my age selective peer group I was still an outcast in many ways. Most just didn't like me and I couldn't figure that out. Would it always be this way?

Maybe these baby snakes would grow up to be mean, like the big one. Was I mean? Was that the reason other boys my age didn't want me around? Was sissy like queer? I'd think about that another time. Cautiously snatching each by the tail I flung them one by one out of the water into the bucket, and trotted as fast as I could to Wild Horse Lake where I dumped them into the dry lake bed. A good riddance!

Relieved to be free of possible death I strolled up the street and on my way home found a stray, a little long-hair black puppy sitting in a clump of Johnson Grass beside the paved road. She seemed lost and afraid. I picked her up. She smelled of burning wood smoke, and puppy breath. I thought maybe she had been in a fire and her masters were killed, as she happily licked my face and squirmed excitedly in my arms. Maybe someone abandoned her like I was abandoned? She needed someone like me to take care of her. She would be a better pet than the serpents. She'd never have to worry about having a home and someone to look after her ever again. I named her Skipper. Now I really was like *"Benjamin Bea."*

That autumn, Harry was expelled from school. He took the sleeping viper out of a shoe box and scared some of the teenage girls on the school grounds. Though the snake was harmless because of the effects of ether, the principal said Harry had jeopardized the safety of the other children. The science teacher identified the snake as a poisonous Cottonmouth. He killed it and placed the specimen in a jar of formaldehyde to be displayed in the science lab. Poor Harry couldn't return to classes for a week. I felt a little guilty about that for him. It was my fault he had the snake in the first place.

As the school year began I enrolled in Mrs. Black's second grade classroom. Kindhearted but stern, Mrs. Black smiled a lot but swatted us with a ruler when we misbehaved. She was a tiny lady with graying short hair. At first I was afraid of her. But soon she took a special interest while spending a little extra time with me so I could understand the work. I was struggling to learn and still behind my new classmates.

I didn't know anyone in the group. Mrs. Black seated us in alphabetical order. Behind me was a husky boy with buck teeth, flat-topped brown-hair and light complection. He had a distinguishable cowlick above his left eye at the hairline. Richie would eventually become my best friend ever.

Wednesday five weeks into the term we had a spelling test. I made the lowest grade in the class. I only spelled two of the ten words correctly. I could barely hold back my tears. Mrs. Black sent a note home with me. I gave the scribbling to Leve and began to cry. She held me on her lap as I told her how stupid I was and how the other kids made fun of me because I couldn't learn. She comforted me and we prayed for God to help me in my schoolwork. As Mrs. Black requested in the letter, Leve supported my studies and spelling with time and patients while I practiced.

We were to have a spelling bee the coming Friday. Dreading it, I knew that once again I would be humiliated in front of my peers.

On Thursday night Leve and I practiced the words. But I was so anxious that I couldn't concentrate enough to spell many of them right. I knew how to spell them but just couldn't seem to find where my brain had filed that information.

On Friday, Mrs. Black chose two team captains for the spelling bee. The captains chose who would be on their team until the whole class was divided into two groups. I was the last one chosen, as always. Embarrassed, when my turn came to go to the blackboard I wanted to run out of the room.

My head held down, I grabbed the chalk, and misspelled the word. I stepped aside in humiliation. Giving the other team a chance. Mary, the smartest girl in class, picked up the chalk. If she misspelled it, I could have one more try. I watched Mary slowly writing down the letters. As I watched, something began to happen inside my head.

My ears buzzed like a swarm of bees. I got dizzy and my vision blurred. Then, as my sight cleared, the buzzing stopped and I heard something that sounded like someone quickly turning a channel knob on a radio and high-pitched squeals inside my head. The sound stopped and my eyes refocused. The pressure inside my head seemed to have been relieved.

Something wonderful had happened! As though someone had turned on the bright light in a dimly lit room I could focus, and retrieving information stored in my mind was no longer a labored chore. My nerves were calm for the first time that I could remember since my parents split up. Peace and warmth surrounded me. I was no longer afraid I'd fail and embarrass myself. Alert and aware, my senses were sharper than ever before. I didn't feel sick or tired anymore. Great joy now filled my heart. And just in time, too. Mary had misspelled the word.

I had another opportunity, and this time I knew the answer. I confidently tapped the piece of white dusty chalk against the blackboard. My lips tight in a straight line. I knew the answer. Smugly I nodded at the teacher and scowling Mary. Then I spelled the word "P-R-E-S-I-D-E-N-T."

Mrs. Black congratulated me. I couldn't contain my smile. The smartest girl in class had been outdone by the dumbest boy in the spelling bee. My teammates began to clap along with the teacher. No words can explain the elation when my peers were cheering me on because I did something right. I won the spelling bee for my team.

In the following weeks I excelled in my class work and began to socialize with the other children without fighting. My self-confidence was building. Now, having fun at school. I was no longer an outcast. I no longer had a problem learning.

I believed God had answered Leve's and my prayers. I'm sure the secure environment Leve and Jake provided for me along with proper nutrition and medical attention contributed to this miracle. But whatever the case may have been, I was healed of my learning disability.

The leaves had fallen off the trees and the lonesome winds whistled through the cracks around the windows where I sat. The day was gray with heavy cloud cover. Winter was on the horizon as autumn slowly losing her temperance grip to the onslaught of coming winter cold. My attentions focused on the multiplication test problems before me on the page. Nine times nine was eighty-one and I wrote the answer down.

Principal Hardin's startling, booming voice broke the classroom silence as he made an announce over the public address box hanging on the wall above the teachers desk. Speaking with a quaver, I heard him swallow the lump in his throat several times. Surmised something was terribly wrong. The other students and I laid down our pencils and gave our undivided attention.

Mr. Hardin said, "Teachers please come to my office immediately. We will be dismissing school within the next fifteen minutes. Have your students put away what they are working on and get ready to go home. I want all teachers in my office immediately."

Mrs. Black grimaced. The look of worry on her face as she scowled and told us to hand in our work. She placed the unfinished test papers on her desk. Smiling, she said, "Gather your things. School will be dismissed shortly. I'm going to the office for a few minutes. You may quietly visit, whisper. Don't be roaming around the room. Stay in your seats." Then she raced out.

When she returned, Mrs. Black was crying. She wiped her eyes with a tissue she drew form the box at the edge of her desk and sat. "Quiet down children. I have something very important to tell you."

At first a hush, then a few sniffles as we watched our teacher crying. Stern Mrs. Black's sorrow infected us all. Her tears saddened me as much as Momma's had and I wept. She got fired? We were too loud? Why was school being dismissed this early? What did she have to say? I sighed and waited while choking back my tears.

Making every effort not to breakdown again, grimacing, she said, "The flag in front of school has been lowered to half-mast. Our President was shot in Dallas. It is not known if he will survive."

We heard wailing drifting up the hallway as other teachers told their students and my classmates began to softly moan, weeping flooded our presence. Mrs. Black said, "Children let us bow our heads for a moment of silent prayer."

Great sadness engulfed my entire being. I didn't know this man. But I knew he was the most important person in America. Kinda like a daddy for the adults? A king of sorts. He was as important to them as my uncle Jake was to me. In a sense this President man was like a father in that his decisions influenced us all. Once again I could not contain my sorrow, and wept.

Mr. Hardin added to our bereavement when he announced that President John F. Kennedy had just died in Dallas. At his grief stricken words the dam burst and unrestrained loud crying, yowls, and howls broke loose. Students and staff in Summit Elementary school along with the nation grieved the loss of our President.

He was with Alvin? Maybe? The bad man who assassinated him will burn for eternity in a lake of fire. Leve said murders go to hell.

Chapter Two

I became known as the spoiled rich kid on the poor side of town, because I had lots of toys and games. My personality changed from the totally frightened insecure little boy to bossy and independent, although the fear of being cast away again lingered always in the back of my mind.

By the second semester in 1964 I was making the highest grades of all my classmates. The first summer there Leve and Jake enrolled me in the local community center where I learned to swim and play ball. With improved health I was enjoying these activities on a regular basis.

Delena and Ricky also enrolled Jane in the summer swimming program and we spent Saturdays together. Jane was changing too and I hardly knew her anymore.

The summer of 1963 Ricky and Delena drove to Loafer's Glory and insisted that Daddy sign adoption papers. Reluctantly he signed. But he was adamant about not allowing Bobby or me to be adopted by anyone, his reasoning being that Jane's name would change someday anyway after she married.

In court the judge discontinued all of Momma's parental rights to any of us. But that didn't matter. She never attempted to contact us after our abandonments. She wasn't in court. She had no say.

Enthused, Delena and Ricky legally adopted Jane. When they returned they bought a house five miles across town and moved. We saw less and less of each other.

Jane was becoming bossy and independent as well but jealous of the new toys I had that Delena and Ricky could not afford to buy for her because Ricky was becoming a sloppy lush and spent most of his extra cash on booze. They barely scrimped by. Delena had chosen the wrong man again.

After a few more months I no longer enjoyed our visits because Rick was drunk, and they had so little. I felt guilty because my situation was better. However, then Jake commenced drinking beer on week ends.

Taking on Delena's domineering, nagging personality, Jane was like a stranger to me. Eventually, our visits were only on special occasions such as birthday parties and at Christmas time. My new friends were becoming more important and I felt a little guilty that my loyalties toward Jane were slipping away. But the fact was at the age of nine the guys were just more fun to play with. Knowing Jane was safe with Delena gave me solace and I did not have to worry about her welfare anymore, other than when Ricky lost his jobs. Though he was a alcoholic, Jane was the apple of his eye, and she loved him.

Within two years of our arrival in Amarillo I had many friends including black schoolmates. Seemed I was drawn to the outcast and underdogs, blacks and whites. The new kids on the block that had a hard time adjusting. I became their friend willingly and cherished ever relationship. They were all special. Realized my black buddies color didn't rub off. They were no different from me other than their culture and dark skin. They had the same human feelings as I did. And the same fascinations with our differences. Some even checked to see if my lighter skin color would rub off too when we first met at school in 1964

Life was good with Jake and Leve most of the time. I was happy there, except for weekends after the first year when Jake drank too much beer. He got mean. But he never hurt me physically. I was afraid of him and I abhorred him when he was drunk.

During the first few vulgar, violent, and turbulent years of my life, most of my male role models were either hateful, violent, controlling, perverts, drunkards, wife beaters, crazy, or religious nuts. Now Jake was turning out to be a great disappointment too.

The women in my life up to that point had been insecure, domineering, harsh spoken, fearful, undereducated manipulators, conniving, selfish, jealous, self-righteous, greedy man haters in that they wanted a man's support, and security but they also wanted to rule the roost. They were bitter. The men in their young lives had hurt them. But Momma's betrayal and abandonment of Jane and me had saddened my heart more than all the others put together. I had worshiped Momma. No greater loss in this son's life than to lose the love of my mother. Jake's rule was her name was to never be mentioned in our home unless I wanted to talk about her.

Jake's dad died before he was born. His momma had abandoned him too. He was raised in seven different homes as a child and had also been raped by a pedophile at age thirteen. Though he never knew Merl had messed with me. I'd never tell. He called women that abandon their children "split-tail bitches." Told me to never let the sons-of-bitches and bastards ever get my anger out of me. He said they were all nuts. He'd talk like that when he was drunk. When sober, he was more disciplined with use of the English language.

All the women and men had character flaws to the extreme in my eyes, all but kindhearted Leve. In her I found stability and balance. She was different. Not weak. She loved me and Jake, and I believed in her. She had never broken my trust. Neither had Jake, except for his boozing problem, and them allowing Delena to take Jane. That was the only broken trust.

Though undereducated, Leve was an intelligent woman with lots of common sense. She was strong willed but not belligerent or domineering. I loved her. She was my momma now, my only security. I guess I was her momma's boy. But more than that she was my most trusted friend.

When Jake got on a rip snorter, Skipper and I hid under the bed or I'd get permission from Leve to let me spend the nights with my best friend Richie and his family who lived up the street. Sometimes Leve and I camped out in the storage shed to get away from Jake's occasional weekend drunken verbal abuse and brawling.

Leve made our hiding into a fun game when we ran from him this way. Why did she stay with him? Love! She believed God would change him one day. He was a good man but alcohol was his demon.

She did her best to help me feel safe in the midst of his intoxicated confusion. Protecting me was her priority. Not until the late spring of 1964 did I actually realize how bad the situation was, especially for Leve.

The bruising on her arms and legs caused me to resent Jake when he was toasted. I couldn't protect her. But I wanted to. I slowly began to lose all respect for him. His drinking escalated. He lost his job and I began to fear for Leve.

Leve didn't use alcohol and he wanted her to be his drinking buddy. She refused. Instead she became his unwilling punching bag while he mocked her faith. He cursed my deceased grandmother Anne's Christian testimony in his inebriate rages. When school was out Leve was determined to make some changes for us. She knew if she didn't she would succumb.

She believed it was the devil using Jake to try and force her to hit the hooch again. Sober for five years when I come to live with them, she was a licensed Full Gospel minister.

Jake certainly hated her reverse attitude against sin and the booze. After all he had met her in a bar having a beer nearly twenty years before. He wanted her to drink with him again. This Jesus to whom she had rededicated her life was boring.

We couldn't continue to live this way, but for me this was heaven compared to the life I had lived in Arkansas, despite Jake's drunkenness. I really didn't want to lose another home. For the first time I had self-pride, friends and wasn't totally ashamed of myself. Although Jake's intemperance was the big problem, I would just avoid him when he was drunk. He was a good guy when sober. I didn't want to be thrown away again.

Chapter Three

Grandmother Anne's spiritual guidance and godly testimony had greatly influenced Leve and Delena. Drawn by the Holy Spirit they each accepted Christ as their personal savior in their early teens, though by 1964 they had thrown the oppressive clothesline holiness doctrines out the window.

After walking in rebellion and backsliding, drinking and sowing their wild oats for several years, the sisters had rededicated their lives to the Lord. But they wore pants, makeup, and cropped their hair short. In the spring of 1964 they were stylish for the times, as best our incomes provided.

Some of the more mainstream holiness religious folks called them backsliding Pentecostal Baptist Jezebels--just as Momma was labeled back in Loafer's Glory. However, the seeds of faith had fallen on good soil and took root in their hearts. They could not get completely away from Anne's raising. Their experiences of salvation were intact still after a period of repentance and they were of Pentecostal persuasion in their beliefs.

My uncles were sloppy lushes, sometimes violent. This made for serious marital problems, much as Anne experienced with grandfather Isaiah. Enduring busted lips and blackened eyes after occasional beatings from their drunkard husbands made my aunts' Christian walks a struggle.

Financial stress due to the loss of jobs for both men cursed our lives and cupboards now and then, but it was more of a problem in Jane's home than mine. Constant turmoil in their relationships eventually would cause both my aunts to backslide in their walk with the Lord again. But on this day in June of 1964 they were on fire for God and full of the Holy Ghost!

Although both Ricky and Jake were good to us children when they weren't drinking, they could be quite abusive to all of us when drunk. Though they never beat Jane and me, the mental and emotional alcohol-induced abuse was horrific. That spring Jake went on a drinking binge that lasted three months.

During one of his drunken stupors, he humiliated us by standing in our yard and screaming obscenities at the neighbors. Holding a can of beer in one hand, giving the neighbors the BIRD with the other, and wearing only the scowl on his face, he stepped off the front porch. Exposing the pride of his full-blown glory in family jewels and ignorance, he bellowed at the neighborhood, "I know all you bastards think you are better than me! I have survived more than you can imagine, protecting your sorry ass' in the battles at Okinawa and Guadalcanal. The blood of my buddies running under my feet on the ship deck! Ugly American Yanks should have let the Japs keep the damn place!"

His violent aggressive shouting went on until late into the night. Leve pleaded with him to hush and not disturb the neighbors as she carried a clean pair of boxer shorts out in the yard and insisted that he put them on. He slapped her but she wouldn't back down.

"Now Jake, the neighbors aren't interested in your feelings or your butt! Now put these on!" she demanded. "Everyone is for certain going to think you are a crazy pervert if you don't stop this yelling and cover yourself."

Hatefully he snatched the shorts out of her hand and bent over to put them on just as a carload of teenaged boys drove by honking with their heads stuck out the windows laughing. Yanking his drawers up he turned around and gave them the BIRD as they passed the house.

Embarrassed Leve convinced him to come inside. His anger turned on her and he continued yelling while punching her around in the bedroom.

I stuck my head through the doorway and yelled at him through my tears, "Leave her alone!"

He staggered after me into the kitchen, pulling a butcher knife off the wall while backing me into a corner where I hunkered down on the floor crying.

When he turned on me, Leve pulled herself off the bedroom floor. Leaving a pool of blood behind on the worn linoleum, she leapt to her feet, grabbed a lamp by the bed, and ran shrieking into the kitchen. Her face wrenched in anger, she whacked Jake good over the back of his bald head. "You won't hurt my boy!" she yelled.

She pounded Jake with one calculated blow after another to the back of his head and shoulders. His bald noggin bleeding, he dropped the knife to the floor laughing in his addled state as we escaped out of the house at two a.m. We locked ourselves inside the storage shed for the remainder of the night. Jake continued his brawling inside the house alone until four a.m.

Our neighbors were used to his weekend exhibitions and drunken scenes. This one had lasted a little longer. It didn't seem to faze them other than a couple of chuckles and the slamming of doors and windows so they couldn't see or hear him. Jake's antics were no worse than some of the other neighbor's escapades in our rough community on the poor side of the railroad track. This was the only time he ever acted violent toward me, though he hadn't touched me. He just enjoyed the terror on my face. I doubt he ever intended to hurt me physically. But who knows what went on in the mind of a drunk?

Inside the shed Leve prayed, whispering to God all night, sitting up in a lawn chair and reading her Bible by flashlight, while I tried to nap on a tarp in the floor. The next morning out of fear and disgust, Leve decided to leave him for a time. She took me with her.

We crept quietly back into the house so not to awaken Jake. Leve's face was swollen and bruised from the night before. We hurriedly and quietly dressed in clean clothing, packed a few things, and left.

That warm Saturday morning during the first week of my summer break from Summit Elementary school, in Amarillo, Texas, Leve walked with me to the local bus stop, suitcases in our hands.

Jake was still passed out naked in the kitchen floor, surrounded by empty beer bottles, blood dried on his hands and head. Leve and I boarded the bus and rode the five miles across town to Delena's and Ricky's place. Neither of us spoke. We huddled close together on the bus.

The other passengers stared at Leve's bruised arms and legs, swollen busted lips, and black-eye. She tried to hide her face behind a newspaper. I glared back at them. They quickly turned away.

Ricky had sobered enough to go to work and wasn't there when we arrived midmorning. I hadn't seen Jane in six weeks. Jane and I, painfully aware of the growing differences in each other, went into the backyard to play.

Jane wore blue khaki baby doll shorts. Delena had made them from the pant leg material of Ricky's worn-out work uniform. She also had on a pale blue second-hand tee shirt purchased from the local junk store. Her black hair had been cut short again to the base of her head and around her face, and her olive complexion now was deep brown from hours of playing outside in the hot Texas sun.

The neighbor's oldest son Robbie, tall, lanky and pimpled with frog-eye thick glasses made fun of Jane's dark complexion. "Nigger! Nigger! Nigger!" he yelled out his back door when he saw her playing in the yard. But his younger sister Gina, a year older than me, was sweet.

Gina secretly played with Jane when her brother wasn't around. She was too embarrassed to be seen with Jane when Robbie was at home because he called her a nigger lover.

The strong bond of mutual survival, motivated by fear and instability that had once ripped through our lives and caused us to cling to each other was almost gone, but I love her. I told Jane that Gina wasn't a friend if she was ashamed to be seen with her. Jane just sighed. No other children lived close enough for her to play with every day since Delena was very protective and wouldn't allow her to stray from the block.

My medium brown hair was greased back like Elvis Presley's and I was proud of my *new* gray store-bought shorts and Beatle tee shirt. In her presence I felt guilty to have new clothes and she wore homemade and junk-store attire.

Inside the older flat-roofed two bedroom house with gray asbestos siding on the outer walls, Leve and Delena began to pray over our home environments and about Ricky and Jake. They were also praying God would give Leve direction in making decisions about our immediate situation and how to handle it.

Jane and I could hear them weeping as they cried out to God in prayer. Sometimes they would speak in tongues. Horribly embarrassed, I feared the neighbors would hear their wails.

For me, the embarrassment of Jake yelling naked in the yard and their loud babbling of nonsense were no different. I was ashamed of both behaviors. Daddy was right--the whole world is nothing but a bunch of crazy chicken dookies! I thought to myself God, were all adults crazy? Jane rolled her eyes and nodded. She must have had the same thought.

"They're at it again, Saul. Sundee alee ho," she said to mock their loud prayer in the unknown tongue. We both giggled.

I patted her on the head. "You're it," I said. Then I took off running around the yard with Jane at my heels. It reminded me of the days when we ran naked through the house after Momma would give us our baths at the old homestead.

Passers by, walking on the street in front of the house, would shake their heads and chuckle at my aunts' loud vocalizations drifting from inside. Humiliated, Jane and I ran behind her storage shed and hid.

After about an hour of their caterwauling, Leve came to the back door and called for me to come inside. "The Lord has spoken!" Leve boldly proclaimed as she smiled and motioned for me to come near.

Apprehensively, I thought is this for real or is she sick like my daddy and hallucinating? I knew God had answered her prayers in the past. She could tell me things that would happen months in advance. These insights came when she had been spending hours in travailing prayer at home while Jake was at work. Curious but a little fearful too, I just didn't understand those loud tongues.

She asked me to come inside again. Reluctantly, I choked back my rebellion and obeyed her. I asked if they were going to pray for Jane too, not wanting to face this alone.

She patted the perspiration from her brow with a lace handkerchief, as she looked down smiling. "We will pray for Jane later."

We walked into the living room. Delena was standing in the corner near a dinning room chair they had move there just for me. Delena was as shabbily dressed as Jane. She too wore blue khaki hand-made peddle pushers made out of material salvaged from Ricky's old work pants and a junk-store flowery blouse with patches sown over the sleeves near the elbows. She seemed exhausted but a sweetness radiated from her as she smiled at me.

"Aunt Delena, may I go next door and play with Gina?" Jane asked.

Delena nodded and smiled while wiping tears from her eyes with one of Ricky's large white handkerchiefs. "Yes if that hateful Robbie isn't home."

I couldn't understand why they had to cry when they prayed.

Smirking, Jane said and darted out the back door, "Bye, Saul. Come and play with us when you're through."

Leve held my hand, still silently crying and smiling while leading me to the chair in the corner. The two didn't seem to go together, the tears and smiles.

Calmly, Leve said, "Son, I feel lead of the Lord to go spend the summer with your aunt Lou in Indiana. I just can't take another beating or endure another night of brawling out of Jake."

I was elated! "When are we leaving?"

She raised her chin and with a lilt in her voice said, "Probably tomorrow."

I would get to see my cousins Alvin, Patsy, and Don, whom I had lived with for almost six months and my mind flooded with fond memories of the fun times we had together a few years earlier. I was glad to be leaving Jake behind.

I had not been looking forward to cleaning up his messes at home when he decided to sober up again. Jake got the squirts when coming off the booze. He would run naked out of his bedroom, vomiting through the dinning room and losing control of his bowels all at the same time, leaving a trail of smelly, nasty stuff on the walls and floor as he rounded the corner into the bathroom. It was always *my* job to scrub the walls before we repainted after Jake's liberal spraying of the house. I didn't even want to think about carrying out all the rubbish and empty bottles that would be left. I was glad to move, instead of having to help Leve clean up after another long alcoholic episode and watch Jake go through the painful withdrawals again.

I missed the man who wasn't there when Jake was drunk. I hated the drunkard. I loved the sober Jake.

Would Leve take me to Lou's house and abandon me as everyone else had? Insecurity gripped my heart. If Leve didn't abandon me in Indiana, perhaps God could fix Jake and answer Leve's prayers. That's what I secretly prayed. I longed for Jake to stop drinking altogether so we could be a normal family. I feared they would eventually divorce, leaving me alone again.

Leve said they were going to pray for my protection before making the long trip. Well, I knew about heavenly protection already and I didn't resist too much but the radical way they prayed really bothered me.

I often wondered if all of these things were contagious and at what age I would begin drinking, beating women, and talking nonsense. I was not looking forward to "growing up." If I did I'd never act like any of them!

Silent rage and loathing stirred within me as I sat in the chair. The loud praying and all the crying and speaking in tongues seemed weird, and I truly thought they had lost their minds. But some reservation tugged at my heart that maybe, just maybe they knew something that I didn't.

Anne had prayed in the unknown tongue on her deathbed and ol' ugly Fanny babbled nonsense when we lived in Wisconsin. Relatives said Momma even had the Holy Ghost and prayed in tongues at one time before she left Daddy but I had never heard her do it. I wanted to believe God was in this, but I had endured abundant pain and suffered many losses. Where was He then? Why did He let that happen if He loved me so much? Iniquity of my forefathers flowed in my veins, the burden of Loafer's Glory gold in my soul. My heart was growing hard. I didn't have much confidence in adults or their religions.

I actually did believe in God at the time, but I also had doubt that He existed. Perhaps He was like Santa Clause for the adults? I didn't believe in Santa. Bewildered and confused, I had seen the destruction of double minded "Christians" in my past, including my parent. I didn't want that kind of relationship, say one thing and do another.

How could their God have allowed all of those bad things to happen to me? But then I remembered many saying it was a miracle when God saved me from death after the accident. I remembered how prayers were answered when He had healed my mind that day in the classroom, and how He heard my whispering prayer and saved Jane and me from my rabid dog Buddy. These things I considered miracles, and surely God was in them. Maybe Jesus did exist, but I didn't know Him? Though I knew I had a guardian angel! I still questioned why I had lost my family if God loved me so much. If Jesus was real, I kinda wanted to meet Him. Maybe He would answer my questions. If they were nuts--I didn't know for certain. Leve had never broken my trust. She couldn't be a lunatic! I didn't know what to expect. Was Jesus real? If He was like the religious folks I knew--I didn't want to meet Him. How do I know what is real and imagination? No more Santa Clause and devil's booger stories! I won't believe them.

As Leve and Delena sat me down in the chair, immediately I wanted to run out of the house as fast as I could, but I didn't. Leve and Delena had treated me better than anyone else in my life. So I decided to bear this to please them and keep my true feelings to myself. I had experienced worse in my earlier homes, and at least they were praying to the same Jesus I had prayed to the day God sent an angel to protect Jane and me from Buddy's attack. Maybe it was the same Jesus. Was He a pompous pious God on duty only part-time? Like the part-time Christians

I knew. Would I meet Him?

Leve and Delena lay their hands upon my head and began to pray loudly. They called upon the name of Jesus. Hot tears streamed down their faces as they spoke in an unknown tongue.

Their prayer of protection turned into praise and worship unto the Lord as they lifted their hands toward heaven. As they prayed, they got louder.

I began to cry. Fight as I did, I could not hold back my tears. This was not in my plan. This was not supposed to happen. I wanted them to get their filthy hands off of me. Now I was angry! They were lunatics! I thought about kicking them and running out of the room. I didn't think I could subdue my tearful volcanic emotions, my crying, or my anger. My sobbing became uncontrollable. The more I resisted the harder I wept.

Then a sweet presence filled the room. I felt that someone powerful and important had entered the house. I couldn't see Him, but I knew someone was standing right behind me. My guardian angel? This was the same presence I had sensed the day Anne had prayed for me before she died. That unexplainable peace I had experienced at the accident when Momma ran over my leg with the car. The same peace I sensed the day I saw my guardian angel. That same peace so many times in the past when I was in great danger or trouble was again all around me.

Leve stopped praying and lifted my hands toward heaven. Then she said, "Son, Jesus is here now. He wants to save your soul today. He is waiting for you to invite Him to come live inside your heart. Lift your hands toward heaven, and praise Him. Tell Him that you love Him. Ask Him to forgive all of your sins and come into your heart to be Lord of your life.

I looked behind me. No one was there that I could see. How could He get inside my heart? Then I remembered Alvin who was now in heaven and our conversation on the teeter totter. But this was not like anything I had imagined back then. Alvin had said, "God is a spirit." I knew someone was in the house, I could feel His presence.

Smiling kindly, Leve said, "Son, the spirit of God is here. He wants you to know how much He loves you."

God is a Spirit? Was that why they called Him Holy Ghost? I nodded while feeling peace and warmth all around me. This had to be the spirit of Jesus. So, with little reservation, I lifted my hands.

Though I did not fully understand what I was experiencing, I knew God was in it. When the chains of my pride were broken, I entered into worship with my aunts. Hot tears streamed down my face. It was as though I had begun to cry away all the hurt, hate, rejection, and fear that I had endured in my few, short years. It seemed like someone strong and powerful was holding me in His arms like the father I never had and loving away all the pain in my broken heart.

I spoke, softly. "Jesus. If you are here, come into my heart and save my soul right now." At those words I traded the family legacy of one hundred years, and a mountain of worthless Loafer's Glory gold for heavenly treasure.

Instantly, I felt an explosion of the love of God as His living rivers of healing peace burst forth from my belly and surged throughout my entire being. I began to scream for joy, through the flood of tears gushed out of my eyes when the power of His cleansing blood washed away the filthiness I had known.

These were great tears of joy. God, the Creator, was intimate with me at that moment. He had come into my heart and had become the Lover of my soul. Jesus set me free that day from all the grief that had gone before. I was free, free indeed. A million pounds slid off my shoulders. I no longer felt dirty and unwanted. I was clean all over, inside and out. The love of God had lit the darkness in every corner of my broken heart and scoured away all the past sorrow. I was truly born again. I was a new creation in Christ Jesus.

Now, God was my father! Dread and insecurity no longer gripped my mind and heart. For the first time in my life I knew what real love was. The burden of shame was gone. Nothing was the same. A veil had been taken off of my mind's eyes and I could see clearly, consumed in the fire of God's total unconditional love and acceptance of His creation. He let me know I wasn't just the unwanted result of two people having sex. There was purpose for my life, His destiny and plan included me and I was able to love myself for the first time ever. I was somebody special because He loved me with a whole heart. Now I was to give back to the world and share what He had given to me. That was His plan for my life.

The people around me looked different. I seemed to be able to discern beyond the outward appearance and sense the content of their hearts, and I loved them despite their character flaws. God had not changed the world but he had changed me.

I got up and went into the back yard. Drunk in the love of God by the presence of Holy Spirit, I could hear a choir singing in the distance. I looked up toward the sky as I rejoiced in my salvation. There, standing on a cloud was a choir of seven angels singing praises unto the Lord. My joy was full!

Jane was in the yard next door playing with Gina. She didn't see anything but she yelled at me across the fence, "Saul, is the church choir practicing?" The Methodist church was directly behind her house across the alleyway.

Calmly smiling, I responded and pointed toward the sky, "It's the angels!" She and Gina giggled when they could see nothing but fluffy scattered clouds overhead and they went back to playing with Gina's dog. But I could see the angels. This was my blessing from God.

The colors of Delena's flowers appeared more brilliant than any I had ever seen before. The smell of her lilacs perfumed the air with the sweetness of God's glory. Drawn to a fragrant, scarlet peony blossom I knelt down and saw splendid detail I had never seen as a fearless monarch butterfly lit on my hand. In awe of God's handy work, I thought the world truly was a beautiful place.

I looked across the fence again. Godly love radiated out of my heart for Gina and Jane while watching them play with the cuddly rag-mop brown puppy.

Walked back inside the house and told Leve and Delena what I had seen. They explained that the angels in heaven rejoice when one sinner repents.

Though their religion may have been muddied with many controversial manmade doctrines the basics of the born again experience were pure. This salvation miracle was the beginning of a very real, personal relationship with the Lord Jesus Christ. He changed my destiny forever. He gave me a sound mind to know right from wrong and the power to overcome evil sent to destroy my life. His unconditional love set me free from the family curses.

Jesus died, was crucified on that cross some two thousand years ago for all the world. He knew, then, there would be a very sad, angry, brokenhearted, frightened, bruised, and lonely nine-year-old boy named Saul living in Amarillo, Texas. He knew little Saul Hotman would accept Him as savior in June of 1964. I was only an insignificant child among billions on the planet. In God's heart on that day I was most important. He gave me a supernatural explosion of His love within my being, making up for all I had never known. His love healed my broken spirit!

Luke 4:18 The Spirit of the Lord is upon me, because he hath anointed me to preach the gospel to the poor; he hath sent me to heal the brokenhearted, to preach deliverance to the captives, and recovering of sight to the blind, to set at liberty them that are bruised.

Praying in the Spirit upon her deathbed, Anne must have imparted her last blessing. Perhaps she sensed the sometimes rocky road my young life would often lead. Maybe her prayer was empowerment for the journey. Now and then I imagine Grandmother Anne praying in the shade of the oaks and willows near the old homestead pond. I can't help but believe from time to time she must look down from the portals of heaven and have to smile knowing her prayers were never in vain.

THE BEGINNING

Epilogue

Jane's and my young years were not a playground of innocence--rather a battlefield. The remainder of our youth was not without problems, though we drew strength from our struggles. Jane never had a spiritual experience such as mine, but she was able to cope. She married, had three sons, and a successful career as a nurse.

Bobby lived all his youth with Sonny. She was a good momma. Loved him like her own. Bobby married an older woman when he was eighteen. They have remained together for twenty-seven years, and have two sons.

Leve never left Jake but succumb to his wishes, fisting, and became his drinking buddy again when I was twelve. That summer, she sent me to live with Delena. It took me many years to get over the pain of losing the one adult in my young life that I trusted most. Losing Leve was worse than Momma's abandonment of us.

I struggled with health problems for years as a direct result of early childhood neglect. Other than that nuisance, I've had a wonderful adult life, surrendering to a part-time ministry when I was twenty-four, and worked as a radio broadcast journalist for many years.

My wife Elisabeth came from a broken home, was a foster child and had lived with nine different families. She understood my passion to help others in need, and being a voice for the many silent victims of abuse. Over the years we raised our three children, and opened our home to thirty-eight foster kids. Today, I teach independent living skills to developmentally disabled and mentally ill adults. I have found there are countless others whose childhood horrors were worse than ours. We are advocates for the rights of children, the disabled, and the mentally ill.

One out of one hundred world wide suffer from schizophrenia. Daddy eventually received proper medication-therapy for the disease. He lived in our home the last fifteen years of his life. Daddy loved Momma, Jane, Bobby, and me until the day he passed away in June, 2000. I will forever miss him. His love was unshakable, always.

When Daddy was first diagnosed with cancer and very nearly died after having a lung removed in 1991, Chad came to our home. Time had mellowed his harsh domineering personality. He wept and asked forgiveness. What he didn't know was that I had forgiven him years before. Chad, a courageous man for humbling himself and apologizing, more noble than to have gone to his grave with out making the effort. His life hadn't been easy either. I admired and loved Chad for his strength. Seemed the hard decisions landed in his lap for the kinsmen after Anne passed away. Tho harsh to the extreme many times, I know he loved Daddy. For years Daddy was his responsibility. That was not an easy task when there was no medication to help.

Jake quit the booze when he was seventy-two, and gave his heart to the Lord. He asked for my forgiveness, and was sober the remainder of his days. Jake died peacefully in my arms at age eighty-nine.

Leve, quit drinking five years after I left their home. She regretted the duality of her nature and the pain it caused. In her old days with humor in her voice, she said, " I was a preacher of the Gospel. Let a lot of people down. Now, here I am old and looking back, I should have been stronger. I pooped in my nest and there I sat. What a waste of my young Christian life." Leve is eighty-five, now she lives with Elisabeth and me.

Delena divorced Ricky after Jane graduated from high school. She returned to the old homestead in Loafer's Glory and lived alone until her death. Ricky joined Alcoholics Anonymous after the divorce. At age seventy he found salvation and spent the next twelve years helping other drunks get free from the ravages of liquor. He died alone in his Amarillo home.

I had no contact with Momma until I was grown. Shortly after our first reunion during the early 1970's, Merl gave her one last beating, leaving Momma for dead under a bridge in Springdale, Arkansas. By the Grace of God she survived one more time. But this time she found the courage to break free from him. He would never beat her physically again, though she refused to press charges, a common behavior for many battered women. Momma never went back to Merl after that. She was the ultimate victim. Her beauty was gone. The hopes and dreams of a strong willed young girl that was--once upon a time, only memories. Momma withered early, like a plucked blossom. Rebellion, bad choices, lack of education, poverty, shame, fear, and abuse robbed her of her youthful potential. I will love Momma always. Our bonds are long-since broken.

Iris and Daniel had thirteen children. Only seven survived. Ten years after the divorce she had a stroke and died at age forty-five.

The drunkard Ku Klux Klansman Elmer Don was found beaten and stabbed to death in Little Rock a few years after Iris passed away.

Daniel and Gert remained together until his death in 1976. Upon his deathbed Daniel made Momma vow to never go back to the devil--Merl Judas. She promised. Then he passed away peacefully. Gert never married again, and at eighty-years-old she died.

Merl's sister Della, her son Rafter, and her other children left Loafer's Glory. While her husband was in prison during the late 1960's she moved to California. Some said she found the Lord Jesus there. He changed her life.

Merl Judas allegedly violated dozens of children during his life span. He left behind a legacy of sorrow, and broken lives. He had betrayed the trust of everyone who loved him. Only one police investigation into Merl's crimes against children ever occurred during his lifetime. Most officials believed the victims but too many years had passed and any physical evidence was gone. Merl Judas was never prosecuted. Estranged from his children and grandchildren, upon his deathbed he was haunted by the ghost of his past. Merl Judas died an agonizing death at age sixty-five. Merl's brother Ely said he repented at the end. Maybe he did.

Our king of terror was dead. Now there was closure. At hearing of Merl's passing Jane broke down, crying she said, "We're free! We're finally free."

Our years of silence were to the determent of many. Silence allows the cycle of abuse to continue for generations. One in three girls and one in seven boys are raped or molested before adulthood. On average one pedophile ravages one hundred children during his life time. NEVER BE SILENT.

Jane and I were survivors! We weren't alone. Just before Merl's death I pondered what good could come from these tragedies. I realized his type evil when shrouded by secrecy of victims empowers his kind to commit more crimes against the innocent. The public scandals with some clergy in certain religious orders today are perfect examples of how decades of silence and covering the shameful crimes perpetuate more evil.

With Delena's and Leve's encouragement, I began writing HOTMAN'S INNOCENCE. Perhaps my words would give others the courage to break the silence, and expose their violators, pedophiles and rapists-- rendering other abusers powerless. The shame ALWAYS belongs to the criminals.

I love my wounded inner child, Little Saul Hotman. I will protect him always. He would say.... "Watch out for the chicken dookies!"

Never again will he be forced to live under tyranny. No more submission through fear/shame, or carrying around nasty-little-secrets to protect an abuser and to cover the disgrace.

I returned to the old breeding grounds a few years ago. Loafer's Glory was once again my home. Today a grand space to be-no more monsters found in this place for me. Her fool's gold was replaced with some education. I saw the past clearly from an adult perspective, and chose to forgive those who hurt Jane and me when we were children. But I never excused their denial. With this writing I found final closure and can forget, now.

The community of Loafer's Glory has changed much over the past forty-five years. Gone are the ramshackle shacks, picker's sheds, outhouses and cisterns. The old replaced with modern homes, paved roads, indoor plumbing, and a public water supply. There are more jobs to be had in the surrounding areas. Though some of the old attitudes remain. Loafer's Glory is not unlike thousands more communities, just by chance she happened to be the place where I was born.

The geographical settings in which one makes his abodes have little bearing on the peace he finds. Whether a large city or rural community the same is true. In any hometown, the content of men's hearts, determine the value of every individual. In that, life can be miserable or blessed. Knowledge, wisdom, and tolerance can rule over ignorance and superstition, if men are willing to take the high road, choose to do good, and resist the powers of evil. Judge with right judgement, and bestow kindness toward the less fortunate. Labeling can come back to haunt.

Peace resides inside my heart. Some say I am a saint, others mock and are not so kind. After all I am the son of the crazy, village idiot preacher, and his little darkey harlot.

They are wrong. I am firm against injustice, evil, abuse, and, destructive behavior in young and old alike. My sharp tongue, though motivated by love and concern can be like a machine gun riddling the flesh with bullets (got that from Delena) to those who mock or abuse the less-fortunate and vulnerable. My words can also be a healing balm of soft spoken kindness for the weak, and those striving to overcome. There is my weakness. Overwhelming compassion for the underdog, trouble souls, and those in need. It gets me into trouble sometimes as the joys of helping and giving over loads available time and cash in the wallet. My words and actions are mis-construed periodically. That's the game plan of the adversary to confuse, and stop a good deed, slander, and say evil of mercy.

God knows who and what I am, and he loves me despite my flaws. Unlike human beings He judges the content of the heart and not by outward appearances, material wealth, or social standing.

Undying love for both my parents. That is what I feel, and in this I honor them. I cherish the few good memories of our short years together during my early youth. Yes, I love the family that should never have been, my biological family--Daddy, Momma, Bobby and Jane. My family was blown to the four winds by the wilds of the devil, and the King of Terror. The cards were stacked against us from the beginning. As far as Momma and Daddy are concerned, I'm proud they were my parents. They taught me the meaning of compassion, love and forgiveness.

Little Saul Hotman was a young prince, stripped of his health, innocence, dignity, and domain. He never forgot who he was and where he came from. Real love began for Saul with God.

I learned to cherish Saul, and in so doing was able to forgive those who were the givers of pain. Love begins at home. Without God, forgiveness of those who hurt Jane and me would not have been possible, as hatred and grudges are the common response. Forgiveness was surely a condition of the human spirit that would have been impossible without the power of God's unconditional love abiding inside my heart.

Not in denial of the truth, I took my will, and chose forgiveness, rejecting bitterness. The reward was tranquility of the soul in the midst of turmoil, while I received hate and resentment from the guilty.

With God's help Jane and I had a life. We were survivors, but we're only two among millions today. There is hope to overcome for any victim.

Wisdom is stifled when a family of wicked deceitful sisters named Lust, Greed, Control, Addiction, Racism, Madness, Slander, Radicalism, and Oppression, violate and rule over the house, or a community. They are murders of the soul. Give them no place.

Be brave, use wisdom , and expose evil. NEVER BE SILENT! The cycles of abuse can be broken!

It is finished! I have my dignity, and closure. Now, I lay down my quill.

Afterward

I am Diana Stevens(pseudonym) and work as a child-abuse investigator with the Crimes Against Children Division (CACD), formerly the Family Protection Division (FPD), of the Arkansas State Police (ASP). I hold a Bachelor of Arts degree in Social Work from Arkansas State University in Jonesboro, AR. Having been with ASP since April 2000, I was a Family Service Worker (FSW)for Children and Family Services prior to accepting this position. Being an FSW meant that I worked to keep children in their homes, even after they had been abused, and worked to reunify children with their parents after the child had been placed into foster care.

My role with CACD is one of gathering information, evidence, and proving that a preponderance of evidence exist to support the allegations being made to the Child Abuse Hot Line. If this evidence does exist the offender is placed on Central Registry and is listed as a Sex Offender or Physical Abuse Offender. If this finding is not appealed, his or her name remains on the Registry for the rest of his life. In the state of Arkansas, a person can be named as an offender if he is ten years of age or older. When a report is found to be True, everything in our investigation is turned over to the local Prosecuting Attorney and by us working with them, charges are then filed.

Some of the different forms of child maltreatment that I, along with the approximately ninety other investigators with ASP, investigate are Sexual Abuse, which includes Oral Sex, Sexual Contact, Sexual Exploitation and Sexual Penetration, Suffocation, Immersions, Burns, and any other form of abuse that is considered severe.

With child victims of abuse, in numerous cases a report is called in to the Child Abuse Hot Line years after the abuse has occurred. By this time, any valuable evidence that would be essential in proving and tying the suspect to the victim is gone. That is why, as the author has done his best to point out, no one should ever be silent regarding child sexual abuse. Report it as soon as you are aware of it! Do not wait because someone else says that they are going to report it, because most of the time, they don't. Many kids feel ashamed and that it must be their fault. That could not be further from the truth. This is what we try to stress in our interviews--the adult was the responsible person, he or she took advantage and did something wrong. It is okay for the victimized child to talk about the abuse and crimes with us, teachers, counselors, the parents of a friend, anyone, as long as they talk to someone they can trust.

This society is too quick to judge the victim. We think there is no way that could have happened in my home, neighborhood, and city. But it does. Day after day, countless children are molested and raped. It is not only a problem in lower socioeconomic families, it is just as likely to happen in a $150, 000 home, where the father is a Deacon in his local church and the mother a school teacher (these are only examples). It is very uncommon to have a suspect who is a total stranger to the child. We need to spend as much time reassuring our children that no matter who has hurt them, that it is okay to talk, as we do warning them about the danger of 'strangers'.

Following are a list of toll-free phone numbers in which anyone can call at any time of the day or night and report suspected child abuse. If you have ever been a victim, some of these numbers may help you in taking that first step to break the silence. Since the author of this book is a native of Arkansas and considering my position, I will post phone numbers for Arkansas and then post national numbers.

Remember that anyone can call and report alleged abuse. You do not have to give your name, phone number, or address. These things are helpful to us, but not necessary. Reporters do remain confidential. Following the guidelines of the Arkansas Child Maltreatment Act, we are not allowed to share that information with anyone, unless we are so ordered by a judge in a court of law.

Arkansas Child Abuse Hot Line (800)-482-5964
Rape Abuse & Incest National Network (800)-656-4673 (HOPE)
National Victim Center INFOLINK (800) FYI-CALL NINE

About the Author
Peter S. Hotman

Peter Saul Hotman was a radio journalist/announcer for many years. Today he works with the disabled and is a free lance writer living in Arkansas with his wife Elisabeth. They continue their work to help ease the suffering of others. His next book is in progress.

Peter encourages you to do your part, support local law enforcement and the Department of Children and Family Services. Help the less fortunate. Perhaps by becoming a foster parent. Choose to make a difference. The rewards are few, and there are no pats on the back from most of the children you may help, (but when they are grown your influence will not be forgotten). Your efforts may save a desperate child's life.

Order Form

To order additional copies of HOTMAN'S INNOCENCE, Please complete the order form below and include your check or money order. Personal order info is not shared, sold or used for any other purpose. All personal information is disposed of after processing.
[Credit card orders can be made through our web site: www.petmegoosepress.net please feel free to contact us by email there and look over our catalogue for more great books.]

PRICING : Paperback
One book: $19.95 + $3.00 shipping and handling [$22.95 total] multiple orders, add $3.00 shipping and handling for the first book and then $1.00 for each additional book after that.
(Your books will not ship until after your personal check clears the bank}

YES ! I want to order HOTMAN'S INNOCENCE. Now ! In case of a processing problem contact me: Email or phone:._____

Please send this number of books [   ]
to the address below:

_____
Your name:

_____
Mailing address: _

_____
City: State: Zip Code:

#of books X $19.95 each: Subtotal: $
$3.00 S&H first copy +$1.00 each additional: S&H: $
payment enclosed: Total: $
Make payment to: Petmegoose Press
Send to this address: Petmegoose Press Publishing
                      HOTMAN'S INNOCENCE
                      HC 80 Box 104 A
                      Marshall, AR 72650

Thank you for your order. Never Be Silent About Abuse !

TEN PERCENT OF PROFIT FROM THE SALE OF HOTMAN'S INNOCENCE, GOES TO AN EDUCATIONAL FUND FOR CHILDREN AT RISK. These monies will be distributed as an incentive and form of encouragement for higher learning to needy students. Education is major step to overcoming poverty, and a troubled childhood. Your support and purchase of this book is appreciated.

Other suggested reading: TWISTED ROOTS OF EVIL by Susan Kesegich
Ordering information:
Twist of Fate Publishing Company
P.O. Box 1445 Destin, FL 32540
850-837-7824 office   850-654-5159 fax
1-877-786-1823 toll free for orders
skesegich@earthlink-net

Your comments to the author are appreciated. PETMEGOOSE PRESS will forward them to Peter S. Hotman.

PLACE YOUR COMMENTS BELOW: